Anonymous

Book-Lore

a magazine devoted to old time literature - Vol. 3

Anonymous

Book-Lore
a magazine devoted to old time literature - Vol. 3

ISBN/EAN: 9783337737979

Printed in Europe, USA, Canada, Australia, Japan

Cover: Foto ©Andreas Hilbeck / pixelio.de

More available books at **www.hansebooks.com**

BOOK-LORE:

A Magazine devoted to Old Time Literature.

All ye who, in these later days,
Love books of days gone by,
Come mount these stairs, shut out the world,
And from its troubles fly.

VOL. III.

DECEMBER, 1885—MAY, 1886.

LONDON:

ELLIOT STOCK, 62, PATERNOSTER ROW, E.C.

1886.

BOOK-LORE.

EARLY ENGLISH BOOK AUCTIONS.

By John Lawler.

HE method and practice of selling books by auction, or " Who bids most," was introduced into England in the year 1676 by William Cooper, bookseller, dwelling at the sign of the Pelican, in Little Britain. The practice had been some time in use in Germany and Holland, and we find John Elzevir selling in this manner part of the stock of Bonaventure and Abraham Elzevir, his predecessors, in the office of the deceased partners in Leyden, in April, 1653. John Elzevir also sold some of his own stock by auction in 1660; and there were several others later on, in 1681, etc. All the catalogues of these early sales are of very great rarity and interest. In June, 1668, Charles Hack, the well-known Dutch bookseller, sold by auction, in Leyden, the library of Dr. Jas. Golius; and the catalogue of this sale appears to have been the model used by Cooper for his first experiment in England.

Cooper was one of the learned booksellers of Charles II.'s time, and was not only a bookseller, but a publisher of alchemical books, and very well read in the science of alchemy and the philosopher's stone. He published in 1673 *The Philosopher's Epitaph*, with a *Catalogue of Chemicall Books*, by W. C.; and two years later amplified the *Catalogue* and issued it separately in three parts. In the following year appeared the catalogue of the first book auction in England, *Cura Gulielmi Cooper Bibliopolæ*. As this catalogue is a great curiosity, it may be interesting to book-lovers to have the full title :—*Catalogus | Variorum et insignium | Librorum | instructissimæ Bibliothecæ | clarissimi doctissimiq Viri | Lazari*

Seaman S.T.D. | *quorum Auctio habebitur Londini* | *in ædilus Defuncti in Area et Viculo* | *Warwicensi, Octobris ultimo* | *cura Gulielmi Cooper Bibliopolæ* | *Londini*

$$apud \begin{cases} Ed.\ Brewster \\ \& \\ Guil.\ Cooper, \end{cases} ad\ insigne \begin{cases} Gruis\ in\ Cœmetario\ Paulino \\ Pelicani\ in\ vico\ vulgariter \\ dicto\ Little\ Britain \end{cases} 1676.$$

It is a small quarto in size (like the Dutch model), and contains title, "To the Reader," and "Index Capitum" (making 3 preliminary leaves), and 137 pages. From the title we learn that the library was sold in Dr. Seaman's own house in Warwick Court, Paternoster Row. In the only consecutive list of English book auctions which the writer has seen—that of Richard Gough, first published in the *Gentleman's Magazine*, and afterwards in Nichol's *Literary Anecdotes*, vol. iii.—a mistake is made in saying that the house in Warwick Lane, where the books were sold, was Cooper's house, a mistake repeated in later notices of the subject. The fact is that Cooper's shop or warehouse was, as stated on this very title, at the sign of the Pelican in *Little Britain*, though it appears that he held none of his early auctions there, but either at the house of the owner of the books, or at other houses, the signs of which are given. That this library of Dr. Seaman was actually the first sold by auction in England, though not definitely stated in the catalogue itself, is proved from the following facts. First, from the preface "To the Reader." "It hath not," says Cooper, "been usual here in England to make sale of books by way of Auction, or who will give most for them ; but it having been practised in other Countreys to the advantage of Buyers and Sellers, it was therefore conceived (for the encouragement of learning) to publish the sale of these books this manner of way ; and it is hoped that this will not be Unacceptable to Schollars ; and therefore we thought it convenient to give an advertisement concerning the manner of Proceeding therein." Secondly, from the preface to the second auction catalogue (the Library of Dr. Thos. Kidner), which was not published until three months after the first. In this preface, Cooper distinctly says that Seaman's was the first library sold by auction in London, and that the sale of Kidner's library in 167¾ was the second. Thirdly, the preface to the auction catalogue of Greenhill's library refers to the "two former attempts in this kind by the sale of Seaman's and Kidner's Libraries." And finally, the preface to the catalogue of Dr. Thos. Manton's library, sold in March, 1678, distinctly states it to be the "fourth" book auction held in this country. Having thus removed all doubt as to the genuineness of the claim of Dr. Seaman's catalogue to priority, a few more details relating to it may be now given. One of the advantages Cooper claims for the method of selling books by auction is, "that having this Catalogue of the Books, and their Editions under their several heads and numbers, it will be more easy for any Person of Quality, Gentlemen, or Others, to Depute anyone to Buy such Books for them as they shall desire, if their Occasions will not permit them to be present at the Auction themselves." The arrangement evidently follows that of the Dutch catalogue already referred to. A kind of classification is adopted, such as "Patres Græci," "Patres Latini," "Biblia Varia," etc., each with subdivisions and separate numeration. The arrangement of names in the various divisions is not alphabetical, so that one might have to read through the whole of the division before finding a particular book. To make confusion still more confounded, surnames come last in each article, and Christian names first. Thus we have "D. Jo. Chrysostomi," "S. Cyrilli," "Jac. Goar," etc., and so even with the Christian names of English authors. As to the conditions of sale, they were very simple, and the most important of them are still retained in literary auction catalogues. Thus we have, "That those which bid most are the Buyers; and if any manifest Differences should Arise, that then the same Book or Books shall be forthwith exposed again to Sale." The books were sold as perfect, and allowed to be rejected if found imperfect before being taken away. The descriptions are of the shortest kind; in very few instances occupying more than a single line for each book. There is no attempt to distinguish editions, nothing about condition or binding. The printers' names are not given, only the place of printing. As to the library itself, it is such a one as a learned divine like Dr. Seaman might be expected to gather, consisting of the works of the Fathers and Schoolmen; learned, critical, and philological works; the writings of contemporary English and foreign divines of the Puritan school; and a goodly number of books and pamphlets printed in the reign of Henry VIII., Edward VI., Mary and Elizabeth, chiefly of the controversial kind. The catalogue is remarkable for the conspicuous absence of Elizabethan poetry, and indeed of all poetry; neither Shakespeare nor Milton being represented in any shape or form. It contains a particular rarity in John Eliot's Indian Bible, printed at Cambridge, in New England, in 1636, which was then thought so little of as to be described as follows, under "Biblia"—*Veteris et Novi Testamenti in Ling. Indica, Cantabr. in Nova Anglia.* It sold for a few shillings, and is now worth £200. Of specimens of early typography the library was quite destitute, the only "fifteener" in it being the Florentine *Homer* of 1488. A copy of the *Complutensian Polyglott* of Cardinal Ximenes and, as usual, the *Walton Polyglott* figure amongst the Bibles.

It was thought that detailed particulars of such an interesting document connected with the history of literary auctions as this first sale catalogue, would be interesting to book-lovers; but a more rapid and general view of the whole subject of this paper must at this time be sufficient. The writer hopes to treat it more in detail in another form. The possession of what is believed to be a nearly complete series of early English book-auction catalogues, extending to 1691, enables us to trace with certainty the history of this method of dispersing Libraries. From an interesting list which Cooper has printed on a blank page of a sale-catalogue of the library of Walter Rea, Esq., we know for certain how many auctions were held between October, 1676, and October, 1682. From this list also may be gathered some information which could not be gleaned from the catalogues themselves. Thus he gives the names of several of the owners of books, which do not appear on the titles of the catalogues. We learn furthermore that thirty sales were held between 1676 and 1682. In this list are included the libraries of many important historical and literary persons, whose names and reputations have lasted to our own time, such as W. Greenhill, author of a *Commentary on Ezekiel*, still read; Dr. Thos. Manton; Brooke, Lord Warwick; Sir K. Digby; Dr. Stephen Charnock; Dr. Thos. Watson; Jo. Dunton, the eccentric bookseller; Dr. Castell, the author of the *Heptaglotton*; Dr. Thos. Gataker, etc.

Between the first and second sales occurred an interval of three months, Seaman's beginning on the last day of October, 1676, and Kidner's beginning February 6th, 167$\frac{6}{7}$. A still longer interval occurs between the second and third sales; and then another auctioneer steps upon the stage in the person of Zacharias Bourne, the library sold being that of the Rev. Wm. Greenhill, Rector of Stepney, Middlesex. This sale took place on the 18th of February, 167$\frac{7}{8}$, rather more than a year after that of Kidner. It is particularly interesting from the fact that it was the first book auction (and the first " hammer " auction) held at a coffee-house. It was sold " in vico vulgo dicto, Bread St. in Ædibus Ferdinandi Stable Coffipolæ ad insigne capitis Turcæ."

Between February, 167$\frac{7}{8}$, and February, 167$\frac{8}{9}$, were issued seven auction catalogues. One of these comprised the library of Dr. Benj. Worsley, and "duorum aliorum Doctorum Præstantium." This catalogue introduces us to two new names as auctioneers, viz.: John Dunmore and Rich. Chiswell, booksellers. The sale was held at the house " over against the Hen and Chickens," in Paternoster Row, and began on the 13th of May, 1678. This is classified, but each class is arranged alphabetically. It is the first example of this mode which is specially referred to by the auctioneers as being adopted " for the more ease and Satisfaction of all Buyers." Two or three other interesting particulars may be gleaned from the preface to this catalogue. First, that the method of the sale of books by auction had " met with good approbation and acceptance from all Lovers of Books." Secondly, that a suspicion had got abroad that a system of " running up," or raising the prices of the books by indirect means—a system perhaps not quite unknown in our own days—was to be resorted to. The auctioneers emphatically deny this, and " affirm that it is a groundless and malicious suggestion of some of our own trade envious of our undertaking;" and they proceed to say that to avoid all suspicion they have refused to accept " commissions " to buy in this sale—the first example of the word being used in this sense. In another sale, November 11, 1678, which included the libraries of Dr. John Godolphin and Dr. Owen Phillips, and of which Cooper again appears as the auctioneer, it may be noted that, according to the preface, the method of selling books by auction was so well established as to need neither apology nor explanation. The place of sale is interesting from a topographical point of view, it having taken place in "Westmorland Court in St. Bartholomew Close, by the *New Alley that leads into Aldersgate Street.*"

The next book-auction catalogue introduces to us an entirely new episode in connection with our subject. The title is, "*Catalogus Variorum Librorum instructissimæ Bibliothecæ præstantissimo doctissimiq. Viri in Angliâ Defuncti : ut et aliorum in omnibus Scientiis atque Linguis insignium, ex Bibliotheca clarissimi Gisbertii Voetii emptorum, cum multis aliis tum antiquis, tum modernis, nuperrimè ex variis partibus Europæ advectis.*" This collection of books was evidently a bookseller's speculation—what would be termed in the auction slang of our day a "*Rig.*" The title gives the names of no less than seven booksellers' at which catalogues could be had, at the head of which is that of Moses Pitt, who was also the auctioneer. Pitt's business as bookseller and publisher was one of the most extensive of his time. He was the agent for the sale of the learned productions of the press set up in the newly constructed theatre of Arch. Sheldon at Oxford; and, as we shall presently see, the first to hold what is known as a trade sale, *i.e.*, a sale of newly published books to the trade only. He was also the compiler or editor of several works, the best known of which is his immense *English Atlas*, an advertisement of which appears in this catalogue. It was in consequence of the expenses of producing this work that he was imprisoned for debt ; and has left behind his interesting little work, called "*The Cry of the Oppressed : being a true account of the sufferings of imprisoned debtors under the Tyranny of Gaolers.*" The books in this sale—which was held at the White Hart in Bartholomew Close, and began November 25, 1678—were "bought out of the best libraries abroad and out of the most eminent seats of learning beyond the seas." Pitt considers it a necessity to insist upon strangers paying at once for the books bought by them at this auction, "that all suspicions may be removed of any strangers appearing there to bid and enhance the price to others, without ever intending to send for what they so buy themselves;" and he further promises that he will "not use any indirect way to advance or promote the sale by commissions or friends." In this catalogue are to be found numbers of *Early Voyages to America*, etc., in foreign languages, which are now of immense value, but which were then thought so little of as to necessitate several of them being put together to make one lot. The method adopted is that of an alphabet of authors for the subdivisions. It is also interesting to note that this is the first catalogue in which "large-paper" copies are particularized.

On the 2nd of December, in the same year, were sold books from the libraries of Brooke, Lord Warwick, and Dr. G. Sangar, which introduces to us another new auctioneer in the person of Nathaniel Renew, bookseller, at the sign of the Kinges Armes in Paul's Churchyard. He notices in his preface the frequency of the "auctionary" way of disposing of books, and gives a passing cut at Moses Pitt's catalogue of *Books from Abroad ;* this collection being, as he says, "not made by any private hand for gain, imputed to some auctions as a reflection, but really belonging to the persons whose names are on the title."

The next auction is that "trade sale" of which mention is made above. It is a catalogue of books printed at the Sheldonian Theatre at Oxford, of which Moses Pitt appears to have purchased the "remainders." The sale was intended for booksellers only. The books were sold in lots of two, four, or six copies, according as the company desired, and were to be paid for at intervals of one, three, six, nine, twelve, and fifteen months, according to the amount of the purchase-money.

John Dunmore sold the library of Sir Edward Bish, or Byssh, Clarencieux King of Arms, in Ivy Lane, on November 15, 1679. By this time the principle and practice of book auctions had become quite familiar, six or seven sales taking place every year; and we can do little more than briefly review the remainder, stopping to notice only some interesting general particulars. Edward Millington sold the stock of two booksellers in Warwick Lane, March 29, 1680. The early auctioneers appear to have chosen any sort of house to conduct their sales in. Thus we find that the library of Dr. Stephen Charnock, Proctor of Oxford University, and a very learned divine, was sold at an upholsterer's house in Cornhill, the sign of the Lamb, in October, 1680—on the catalogue of which the name of the auctioneer does not appear. A sale which took place at "Bridge's Coffee-House," in Pope's Head Alley, November 22, 1680, is the first with the catalogue title in English. It is also interesting as the first sale which took place at this well-known coffee-house, which was several times afterwards used for the same purpose. The custom of selling books by auction at coffee-houses soon became frequent, and besides that of Bridge's, the following houses were used: "Jonathan's," in Exchange Alley, Cornhill; "Tom's," in Pope's Head Alley (who may have been Bridge's successor); "Sam's," "Roll's," and others. Besides these places there appear to have been at least three houses recognised as "auction-houses" (*Domus Auctionarii*). One in Warwick Lane, opposite Coxe's Rents; another in Ivy Lane, kept by John Dunmore, the bookseller and auctioneer; and a third opposite the Black Swan in Ave Maria Lane.

A very interesting episode in the history of early English book auctions is that of the introduction of the method into the provinces. Millington, the auctioneer, took down with him to Stourbridge, near Cambridge, at fair-time, in September, 1684, a quantity of miscellaneous books, which he sold by auction in a booth, appealing to the learned of the University to patronize him. He appears to have succeeded well enough to encourage him in a second attempt in the same place the next fair-time; and in the year following he sold in the City of Cambridge itself the library of the learned Dr. Castell, who assisted Brian Walton with his *Polyglott Bible*, and composed its indispensable handmaid, the *Lexicon Heptaglotton*. Millington was also the introducer of auctions into Oxford jointly with William Cooper, they together selling the stock of the Oxford bookseller, Richard Davis, in April and October, 1686, after which several sales were held in the University City. Indeed, such was the roving nature of Millington, that we find him treating the inhabitants of Norwich to a sale of books by auction, "at Mrs. Elizabeth Oliver's house," December 16, 1689; and in 1692 he travelled to Abingdon, and made a sale in the Town Hall, most likely under the patronage of the Mayor himself, since he makes a neat dedication to him in his catalogue. In this preface he mentions "having made sales of this nature in many places in this kingdom," so that he probably issued several other catalogues which are now lost. On the whole, Millington's career as a travelling book-auctioneer is most interesting, and worth treating in detail, which may possibly be done on another occasion. The manner of conducting these early sales was somewhat different to that which prevails in our own day. Instead of the catalogues being divided into "days," in which a stated number of lots should be sold, the first auctioneers sold as many lots as they could in a stated time. Thus they began at a certain time, and left off at a certain time, and so continued day by day until all the lots were sold. There is only one early auction catalogue from which we can gather particulars of the time occupied in selling. It is a sale of the library of Dr. Paget, conducted by Cooper in October, 1681. This catalogue contains 2,178 numbers, and he informs us that he hopes to dispose of the whole in four days. This gives 544 numbers in a day. The hours of sale were from eight o'clock in the morning until twelve, and again from two o'clock until six, the actual time occupied in selling being eight hours. This gives us about sixty-eight lots as the average number sold in each hour. With regard to biddings, Gough says that he noticed in one catalogue that penny biddings were taken; it is certain that up to ten shillings twopenny biddings was the usual custom, but no rule with regard to them appears to have been made by the auctioneers. There was much heart-burning upon a subject which afflicts as well auctioneers in our own day. Impecunious people attacked with bibliomania very soon got into the way of having books knocked down to them, without the slightest intention of paying for them. Cooper complains greatly of this; and Millington, in the preface to a catalogue issued in May, 1681, goes so far as to threaten to prosecute all such "according to law." The early hour in the morning at which Cooper began his sales naturally led to a poor attendance, and he was soon compelled to require as a condition of beginning at the appointed time that twenty people should be present. Later on the time was altered to nine o'clock, at which hour it remained for some time, when the morning sales were dropped, and the time altered to twelve, one, and two o'clock, as it prevails in our own time. The last book auction of the seventeenth century was that of the Library of Dr. Wm. Hopkins, Prebendary of Worcester Cathedral, which was sold in Oxford, February 10, 170⁰/₁.

The subject of early English book auctions is far from being exhausted in this paper, and is certainly of sufficient interest to call for its treatment in greater detail. But time and space forbid it to be done here; and in the meantime this hasty sketch may not be ungratifying to readers of *Book-Lore*.

A FORECAST OF PHOTOGRAPHY AND TELEPHONY.

AMONGST the industrious and once popular writers who have descended into oblivion, we must include the name of Charles François Tiphaigne de la Roche. Very little is known of his personal history, but we know that he died in 1774 at Montebourg, his native place, at the age of forty-five, having attained some local distinction as a physician. His scientific tastes, which probably led to his election as a member of the Academy of Rouen, are evidenced by his writings on agriculture, and on the western seas of his native country. He wrote also a number of philosophical and speculative books, and of these the most curious is *Giphantié*. The curiosity of the book begins with the title, for it is an anagram of the author's name. The book is an account of an imaginary kingdom in Africa, which was given to the "elementary spirits" before the Garden of Eden was allotted to mankind. One of its mechanical adjuncts looks a little like an anticipation of the telephone.

The President of Giphantié, speaking of the elementary spirits, says :—

"No sooner are they out of the probation-column, where they are purified, but they return to their usual labours : and to see where there presence is most necessary, and where men have most need of their assistance. At their coming out of the column they ascend this hill. There, by a mechanism which required the utmost skill of the spirits, everything that passes in all parts of the world is seen and heard. Thou art going to try the experiments thyself.

"On each side of the column is a large staircase of above a hundred steps, which leads to the top of the hill. We went up, and were scarce half-way, when my ears were struck with a disagreeable humming, which increased as we advanced. When we came to a platform, in which the hill ends, the first thing that struck my eyes was a globe of a considerable diameter. From the globe proceeded the noise which I heard. At a distance it was a humming; near, it was a frightful thundering noise, formed by a confused mixture of shouts for joy, ravings of despair, shrieks, complaints, singing, murmurs, acclamations, laughter, groans, and whatever proclaims the immoderate sorrow and extravagant joy of mortals.

"Small imperceptible pipes (said the Prefect) come from each point of the earth's surface and end at this globe. The inside is organized so that the motion of the air, which is propagated through the imperceptible pipes, and grows weaker in time, resumes fresh force at the entrance into the globe and becomes sensible again. Hence these noises and hummings. But what would these confused sounds signify if means were not found to distinguish them? Behold the image of the earth painted on the globe; the islands, the continents,·

the oceans which surround, join, and divide all.　Dost thou not see Europe, that quarter of the earth that hath done so much mischief to the other three? Burning Africa, where arts and the wants that attend them have never penetrated? Asia, whose luxury, passing to the European nations, has done so much good, according to some, and so much hurt, according to others?　America, still dyed with the blood of its unhappy inhabitants, whom men of a religion that breathes peace and good-will came to convert and barbarously murder?　Observe what point of the globe thou pleasest.　Place there the end of this rod which I give thee, and putting the other end to thy ear, thou shalt hear distinctly whatever is said in the corresponding part of the earth."

The mortal visitor is one day taken by the Prefect into a hall, and looking through the window, as he supposes, he is astonished at the sudden change which has converted a smiling day into one of cloud and storm.　" By what miracle," he asks, "has the air, serene a moment ago, been so suddenly obscured?　By what miracle do I see the ocean in the centre of Africa?" Intent upon further investigation of this remarkable change in the weather, he attempts to put his head through the window for an external survey, but instead knocks it against something that felt like a wall, and then found that the dark and frowning landscape was only a picture.　The method in which this had been executed is then described by the Prefect.　This passage must be quoted in full:—

" The elementary spirits (said the Prefect) are not so able painters as naturalists; thou shalt judge by their way of working.　Thou knowest that the rays of light, reflected from different bodies, make a picture and paint the bodies upon all polished surfaces—on the retina of the eye, for instance, on water, on glass.　The elementary spirits *have studied to fix these transient images;* they have composed a most subtile matter, very viscous, and proper to harden and dry, by the help of which a picture is made in the twinkle of an eye.　They do over with this matter a piece of canvas, and hold it before the objects they have a mind to paint.　The first effect of the canvas is that of a mirrour; there are seen upon it all the bodies far and near whose image the light can transmit.　But what the glass cannot do, the canvas, by means of the viscous matter, retains the images. The mirror shows the objects exactly, but keeps none; our canvases show them with the same exactness, and retain them all.　This impression of the images is made the first instant they are received on the canvas, which is immediately carried away into some dark place: an hour after the subtile matter dries, and you have a picture so much the more valuable, as it cannot be imitated by art, nor damaged by time.　We take, in their purest source, in the luminous bodies, the colours which painters extract from different materials, and which time never fails to alter.　The justness of the design, the truth of the expression, the gradation of the shades, the stronger or weaker strokes, the rules of perspective, all these we leave to Nature, who, with a sure and never-erring hand, draws upon our canvases images which deceive the eye, and make reason to doubt whether what are called real objects are not phantoms which impose upon the sight, the hearing, the feeling, and all the senses at once. The Prefect then entered into some physical discussions: first, on the nature of the glutinous substance which intercepted and retained the rays; secondly, upon the difficulties of preparing and using it; thirdly, upon the struggle between the rays of light and the dried substance—three problems which I propose to the naturalists of our days, and leave to their sagacity."

It is only necessary to add that this fantastic prevision of the processes of photography was published in French at the Hague in the year 1760, and that an English translation, from which our quotation is taken, appeared in London in the following year. Truly, the book is such stuff as dreams are made of; but there is something remarkable, when all deductions have been made, in the manner in which the Frenchman's fairy-tale, in however fantastic a fashion, anticipates the sober reality of the present day.

WORKS OF THOMAS TAYLOR THE PLATONIST.

By Orlin Mead Sanford.

II.

PLOTINUS. *An Essay on the Beautiful.* From the Greek of Plotinus. Beautiful and rare frontispiece of a female figure. In original boards, with errata, uncut edges, 1 vol. 12mo., pp. 47. Printed for the author. London, 1792.

[*n.* Either this is a 2nd edition, or it is the old one of 1787, supplied with a new and different title-page. Page 37 is, by mistake in *each*, printed 27, and this would favour the latter view. This is not mentioned in Edward Peacock's list, and is excessively scarce.]

Plotinus: Five Books of, viz.: On Felicity; On the Nature and Origin of Evil; On Providence; On Nature, Contemplation, and The One; and on the Descent of the Soul. Translated from the Greek, with an Introduction, containing Additional Information on these Important Subjects. By Thomas Taylor. 1 vol. 8vo., half calf, large paper. London, 1794.

Plotinus: Select Works of. The Great Restorer of the Philosophy of Plato; and Extracts from the Treatise of Synesius on Providence. Translated from the Greek. With an Introduction containing the substance of Porphyry's Life of Plotinus. By Thomas Taylor. 1 vol. 8vo., full white vellum, with tooling, very choice copy. Printed for and sold by the author, and by Black and Son. London, 1817.

[*n.* We learn from an article in the *Atlantic Monthly* for June, 1883, upon "Mr. Emerson in the Lecture Room," that, "Mr. Emerson read carefully selected passages from Plotinus, and afterward gave the history of his life so far as it is known; then, taking up an octavo volume, translated by Thomas Taylor, of Norwich, which contained the Essay of Synesius on Providence, he spoke of its untold value to the world."]

Plotinus: Translations from the Greek, of the following Treatises of Plotinus, viz.: On Suicide; to which is added an extract from the Harleian MSS. of the Scholia of Olympiodorus on the Phaedo of Plato respecting Suicide, accompanied by the Greek Text; two books on Truly Existing Being; and Extracts from his Treatise on the Manner in which the Multitude of Ideas subsists, and concerning the Good; with additional notes from Porphyry and Proclus. By Thomas Taylor. 1 vol. new half calf, uncut edges, gilt top. Printed for the translator, 9, Manor Place, Walworth. London, 1843.

[*n*. In his preface to the above, Mr. Taylor speaks of the brevity of diction which applies to the writing of Plotinus, and of the many beautiful passages therein, and of him as "this most extraordinary man who was the first that brought to light the divine wisdom of Plato, after it had been in oblivion for 500 years."]

Porphyry: Select Works of. Containing his four books on Abstinence from Animal Food; his Treatise on the Homeric Cave of the Nymphs, and his Auxiliaries to the Perception of Intelligible Natures. Translated from the Greek by Thomas Taylor. With an Appendix explaining the Allegory of the Wanderings of Ulysses. By the translator. 1 vol. 8vo., half calf. London, 1823.

Proclus: Commentaries of, Philosophical and Mathematical, On the First Book of Euclid's Elements; to which are added, a History of the Restoration of the Platonic Theology, by the Latter Platonists; and a translation from the Greek of Proclus's Theological Elements. Dedicated "To the Sacred Majesty of Truth." 2 vols. 4to., calf, with beautiful vignettes. Pub., in boards, at two guineas. Printed for the author. London, 1792.

[*n*. In his study of these commentaries it is said that Mr. Taylor read them through thrice, a task, perhaps, never performed by any other man.]

Proclus: Two Treatises of. The Platonic Successor; the former consisting of Ten Doubts concerning Providence, and a Solution of those Doubts; and the latter containing a Development of the Nature of Evil. Translated from the edition of these works by Victor Cousin. By Thomas Taylor. Printed for the translator, and sold by William Pickering. Only 250 copies printed. Dedicated to Charles Atwood, Esq. 1 vol. London, 1833.

[*n*. Upon the fly-leaf of this volume appears the following inscription in Mr. Taylor's writing: "Presented to I. P. Cory, Esq., by the Translator, with his best respects." Isaac Preston Cory was a friend of Taylor's, and author of *Ancient Fragments.* Bound up with *Fragments of Lost Writings of Proclus;* and the 1805 edition of *Miscellanies.*]

Proclus: The Six Books of. The Platonic Successor, On the Theology of Plato, translated from the Greek; to which a Seventh Book is added, in order to supply the deficiency of another book on this subject, which was written by Proclus, but since lost. Also a translation from the Greek of Proclus' Elements of Theology. To which are added a Translation of Extracts from his Treatise, entitled Ten Doubts Concerning Providence; and a translation of Extracts from his Treatise on the Subsistence of Evil; as preserved in the Bibliotheca Gr. of Fabricius. By Thomas Taylor. 2 vols., heavy full calf, tooled. Pub. at £5 10s. Printed for the author. London, 1816.

[*n.* Dedicated "To William Meredith, Esq., who with a firmness and muni-ficence, unparalleled in modern times, has patronized the Philosophy of Plato and Aristotle, and its English promulgation; as an acknowledgment of no common esteem for his character, and a tribute of the warmest gratitude for his patronage, this work is dedicated by the translator, Thomas Taylor."]

Proclus: Lost Writings of. The Fragments that remain of Proclus, surnamed the Platonic Successor. Translated from the Greek. By Thomas Taylor. 1 vol. Dedicated to Mrs. Elizabeth Howard. Printed for the author. London, 1825.

[*n.* Only 250 copies. This is bound in with the *Two Treatises of Proclus,* and the 1805 edition of *Miscellanies in Prose and Verse,*" both of which are autographic presentation copies. Among these Fragments, there are narrated five very remark-able instances of persons who have returned to life after they have been for a considerable time buried. See p. 109.]

Proclus: Commentaries of. On the Timaeus of Plato, in five books; Containing a Treasury of Pythagoric and Platonic Physiology. Translated from the Greek. By Thomas Taylor. 2 vols., heavy full calf, tooled. Pub. at £5 10s. Printed for and sold by the author. London, 1810.

[*n.* There is a curious discussion of the Atlantis Theory and the Atlantic Island, in the 2nd vol., pp. 147, etc.]

Sallust on the Gods and the World; and the Pythagoric Sentences of Demophilus. Translated from the Greek; and Five Hymns, by Proclus, in the original Greek, with a poetical version. To which are added Five Hymns by the translator. 1 vol. 8vo., half calf. London, 1793.

[*n.* Apparently large paper.]

THE ROSICRUCIANS.*

R. PLOT, in his well-known *History of Staffordshire*, relates a strange story of a countryman, who being employed in digging a trench, struck his spade on a large oblong stone with an immense iron ring fixed at one end in a socket. Raising this stone, after considerable difficulty, he descended a flight of steps as befitted a man of courage, and found himself, when deep in the bowels of the earth, at the entrance of a long corridor. Pursuing his way through many tortuous windings, he came at last to a vaulted chamber hewn out of the solid rock, in which sat an aged man reading a book. The vault was brilliantly illuminated from above, and on every side rose columns carved with fantastic and weird devices. The strangeness of the scene so alarmed the poor man that he gave an involuntary cry, and immediately the figure, rising in awful majesty, shattered the lamp to atoms with an iron *bâton*, leaving the place in utter darkness. This was the end of the terrifying adventure. Only a long, low roll of thunder seemed to begin from a distance, gradually increasing to a climax, when it rumbled suddenly to sleep through unknown and inaccessible passages. How the countryman found his way out is not related; but get out he certainly did, for the place became afterwards famed as the sepulchre of one of the brethren of the Rosy Cross, or for want of a more distinct recognition the people called "Rosicrucius."

This and similar tales, one of them bordering on, if not exceeding, the limits of credibility, point to a certain vague and lingering belief, even yet not entirely dissipated, in a coterie of sages brought up and trained through the centuries in all the *arcana* and hidden mysteries of nature.

The Rosicrucian philosophers, so-called after the name of their master Christian Rosencrentz, are supposed to have been a sect of Hermetic adepts, and are described by Mr. Hargrave Jennings as wedded to poverty and chastity. Sole possessors of the philosopher's stone, they could make gold at pleasure, and yet preferred to be poor; masters of the *elixir vitæ*, they chose death to eternal life.

If any student of the mysterious should endeavour to pry into the hidden history of these sages, he would find his efforts frustrated almost at the onset. No one ever yet saw a Rosicrucian knowing him to be such, while the writings the very few who have deigned to enlighten the outer world abound in such mysterious and equivocal directions that it is absolutely impossible to understand a single phrase that is penned. If Artephius was a member of the brotherhood,

* *Tractatus Apologeticus integritatem Societatis de Rosea-Cruce defendens*, by Robert Flood, Leyden, 1617; *The Rights and Attributes of the True Rosicrucians*, by J. Von D——; *The Rosicrucians, their Rites and Mysteries*, by Hargrave Jennings. London: Chatto and Windus, 1879.

he was clearly determined that no one else but himself and others like him should derive the least benefit from his explanations. The same may be said of Vaughan, and even of Flood.

Mr. Jennings, who studied the subject for more than thirty years, and whose book, *The Rites and Mysteries of the Rosicrucians*, is undoubtedly the standard work on this particular branch of necromantic lore, admits that he knows nothing. He has, it is true, traced to their source many quaint and apparently meaningless devices, showing at the same time how those devices have been perpetuated through many hundred years, from one generation to another, until they assume their present form ; but of the philosophers themselves, who they are, when they lived, or whence they came, he is entirely ignorant.

Where Mr. Jennings has failed, it would be useless for us to endeavour to succeed ; and so far as we are concerned the brethren of the Rosy Cross, who " come like shadows, so depart," must ever remain in their wonted obscurity.

In addition to the books already mentioned in this article, the inquisitive reader may wade, if he can, through the doctrines laid down by Paracelsus. The works of this voluminous author—still, according to his disciples, " living in his tomb, whence he retired disgusted with the vices and follies of mankind,"—were published complete in two volumes, folio, Geneva, 1658 ; and though not of frequent occurrence, may still occasionally be met with.

Paracelsus was a Rosicrucian, if ever there was one ; and it is a matter of curious comment that this "immortal man," the master of the philosopher's stone and the elixir of life, beside other things too numerous to mention, should have died, as he had generally lived, drunk in an inn at Saltzburg, having barely attained his fortieth year.

Flood, another disciple of Rosencrentz, died at the age of sixty, and lies buried in the church at Bersted in Kent, having left behind him numerous works, which perhaps, beyond all others of the class, are the easiest to understand. The following list comprises the most important of his productions :—

1. *Utrius que cosmi, majoris et minoris, Technica Historia.* 2 vols., folio. Oppenheim, 1617.

2. *Tractatus Apologeticus integritatem Societatis de Rosea-Cruce defendens.* Folio. Leyden, 1617.

3. *Monochordon mundi symphoniarum, seu replicatio ad apologiam Johannis Kepleri.* Folio. Francfort, 1620.

4. *Anatomia Theatrum triplici effigie designatum.* Folio. Francfort, 1623.

5. *Philosophia Sacra et vere Christiana, seu Meteorologia Cosmica.* Folio. Francfort, 1626.

6. *Medicina Catholica, seu, Mysterium Artis Medicandi Sacrarium.* Folio. Francfort, 1626.

7. *Integrum Morborum Mysterium.* Folio. Francfort, 1631.

8. *Clavis Philosophiæ et Alchymiæ.* Folio. Francfort, 1633.
9. *Philosophia Mosaica.* Folio. Goudæ, 1638.
10. *Pathologia Dæmoniaca.* Folio. Goudæ, 1640.
11. *Fasciculus Geomanticus, etc.* Folio. Verona, 1704.

Beyond the works of Flood and Paracelsus, there is hardly anything which touches on the peculiar doctrines held by the Rosicrucians. References to the subject are frequently met with in the pages of those quacks and charlatans who in the Middle Ages passed for magicians; but the reader of such lore will find just as great a difficulty in understanding the allusions, as the authors had in comprehending what they had written.

THE GENIUS OF THE BOTTLE.

There's a queer little bottle stands here on my desk,
It is shaped like a boat, and is quite picturesque,
With a figure-head just the least trifle grotesque.
It holds in its depths, though you never may know it,
And I may not clearly be able to show it,
The treasures of romance, pundit and poet.
There are positive facts for the solemn and wise,
And fables for those who like truth in disguise,
And many a fancy that floats to the skies.
There are songs that are sweet as the songs of the lark,
And jests dating back to the days of the ark;
There are arrows of wit that fly straight to the mark.
And tales of devotion and honour and truth,
And stories of danger and beauty and ruth,
That quicken the pulse in the bosom of youth.
There are truths that flash out like a sword in the fight,
That shine like a star in the darkness of night,
To guide straying feet from the wrong to the right.
There are true-lover songs full many, I ween,
There is solace for sorrow, and praises serene,
And the strong staff of Hope, whereon weakness may lean.
Of the Genius who holds of this bottle the keys,
I speak in a parable now, if you please,
I pray, on my bent—metaphorical—knees,
Every day for the secret by which to extract
The song, the romance, the wit, wisdom and fact,
With which, to my knowledge, this bottle is packed.
And oft, as I raise my importunate plea,
He touches my lips with a chrism none see,
And then, when he hears me—why then, you hear *me;*
For, whatever he gives of his marvellous store,
With pride that is humble I bring to your door,
And, grateful and happy, I pray evermore,
O Genius, who stands on the strange bottle's brink,
Aid me forever and ever to link
My heart to the world's with a drop of its ink.

CARLOTTA PERRY.

The Independent.

NOTES ON WELSH BIBLES.

By J. R. Dore.

I.

S a new version of the Bible in the Welsh language is now being prepared, a few notes may be interesting anent the editions that have already appeared. These are not numerous. During the sixteenth century only one translation of the New Testament by itself, and one of the whole Bible, were issued; the first in quarto, and the second in small folio. For nearly one hundred years after the Reformation, no Welsh Bible of a convenient size was in existence; and during the whole of the seventeenth century, and a good way into the eighteenth, there were but two folios and four octavo editions printed. None of these editions consisted of a considerable number of copies. It is estimated that the whole of the impressions did not amount to more than 30,000; a very small number for the use of 300,000 persons.

Only one manuscript translation of any part of the Bible into Welsh is known, and that is a Welsh version of the Pentateuch.

In the year 1551 some detached portions of the Bible were translated from the Vulgate into the Welsh language. They are entitled : *Certain portions of Scripture appointed to be read in Churches in the time of Communion and Public Worship.* In the year 1562 it was enacted by Parliament (5 Eliz., c. 28), " That the Bible, containing the New Testament and the Old, together with the Book of Common Prayer and the administration of the Sacraments, should be translated into the British or Welsh tongue . . . should be viewed, perused, and allowed by the Bishops of S. Asaph, Bangor, S. David, Landaff and Hereford . . . should be printed and used in the churches by the 1st of March, in the year 1566, under a penalty, in case of failure, of forty pounds, to be levied on each of the above Bishops. That one printed copy at least of this translation should be had for and in every cathedral, collegiate, and parish church and chapel of ease throughout Wales, to be read by the Clergy in time of Divine service, and at other times for the benefit and perusal of any who had a mind to go to church for that purpose, as the inhabitants of Wales, being no small part of the realm, are utterly destituted (*sic*) of God's Holy Word, and do remain in the like, or rather more, darkness and ignorance than they were in the time of Papistry." " That till this version of the Bible and Book of Common Prayer should be completed and published, the Clergy of that country should read in time of worship, the Epistles and Gospels, the Lord's Prayer, the Articles of the Christian Faith, the Litany, and such other parts of the Common Prayer Book, in the Welsh tongue, as should be directed and appointed by the above-mentioned Bishops."

" And not only during this interval but ever after, English Bibles and

Common Prayers should be had and remain in every church and chapel throughout that country, with the Welsh translation, so that such as do not understand the English language may, by conferring both tongues together, the sooner attain to the knowledge of the English tongue, anything in this Act to the contrary notwithstanding." One year after the expiration of the time appointed by the above Act of Parliament, namely, in the year 1567, the first New Testament in Welsh was issued. It was printed by Henry Denham, at the cost and charges of Humphrey Toy, in a handsome quarto volume of 399 leaves, similar to the Blank Stone, Mole, and Engraver's-mark editions of Tyndale; black-letter type, not divided into verses, but with arguments and contents to each chapter and book. In the margins are explanations of difficult words, but no references to parallel passages. In the preliminary matter is a "calendar" and a dedication in English to "the most vertuous and noble Prince (*sic*) Elizabeth, and a long Epistle in Welsh, by the Bishop of St. David to his countrymen. This version is said to have been made from the original Greek, and the Vulgate. This *Editio princeps* being now excessively rare, it may be worth while to append its dedication :—

"To the most vertuous and noble Prince Elizabeth, by the grace of God of England, France, and Ireland, Queene, defender of the Faith, etc.

"When I call to remembrance, as well the face of the corrupted religion in England, at what tyme Paules Churcheyarde in the citie was occupied by makers of alabaster images to be set up in churches; and they of Pater-noster-rowe earned their lyving by makyng of Pater-noster bedes only; they of Aue-lane by selling Aue-bedes; of Crede-lane by makyng Crede-bedes: As also the vaine rites crepte into our countrey of Wales, whan, instead of the lyving God, men worshipped dead images of wood and stones, belles and bones, with other such uncertain reliques I wot not what; and withal consider our late general revolt from Goddes most holy worde once receaued, and dayly heare of the lyke enforced uppon our brethern in forain countryes, having most piteousely susteined great calamities, bitter afflictions and merciles persecutions; under which verye many doe yet styll remain; I cannot, most Christian Prince, and gracious Soueraine, but even as dyd the poore blynde Bartimeus or Samaritane lepre to our Sauiour, so I com before your Maiesties feete, and there lying prostrate, not onely for myself, but also for the deliuery of many thousandes of my countrey folkes, from the spiritual blyndnes of ignoraunce and fowl infection of the old idolatrie and false superstition, most humbly and dutifully to acknowlege your incomparable benefite bestowed upon vs in graunting the sacred Scriptures (the verye remedie and salve of our ghostly blyndness and leprosie) to be had in our best knowen tongue; which as far as euer I can gather (thoughe Christ's trewe religion sometyme floorished emong our auncesters the old Britons) yet were neuer so entierlye and uniuersallye had, as we now God be thanked haue them.

"Our countreymen in tymes passed were indede most loth (and that not wythout good cause) to receaue the Romish religion, and yet haue they nowe synce (such is the domage of euyll custome) bene loth to forsake the same, and to receaue the gospell of Christ. But after that thys nation, as it is thought, for their apostasie had ben fore-plagued wyth long warres, and finally vanquished, and by rigorous lawes kept under, yet at the last it pleased God of his accustomed clemencie to looke down agayne upon them, sending a most godly and noble David and a wyse Solomon, I meane Henry the Seventh and his sonne Henry the Eighth (both kynges of most famous memorie, and your Grace's father and grandfather), who graciously released their paynes and mitigated their intolerable burthens, the one with charters of liberties, and the other with Acts of Parlya-ment, by abandoning from them al bondage and thraldom, and incorporating them wyth his other louing subjects of England.

"Thys, no doubt, was no small benefit touchyng bodyly welth ; but thys benefit of your Maiesties prouidence and goodnesse excedeth that other so far as the soule doeth the bodye. Certaine noble women (whereof some were chiefe rulers of thys nowe your isle of Britain), are by antiquitie vnto us for their singuler learning and heroical vertues highely commended, as Cambra the Fayre, Martia the Good, Bunducia the Wariar, Claudia Rufina mentioned in S. Paules epistle, and Helena, mother of the great and first Christian emperor Constantinus Magnus, and S. Ursula of Cornwals, with such others who are also at thys day styl renowned ; but of your Maiestie, I may as I thynk, right well use the wordes of that king who surnamed himself Lemuel. Many doughters have don vertuously ; but thou surmountest them all. Fauour is deceiptfull, and beautie is vanitie : but a woman that feareth the Lord, she shall be praysed. For if M. Magdalen for the bestowing of a boxe of material oyntment, to annoynt Christes carnal body, be so famous throwe out all the world where the gospell is preached, howe muche more shall your munificence by conferring the unction of the holy ghost to annoynct his spiritual body the churche, be ever had in memorie ?

"But to conclude and to drawe neare to offer up my vowe : where as I, by our most vigilant pastours the Bishopes of Wales, am called and substituted, though unworthy, somewhat to deale in the perusing and setting fourth of thys so worthy a matter, I thynk it my most bounden ductie here in their name, to present to your Maiestie (as the chiefest fyrst fruict) a booke of the New Testa-ment of our Lorde Jesvs Christ, translated into the British language, which is our vulgare tongue, wyshing and most humbly praying, if it shall so seme good to your wysedome, that it myght remayne in your M. Librarie, for a perpetual monument of your graciouse bountie shewed herein to our countrey, and the churche of Christ there. And would to God that your Graces subiectes of Wales might also have the whole booke of God's woord brought to like passe : then might their felow subiectes of England reioycingly pronounce of them in these wordes, The people that sate in darknes, have seen a great lyght ; they that dwelled in the land of the shadowe of death upon them hath the lyght shyned.

3—2

Blessed are the people that be so, yea blessed are the people whose God is the Lord. Yea than wold they both together thus brotherly say, Come, and let us go up to the mountaine of the Lord, and he wyll teache us hys wayes, and we wyll walke in his pathes, &c.

"And thus to ende, I beseeche Almyghtye God, that as your Grace's circumspect providence doth perfectlye accomplish and discharge your princely vocation and gouvernaunce towardes all your humble subiects, that we also on our part may towards God and your highness demeane ourselves in such wyse, that His iustice abrydge not these halcyons and quiet days (which hetherto since the begynning of your happie reigne have most calmely and peaceably continued) but that we may long enioy your gracious presence and most prosperous reigne over us : which we beseche God, for our Saviour Jesus Christes sake moste merci-fullye to graunt us. Amen.

Your Maiestie's

Most humble and

Faithfull subiect

WILLIAM SALESBURY."

The translators of this Testament were :

W. S.—William Salesbury ;

T. H. C. M.—Thomas Huet-Chantor, Menew ;

D. R. D. M.—Dr. Richard Davis, Menevensis.

The Bishop of S. David took the second Epistle to S. Timothy, the Hebrews, S. James, and the first and second Epistle of S. Peter ; Thomas Huet, Precentor of S. David's, translated the Apocalypse ; and William Salesbury the rest of the book. All three were men of eminent learning, and their work has ever been regarded as accurate and elegant. Dr. Davis was a native of Denbigh, and was educated at Oxford. He left England at the death of Edward VI. On his return early in the reign of Elizabeth, he was consecrated Bishop of St. Asaph (January 21st, 1560), and translated to the See of S. David May 21st, 1561. He was one of the Bishops selected by Archbishop Parker to revise the Bible of 1568, commonly called the Bishops' Version. His share was the books of Joshua, Judges, and Ruth. He died November 7th, 1581, aged eighty years.

(*To be Continued.*)

REVIEWS.

———

The Bibliography of the Rev. George Oliver, D.D., of Exeter. By T. N. BRUSHFIELD, M.D. Reprinted from the Transactions of the Devonshire Association for the advancement of Science, Literature, and Art, 1885. 8vo., pp. 11.

DR. BRUSHFIELD has done a real service to bibliography by this tract, in which he carefully discriminates between the works of the two writers, each of whom was the Rev. George Oliver, D.D., whilst one was an Anglican clergyman, and the other a priest of the Church of Rome. The confusion which has resulted from the identity of names extends to such works as Lowndes and Allibone; but henceforth each Oliver will enjoy his own rights.

Index to Recent Reference Lists, 1884-5. By WILLIAM COOLIDGE LANE. Republished from the *Bulletin* of Harvard University. Cambridge: Mass., 1885. 8vo., pp. 8.

THIS latest issue of the *Harvard Bibliographical Contributions* is a very useful one. Dante, Skating, Temperance, and Chaucer are amongst the varied topics dealt with by the bibliographers whose labours are here chronicled.

Steele's Selections from the Tatler, Spectator, and Guardian. Edited, with introduction and notes, by AUSTIN DOBSON. Oxford: at the Clarendon Press, 1885. 12mo.

THE 133 essays in this selection are arranged, without regard to the original order of publication, under four heads—Moral and Didactic, Social, Theatrical, and Miscellaneous, and include all the more interesting of Sir Richard Steele's contributions to the *Tatler, Spectator,* and *Guardian.* In the valuable notes at the end of the volume Mr. Dobson has collected some curious matter, and identified many of the persons described, under false names, in the essays. The index unfortunately refers only to these notes, and not to the body of the work. A useful life of Steele forms the introduction to the volume.

Jacob Boehme: his Life and Teaching; or, Studies in Theosophy. By the late DR. HANS LASSEN MARTENSEN, Metropolitan of Denmark. Translated from the Danish by T. RHYS EVANS. London: Hodder and Stoughton. 8vo., pp. xvi. 344.

AMONGST the mystics a high place must be assigned to the shoemaker Böhme, who was born in 1575, and died in 1624. Before his first book—the *Aurora*—was printed, it brought him persecution. Some MS. extracts fell into the hands of a clergyman, who denounced the author in a furious sermon against false prophets. The pastor induced the magistrate to banish Böhme from the town; this sentence was revoked before it was executed; but the mystic was ordered to cease writing, and as a shoemaker to stick to his last. But the persecution brought him friends, who were not only higher in the social scale, but men of learning and science. For five years he refrained from writing, and then broke silence. His theosophical speculations are to be found in a series of volumes which have been translated into English by William Law. But in Böhme's own days he had admirers in this country, and a life of him with a catalogue of his works appeared in 1644. Dr. Martensen's book is an appreciative exposition of the theological views of Böhme. How variously this system has been estimated may be judged by two sentences. Richter, the virulent antagonist of Böhme, declared that "there are as many blasphemies in this shoemaker's book as there are lines." Angelus Silesius, on the other hand, declared:—

> In water lives the fish, the plant in the earth,
> The bird in the air, in the firmament the sun;
> The salamander must subsist in fire,
> And the heart of God is Jacob Böhme's element.

We may express our regret that Dr. Martensen has not given any bibliographical detail, though it may fairly be claimed that such information did not come within the scope of his plan, which is to expound as a connected system the mystical thoughts of the quaint, pious, honest disciple of St. Crispin, to whom has been given the name of the Teutonic Philosopher. As such, Dr. Martensen's book is highly to be commended.

WE have received the following catalogues :—W. Downing, 74, New Street, Birmingham ; Brook and Chrystal, 11, Market Street, Manchester ; Thomas Wilson, 142, Oxford Street, Manchester ; Arthur Reader, 1, Orange Street, Red Lion Square, London, W.C. ; H. Gray, 25, Cathedral Yard, Manchester ; Parry and Co., 46, Mount Pleasant, Liverpool ; John Wilson, 12, King William Street, London, W.C. ; Thomas Simmons, 164, Parade, Leamington ; Walter Scott, 7, Bristo Place, Edinburgh ; James Fawn and Son, 18, Queen's Road, Bristol ; Charles King, Torquay ; R. H. Sutton, 25, Princess Street, Manchester ; Henry Young, 12, South Castle Street, Liverpool ; James Wilson, 35, Bull Street, Birmingham ; James Roche, 1, Southampton Row, Holborn, London, W.C. ; Kerr and Richardson, 89, Queen Street, Glasgow ; Henry Gray, 25, Cathedral Yard, Manchester (Family History) ; H. Grevel and Co., 33, King Street, Covent Garden, London, W.C. ; Albert Cohn, 53, Mohrenstrasse, Berlin (Theoretischer und praktische Musik and Musiker autographen) ; Karl W. Hiersemann, 1, Turnerstrasse, Leipzig (Goethe, Orientalia) ; A. Iredale, Torquay ; J. E. Cornish, 33, Piccadilly, Manchester ; Robson and Kerslake, 23, Coventry Street, Haymarket, London, W. ; James Coleman, 9, Tottenham Terrace, White Hart Lane, Tottenham, N. ; James Fawn and Son, 18, Queen's Road, Bristol ; H. Sotheran and Co., 49, Cross Street, Manchester ; Albert Cohn, 53, Mohrenstrasse, Berlin (Incunables) ; Karl W. Hiersemann, 1, Turnerstrasse, Leipzig (Numismatik, etc.) ; C. Herbert, 319, Goswell Road, London, E.C. ; Bertram Dobell, 66, Queen's Crescent, Haverstock Hill, N.W. ; Kelley, the Albion Club House, King Street, opened March ; J. Yule, 7, Aberdeen Walk, Scarborough.

CORRESPONDENCE.

CRANMER'S BIBLE.

IN the notice of Cranmer's Bible, in the July number of *Book-Lore*, it was shown that the version of the Psalms which appeared in the Prayer Book of 1662 was not taken from that of the great Bible of 1539, but from one of the editions of Cranmer's Bible, which had been followed in the Bishop's Bible of 1602. I had too hastily come to the conclusion that the particular edition followed was that of April, 1540. Mr. John R. Dore, of Huddersfield, has called my attention to the fact that there are two or three misprints in the Psalms as they appear in 1662, which pretty conclusively show that the copy was made from the edition of November, 1541. The principal mistake is so curious and has been so often repeated that it is worth recording.

In Psalm lxviii. 4, the word *yea* has been substituted for *Jah*, and the mistaken reading found its way into the Prayer Book of 1662, from which it was copied in all subsequent editions, as far as I know, till the year 1708. In that year a duodecimo Prayer Book was published at Oxford with the right reading, which, however, was not adopted in the books published by the Queen's printer in London, for the erroneous reading *yea* appears in a London folio of 1711, and also in a 4to., which was published later than June 13, 1715, though I cannot fix the date, as the book has no title, and again in a 12mo. of 1719. An earlier Oxford edition, bearing date 1697, has the erroneous reading *yea;* but I have not been able to collect any between 1697 and 1708.

There are other points connected with changes introduced into the Prayer Book, published since 1662, which I should like to see cleared up. If any of your correspondents would examine the Prayer Books bearing date about the beginning of the eighteenth century, it might be determined where first the unauthorized insertion of the Thirty-nine Articles was effected. I have seen them in the Oxford edition of 1697, where they certainly form part of the last sheet, though the heading of them does not appear in the contents as printed at the back of the title. But they do not appear in another edition printed at Oxford in 1708, but are printed in the London edition of 1719 above referred to.

There is also another variation in the first Rubric at the end of the Communion Service, which was commonly printed till the end of the seventeenth century—" For the good estate of the Catholic Church of Christ," instead of as it was in the sealed book, and in Prayer Books as printed now, " For the whole state of Christ's Church militant here on earth." When the proper form was first restored to the Prayer Book might be easily ascertained by anyone who had access to books which may be found in the British Museum, and anyone who would take the trouble to investigate it would be doing a service to the cause of bibliography.

NICHOLAS POCOCK.

SIMILARITY OF NAMES.

SIMILARITY of authors' names has often proved a source of much trouble to bibliographers and others in assigning the proper works to each, so that it is of considerable literary importance to correct any errors arising from this cause, and as soon as possible. During the last few years I have on several occasions noticed in booksellers' catalogues an error of this kind in an advertisement of the following book :—

Hughes (T., Author of *Tom Brown) Stranger's Handbook to Chester and its Environs*, including the Walls, Cathedral, Castle, and Eaton Hall, numerous steel plates and wood engravings. 8vo., cloth. 1856.

The name of the author of *Tom Brown's School Days* is sufficiently world-wide famous without having ascribed to him works written by others of the same name, as in the instance of the one just cited. Mr. Thomas Hughes, the writer of the *Stranger's Handbook to Chester*, is well known in northern literary circles as the editor of the *Cheshire Sheaf*, of an abridgment of *King's Vale Royal* (1852), and of Batenham's etchings of *Ancient Chester* (1880); and to archæologists as F.S.A., and Secretary of the Chester Archæological Society. Mention of this in *Book-Lore* will probably arrest the perpetuation of this bibliographical error.

T. N. BRUSHFIELD, M.D.

B. Salterton, Devon.

BIBLIOPHILE'S KALENDAR.

THE Clarendon Press will publish immediately *The Governance of England*, by Sir John Fortescue; a revised text, edited with introduction, notes, and appendices, by Mr. Charles Plummer. The Introduction is divided into three parts—historical, biographical, and bibliographical; and it is believed that in each section some facts have been brought to light which have escaped previous investigators. The appendices consist of writings of Fortescue hitherto inedited or imperfectly edited. One of these is of especial interest, as containing an earlier draft of a considerable portion of the present treatise, drawn up in the shape of a programme for the Lancastrian Restoration of 1470. The text of the work has been carefully revised throughout, and is based on the oldest existing MS., collated with all other MSS. the existence of which was known to the editor. The whole is furnished with indices, glossarial and general, and a chronological table.

MESSRS. GEORGE ROUTLEDGE are issuing a series of volumes which are at once cheap and attractive. Thackeray's *Paris Sketch Book* and Bret Harte's *Poetical Works* have already appeared. From the last-named we quote some charming lines :—

ON A PEN OF THOMAS STARR KING.

This is the reed the dead musician dropped,
  With tuneful magic in its sheath still hidden;
The prompt allegro of its music stopped,
  Its melodies unbidden.

But who shall finish the unfinished strain,
  Or wake the instrument to awe and wonder,
And bid the slender barrel breathe again,
  An organ-pipe of thunder?

His pen! what humbler memories cling about
  Its golden curves! what shapes and laughing graces
Slipped from its point, when his full heart went out
  In smiles and courtly phrases?

The truth, half jesting, half in earnest flung;
  The word of cheer, with recognition in it;
The note of alms, whose golden speech outrung
  The golden gift within it.

But all in vain the enchanter's wand we wave;
  No stroke of ours recalls his magic vision;
The incantation that its power gave
  Sleeps with the dead magician.

THE handsome November *Magazine of American History* is entertaining and informing. It would be difficult to point out the part of it that would entice and interest the larger audience. It will surprise the public to read of "Witchcraft in Illinois," but the paper of John H. Gunn speaks for itself. "The Burning of Washington in 1814," by Hon. Horatio King, is a graphic account of an event never before so clearly and forcibly represented. The Civil War Studies comprise the second of General W. F. ("Baldy") Smith's series of papers on "The Campaign of 1861-62 in Kentucky—as Developed through the Correspondence of its Leaders." "A Ride with Sheridan," by Dr. A. D. Rockwell, who was a surgeon in Sheridan's division of the army, is exceedingly readable, and presents aspects of the war from a fresh point of view. Among the shorter articles is one from Col. W. L. Stone, pointing out the relics to be seen at the present time on the Saratoga battle-fields.

To the "Canterbury Poets," Mr. Walter Scott has added a volume of selections from *Cowper*, and another from *George Herbert*. Miss Eva Hope writes an introductory notice of Cowper, and Mr. Ernest Rhys of Herbert.

THE importation of American pirated reprints of the works of Mr. Ruskin has been made the subject of an action at law. This was brought by Mr. Ruskin against Messrs. Robinson, Low, and Fisher, auctioneers, New Bond Street, London, to restrain the defendants from selling or disposing of certain pirated copies of the plaintiff's works which had been brought from New York for sale by public auction. The books, including *Stones of Venice* and *Modern Painters*, were catalogued for sale on the 22nd of October, and on the morning of that day the plaintiff obtained an interim order restraining the sale of the books, which were only formally put up and bought in. Mr. Justice Pearson granted an injunction, and ordered the books to be given up to the plaintiff, and the defendants to pay costs.

THE *Critic* says that Mr. Henry Du Bois, formerly known as Henri Pène Du Bois, has written a book called *The New York Bibliophile*, which will be furnished with illustrations by E. J. Meeker and T. de Thulstrup, and published in Paris by Quantin, and in this City by John Delay next January. Mr. Delay has just issued his full catalogue of rare and curious books. It contains nearly 700 titles, some of them dating back to the sixteenth century.

DR. G. BÜHLER, in the course of a description of the Archduke Rainer's papyri, observes:— "Perhaps the most important find made is a strip of paper, 42 centimeters by 8·5, containing Arabic prayers, among them one by a companion of the Prophet Abû Dujâna. It dates from the ninth century. The whole text, as well as some marginal ornaments, *have been printed from a block of wood.* It thus appears that the art of block-printing was known to the Arabs more than 500 years before it came into use among the Western nations. Perhaps we may assume that the Arabs received it from the Chinese and communicated it, like so many other elements of civilization, to their European neighbours."

THE *Co-operative Index to Periodicals* continues its useful career. It is a fine example of public spirit wisely directed.

THE *Complete Poems of Charles Dickens* is the title of a volume recently issued at New York.

ERRATUM.—In No. 12 *Book-Lore*, November, 1885, "Iyväskylä" should be "Jyväskylä."

"THE ESSAYS AND DISCOURSES OF FATHER FEIJOO."

By F. R. McClintock, B.A., Author of "Holidays in Spain."

"Ask to see the cell of Padre Feijoó, one of the brotherhood, whose critical essays, about a century ago, dispelled some of the gross popular errors of Spain."—*Ford's* "*Handbook for Travellers in Spain.*"

N a well-known passage in one of the "Letters from a Citizen of the World," the Chinese philosopher expresses astonishment "that there should be any demand for new books before those already published are read." But on further consideration of the matter, he comes to the conclusion that it may be well "first to learn to know what belongs to ourselves, and then, if we have leisure, to cast our reflections back to the reign of Shonou, who governed twenty thousand years before the creation of the moon."

Thinking with our Chinese philosopher that the goods of antiquity are often "better than any of modern manufacture," and having recently had some leisure-time at our disposal, we have utilized it in making ourselves acquainted with certain volumes of a bygone age, and we now ask leave to communicate the result of our researches. We have not, however, thought it necessary to cast our reflections quite so far back as the epoch of the aforesaid Shonou, but only to the first half of the last century, when the eminent man, whose works we have occupied ourselves in examining, lived and laboured in the mountainous region of North-western Spain.

We are rather inclined to fear that the *Essays and Discourses of Father Feijoó* may be reckoned among the "thousands of volumes in every large library which are unread and forgotten;" and it may not have occurred even to those who have interested themselves somewhat in the matter of Spanish literature to dip into the works of the learned Benedictine. And yet his efforts for the enlightenment of his fellow-men are, it appears to us, well deserving of remembrance even now, although no doubt much of what he wrote has become antiquated, and may be cast aside as lumber. Towards the close of the last century his merits attracted no small amount of attention in this country, and many of his essays were translated into English. The celebrated author, from whom we have quoted above more than once, awards a tribute of just praise to Father Feijoó, and relates how, on his happening to pass through a small town of the kingdom of Valencia, he showed the credulous inhabitants of the place that a light which had appeared in the parish church, and which they looked upon as miraculous, was in reality due to exceedingly simple natural causes.*

Who, then, was this Father Feijóó, and what is his title to be held in remembrance by us in this present highly cultivated and ultra-scientific age?

At a time when Spain was reduced to the lowest state of ignorance and mental decrepitude, Benito Jerónimo Feijóó was born on the 8th of October, 1676,† at Casdemiro, a small town in the diocese of Orense, on the banks of the river Miño, a little below its junction with the Sil. His parents both belonged to families of distinction located in that part of the country. But, although Benito Jerónimo was their eldest son, they did not think the law of primogeniture absolved them from encouraging the boy's strong love for study, or obliged them to devote his time and talents exclusively to the duty of sustaining the honour of the family, and enjoying the revenues of the ancestral estate. At the early age of fourteen his future career was decided upon, and in 1688 he received the habit of the Benedictine Order in the Monastery of St. Julian de Samos. He afterwards pursued his monastic studies in the colleges of Lerez, near Pontevedra, and at Salamanca; after which he returned to Samos, where he fulfilled the duties of lecturer and professor in the monastery at that place. From thence he proceeded to the Benedictine Convent at Oviedo, where he lived for forty-seven years in as strict retirement as his professional and other monastic duties permitted.

In this secluded retreat he devoted himself with ardour to the pursuit of knowledge of all kinds, and zealously occupied himself in its dissemination by means of the press for the enlightenment of his countrymen. His first important work was the series of essays on a variety of subjects, known as the *Teatro Critico Universal*, or *Critical Theatre* for the detection of vulgar errors, published between the years 1725 and 1740, which was followed in 1742 by the *Cartas eruditas y Curiosas*, or *Learned and Inquiring Letters*—making up, together with the replies and rejoinders they provoked, some fifteen or sixteen volumes in all.

Now, in order to form a just estimate of the value of the work performed by Feijóó, it behoves us to know something of the epoch in which such work was done, and to consider as carefully as we can the condition of the people among whom he lived.

The power of Spain may be said to have reached its greatest height towards the end of the sixteenth century. The reunion of the two crowns of Aragon and Castile by the marriage of Ferdinand and Isabella, and the discovery of America

---

° See *The Bee*, No. III., Oct. 20, 1759; also *Inquiry into the Present State of Polite Learning*, chap. v.

† Not on the 16th Feb., 1701, at Compostella, as is stated by Lemcke (*Handbuch der Spanischen Litteratur*) and others.

in the latter part of the preceding century, had prepared a new era of wealth and glory for the nation. By the conquest of Portugal in 1580 the entire peninsula was amalgamated into one kingdom. Vast possessions, moreover, had been acquired in the New World, while on the Continent of Europe Spain was mistress of the kingdom of the two Sicilies, of the Low Countries, of Franche Comté, and of Artois. Such extensive dominions almost seemed to justify the dream of universal monarchy. The literary greatness of the country began about this time to rise to a higher pitch of excellence than it had ever before reached. The sixteenth century may be said to inaugurate the most brilliant period of Spanish literature, and the seventeenth throughout its greater portion worthily continued the glory of its predecessor. In 1600 Lope de Vega had attained the height of his fame, and Calderon's genius was soon to add new lustre to the national drama.

But the seeds of decay, profusely scattered even as early as the reign of Ferdinand and Isabella, had taken root, and began from henceforward to grow apace. The deadly influence of the Inquisition, the censorship of the press, so wittily scathed by Beaumarchais,* and the abridgment of the ancient rights and liberties of the people bore their legitimate fruit. Freedom of inquiry was banished; every spark of civil and religious liberty was extinguished, and despotism, supported by superstition and intolerance, held full sway. "The Spanish writers," says Sismondi, "abandoned themselves to apathy and rest; they bowed the neck to the yoke; they attempted to forget the public calamities, to restrain their sentiments, to confine their tastes to physical enjoyments, to luxury, sloth and effeminacy. The nation slumbered, and literature, with every motive to national glory, ceased."† On the death of the imbecile Charles II., the last prince of the Austrian line, the ruin and debasement of the country seemed complete.

In 1700 Philip V. of Bourbon was proclaimed King of Spain. With the new dynasty but few signs of improvement are discoverable. The Spanish Academy, founded in 1714, after the model of the famous French Institution, and the other kindred associations which sprang into being about this time, could produce no immediate effect on the general culture of the country. Abuses so deeply rooted as those under which the nation groaned could not be eradicated all in a moment. In literature, false taste, affectation, and bombast were the prevailing characteristics; the monks were ignorant, and the clergy licentious, while the people generally were sunk in a chaos of superstition and vulgar delusions.

But darkness is not of endless duration, even in the blackest regions. When things are at their worst, deliverance often comes from some quiet and unex-

---

° *Mariage de Figaro*, Act V.
† *Historical View of the Literature of the South of Europe.*

pected quarter. It was so in this case. From his lonely cell, in the Convent of St. Vincent at Oviedo, the Benedictine Father Feijoó sent forth his contributions towards the healing and advancement of his fallen and degraded fellow-citizens.

It was well for his countrymen that the author of *The Critical Theatre* was a sincere and devout Catholic, as otherwise his researches might have led him into regions of thought far too advanced to have been welcome to their restricted field of intellectual vision, and his labours for their improvement would indubitably have been put a stop to at the outset. As it was, he did not escape being arraigned before the Tribunals of the Inquisition as being tainted with the various heresies which had arisen since the fifteenth century, and even of that of the ancient Iconoclasts. Had he lived under the despotic rule of Philip II. he would certainly have been consigned to the dungeons of the Holy Office. But "persecution," to quote Goldsmith once more, "is a tribute the great must ever pay for pre-eminence." The orthodoxy, however, of Feijoó was above suspicion, and the Inquisitors denounced him in vain.

The seclusion of his monastic retreat afforded Feijoó ample time and opportunity for study. He gave, we are told, barely four hours to sleep, and only appeared in the world when obliged to do so by the demands of business, or when called upon to exercise the duties of his ministerial office. That a man who lived so much apart from his fellow-men should have understood them so thoroughly, and have shown such enlightened zeal for their intellectual emancipation, is a matter for no small astonishment. We do not usually expect largeness of mind and liberal views to emanate from the cell of a Spanish monk. Yet so it was in the case before us.

When he was fifty years of age, Feijoó came to Madrid to enter into negotiations for the publication of the first volume of his *Teatro Critico*. The whole work was eventually completed in eight volumes in 1739. It consists, as has been seen, of dissertations on an endless variety of subjects, somewhat after the manner of *The Spectator*—so much so, that the author has been called the Spanish Addison. The profound erudition which Feijoó had acquired in almost every branch of human knowledge, extending far beyond the ordinary routine of monastic studies, enabled him to combat with success the common prejudices and charlatanisms of the ages; and in the best passages of his essays, a few extracts from which we now propose to give, we are made to feel that a man of no ordinary integrity and energy of character is addressing us.

In the very first of his discourses,* which may be taken as a favourable specimen of his style and manner, he energetically declaims against the commonly received idea that the voice of the people is the voice of God—an error, he says, "which is the parent of many others." "'Æstimes judicia, non numeros,' said

---

* On *The Voice of the People.* *Voz del Pueblo.*

Seneca. The value of opinions should be computed by the weight, not by the number, of the minds who give utterance to them. The ignorant, although they be numerous, do not on that account cease to be ignorant. (*Los ignorantes, por ser muchos, no dejan de ser ignorantes*) . . . . A man of wisdom and discretion will always be raised above a great crowd of fools: as a single eagle will see more of the sun than a whole army of owls." In these days when we hear it loudly proclaimed in high places that "for good or for evil, the democracy has established itself in the seat of authority," and that "the Government of the many is about to be substituted for the Government of the few," it cannot be said that warnings such as those uttered by the Monk of Oviedo in this discourse are unworthy of consideration. The whole essay may still be read with profit.

Feijoó, however, was no hero-worshipper, as abundantly appears in his discourse on *Ambition in Sovereigns* (*La Ambicion en el Sólio*). In his estimation "the most unjust adoration the world bestows, is that which is given to, and received by, conquering princes, they being only deserving of the public hatred; while living mankind pay them a forced obedience, and when dead a courteous applause; the first is necessity, the second folly." "What," he goes on to say, "is a conqueror but a scourge, which the divine anger has sent among us for our chastisement? What, but an animated pestilence, both to his own kingdom, and those of the princes his neighbours also? A malignant star, which rules and influences nought but murders, robberies, desolations, and conflagrations; a comet, which equally threatens the destruction of cottages and of palaces; and, to sum up the whole, a man who is the enemy of all other men, because in the prosecution of his ambitious views he would deprive all mankind of their liberty, and take from many their lives and fortunes."

But for true greatness, especially when combined with unostentatious virtue, Feijoó had a profound respect; while for "those ridiculous scarecrows who led a kind of hermitic life, and are called sanctified or holy men," his scorn was unbounded. In the following extracts from his essay on *The Semblance of Virtue, or Virtue in Appearance* (*Virtud aparente*), which, though somewhat long, I cannot resist the temptation to quote *in extenso*, he pays an eloquent tribute to the high merits of our countryman, Sir Thomas More.

"I have," he says, "taken notice of a thing which is very remarkable, and that is, that great virtues are less perceptible than small ones. This is derived from the exercise of them not being so frequent, and the value of them not being generally understood. Regular attendance at church, exterior modest deportment, taciturnity and fasting, are virtues which strike the eyes of everyone, because they are daily practised, and everybody knows them. There are other virtues that are more substantial, and which spring from more noble roots that the vulgar are unacquainted with, because they are carried about by those who are masters of them, like ladies who go abroad *incognitas*, without the ostentatious parade and show of equipage. There are men (would to God there were more of them !) bearing an open carriage, and holding the free correspondence and inter-course of an ordinary life, who seem unaffected with mysterious niceties, but who nourish within their breasts a robust virtue and solid piety, impenetrable to the most furious batteries of the three enemies of the soul. Let Sir Thomas More, that just, wise, and prudent Englishman, whom I have always regarded with profound respect, and a tenderness approaching to devotion; I say let this man serve as an example to all men, and stand as a pattern to future ages of all the virtues and excellences I have been describing.

" If we view the exterior part of the life of Sir Thomas More, we see only an able politician, simple in his manners, engaged in a department of the state, and attentive to the affairs of the king and kingdom, always suffering himself to be wafted by the gale of fortune, without soliciting honours, and without refusing to accept them; in private life, open, courteous, gentle, cheerful, and even fond of a convivial song, frequently partaking, in the halls of mirth, of the jovial relaxations of the mind, and in the circulation of wit and pleasantry, always innocent, but never showing the least symptom of austerity. His application in literature was directed, indifferently and alternately, to the study of sacred and profane learning, and he made great advances in both the one and the other. His great applica-tion to, and proficiency in the living languages of Europe, represent him as a genius desirous of accommodating himself to the world at large. His works, except such as he composed in prison during the last year of his life, seemed more to favour of politics than religion. I speak of the subject of them, not of the motive with which he wrote them. In his description of Utopia, which was truly ingenious, delicate, and entertaining, he lets his pen run so much on the interests of the state, as makes it seem as if he was indifferent about the concerns of religion.

" Who, in this image or description of Sir Thomas More, would recognise that glorious martyr of Christ, and that generous hero whose constancy to the obligations of his religion could not be bent or warped, neither by the threats or promises of Henry VIII., nor a hard imprisonment of fourteen months, nor the persuasions and entreaties of his wife, nor by the sad prospect of seeing his family and children reduced to misery and beggary, nor by the privation of all human comfort in taking from him all his books, nor finally of the terrors of a scaffold placed before his eyes? So certain is it that the qualities of great souls are not to be discovered but by the touchstone of great occasions, and, like flints, only give out their fires under the stimulating influence of hard blows.*

" Sir Thomas More was the same while he was a prisoner of state as when he was High Chancellor of England; the same in adverse as in prosperous fortune; the same ill-treated as in high favour; the same in the prison as seated at the head of the Court of Chancery: but adversity manifested and made

* "Al excitativo de los golpes."

visible his whole heart, of which the greatest and best part had before lain hid. This great man used to give to his own virtues an air of humanity and condescension, which in the eyes of the vulgar abated their splendour; but in proportion as it obscured the lustre of them to their view, it augmented it in the sight of all men of discernment and penetration."

After reciting an anecdote in proof of the dignity and courtesy displayed by More, when High Chancellor, towards a suitor in his court who sought to influence him by a bribe, the worthy Padre proceeds as follows:

" It is clear that the heroic constancy with which in the time of trial he supported his adherence to his religion, was not the effect of a strained violence on his nature, but proceeded from innate virtue, which acts in all things, and on all occasions, according to the habitual dispositions of the mind; for always, to the very crisis of his suffering, he preserved the native cheerfulness of his disposition. He did not appear less festive nor less tranquil in chains, than he had before appeared in the banquet-room. During the time of his trial he was all composure; and when it was drawing near a conclusion, and those iniquitous judges, who had already sacrificed their consciences to the will of the sovereign, were on the point, to please and flatter him, of delivering that innocent man as a victim to his resentment, the barber came to take off his beard, which was somewhat long. But just as he was going to begin his work, Sir Thomas recollected himself, and said: '*Hold! as the king and I at present are contending to whom this head belongs, in case it should be adjudged to him, it would be wrong for me to rob him of the beard, so you must desist.*' Being about to ascend the scaffold, and finding himself feeble, he begged one who was near to aid him in getting up the ladder, saying to him at the same time: '*Assist me to get up, for be assured I shan't trouble you to help me down again!*' O eminent virtue! O spirit truly sublime, who mounted the scaffold with the same festive cheerfulness that he would sit down to a banquet! Let men of little minds and narrow souls contemplate this example, and learn to know that true virtue does not consist in the observance of forms and scrupulous niceties."*

The knowledge Feijoó had acquired of the labours of such men as Galileo, Bacon, Newton, Leibnitz, Pascal and Gassendi, although it in nowise emancipated him from the tenets of Catholicism, raised him far above the grosser credulities of his age and country. Among other superstitions he exposed the use of divining arts, of magic, the belief in witches and familiar spirits, and divers kinds of pretended enchantments. It would seem that much that Feijoó had to say on these heads is not yet out of date even among ourselves. Beliefs in divining arts and in familiar spirits still prevail. The sieve and shears and the key and Bible are still appealed to as oracles by the ignorant. Even among persons "accustomed to good society," and otherwise disposed to be rational, we

---

* Compare also *Spectator*, No. 342.

have here and there detected a lingering tendency to credit stories of ghosts and præternatural appearances. We boastfully proclaim ourselves the "heirs of all the ages;" but alas! as Schiller says, "let as many friends of truth as you will instruct their fellow-citizens in the pulpit and on the stage. the vulgar will never cease to be vulgar, though the sun and moon may change their course, and heaven and earth wax old as doth a garment."*

The low state of the healing art in Spain, at the time of which we are speaking. might readily be imagined even if positive evidence of the fact were not so abundantly forthcoming. Feijoó resolutely set himself to correct some of the errors which the multitude had too readily imbibed with regard to the powers of physicians to cure the ailments to which our flesh is heir. The quaint shrewdness of many of his remarks on this head makes them worth quoting. even when we remember how great an advance has been made in the theory and practice of the science since his day. They occur in his essays on *Medicine*, and on *Rules for Preserving Health.* A few short extracts must suffice.

" The too great confidence placed by the world in the efficacy of medicine is vexatious to physicians and hurtful to patients. For physicians it is vexatious because, owing to the hope with which their patients are inspired that prompt relief may be found in medicine for every kind of disorder, they are obliged to pay a number of visits, from the greater portion of which they might be excused ; thence it unfortunately happens that but little time is left to them for study, and none at all for reflection, which is the principal part of study. For the sufferers it is hurtful, because out of this confidence arises the habit of heaping remedy upon remedy, the taking of which in such quantities is always hurtful and often fatal. So much so that as the Emperor Adrian ordered it to be written upon his tomb that he perished by the multitude of his physicians, so on the graves of many it might be inscribed that they succumbed to the too great number of the remedies they adopted."

Later on the learned Father utters some useful words of warning on the uncertain and imperfect state of the art :—" One physician abhors a remedy which another idolizes. To this uncertainty we may add the change of fashion. which has not less power over this science than it has over our manner of dressing.

" While some remedies lose their vogue, others are coming into it. The same thing happens to physic, with regard to the remedies it proposes, as to Alexander in his conquests, who, while he was submitting new provinces to his yoke, lost those which he left behind his back. All remedies upon their first invention have been famous ; hence are derived the magnificent names that are given to them, of the Angelic Water, the Golden Julep. and others of a like nature. But nowadays neither the Golden Julep, nor the Angelic Water. nor the pills *sine quibus*, nor a number of other equally famous compositions dare to hold up their heads before English Salts."

Our Benedictine, we regret to say, has no opinion of English Salts, which he esteems a doubtful remedy for the reasons stated.   But he consoles himself with the reflection that "both this and other medicines, which are now in vogue, will be dethroned by fresh nostrums which time will produce; for it is the fate of the science to be in a state of perpetual fluctuation. *Mutatur ars quotidie interpolis, et ingeniorum Graciæ statu impellimur.*"

" I do not know," he says, " whether this exposure which I am now making public of the uncertainty of medicine will please the faculty.   Indeed, I expect to bring the anger of some of them upon my head.   I have no doubt that all those of little learning, and of still less understanding, will attack me with violence, as they think they possess a treasure of infallible doctrine in that author whom they follow.   Besides, if persons give up taking medicine, they will also be likely to give up consulting doctors: in which case some of them will be discarded.   But they may be very easy upon this head, for the world will always be the same; nor is any engineer capable of turning the course of the impetuous rivers of prejudice and universal custom.   How much, and indeed even beyond truth, has Quevedo written against physic and physicians in Spain; Petrarch in Italy, and first Montaigne, and afterwards Moliére, in France!   Their works are read and commended; but things go on in the same manner as before.   I shall be content if I can persuade only a few that they may ruin their health by those very means they make use of to preserve it."

There is much more in a similar strain, but further quotation is needless. The outcome of it all is that too much reliance should not be placed on the powers of drugs to cure diseases; that physicians, however skilful, are by no means omnipotent; that we should do well to leave minor ailments to nature, relying rather on a well-regulated diet than on medicine in those disorders which belong to the constitution, which no physicians in the world can cure, however much they may talk of eradicating them.

We are inclined to think that imaginary invalids and persons of hypochondriacal and unduly nervous temperaments might derive much profitable, if not altogether palatable, counsel from these admonitions of the Spanish monk.

The subjects treated of by Feijóo in his two principal works are so numerous and of so varied a character that anything like an adequate analysis of them would be quite impossible within the limits at our disposal.   He ranges with equal freedom and discernment over such opposite fields of inquiry as science, religion, the arts, letters, history, philosophy, jurisprudence, and medicine.   He defended women; he ridiculed the absurd dictates of fashion; he exposed the pretensions of superficial learning; though so devout a Catholic, he steadfastly set his face against mendicity, and the pernicious practice of indiscriminate almsgiving; in short, as Mr. Ticknor says, he, " in all respects, came forth to his

5

countrymen as one urging earnestly the pursuit of truth and the improvement of social life." *

It may be said that he was not a man of genius, and that he was unequal to the task of inventing new systems of metaphysics and philosophy. Perhaps not. But he was, what was even more to the purpose at the time when he appeared, a man of sense, judgment, energy, and courage. It would be a mistake to consider him merely as a critic of ordinary learning and attainments, whose works are to be held as of no value outside the limits of his own time and country. Much, we do not say the whole, of what he wrote is good still, inasmuch as the errors and prejudices which he so ably attacked are still prevalent in a greater or less degree even among the most civilized nations. His style, although occasionally somewhat prolix, is—certain Gallicisms apart, imbibed from the numerous French writers he was in the habit of consulting—clear, simple, vigorous, and without the least trace of affectation. Here and there, moreover, a quiet vein of humour displays itself in his discourses; no unfrequent sign, we take it, of strong sense and practical wisdom.

The talents of Feijoó brought him under the notice of the most distinguished men of his time. He was especially befriended by the celebrated Campomanes, Minister of State under Charles III., who vainly sought to induce him to abandon the cloister and to accept certain high ecclesiastical posts and dignities. But so far was he from desiring promotion, that he resigned his position as abbot of his monastery in order to devote himself exclusively to his studies, and to the great task he had taken in hand.

Feijoó closed his long and useful career on the 16th May, 1764, at the ripe age of eighty-eight, regretted, not less for his unquestionable learning and varied attainments, than for the purity of his character and the genial affability of his disposition. The eulogy pronounced upon him by a distinguished French traveller and antiquary will hardly be deemed too highly pitched. "Feijoó," says the Count de Laborde, "arose from the midst of ignorance at a time when literature, science, and the arts were absolutely neglected and unknown in his native country. His versatile genius embraced all subjects: theology, jurisprudence, philosophy, and medicine; with all of which he acquired an intimate acquaintance. His style was pure, simple, perspicuous, and methodical, though at times prolix; his genius was fertile, bold, and sincerely attached to truth; in consequence he freed both himself and his nation from the dominion of many mischievous and disgraceful prejudices. To him Spain is deeply indebted for the restoration of literature, good taste, and the love of study. He overthrew judicial astrology, and combated with success the superstitious and popular dread of comets, eclipses, ghosts and goblins; he declared war against the practice of indiscriminate almsgiving; against the cheats and absurdities of the

---

* *History of Spanish Literature*, vol. iii., period iii., chapter ii.

divining-rod, hydroscopy, and the healing of madness by touch, joined to the repetition of certain secret and mysterious prayers. The only reproach," adds M. de Laborde, "we can bring against him is that, in combating the prejudices of his countrymen, he was at times unable to resist some of those with which his circumstances and his education had imbued him."

The shortcomings of such a man as Feijoó, like the immaturities of style of the early painters, may well be looked upon as less his own than as those of the times in which he lived. From such influences no man, however great, can altogether free himself. In any case the memory of one who accomplished so much in so backward an epoch of his country's history well deserves to be held in grateful recollection by all who are interested in the mental advancement of their fellow-creatures.

ON THE FLY-LEAF OF A BOOK OF OLD PLAYS.

At Cato's Head in Russell Street
  These leaves she sat a-stitching;
I fancy she was trim and neat,
  Blue-eyed and quite bewitching.

Before her in the street below,
  All powder, ruffs, and laces,
There strutted idle London beaux
  To ogle pretty faces;

While, filling many a Sedan-chair
  With hoop and monstrous feather,
In patch and powder London's fair
  Went trooping past together.

Swift, Addison, and Pope, mayhap
  They sauntered slowly past her,
Or printer's boy, with gown and cap
  For Steele, went trotting faster.

For beau nor wit had she a look,
  Nor lord nor lady minding;
She bent her head above this book,
  Attentive to her binding.

And one stray thread of golden hair,
  Caught on her nimble fingers,
Was stitched within this volume where
  Until to-day it lingers.

Past and forgotten, beau and fair;
  Wigs, powder, all outdated;
A queer antique, the Sedan-chair;
  Pope, stiff and antiquated.

Yet as I turn these odd old plays,
  This single stray lock finding,
I'm back in those forgotten days,
  And watch her at her binding.

WALTER LEARNED.

NOTES ON WELSH BIBLES.

By J. R. Dore.

II.

HE first complete Bible in Welsh is known as "Morgan's" Bible. It is small folio size, and is dated 1588. It contains the Old Testament, Apocryphal and New Testament. The chapters are divided into verses. It has a table of contents prefixed to each chapter, and marginal references. A long dedication in Latin, to Queen Elizabeth, signed GVLIELMVS MORGANVS, also a calendar and other tables. Like the Welsh New Testament of 1567, it is numbered, not by pages, but by leaves, of which there are 553. It was printed at London by Christopher Barker. The title is, *Y Beibl Cyssegr-Lan, Ses yr hen Destament a'r Newydd.*

It has always been uncertain by whom Myles Coverdale was employed to translate the first English Bible, and it is equally doubtful by whom Morgan was induced to undertake the task of translating the Bible into Welsh. He mentions in his preface the support and encouragement he received from Whitgift, Archbishop of Canterbury. He would have sunk, he says, under his difficulties and relinquished the work, or would only have published the five books of Moses, had it not been for the Archbishop's help. Nothing is known of Coverdale's assistants in the work of translating, although it is almost impossible he could have accomplished it single-handed, and Morgan's assistants are equally unknown. Morgan speaks of, as his patrons, the Archbishop of Canterbury, the Bishops of St. Asaph and Bangor; Dean Goodman, of Westminster; Dr. David Powell; Archdeacon Edmund Pryse, of Merioneth, author of the Welsh Psalms in metre; and the Rev. Richard Vaughan, Rector of Lutterworth, afterwards Bishop of Bangor, Chester, and of London. During the time the book was going through the press, Morgan resided with the Dean of Westminster. The exact number of copies of which the edition consisted is not known; there is reason to believe they did not exceed one thousand. The statute of 1562 evidently does not contemplate a household Bible but one for church use. A quarto edition of the Prayer-Book and Psalter, beautifully printed in black-letter, was printed the same year (1588). It is now a very rare book, much more difficult to procure than Salesbury's Testament, or Morgan's Bible.

At the commencement of the seventeenth century, a revision of Morgan's Bible was undertaken by his successor in the See of S. Asaph, Dr. Richard Parry. This new version was printed in London in 1620, by Bonham Norton and John Bill, who had purchased the patent right of Robert Barker to print the Bible. It is a grand folio volume, printed in clear black-letter type, on good paper. The marginal references are taken from King James's Bible of 1611. The signatures of the Old Testament and the Apocrypha run to Eeee 3, and the New Testament from A to Y 2. Bishop Parry dedicated his Bible in Latin, to the Most Holy and Undivided Trinity, and to King James I. In it he says, that the copies of Morgan's Bible being exhausted, and many or most of the Welsh Churches being without Bibles, or having only worn or imperfect copies, he set about revising the Welsh Bible, as the English Bible had recently been revised, for the sake of providing for his countrymen a better and more correct version than they had ever possessed. Dr. John Davis, the learned Chaplain of the Bishop of St. Asaph, had a considerable share in the work of revision. He was admirably suited for the purpose, being well versed in Hebrew and Greek, and complete master of the Welsh language. This is important, as from one rendering in the Apocalypse it has been supposed it was translated solely from the English version into Welsh, without the original languages being consulted. The verse referred to is the eighth of the fifth chapter of the Revelation, which, both in Morgan's Bible of 1588, and Parry's of 1620, reads: "The four-and-twenty elders fell down before the Lamb, having every one of them harps and golden fiddles full of odours," etc. "Crythau," which signifies fiddles or violins, being used instead of "phialau," the Welsh word for vials. The translator, it has been imagined, having only the English Bible before him, mistook "vials" for "viols." This may have been a printer's error, like one recently made in a rubric of a French Canon of Mass, which orders that "*Ici le prêtre ôte sa culotte,*" instead of "*Ici le prêtre ôte sa calotte.*"

The first octavo Bible in the Welsh language is said on the title-page to be "Printiedig yn Llvndain. Robert Barker, Printiwr i Ardderchoccaf fawrhydi y Brenin: a chan Assignes Iohn Bill, A.D. 1630." It has four pages of Bishop Parry's Latin dedication; this is followed by four pages in smaller type of Morgan's address to "Illustrissimæ, Potentissimæ, serenissimæque Principi Elizabethæ D.G. Angliæ, Galliæ et Hiberniæ Reginæ, fidei veræ, et Apostolicæ Propugnat," etc.; then an address in Welsh of two pages, and on recto of last leaf of preliminary, "Nomina eorum qui præ cæteris hoc opus promouere conati sunt;" and on verso, "Henwav a threfn Uyfrav 'r hen Destament a'r Newydd, a rhisedi pennodau pol Uyft." The text is printed in Roman type. The only woodcut is the "Temptation in the Garden of Eden." The book is without pagination, and is printed in double columns, having seventy-three lines to a full column. It was undertaken, like other Welsh Bibles, not by any public authority, but by private individuals, on their own responsibility and risk. Sir Thomas Middleton, and Mr. Rowland Heylyn, both Aldermen of London, and natives of Wales, co-operating with two other gentlemen, undertook to supply the great want that had been so long felt of a Bible of a size suitable for family and private reading.

The reason the Bible in Welsh was so sparingly supplied, was to induce the Welsh people to study the English language for the sake of obtaining a knowledge of the Scriptures, and thus gradually to banish the ancient British language from the principality, and to substitute for it the English tongue. The third folio edition of the Holy Scriptures in Welsh is commonly known as "Lloyd's" Bible. It was printed at the Theatre, Oxford, 1690, in Roman letter. It has two title-pages to the Old Testament; one, the full-plate engraving usual in Oxford Bibles of this date; the other a letter-press title. There are also two titles to the New Testament. It is well printed, on good paper, but not nearly so handsome a book as Parry's Bible of 1620.

Why Bishop Lloyd should have the credit of this edition it is difficult to say. It was brought out under the superintendence of Mr. Pierce Lewis, an Anglesea man, who discharged his trust accurately and well. It does not pretend to be a new translation, but merely a faithful reprint of the Bible of 1620.

The octavo edition of the Welsh Bible, issued in 1654, consisted of 6,000 copies. This is the first record we have of the exact nnmber of copies of which any edition was made up. Numerous as it was, it soon became exhausted, and in 1677 another octavo edition was produced of 8,000 copies. One thousand were distributed gratuitously among the poor, and the remainder were offered for sale at four shillings each. An edition of the Book of Common Prayer in Welsh was published in 1664 in black-letter. Many errors having been made in reprinting one edition after another, Mr. Stephen Hughes, of Swansea, undertook to act as editor of the 1677 octavo, and a better man for the purpose could not have been selected, as he had long been engaged in publishing Welsh literature, amongst other books the popular Welsh poetry of the Rev. Rys Richard, of Llandovery. A great many copies of this edition were put into circulation by Mr. Thomas Gouge, a benevolent man, who always gave away two-thirds of his income, and managed to live on the remainder, which amounted to rather less than a pound a week. When over sixty years of age he used to travel about Wales, and personally distribute his bounty among the poor and needy. His funeral sermon was preached by Archbishop Tillotson, and afterwards published. In this sermon Tillotson states that, aided by the contributions of others, Mr. Gouge established a great number of schools in the principality, and liberally supplied them with Welsh books, particularly with the Prayer-Book, the New Testament, and the octavo Welsh Bible. Mr. Gouge died in 1681, and his colleague, Mr. Hughes, in the year 1687.

Sir Thomas Middleton and Mr. Rowland Heylyn were not the only Aldermen of London who exerted themselves to supply the inhabitants of Wales in their mother tongue, for in a copy of this Bible in Earl Spencer's library there is the following note:—"Presented by the Publisher to Sir Richard Clayton, of the City of London, Knt., Alderman and Mayor thereof, anno 1679, in thankfull acknowledgement of his former bounty to Wales, in contributing towards the printing of this Bible, and teaching many hundreds of poor children to read, and some to write."

The next edition of the Welsh Bible came out in quarto, in the year 1689, and was the last issued in the seventeenth century. It was printed by Bill and Newcombe, London, on rather poor paper, and from small and badly cast type. Its editor was Mr. David Jones. A considerable portion of the expense was defrayed by the Earl of Warton, once a member of Queen Anne's Cabinet. Ten thousand copies of this edition were speedily distributed.

The first edition, issued in the eighteenth century, was an octavo one, dated 1718. It has two engraved maps, signed, "Llundain, Ioan Baoged." It was edited by the Rev. Moses Williams, Vicar of Dyfynog, Brecon, an excellent scholar, who assisted Dr. Wotton in publishing the *Leges Wallicæ*. He added to this Bible a table of interpretation of Hebrew and Greek names into Welsh. To the Society for Promoting Christian Knowledge is due the honour of publishing this and the two following editions. The second edition is dated 1727. This is small octavo size, without contents of chapters or marginal references, and was for this reason very little valued by Welsh people. The next was printed by J. Bentham, Caer Grawnt, 1746, in octavo. In addition to the Apocrypha, the Old and New Testament, it has the Prayer-Book, and a Metrical Psalter, by Archdeacon Pryce. This Prayer-Book contains the Acts of Uniformity of Elizabeth and Charles II. The table dates from 1746 to 1785. Great prominence is given to the ornaments rubric. It is printed in larger type than any other part of the book, and occupies an entire page. The Epistles and Gospels are all given in full. The authorization of the State services is signed, "Towns-hend, 1728;" then follows the Ordinal and Canons of 1603. The last page has a table of affinity and consanguinity that "let" marriage. At the end of the New Testament are twenty-three pages of chronological and five of other tables. The Psalter has a fresh signature, and after it are sundry prayers.

In 1752, under the care of Mr. Morris, Baskett produced an octavo edition, which could not be spoken of as some of Baskett's Bibles have been, as Basketfuls of errors, for it is considered the most correct Welsh Bible ever printed.

In 1779 a quarto was printed at Carmarthen with a Welsh concordance, some passages of which were supposed to favour Sabellianism.

The last Welsh Bibles to be mentioned are the octavos of 1770 and 1799. The latter consisted of 10,000 copies, and, like the 1746 issue, contained the Book of Common Prayer and the Psalms in metre. The Psalms in metre were published separately several times—Thomas Galesbury's version in 1603, and Archdeacon Pryse's in 1648. The New Testament was also issued by itself in 1647 in 12mo.; in 1654 in 4to.; in 1672, and again by the Society for Promoting Christian Knowledge, in 1752 and 1769.

KING JAMES I. AS AN AUTHOR.

ILTON has remarked that kings, though strong in legions, are weak at arguments; but James I. of England, so far at any rate as his own person was concerned, can hardly be considered as having been strong in anything, except possibly his overweening vanity and self-conceit.

In these qualities he was a proficient, and nowhere are they so conspicuous as in his writings.

The royal author commenced his literary career in 1584, by the publication of a volume entitled *Essayes of a Prentice in the Divine Art of Poesie*, and considering that at the time he was only eighteen years of age, his Majesty might lay claim to considerable credit, for the verses contained in this volume are by far the best he ever wrote.

His *Short Treatise containing some Rewlis and Cautelis to be observit and eschewit in Scottis Poesie*, which next saw the light, is acknowledged without any difference of opinion to be choked with absurdities both of matter and style. We say "without any difference of opinion" advisedly, for although it is true that many of his contemporaries professed to be charmed with the *Rewlis and Cautelis*, we do not regard their avowals at all in the light of an opinion, but rather as part of that homage which monarchs usually succeed in obtaining from their dependents. Seriously and impassionately judged, the effusion may be pronounced as puerile and ridiculous, and no attempt has been made, at least in modern times, to prove the contrary.

In 1591 there appeared *Poeticall Exercises at Vacant Houres*, and later still a paraphrase in verse of the Revelation of St. John, and an adaptation, also in verse, of the Psalms.

As already stated, the *Essayes of a Prentice* are altogether superior to any of the author's poetical attempts; and one of the pieces, entitled "Ane Schort Poeme on Tyme," taken from this same volume, is really so commendable that we give it in the original spelling:—

I.

As I was pausing in a morning aire,
   And could not sleip nor nawyis take me rest,
Furth for to walk, the morning was so faire,
   Athort the fields, it seemed to me the best.
    The East was cleare, whereby belyve I gest
That fyrie Titan cumming was in sight
Obscuring chaste Diana by his light.

2.

Who by his rising in the azure skyes,
   Did dewlie helse all thame on earth do dwell.
The balmie dew through birning drouth he dryis,

Which made the soile to savour sweit and smell,
By dew that on the night before downe fell,
Which then was soukit up by the Delphienus heit
Up in the aire: it was so light and weit.

3.

Whose hie ascending in his purpour chere,
Provokit all from Morpheus to flee;
As beasts to feid, and birds to sing with beir,
Men to their labour, bissie as the bee;
Yet idle men devysing did I see
How for to drive the tyme that did them irk,
By sindrie pastymes, quhile that it grew mirk.

4.

Then wondered I to see them seik a wyle
So willingly the precious tyme to tine;
And how they did themselfis so farr begyle,
To fushe of tyme, which of itself is fyne.
Fra tyme be past to call it backwart syne
Is bot in vaine; therefore men sould be warr,
To sleuth the tyme that flees fra them so farr.

5.

For what hath man bot tyme into this lyfe,
Which gives him dayis his God aright to know?
Wherefore then sould we be at sic a stryfe,
So spedelie our selfis for to withdraw
Evin from the tyme, which is on nowayes slaw
To flie from us, suppose we fled it noght?
More wyse we were, if we the tyme had soght.

6.

But sen that tyme is sic a precious thing,
I wuld we sould bestow it into that
Which were most pleasour to our heavenly King.
Flee ydilteth, which is the greatest lat;
Bot, sen that death to all is destinat,
Let us employ that tyme that God hath send us
In doing well, that good men may commend us.

This poem constitutes the one metrical production which can in the slightest degree be considered as rising above the common level of inferiority, and we shall not therefore trouble ourselves with any further reference to this branch of the author's efforts.

As the King deemed it his duty to give to the world his opinion upon almost every topic which at the time agitated the minds of his subjects, it is no exaggeration to say that his prose disquisitions are legion. Many of these are of little moment, and have long since been forgotten, passing away with the incidents which gave rise to them; but others are still occasionally read, not so much on account of their intrinsic value, as by reason of the curious nature of the subjects enlarged upon, and the author's method of handling them. Chief among these works rank the *Dæmonologie*, published in 1597; and the *Basilicon Doron*, published in 1599; and the famous *Counterblast to Tobacco*, 1616.

Before commenting upon these treatises, we digress to examine the so-called complete edition of the author's works, published at London in the year 1616.

The volume, which is in folio, has a full length portrait, by Simon Pass, of the King sitting in his robes of state; and on the opposite leaf is an elaborate title-page, the scroll-work surrounding the letterpress being engraved by Elstrack. Both the portrait and the scroll-work are beautifully executed, and ill-natured persons might possibly incline to the opinion that these engravings constitute the most important part of the work.

In the centre of the scroll is the title, which runs as follows :—

The | workes | of the most high | and mighty Prince | Iames | By the Grace of God Kinge | of Great Brittaine | France & Ireland | Defender of y^e | Faith &^c | Published by Iames Bishop of | Winton & Deane of his | Ma^ts Chappell Royall | 1 Reg. 3, 12 v. Loe I have given thee | a wise and an understanding heart | London | Printed by Robert | Barker & John Bill | Printers to ye Kings most | Excellent Maiestie| 1616 | Cum privilegio |

On the leaf immediately following the same title is displayed, but in much larger letters, and following this a separate page is devoted to a representation of the Arms of England, Scotland, Ireland, and France, quartered within a shield, and surrounded by the garter and motto.

Next follows the dedication of the Bishop of Winchester (3 pages)—the editor of the work—to "the thrice illustrious and Most Excellent Prince Charles, the onely sonne of our Soveraigne Lord the King ;" and above the dedication on the same page appears a medallion portrait of Prince Charles, engraved by Simon Pass.

The Preface to the Reader, also by the Bishop of Winchester, occupies 28 pages; and the table of contents, arranged in chronological order, 2 pages. This table details the list of his Majesty's works, consisting of :—

1. Two Meditations. First, on the 7th, 8th, 9th, and 10th verses of the 20th Chapter of Revelations. Second, on the 25th, 26th, 27th, 28th, and 29th verses of the 15th Chapter, first Book of Chronicles.

2. The Books on Dæmonologie.

3. Basilicon Doron.

4. The Trew Law of Free Monarchies.

5. A Counterblast to Tobacco.

6. A Discourse of the Powder Treason.

7. An Apologie for the Oath of Allegiance.

8. A Præmonition to all Christian Monarches.

9. A Declaration against Vorstius.

10. A Defence of the Right of Kings.

11. Five Speeches.

Immediately following the table of contents comes the body of the work, comprising 569 pages of matter, and usually, but erroneously, described as constituting the complete works of the King. That this is so will be apparent from the fact, that none of the author's poetical effusions are included in the volume ; and further that in the Latinized version of the same book, published three years later by the Bishop of Winchester, other pieces are given, which we search for in vain in the former edition.

This Latin translation, also in folio, contains the engravings by Pass and Elstrack, very much worn, and the following title in the centre of the scroll-work, repeated on the succeeding leaf as in the former instance :—

Screnissimi et | Potentissimi | Principis | Jacobi | Dei gratia magnæ Bri | tanniæ Franciæ et Hiber | niæ Regis Fidei Defensoris | Opera | Edita ab Jacobo Montacute | Vintoniensi Episcopo et sacelli regis Decano | 1 Reg. 3, 12 | Ecce do tibi animum sapientem et intelligen | Londoni | Apud Bonhamñ Nor | tonium et Johanne Bil | lium Typographos regios | 1619 | Cum privilegio |

The succeeding matter, of course Latinized, is precisely the same as in the edition of 1616, with the following exceptions :—The Preface to the Reader occupies 27 pages instead of 28, and the body of the work 644 pages instead of 569.

The table of contents is altered to include (after the declaration against Vorstius) the " Responsio ad Epistolam Cardinalis Perronii," the " Meditatio in Orationem Dominicam," and the " Hypotyposis inaugurationis Regiæ," the two latter pieces occupying the concluding portion of the work. His Majesty is likewise credited with an additional speech.

To whatever extent it may be fashionable to abuse the literary efforts of King James I., it must not, as is pointed out by Isaac D'Israeli in his " Literary and Political Character of the King," be forgotten that the times in and the circumstances under which he lived were exceedingly unfavourable to any author whose talents were not of the highest order. The genius of Shakespeare, as well as of a score of minor stars which illumined the Elizabethan age to such an extent as to be quite exceptional in the annals of our history, caused other and lesser lights to pale. James would have been nothing had he not been a king, and it is the very fact of his being so that gives his writings a prominence equal to those of far more gifted authors. Comparisons are in this instance unfair, for the circumstances are highly exceptional, and vastly to the King's disadvantage.

Some excuse may also be found for the *matter* of his productions, as well as for his peculiar and often trivial diction and style. We laugh in the nineteenth century at the author who treats of witchcraft as if it were genuine, and looks upon magic as the peculiar province and will of the devil ; but in the seventeenth century such beliefs were universal, and the person who confessed his inability to subscribe to this and similar doctrines was looked upon as impious, a traverser of the sacred truths of the Gospel, perhaps in league with the arch-enemy himself.

The King therefore merely fell in with the popular belief, and it is greatly to his credit that, having at last discovered the numerous impostures he had often referred to as authorities, he grew suspicious of the whole system of *Dæmonologie*, and at last recanted it altogether.

With regard to his opinions upon smoking, which he described as a beastly practice, "emitting black fumes nearest resembling the horrible Stygian smoke of the pit that is bottomless," it is surmised that he would not be without sympathizers even at the present day. And so on of the other works, all of which portray the opinions of the time, and only seem ridiculous on account of the extremes of puerility and seriousness in which the King alternately indulged.

The preface to the *Dæmonology* tells us that "the fearful abounding at this time in this country of these detestable slaves of the devil, the witches or enchanters, hath moved me, beloved reader, to dispatch in post this following treatise of mine, not in any wise, as I protest, to serve for a show of my learning and ingine, but only, moved of conscience, to press thereby, so far as I can, to resolve the doubting hearts of many, both that such assaults of Sathan are most certainly practised, and that the instruments thereof merit most severely to be punished; against the damnable opinions of two principally in our age, whereof the one called Scot, an Englishman, is not ashamed in public print to deny that there can be such a thing as witchcraft, and so maintains the old error of the Sadducees in denying of spirits. The other called Wierus, a German physician, sets out a public apology for all these crafts-folk, whereby procuring for their impunity, he plainly bewrays himself to have been one of that profession."

The Scot, or more properly Scott, here referred to wrote the famous *Discoverie of Witchcraft* (London, 4to., 1584), in which he disputed the whole theory of apparitions and devils, suggesting that the confessions of reputed witches were wrung from them by means of torture, and that those enchanters who made a profession of their pretended arts were moved to do so by the foolishness and credulity of the age. In other words, that the witches, like other impostors, lived on the ignorance of their dupes.

Wierus, the German physician, in his book, *De Prestigiis Dæmonum* (Basle, 4to., 1583), on the contrary, as King James asserts, admitted his belief in the Satanic influence, and then endeavoured to prove its lawfulness, if used in a certain manner. This, no doubt, was highly improper; at any rate the author would have every reason to congratulate himself that he lived in Germany and not in Scotland.

The preface subsequently proceeds to explain the arrangement of the work into three parts; the first "speaking of magic in general, and necromancy in special; the second, of sorcery and witchcraft; and the third contains a discourse of all those kinds of spirits and spectres that appears and troubles persons, together with a conclusion of the whole work."

It would indeed be an unusual circumstance if a treatise upon magic omitted to give a list of the reasons which prompt the author, in common with all good men, to regard strange and monstrous prodigies as undoubted facts, and accordingly the remainder of the preface is devoted to refreshing the memory of the reader on such incidents as the competition between Moses and the magician, the vagaries of Simon Magus, and the powers of necromancy displayed by the Witch of Endor.

These and other narratives are usually taken as proofs of the existence of the baneful art, and as being of themselves sufficient to stamp anyone who failed to perceive their applicability as a friend and associate of the devil.

The preface concluded, the ball commences in real earnest by a number of interrogatories put by Philomathes to Epistemon, who indeed carry on the conversation to the end of the treatise.

Philomathes being blankly ignorant on the important subject of witchcraft, doubtless through reading Mr. Scott's *Discoverie*, comes to Epistemon to be enlightened, and forthwith propounds the question, whether it was the actual ghost of Samuel which was raised by the Witch of Endor, or whether she did not rather describe the appearance of the old man, and by imitating his voice impose on the terrified senses of Saul.

Epistemon, shocked beyond measure, scouts the impious suggestion; for, says he, "it is said in the text that Saul knew *him* to be *Samuel*, which could not have been, by the hearing tell onely of an old man with a mantell, since there was manny moe old men dead in Israel nor Samuel: And the common weil of that whole country was mantils." With this lucid explanation Philomathes appears to be satisfied, and after a slight and comparatively speaking unimportant discussion on other topics, the first chapter ends clearly in favour of the powers of darkness.

It would be an invidious and profitless task to reproduce the vagaries contained in the royal author's production; for the very same arguments, if they can be so called, are to be found in almost every work which professes to treat on the subject of witchcraft. It may be entertaining, however, to give an idea of the punishment which in the opinion of James should be unsparingly inflicted upon everyone proved to be guilty of conspiring with spirits and demons:

"*Phil.* What sort of punishment, thinke ye, merite those magicians and witches: For I see that ye account them to be all alike guilty?

"*Epi.* They ought to be put to death according to the Law of God, the civall and imperiall Law and municipall Law of all Christian nations.

"*Phil.* But what kinde of death, I pray you?

"*Epi.* It is commonly used by fire, but that is an indifferent thing to be used in every country according to the Law or custome thereof.

"*Phil.* But ought no sexe, aage, nor rancke to be exempted?

"*Epi.* None at all; for it is the highest point of Idolatry wherein no exception is admitted by the Law of God.

"*Phil.* Then barnes may not be spared?

"*Epi.* Yea, not a haire the lesse of my conclusion, for they are not that capable of reason as to practise such things : And for any being in company and not reveiling thereof, their lesse and ignorant aage will no doubt excuse them."

This conversation assumes a melancholy significance when it is remembered that a large number of persons were actually put to death upon these or similar grounds ; and in many cases upon the evidence of hysterical women, who swore they had been transported at night to *Sabbaths*, and other resorts of the witches :

"*Phil.* And what may a number then of guilty persons' confessions worke against one that is accused ?

"*Epi.* The Assize must serve tor interpretation of our law in that respect. But in my opinion, since in a matter of treason against the Prince, barnes, or wives, or never so diffamed persons may of our law serve for sufficient witnesses and prooves, I think, surely, that by a farr greater reason such witnesses may be sufficient in matters of high treason against God : For who but witches can be prooves, and so witnesses of the doings of witches ?

"*Phil.* But what if they accuse folke to have been present at their Imaginar conventions in the spirit when their bodies lye senceless as ye have said ?

"*Epi.* I thinke they are not a haire the less guiltie : For the Divel durst never have borrowed their shadow or similitude to that turne, if their consent had not beene at it. And the consent in these turns is death of the law . . . . There is the confession of a young lasse troubled with spirits, laid on her by witchcraft, that although she saw the shapes of divers men and women troubling her, and naming the persons who these shadowes represent, yet never one of them are found to be innocent, but all clearely tryed to be most guiltie, and the most part of them confessing the same. . . . There are two good helpes that may be used at the triall. The one is the finding of the mark and the trying of the insensibleness thereof. The other is their fleeting on the water ; for as in a secret murther, if the dead carkasse be at any time thereafter handled by the murtherer, it will gush out of bloud, as if the bloud were crying to the heaven for revenge of the murtherer. God having appointed that secret supernaturall signe for triall of that secret unnaturall crime, so it appears that God hath appointed for a super-naturall signe of the monstrous impietie of witches that the water shall refuse to receive them in her bosom that have shaken off them the sacred water of baptisme, and wilfully refused the benefite thereof. No! not so much as their eyes are able to shed teares (threaten and torture them as ye please), while first they repent (God not permitting them to dissemble their obstinacie in so horrible a crime), albeit the womenkind especially be able other wayes to shed teares at every light occasion when they will, yea, though it were dissemblingly like the crocodiles."

Thus pleasantly and profitably did King James beguile the hours with the learning of Cornelius Agrippa, and the wisdom of the *Malleus Malificarum.*

(To be continued.)

"WHO HAS NOT LOVED AN ELZEVIR?"

*(Lines suggested while cutting " Wordsworth," vol. i., in " The Miniature
Library of the Poets.")*

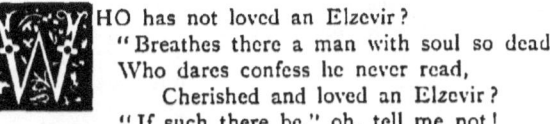

HO has not loved an Elzevir?
   "Breathes there a man with soul so dead,"
   Who dares confess he never read,
      Cherished and loved an Elzevir?
   "If such there be," oh, tell me not!
Better his name should be forgot;
Why sadden history with his lot
   Who never loved an Elzevir?
Who has not, like our Wendell Holmes,
Tenderly loved these fairy tomes?
That dear little book in 32mo.,
"Erasmi Colloquia," surely you know,
"Typis Ludovici Elzevirii,"
Date " 1650, Amstelodami,"
With little ribbed back, all bound in black,
And the cleanest type you ever did see;
You'll remember too, on the title-page,
That William Cookeson, late of All Souls,
Had writ his name, for a later age;
But alas! Oblivion ever rolls
Its tide along, and this man of All Souls
Had been quite forgot, had not Wendell Holmes
Fallen in love with these fairy-like tomes.
Well, it's quite agreed that all you who read
Have felt what I mean, and there's no further need
   To ask, Have you loved an Elzevir?
So I'll pass along in my random way,
And come to the point of my bookman's lay.
As you've sat at night in that little room,
   So cosy and snug, the "sanctum" you love
   All other places on earth above,
With its "learned dust" (forfend the broom!)
Where the light of the lamp as softly falls
   As music on weary souls, and around,
   Above and below, not an inch is found

Uncovered by books, for of course the walls
From ceiling to floor, from window to door,
Are packed with the trophies of many old stalls,
And vainly you'll search for table or chair
Unblessed with its burden of learning to bear.
But one little spot there is that is not
Thus weighted with tomes—that corner, I mean,
Defended with folios huge for a screen,
Not too large a bit that armchair to admit,
The cosiest armchair that ever was seen.—
Well, reader, so gentle, patient and kind—
When was there a reader accused as unkind?—
When, snugly ensconced in your sheltered nook,
You fondly pore on that dear little book,
With the magic of Elzevir's name
On the front, and the print so wondrous small,
Did you never at such a moment fall
A-sighing for past days, never exclaim,
"Would that the Elzevirs could live to-day!
What joy were deep enough if only they
Could print for us the poets that we love
From Shakespeare to our day, how far above
His daily task, his common round of cares,
And all the frets of life, would be that man
Whose blessed privilege it was to scan
Shelley and Keats in fairy type like theirs!"
Oft have I sighed, but always sighed in vain,
It seemed to me that aching void of pain
Would never fill, my blood ever run cold
At " popular editions " thick with gold,
Or " éditions de luxe" one dare not touch.
But, heaven be thanked, deliverance comes at last,
The days of "cheap-nasty" are now of the past;
To-day I have seen for only 10 d.,
The sweetest small book you ever did see.
And soon as I saw it on bookseller's stall,
" Pythagoras, then, was right after all,"
I said to myself; for surely the man
Who printed this can be no other than
An Elzevir born in this world again
To save us poor bookmen that aching pain
Begot, as I told, of editions in gold,
And " éditions de luxe " one dare not touch.

'Tis a dear little book in 32mo,
"The Poems of Wordsworth," surely you know,
With parchment back, sweetly lettered in black,
And with type so neat and margin so fair,
That no other man, you are ready to swear,
    Could have printed this but an Elzevir.
I'm so sure of this that all I doubt is
    Which Brother Elzevir this one may be
Who's left spirit homes to print fairy tomes,
    All those paradise-blisses deserted that we
    Might buy such a book for the sum of 10 d.
But such an inquiry might prove too long
For patience wearied enough with my song,
So not to-day will I venture to say,
But leave it with thee to find out for me
    Which Brother Elzevir this one may be.

                        RICHARD LE GALLIENNE.

From the " Nook in my Study."

WOODSTOCK, PRENTON LANE, BIRKENHEAD.
    2 *October*, 1885.

VICTOR HUGO IN ENGLISH VERSE.*

.   .   .   .   quella fonte,
Che spande di parlar si largo fiume.—DANTE.

HE passing away of Victor Hugo has been followed by two distinct
efforts to make the overflowing wealth and massive strength of his
poetry known by means of English translations.   Perhaps the most
remarkable circumstance is that a task so fascinating, in spite of its
difficulty, was not undertaken years ago.   Many translations from
separate poems of Hugo have appeared in English periodicals, but not in separate
form, with the exception of a pamphlet of political poems. This is now a somewhat
rare tract.   The poems were first published in the *Morning Star*, and then printed
in this somewhat ephemeral form with a preface by Mr. G. J. Holyoake.   The
Oxford graduate signed only the initials, E. A., but collectors of modern poetical
literature may be glad to recognise in him Mr. Edwin Arnold, who has since given
The Light of Asia to the world.

The difficulty of an adequate translation of Victor Hugo is greater than that
of almost any poet who could be named.   It is emphatically true of him that the
style is the man, but the man and the style are so multifarious, as well as so
splendid in their developments, that no translator could hope to reflect in his
version the kaleidoscopic change and brilliant variety of the original.   Only himself could be his parallel, and a British Hugo alone could make English the
profundity, the glitter, the pathos, the ever-varying charm of the poetry which for
nearly eighty years flowed from the fountain of his fertile genius.   Only one of
our insular poets can reproduce in their fulness the rich gifts which Hugo has
showered upon the literature of France.   Since Mr. Swinburne has not essayed
the task, the most obvious method of presenting Hugo in an English dress is that
adopted by Mr. H. L. Williams, who has collected from various sources the best
versions he could find.   Some of them are from old magazines, perhaps not too well
known when new, and now covered with dust in nooks and corners of libraries—
when they have not been entirely read away.   Probably the greater part of these
versions have been made from a genuine impulse, and not as task-work, or even
as the necessary completion of an undertaking.   They vary greatly in quality ;
and some might be detected which are rather travesties than translations, since
they miss both the matter and manner of the great original.   Some of the most

* *Political Poems*, by Victor Hugo and Garibaldi.   Done into English by an Oxford Graduate.
Reprinted from the *Morning Star*.   London, 1868. 8vo., pp. 16.
    Translations from the Poems of Victor Hugo, by Henry Carrington, M.A., Dean of Bocking.
London : Walter Scott, 1885. 12mo., pp. 325.
    Selections, chiefly Lyrical, from the Poetical Works of Victor Hugo, translated into English
by various authors.   Now first collected by Henry Llewellyn Williams. London : George Bell and
Sons, 1885. 8vo., pp. xix. 321.

spirited versions in Mr. Williams's anthology are from the pen of Mr. G. W. M. Reynolds, who, in addition to being perhaps the most prolific of novelists, was, in his early days, a hard student of French literature, moved thereto, it may be, by political as much as by literary affinity. Some of the subtlest are by Toru Dutt, that Muse of Hindostan, whose early death was a loss alike to East and West.

Mr. Williams would have been well advised to have included in his anthology the vigorous renderings by the late R. B. Brough of some of the *Odes et Ballades*. It has not, we think, been pointed out that one of the stories in the first Christmas Number of Brough's magazine, the *Welcome Guest*, is a prose version of *Les Pauvres Gens*, from the *Légende des Siècles*.

As a sample of graceful French turned into graceful English, let us take Mr. A. Lang's version of

THE ROSE AND THE GRAVE.

The Grave said to the Rose :
" What of the dews of dawn,
Love's flower—what end is theirs ?"
" And what of spirits flown,
The souls whereon doth close
   The tomb's mouth unawares ?"
The Rose said to the Grave.

The Rose said : " In the shade
From the dawn's tears is made
   A perfume faint and strange,
Amber and honey sweet."
" And all the spirits fleet
   Do suffer a sky-change,
More strangely than the dew,
To God's own angels new,"
   The Grave said to the Rose.

With this we may compare Dean Carrington's Translation :

THE TOMB SAID TO THE ROSE.

The Tomb said to the Rose,
" With the dews thy leaves enclose
   What dost thou, Love's own flower ?"
The Rose said to the Tomb,
" Tell me what is the doom
   Of hosts thy depths devour ?"

Said the Rose : " Of every drop
That in my bloom doth stop
   Sweet perfume I distil."
Said the Tomb: " I make the souls
My dreaded reign controls,
   Angels that heaven fill."

Neither Mr. Williams nor Dean Carrington have essayed a rendering of the splendid passage in *L'Année Terrible*, descriptive of the burning of a library by the Communists. A spirited version by Miss Mathilde Blind is given in Mr. Ireland's *Book-lover's Enchiridion*.

Dean Carrington's little volume is, of course, more uniform in its texture than that of Mr. Williams, and if it does not rise so high, it does not fall so low. It is a book that no lover of Hugo will willingly spare from his shelves. We hope that these two books—which are both commendable—will increase the number of Victor Hugo's admirers, and lead them to study in his own tongue a poet unsurpassed for fertility of expression and grandeur of thought.

REVIEWS.

Les Livres à Gravures du XVI. Siècle. Les Emblèmes d'Alciat. Par GEORGES DUPLESSIS. Paris : J. Rouam, 1884. 8vo., pp. 64.

SOMEWHAT late in the day we have the pleasure of calling attention to the monograph of M. Duplessis on the famous emblems of Alciat. Regarded from an iconographical point of view, M. Duplessis has done his work with skill, accuracy and *esprit*, and he has given full credit to the late Rev. Henry Green for the investigations which have again made the name of Alciat familiar to book-lovers.

Le Musée de Cologne. Par EMILE MICHEL. Paris : Librairie de l'Art.

M. MICHEL has produced a companion to the Cologne Gallery, which may be used either as a guide for a visit, or kept for permanent reference as a reliable account of an important collection.

Popular County Histories : A History of Norfolk. By WALTER RYE. London : Elliot Stock, 1885. 8vo., pp. viii. 316.

THIS is the first of a series of " Popular County Histories," and if the succeeding volumes equal Mr. Rye's *History of Norfolk*, they will form an important and valuable addition to our knowledge of local history. Mr. Rye's theory of an invasion and settlement of Norfolk by the Danes before the Roman Conquest, is founded on the large number of Norfolk place-names, to which, either in whole or in part, can be assigned a Danish origin. Mr. Rye thinks it absurd that the very large proportion of Danish place-names in Norfolk can possibly be accounted for by the intermittent raids of the ninth and tenth centuries, and he asks, " If the similar raids in France and Normandy have left next to no trace on their maps, why should the invasions on our east coast have left such strong evidences ?" There are a few references to books and libraries, and from these we learn that " the first Norwich book was printed by ' Anthony Solen, prynter,' in 1570. His real name was Anthonius de la Solemne, ' Tipographus,' and he came from Brabant in 1567, with his wife and two children." The materials at our disposal for discovering the literary tastes of the early gentry are very scanty, but some of their wills contain bequests of books. From one of these wills Mr. Rye finds that " a testator who died in 1482, had *La Belle Dame saunce mercye; The Death of Arthur;* a book on the blazoning of arms; Tully *De Senectute;* and—oh that it were rightly so now !—*A Boke in preente off the Playe of the Chess !*" Mr. Rye doubts that the parsons lived very studious lives, for " books were too scarce and too dear for their purses. Of course there were exceptions ; and sometimes we find clergymen leaving books by their wills, as when Richard Wygelworth, parson of Waxtonesham, in 1370, left all his library, except *Sermones parati,* and *Manipulus Curatorum,* to Hickling Priory. Robert Barwell, parson of Thuxton, in 1531, must have had a fair library, for he mentions *Itercalyn to Jherusalem, The Constitutions Provincial* (two copies), *Josephus de Antiquitatibus, Postilla super Epistolas et de Evangelia, Gemma Predicantium, The Fall of Princes, Geoffrey de Historia Britanniarum,* and *The Cronycles of Ynglond,* besides an ordinal, which he left to St. Peter Mancroft, Norwich. Of course many of the city clergy, like the rector of the parish just named, had access to good, and in St. Peter's case to fine, libraries." The statement on p. 187, that " illegitimacy was then [sixteenth century], as now, a bar to taking orders," is incorrect, Cardinal Beaufort, in the Roman Church, and the Rev. Henry Wellesley, D.D., in the English Church, both being bastards and in orders. It was only the natural sons of priests who were incapable of taking Holy Orders. The volume concludes with an interesting chapter on Superstitions, Folk-Lore, and Dialect.

Bibliotheca Arcana seu Catalogus Librorum Penetralium : being brief notices of books that have been secretly printed, prohibited by law, seized, anathematized, burnt or Bowdlerized. By SPECULATOR MORUM. London : George Redway, MDCCCLXXXV. Small 4to., pp. xxii. 141 and xxv.

WE are always ready to hail with a cordial welcome every book on bibliography, of which the notices are at first-hand, done conscientiously, and *de visu.* This seems to be the case with the *Bibliotheca Arcana*, although we must take exception to it on other grounds. The books noticed, the nature of which is sufficiently explained on the title-page, are of a kind which renders it desirable that they should not be made very generally known. Many hold that every book has a utility of some sort, *nullus est liber tam malus qui non ex aliqua parte prosit ;* others that all books, irrespective of their subjects or tendencies, should be catalogued. It is not for us to argue either point here, and as the *Bibliotheca Arcana* is an expensive publication, is issued, we believe, to subscribers only, and is well printed on excellent paper, its existence may for these reasons be condoned. But we fear it will be found of little service to the bibliophiles, for whom it is evidently destined : it is put together without system or classification ; the entries are undigested, and have more the appearance of cuttings from a bookseller's catalogue than notices by a bibliographer ; neither are the works by the same author or the various editions of the same book brought together, but are dispersed in various articles, and spread over several pages ; translations are served up as original works ; books issued at different times with different titles are treated as distinct works ; there are numerous errors which we cannot in this journal point out. In fact, the compilation (it is nothing better) displays neither grasp of the subject, critical acumen, nor bibliographical treatment. "The entries," we are told, "have been arranged (?) without any reference either to subjects or authors. The index which is appended will enable the student to classify for himself." This is all very well, but it is not for the guest to arrange the entertainment to which he is invited.

The preface is the best part of the book. "It would be an interesting task," writes Speculator Morum, "for an essayist to describe the progress and fortunes of the erotic in art and literature from the earliest times down to the present day, to show how eroticism was in some mysterious way at the root of all ancient religions ; and to point out how, instead of being looked askance upon, it was actually favoured and patronized by priests, poets, sculptors, dramatists, and philosophers in the classic ages, which have handed down to us not only literature, but also pictures, statues, and gems, tinged with the most extreme eroticism, and yet truly lovely in their design and workmanship." Interesting as such a task might be, we doubt whether the author is to be found, at any rate in England, likely to undertake it. We cannot but think that we trace, both in the preface and in the general idea and form of the book itself, the influence of two much more important and thoroughly done bibliographies of the same description of books, lately privately printed, and which are noted in arts. 6 and 7 of the *Bibliotheca Arcana.* As in the *Bibliographie des Ouvrages relatifs à l'Amour* of Gay, many books have been introduced which are foreign to the scope of the work ; so in Mr. Redway's compilation there are several articles, among which we may instance Nos. 323, 330, 435, 437, 556, 595, of which we fail to see the *raison d'être.*

WE have received the following catalogues :—Henry Gray, 25, Cathedral Yard, Manchester ; William Downing, 74, New Street, Birmingham ; Black and Johnston, 40, High Street, Brechin ; Karl W. Hiersemann, 1, Turnerstrasse, Leipzig ; Thos. Simmons, 164, Parade, Leamington ; J. Salisbury, 4, Paternoster Row, London, E.C.

CORRESPONDENCE.

RUSKIN'S "PRÆTERITA."

IT may interest some of your readers to know that the title of Mr. Ruskin's autobiography is not, like most of his titles, a *new one.* It was made use of more than 200 years ago ! I have in my possession an old work, called *Præterita, or a Summary of several Sermons : The greater part preached many years past, in several places, and upon sundry occasions.* By John Ramsey, Minister of East-Rudham, in the County of Norfolk. London : Printed by Thos. Creake, for Will. Rands, over against the Bear Tavern, in Fleet Street, 1659. Small 4to., pp. viii. 323.

FRANK MURRAY.

Moray House, Derby.

CONTEMPORARY REFERENCE TO MILTON.

THE following curious extract is taken from Winstanley's *Lives of the Poets*, published in 1687, p. 195 :—

John Milton was one, whose natural parts might deservedly give him a place amongst the principal of our English Poets, having written two Heroick Poems and a Tragedy ; namely, *Paradice Lost, Paradice Regain'd,* and *Sampson Agonista.* But his Fame is gone out like a Candle in a snuff, and his Memory will always stink, which might have ever lived in honourable Repute, had not he been a notorious Traytor, and most impiously and villanously bely'd that blessed Martyr King *Charles* the First.

How curiously has the prophecy of this critic been belied by posterity.

S. A. A.

◆◇◆

BIBLIOPHILE'S KALENDAR.

THE death is announced from Boston of a notorious book-thief on 30th October last. In a cell in the Brattle Square (Cambridge) Police Station, Boston, a policeman found lying dead, but with the body still warm, a young man who had been arrested the night before for the larceny of an overcoat. A whitish powder sprinkled over his clothing and about him told the story of suicide by poison. The suicide was until quite recently a student at the Harvard Divinity School, and had been variously known as Otto Funk, Otto Boehms, J. A. Helbut, and J. A. Talbot. Not long ago he created a sensation in Chicago, where he was a student at the university, by elaborate preparations for an attempt to destroy the University buildings. He had constructed a tunnel and laid a train of dynamite under the college-yard for this purpose. In addition to this escapade he was detected in the theft of a number of valuable books from the Public Library of Chicago, and was tried for these offences, acquitted on the ground of insanity, and committed to the Elgin Insane Asylum, from which he made his escape. At the opening of the Fall term of Harvard University he applied for admission to the Divinity School, offering letters of indorsement from many prominent citizens of Chicago, including officers of the University, which were later found to be forgeries, as their dates had been changed from 1883 to 1885. Before this discovery he had, however, been admitted as a student. Soon books were missed from the library. He was suspected, and left the school. Still later he surreptitiously entered the Divinity Library, and books were abstracted from there. He was found in a stolen overcoat and arrested, but escaped from the officers while crossing to Cambridge in a horse-car. Sacks containing several hundred books belonging to the Harvard Library were found secreted in Norton's Woods, behind the Agassiz Museum, and packages of books ready for shipment were found at the express office. At the Old Colony Station in Boston was also found a trunk containing valuable surgical instruments, stolen from Dr. Wesselhoeft, of Cambridge, and other purloined property. Later it was found that "Talbot" was the man who some days since stole the doctor's horse and carriage, drove to Waltham, and there clipped the horse, and changed his colour and markings in several places by the use of nitrate of silver. These and other pranks undoubtedly prove the young divinity student to have been insane. As he lay in his cell, there was found on the floor, crumpled as if it had fallen from his hand when death loosened its grasp, a soiled bit of coloured paper, upon which was written : "Mr. Peabody : Will you please forward my trunk to my sister, Bertha Tabel, No. 47, West Blackhawk Street, Chicago, Ill. Tell her what has happened."

THE subject of book-thieves was discussed in some detail at the first meeting of the New York Library Club, when William T. Peoples, of the Mercantile Library, said that many books were lost through subscribers, who carried them home and failed to return them. He instanced the case of a German school-teacher, who kept a book for four years and resisted every effort to recover it. George Hannah, of the Long Island Historical Society, said that while he was connected with the Astor Library a wealthy and well-known man, who had been an habitual visitor to the library, died suddenly. From his library Mr. Hannah picked out nearly 200 volumes that he had carried away from the Astor Library at different times. Mr. Pool, of the Young Men's Christian Association, employed a detective on one occasion to watch a Frenchman, who was suspected of stealing books. The man's method was to procure a book, sit down to read it, wrap it up in his overcoat after a little while, and then take up a paper or a magazine. After he had satisfied himself that he was unobserved, he would take up his overcoat and walk out. He was arrested in the act, and some of the books he had stolen were recovered from an old book-store near Washington Square. They were identified by a private mark, and the bookseller told Mr. Pool that he ought to make his private mark public, so that booksellers could know when they were offered stolen books. In the same store were found a number of Astor Library books that had been stolen by the same man. Mr. Hannah spoke of the mania that some people have for collecting old directories, and said that he had detected a respected citizen of Brooklyn in the act of enriching his collection at the expense of the Long Island Historical Society. Mr. Melvil Dewey, Librarian of the Columbia College Library, advocated the adoption by the club of a system of information through which one library would give notice to another of known thieves and suspected persons. Miss Coe said she had prepared a black list for the use of her library, and should take pleasure in furnishing it to other libraries. Mr. Hannah said that he had detected a prominent lawyer, formerly a resident of Brooklyn, stealing newspapers from his library. Dr. Buel, of the Union Theological Seminary Library, said his library had suffered severely at the hands of clerical book-fanciers. A prominent clergyman of this city kept one book for twenty-three years, and finally, after much importunity, returned it with the remark that he had obtained a better one. Mr. Peoples said he also had discovered that clergymen were not to be trusted any more than other persons. They were also uncommonly addicted to defacing books by marks and marginal notes. A prominent Episcopal clergyman, whom he detected by recognising his handwriting, frankly admitted that he had defaced a book with marginal notes, and complacently remarked that he considered the book more valuable since he had annotated it than it was before. Mr. Peoples thereupon remarked that since the value of the book had been enhanced he would be very glad to let him take it and furnish another in exchange. Much testimony was also given as to the necessity for watching ladies. Mr. Hannah said he was once warned by the President of one of the largest female seminaries in Brooklyn that all schoolgirls would steal books, and Mr. Peoples told of detecting the daughter of a very wealthy man in the act of carrying off five books under her cloak, and the wife of a Professor, known to everybody in the literary world, as she was about to put several books into her satchel. Secretary Nelson was moved by these revelations to remark that there seemed to be a curious connection between bibliomania and kleptomania. Mr. Schwartz gave some remarkable examples of the devices resorted to by persons to put themselves on the free list in the Apprentices' Library before the library was made free to everyone. It was found that some school-teachers receiving large salaries had put themselves down on the list as dressmakers. The wife of a prominent manufacturer had made use of her husband's office-boy to procure books free for her own use. It appeared from the experience related by Mr. Hill, formerly of the Lowell (Mass.) Library, that factory hands and working people were much less liable to steal books and mutilate newspapers than people in more comfortable circumstances, and Mr. Peoples said that harmonized with his own experience in the Mercantile Library.

THE *Athenæum*, in the course of a review of *Die Scheibaniade*, an Uzbek epic poem in seventy-two cantos, by Prince Muhammad Sálih of Khwárizm, which has recently been published in a German dress by Arminius Vambéry, has some interesting remarks upon royal authorship in the East :—" If the name of the professed writer on the title-page of a book be accepted as sufficient proof of authorship, then may it be said that emperors, kings, and ministers in the East acquire literary reputation as frequently as they do in the West. The argument will apply with greater force to a bygone age than to modern times, though it may be fairly used in reference to both. Naushirwán the Just, the Sassanian monarch of Persia, not only said, but wrote, thirteen hundred years ago, things which are still reverently quoted by his countrymen ; and quite recently, in our own days, two diaries by a living Shah have been translated and published in Europe. The authenticity of Timur's memoirs may be disputed ; Abul Faẕl may have been the mouthpiece of Akbar and the genius of his reign ; and there may be doubt as to what part of his 'autobiography' was actually written by Jahángir ; but the *Malfúzát* and *Tuzukát* of the first, the *Aiyn* of the second, and the *Jáhángir-Náma* seem to connect inseparably the sovereigns named with Oriental literature. So in the case of the soldier-poet Prince Muhammad Sálih of Khwárizm. He has not, like 'Antar, suspended his poem (*kasída*) on the temple (*Kaba*) of Makka, but he has left behind him a fine specimen of native poetical power, to be interpreted four centuries later in vigorous German for the edification of Western critics. It would be interesting to trace his career from the period at which the narrative of the *Shaibáni-Náma* is broken off. M. Vambéry does not believe that he voluntarily withdrew from his literary task, and assumes that he fell in action before Balkh, the year after the taking of Urganj. It is certainly quite probable that he was killed in one of those battles or skirmishes, the prospect of which so frequently and readily aroused his military ardour. As commandant of Chárjúi, on the Oxus, he seems to have displayed high soldierly qualities, and more than once distinguished himself by personal bravery. Baber, in his *Memoirs*, mentions having met him on one occasion only, but he gives no particulars to mark his personality, nor do any other known authors throw light on the subject. The death of Muhammad Shaibáni himself occurred in A.D. 1510, at Merv, whither he had been pursued after unsuccessful encounters with the Persian troops under Shah Ism'aïl Súfi. We learn that in that same year a beautiful manuscript of the *Shaibániad*, embellished with coloured drawings of sieges, battles, and revelries, was prepared; that it is now to be seen in the Imperial Library at Vienna; and that the 'Toorki' text of the volume under review is a copy of this original."

THE Rev. Dr. Stockbridge, of Providence, is engaged in preparing, with copious biographical and bibliographical notes, a catalogue of *The Harris Collection of American Poetry*, the gift to Brown University, Providence, Rhode Island, of the late Senator Anthony. The collection is a valuable and important one, and Dr. Stockbridge is well equipped for the work.

Il Bibliofilo gives some curious particulars respecting astrological almanacs in the seventeenth century.

THE eleventh annual report of the Swansea Public Library and Gallery of Art records a year's progress. The most liberal donor is Mr. Deffett Francis, who has presented, since the foundation of the institution, no less than 6,920 volumes.

IN the *Neuer Anzeiger* the principal topics discussed are the Examination for Library Assistants by the Library Association.

WE learn from *Polybiblon* that M. Henri Harrisse is writing a pamphlet on the *Grandeur et Decadence de la Colombine*, of Seville, a library about which some singular stories have recently been told.

To the Canterbury Poets has been added a handsome volume of Shakespeare's *Songs, Poems and Sonnets*, with a careful introduction by Mr. William Sharp.

THE *Western Antiquary* contains a portrait of the late Mr. Cornelius Walford.

"MR. HALLIWELL-PHILLIPPS," says the *Nation*, "still brings forth fruit after his kind. Writing to an American friend in the last week of October, he says: 'I have had one piece of luck of late, in buying a deed of 1579, with the signature and beautiful handwriting of Walter Roche, who was Master of the Grammar School at Stratford-on-Avon, when Shakespeare was a little boy there. Only one other specimen of his handwriting—that in the Museum at the birthplace—is known to exist. Another acquisition: I am not fond of mulberry-tree relics, wanting faith, but, by the death of my father's last surviving relative in Lancashire, I come into possession of one which was purchased by my grandmother at Stratford from Sharp himself in the last century, and so far has an undoubted pedigree.' Sharp will be remembered as the relic-carver who, on the cutting down of Shakespeare's mulberry in 1758 by Rector Gastrell, the then owner of the estate, 'purchased the greatest part of it'—as he declared in a formal death-bed affidavit in 1799. The autograph of Roche, as the first schoolmaster the future dramatist ever saw, and one so nearly unique, deserves a station in Hollingbury Copse beside the signature of Shakespeare's friend and patron, the Earl of Southampton, and that of Sir Thomas Lucy of Charlcote, who was perhaps in truth a still greater friend, albeit in the disguise of driving the poet to his field of future fame by a prosecution for deer-stealing. The free school, of which Roche was master, and which gave Shakespeare his 'small Latin and less Greek,' has been shown by a recent writer in *Notes and Queries* to have been endowed before the year 1453. The master's salary was fixed at £10, and he was forbidden to receive any fees from pupils. Mr. Phillipps, while remarking that he would as soon think of making money by keeping a yacht as by the sale of his Shakespeare *Outlines*, adds that the fifth edition of that work is already out of print, and that he shall soon be at work on the sixth."

WE learn from the *Courier de l'Art* that M. Paturet has received at the school of the Louvre the diploma of *Docteur en droit Egyptien* for his thesis on the *Condition juridique de la femme de l'ancienne Egypte*.

BY the same authority we are informed that the widow of General Octave de Bastard has made an important gift to the Bibliothèque Nationale of sketches, charters, seals, and other documents, illustrative of history, painting, and illumination.

THE annual report of the Leamington Free Library shows an increase in the prosperity of the institution. It now contains 12,729 vols.

THE excellence of *L'Art* is too well known to need emphasising. The taste and delicacy of the illustrations, and the solid information of the articles, commend this periodical to all who are interested in the history and literature of art.

THE LAST OF THE CROMWELLS.

THE history of the Cromwell family is very remarkable. From a rather obscure beginning the Cromwells rapidly attained power, first as landed gentry, afterwards as supreme rulers of the Commonwealth, and then as rapidly decayed till they became extinct, in the male line, in the subject of this notice. The family was of Welsh origin, but, owing to some connection with Thomas Cromwell, Earl of Essex, Sir Richard Williams assumed the name of Cromwell. His son, Sir Henry, known as the "Golden Knight," had several sons, among whom were Sir Oliver, M.P., Robert, M.P., Sir Philip, M.P., and Richard, M.P. Robert Cromwell, who was M.P. for Huntingdon, was father of the Protector, Oliver Cromwell, whose second son, Henry, was, during the Commonwealth, Lord Deputy of Ireland, a position that he resigned shortly before the Restoration, after which event he purchased the estate of Spinney Abbey, where he lived a retired life. He was succeeded in that property by his son Henry, who sold his inheritance, and after experiencing great pecuniary distress, obtained a commission in the army and died, a major, of fever in 1711. Of Major Cromwell's sons, Richard, the fifth, was an attorney. Thomas Cromwell, the Major's seventh son, was born at Hackney, on August 19, 1699, and became a grocer, or, according to Cussan's *Hertfordshire*, a "merchant and sugar-refiner," on Snow Hill. He was twice married, secondly to Mary, daughter of Nicholas Skinner, merchant. He is described in the *Gentleman's Magazine* as "a person of an exemplary life, and it was also said of him that "his virtues deserved a more elevated employment." He died in Bridgewater Square, London, on October 2, 1748. By his second wife he had, with other issue, two sons, Thomas and Oliver. Thomas was apprenticed to an ironmonger, but as soon as his term had expired he obtained a commission in the East India Company's Army, and having attained the rank of lieutenant, died unmarried in 1771. Oliver Cromwell, the other son, was born about 1742, and along with his younger brother, Thomas, entered St. Paul's School on December 4, 1751, they being described as sons of Mary Cromwell, widow, of Paternoster Row. He was bred an attorney, and was in partnership with Mr. Morgan Morse, whose daughter he married. He became a solicitor in Chancery, and clerk to St. Thomas's Hospital, in London, and practised in Essex Street, Strand, "having," says the Rev. Mark Noble, "some of the first noblesse his clients." He is said to have been "very much and very justly esteemed by his numerous acquaintance;" and Mr. Noble was informed by many who knew Mr. Cromwell well, that this character was "rather below than above his merit." Late in life Mr. Cromwell gave up his profession, and retired to an estate at Theobald's, Hertfordshire, which he had inherited from his cousins, the Misses Cromwell, and occupied himself chiefly with the duties of a country gentleman. He seems to have felt keenly the abuse that successive biographers had levelled at his great ancestor, the Protector, and, as an act of justice to a man he greatly admired, wrote a book, which was published under the title of *Memoirs of the Protector, Oliver Cromwell, and of his sons Richard and Henry, with Original Letters and other Family Papers. By Oliver Cromwell, Esq., a Descendant of the Family.* London: 1820. 4to., pp. 733. A second edition of these *Memoirs* was issued in two volumes, 8vo., in 1821, and a third was called for in 1823. The first part of this work is taken up with an account of the times in which the Cromwells lived. Then follows an account of Oliver's family, paternal and maternal, both of which were illustrious. Mr. Cromwell took the pedigree given by Mr. Noble as correct, and evidently believed with everybody else at the time that Cromwell's mother was of royal descent, that Sir Richard Williams did marry the sister of Lord Cromwell, and that the Cromwells could show a pedigree from 1066. Mr. Cromwell says that less would have been said of the family pedigree "had not Lord Clarendon and some other writers of the royal party shown themselves anxious of every opportunity to treat slightingly and contemptuously Cromwell's descent and family connections and consequence, in the outset of his life." Mr. Cromwell had a special grievance against Lord Clarendon and Sir Philip Warwick, both of whom agree in considering Oliver to have been careless of his dress, and coarse in his manner, when first they knew him in the House of Commons. After disposing of the charge of lowness of birth, Mr. Cromwell next treats of Oliver's reported disagreement with the Duke of York at Hinchinbrooke, and considers it incredible that Oliver should have at any time of his life so far forgotten himself as to strike his prince, though where the incredibility comes in Mr. Cromwell does not inform us. He replies to Warwick's statement that Oliver Cromwell was dissolute in his early manhood, and shows that the stories of his excesses whilst in town, in Lincoln's Inn, must fall to the ground, because Cromwell never was there. Another alleged failing of the Protector's was his indistinct pronunciation; but Mr. Cromwell quotes a letter written by Beverning, the Dutch deputy in England, in which he says: "Last Saturday I had a discourse with his Excellency Cromwell above two hours, being without anybody present with us. His Excellency spoke his own language so distinctly that I could understand him. I answered again in Latin." Mr. Cromwell also points out that the Protector was a patron of learning, that he erected and endowed a college at Durham for the benefit of the Northern counties, that he settled one hundred pounds a year on a divinity professor in Oxford, and purchased and gave twenty-four rare Greek manuscripts to the Bodleian Library. Another instance of his generosity was his treatment of Archbishop Usher, to whom he granted an annuity, and whose funeral expenses he defrayed. One of the Protector's letters to his eldest son is quoted in this work, and contains the following passage : " Recreate yourself wth Sr Walter Raughley's *Historie ;* its a bodye of historie, and will add much more to your understandinge than fragments of storie." Another charge of Warwick's was that Oliver Cromwell plundered his uncle's estate ; but Mr. Cromwell shows that Cromwell was only carrying out the orders of the Parliament directing a disarming of the recusants. Sir Oliver Cromwell, the uncle in question, was a royalist, and came within the meaning of the order, and Warwick's own account shows that Oliver did an unpleasant business in as polite and gentle a manner as possible. After these details of the private life of Cromwell follows an account of his public life. Mr. Cromwell next deals with Richard Cromwell, and endeavours, to our mind unsuccessfully, to prove that he was not the weak, effeminate man he is usually said to have been. Of Henry Cromwell he gives a short account. Of Mr. Cromwell's own opinions we get some knowledge from this book. We find that he was a member of the Established Church of England, and that he considered a monarchy to be preferable to a republic, but acknowledges that the Restoration did not produce the good effects to be hoped and expected from it. On the whole, the defence of Cromwell is a very good piece of work. Mr. Cromwell married Mary, daughter of Morgan Morse, and had two sons, who died in infancy, and a daughter who married Thomas Artemidorus Russell, and had a large family. Having been deprived by death of his two sons, Mr. Cromwell, being naturally disposed to wish that the name of his great ancestor should not expire with himself, made application in the usual quarter for permission that his son-in-law should assume the surname of Cromwell ; but, to his astonishment, the permission was, by the enlightened personages applied to, refused. It would be interesting to know who was responsible for this remarkable example of official stupidity. Mr. Cromwell, who much resembled his great namesake, died at his residence, Cheshunt Park, Theobald's, Hertfordshire, on the 31st of May, 1821.

BOOKS UPON "CHANCE."

R. JOHN VENN is the only English author who has satisfactorily dealt with what is commonly though erroneously termed chance. His work, entitled the *Logic of Chance* (London: Macmillan and Co., 1866), is a wonderful example, not only of learning, but of his capacity to handle an unusually difficult subject in a popular manner.

The earliest book which touches the doctrine was published at the beginning of the eighteenth century, and is entitled *De Ratiociniis in Ludo Aleæ*. It is by a Mr. Huygens, and consists of a number of mathematical calculations, some of which, however, are not demonstrated. Still this work, the first which treated the subject methodically, forms the basis of many others, chief among which may be mentioned *L'Analyse des Jeux de Hazard*, by M. Moumort (1708). Both these books are devoted to a calculation of the odds arising in certain games of cards, or as the authors prefer to put it, of chances at play.

Passing by Bernoullis's *De Arte Conjectandi* (1713) as a work of little importance and doubtful accuracy, we come to De Moivre's treatise on the *Doctrine of Chances*, a book consisting, like the others, of mathematical problems; but unlike them, proceeding from simple to complicated cases. The second edition, which was published in 1738, forms the best gambler's *vade mecum* in the English language, and has perhaps emptied more pockets in the shortest possible space of time than any other production of a similar nature whatever.

We have no intention of critically examining these works, and only refer to them as examples of the class of literature which is likely to attract the reader in his search for a guide on the subject to which we allude.

A similar remark will apply to Simpson's *Nature and Laws of Chance* (1740), and William Saint's exposition on the *Doctrines of Chance* (1810); both are mere systems of calculation, and do not in any appreciable degree explain the laws which govern the causation of the results they affect to compute.

Putting aside Todhunter's *History of the Theory of Probabilities* as being a history and nothing more, we come to Mr. Venn's work; and here, for the first time to our knowledge, the subject is treated from its proper standpoint of critical inquiry into the *cause*, as distinguished from the *event*. An illustration will make the distinction clear.

There is a story told by Plutarch of a painter who, unable to portray the appearance of foam at the mouth of a horse, flew into a violent passion, and throwing a saturated sponge at the canvas, did by "accident" what he could not do by design.

If we wished to know how long it would be before the painter could again produce a similar result in the same way, we could arrive at a reasonable "probability" by measuring the picture and the circumference of the sponge, and calculating accordingly. The computation would be extremely uncertain, it is true, but still it might be made.

Now De Moivre, who deals with *events*, could not effect this or any other calculation of a like nature, unless the original conditions were preserved in their entirety; the painter must stand at the same distance from the canvas, must throw the sponge (properly saturated) with the same force, and then, and then only, could he speculate on the probability of the event happening again.

No *chance* is involved here; on the contrary, everything is a matter of absolute certainty. For, given the conditions, the event *must* follow; the only speculation possible is upon the skill of the painter in throwing the missile.

On the other hand, if the inquiry had been into the *cause* of the event certain, it would be necessary to gauge the elements which form the combination upon which the event depends.

De Quincey, in his description of the wonders displayed by Lord Ross's telescope, follows his imagination through space to distant suns unknown to man; for billions and quadrillions of miles, in death-like silence and absolute darkness, he pursues his flight until another sun is seen revolving in its course; he passes it, it is gone; the minutes become hours, the hours days, the days years, and still the lightning-flash of imagination, which knows no earthly bounds, is fettered and confined in abysmal depths, until at last it is annihilated in the immensity of space, and everything becomes a blank.

De Quincey's mind, when it dealt with such a subject, was finite a little way above his head; but it was expansive compared to what it would have been had he sought to fathom the endless permutations which create even the simplest cause.

Assume, for the sake of example, a large concourse of people gathered together to witness a spectacle of any kind. The philosophical cause of their being where they are is not the show, for if it were, the next time a similar exhibition was held the very same people would attend, since an identical cause must produce an identical result. The real cause is made up of the precise number of reasons which prompted the individuals to be present as a whole. One man came because he was in the vicinity and had nothing else to do, another because he wished to see a friend whom he knew to be in a certain spot; a third might find his progress barred, and so was forced to remain against his will.

These, and perhaps twenty thousand other varying reasons, make up the cause of that great crowd being where it is, and any attempt to calculate the possible recurrence of such factors would be futile and vain. Still there is no "chance" involved; let the same reasons prompt each individual at the same time and under the same circumstances, and they would again be present as before, a spectral crowd grey with the lapse of unnumbered ages.

Neither Mr. Venn, nor anyone else that ever lived, could advance a step in the solution of such problems, and if the adjustment of the various agencies involved did not in a sort of way balance each other and produce something of uniformity, the whole subject would be altogether beyond our reach. As it is, each agency becomes in its turn a cause, and is "interwoven inextricably with an indefinite number of other causes, and the same kind of uniformity is in this way propagated amidst endless variations through all nature."

The study of these resemblances is by no means an exclusively modern occupation, for Aristotle in his *Ethics* (Lib. iii., c. 3), enumerates the action and efficient causes of all events, among which is what he calls "chance." Seneca again, in his work entitled *De Remediis Fortuitorum*, touches the subject; and Milton, so far from acknowledging that chance arises from the mere absence of any law or order, distinctly recognises it as an arbiter.

> . . . . Next him high arbiter
> Chance governs all.—*Paradise Lost*, Book ii., l. 910.

Mr. Venn has been the first to reduce the known laws governing the doctrine into something like order, and in doing so he takes his stand upon the fundamental axioms that it is only our ignorance which leads us to attribute things to chance, which have in reality necessary and determinate causes, and that when we say a thing happens by chance, we mean only that its cause is unknown—not that chance itself can be the cause of anything.

Disprove these premises and we are involved in chaos everlasting.

SOME CHINESE BOOK-LORE.

O little is known, except by the specialist, of Chinese books, their producers and purchasers, that we may give a hearty welcome to the pleasant little work in which M. Maurice Jametel gives the result of his own experiences in the Middle Kingdom, especially in the character of a collector.* The Chinese are by no means without a love of money, but their contempt for the "red-headed foreign devils" is greater even than their avarice, and M. Jametel found that in one quarter of Pekin the keepers of the old curiosity shops would not deal with him, either giving a blank refusal or asking a price at which even extortion would turn pale. There are collectors in China who devote themselves to the accumulation of sticks of what in England we call Indian ink. This is really a Chinese manufacture, and is the instrument by which for centuries the *literati* of the Middle Kingdom have recorded their traditions and speculations. These *bâtons* have their sides decorated with artistic designs, and with the signature of the maker. Sticks of ink of great antiquity and of famous manufacturers are eagerly desired by native antiquaries, bibliographers, or whatever they are to be called. Of course the sticks are never degraded by their collectors to the uses for which they were made. There are no bookshops in the city of Pekin, and the booksellers row is outside the walls in a south-eastern suburb. M. Jametel gives a curious account of the companion who accompanied him. Yang-King-Chong was a retired merchant, who had made a fortune by the sale of more or less sham antique pottery to Europeans, and whose household arrangements were in two parts, each kept distinct from the other. In one section he had his many wives, his collection of Chinese books and curiosities, where everything was in the national taste and without admixture. The other part of the house was furnished exclusively in the European fashion, and included a small library of illustrated books of science in French, English, German, Russian, and even Swedish. He could not read any of these languages, but pored over their illustrations, and when one specially excited his curiosity called in the aid of his secretary, who had been partially educated at the Catholic Mission, but who had renounced at once celibacy and Jesuitism. The bookshops of Pekin are more like private libraries than magazines of commerce. The books are in paper packages, each with a title written on the outside, and are piled up on the shelves. Seated upon a sofa, with the inevitable small table and tea upon it, the visitors were shown some of the richest treasures of Chinese typography—books printed by the imperial orders—of past generations, and notable for their luxurious covers of yellow

---

* *Souvenirs d'un Collectionneur : La Chine inconnue*, par Maurice Jametel. 3e. édition. Paris : J. Rouam, 1886. 8vo., pp. 250.

silk, and Buddhist liturgies in boxes of perfumed woods. One shown to him was the *Book of Annals*, printed at Nanking in 1282. For this the bookseller asked 600 francs. Another curiosity was a book printed under the direction of the Emperor Kang-Chi in 1685. The text is in black ink; the annotations, by authors who were dead when it was executed, are in blue ink, for blue is the colour of mourning; the notes of the Emperor are printed in yellow, for that is the imperial colour; those of his tutors are in pale green, and those of the *literati* who were living at the time this book came from the press are in red ink. The harmonious arrangement of these colours is described by M. Jametel as a triumph of art. They were shown a copy of the *Kin-ping-mëi*, a romance prohibited by the censor for the licentiousness alike of text and illustrations. A more respectable example of Chinese literature is a description of the empire in 124 quarto volumes, which appeared in 1744. Finally, M. Jametel contented himself with the purchase of a collection of the hymns chanted in the imperial palace in the reign of Kang-Chi—a book not printed for sale, and now of course very rare. The next visit was to a dealer in engravings, who promptly displayed prints religious and irreligious. For this ancient civilization of the East, like the modern civilization of the West, has its pornographic literature and art. M. Jametel has other matters to describe, and describes well; but this glimpse of the old book-world of China will have most interest for the readers of *Book-Lore*.

THE POINT OF VIEW.

Whene'er I take my works abroad,
  The publisher to see,
I inly feel a deep desire
  To punch the head of he.

          Irate Author.

Whene'er he takes his works abroad,
  And brings them me to buy,
I inly feel, but rarely say,
  "You'll be the death of I."

          Patient Publisher.

THE GOLDEN LEGENDE.

ACOBUS DE VORAIGNE, Archbishop of Genoa, composed the *Legenda Aurea* in Latin about the year 1260. In the fourteenth century it was translated into French by Jean de Vignay, and from this French translation it was converted into English by Caxton.

Those particulars, though meagre in the extreme, represent almost every-thing that can with certainty be said with regard to the authorship of this curious and at one time popular book.

From a bibliographical point of view, however, the English-printed editions of the work are of the utmost possible importance, all are excessively scarce, and as specimens of the typographic art have but rarely been equalled, and never surpassed.

While admitting that there is much which might possibly be discovered, relating to the historical circumstances connected with the production of *The Golden Legende*, it is purposed to regard the book from a bibliographical stand-point, and consequently to ignore all extraneous questions. These woven out of the mist which envelops the introduction of printing into this country would in all probability never be satisfactorily settled.

Before proceeding to examine the seven or perhaps eight English editions which were issued between the years 1483 and 1527, it may be convenient to explain the object of the work as well as to glance at its contents.

The Golden Legende, described as exceeding all other books as gold passeth in value all other metals, contains, when in its most complete form (some editions are fuller than others), the lives and histories of certain personages mentioned in the Bible, namely, the lives of Adam, Noah, Abraham, Isaac, and Joseph; and the histories of Moses, Saul, David, Solomon, Roboas, Job, Tobit, and Judith. The passions of the Saints and an historical account of the Feasts of the Church occupy, however, the major portion of the book, which may be described as, and was no doubt intended for, a guide to the Scriptures.

As it appears tolerably certain that Caxton sent some twenty copies to St. Clement's Church, it may fairly be taken for granted that his object was to distribute the book among the ecclesiastics, who, there is every reason to suppose, read passages to the people as opportunity offered. If this surmise is correct, an impression of the *Legende* would be found in most churches in the vicinity of the metropolis, and would be regarded as supplementary to the Bible, and carefully preserved as such.

As a compilation the *Legende* is orthodox, frequently following the exact words of the Bible, and never departing from the meaning ascribed to it by the Church of the day.

9

In connection with this statement, it is a very curious fact that the translator, Caxton, used the word "breches" in his rendering of Genesis iii. 7. He says, "And thenne they toke fygge levys and sewed theym togyder for to cover theyr membres in the maner of breches."

This, it may be observed, shows that the Genevan version is not, as is generally supposed, the originator of this quaint expression.

The original French manuscript of Jean de Vignay, or what passed as the original, was sold at the Heathcote sale in 1803 to the then Duke of Norfolk for £63. The Catalogue (lot 1,090) describes it as "an immense folio volume, perhaps the most curious work of the kind in the world; every leaf on the finest vellum, all the capital letters illuminated with gold and rich colours, with upwards of 200 miniatures of the different saints, etc., etc." It would be interesting to speculate on the fate of this manuscript should it ever find its way to the market again.

We now propose to collate each English edition of the *Legenda Aurea* in order of date. The descriptions have, save where otherwise stated, been taken from the original sources.

1. The edition of 1483 (large folio).

The first leaf (not numbered) is almost entirely occupied with a large woodcut representing an assemblage of Saints. No title. At the foot of the leaf commences Caxton's prologue: "The holy and blessed doctour Saynt Ierom sayth," etc.

On the second leaf there is a rude woodcut of a galloping horse, and underneath Caxton's preface as follows (in black-letter) :—

"And for as moche as this | sayd werke was grete & over | chargeable to me taccomplisshe | I feryde me in the begynnynge of the | translacyon to have contynued it by | cause of the longe tyme of the transla | cion & also in thenpreyntying of yᵉ same | & in maner halfe desperate to have ac | complissd it was in purpose to have | lefte it after that I had begonne to | translate it & to have layed it aparte | ne had it be at thynstaunce & requeste | of the pryssant noble & vertuous erle | my lord wyllyam erle of arondel whi | ch he desyred me to procede & contynue | the said werke & promysed me to take | a resonable quatyte of them when they | were achyeued & accomplisshed and | sente to me a worshypful gentylman | a servaunte of his named Iohn Stan | ney which solycyted me in my Lordes | name that I shold in no wyse leve it | but accomplisshe it promyssing that my | sayd lord shold duryng my lyf geve | & graunte to me a yerely fee that is | to wete a bucke in sommer & a doo in | wynter with which fee I holde me | wel contente. Thenne atte contempla | cion & reverence of my sayd lord I | have endevoyred me to make an ende | & fynysshe thys sayd translacion and | also have emprynted it in the moost best | wyse that I have coude or myght and | presente this sayd book to his good & | noble lordshyp as chyef causer of the | achyeuvyng of hit praying hym to take | it in gree of me Wyllyam Caxton hys | poure servaunte & that it lyke him to | remember my fee & I shal praye unto | almyghty god for his longe lyf and | welfare & after this shorte and transy | torye lyf to come in to everlastynge joye | in heven the which he sende to hym & | me & unto al them that shal rede and | here this sayd book that for the love and | feythe of whom al these holy sayntes | hath suffred deth & passyon. Amen."

On the last leaf of the volume (ccccxliiii), right-hand column, is the following colophon:—

" Thus endeth the legende named | in latyn legenda aurea (that is to saye | in Englysshe the Golden legende) For | lyke as golde passeth in valelue alle | other metalles so this legende excedeth | alle other bookes wherin ben contey | ned alle the hygh and grete festys of | our lord, the festys of our blessyd la | dy the lyves passyons and myracles | of many other sayntes and other hys | torys and actes as al allonge here | afore is made mencyon whiche werke | I have accomplished at the Commaundemente and requeste of the noble and | puyssaunte erle, and my special good | lorde Wyllyam erle of arondel and have | fynysshed at Westmestre the twenty | day of Nouembre the yere of our lorde | M.CCCC.lxxxiij, and the fyrst yere | of the reygne of Kyng Rychard the | thyrd. By me Wyllyam Caxton."

This work is, without exception, one of the most elaborate, skilful, and magnificent specimens of printing which ever issued from Caxton's press. It is printed with double columns in large folio, 444 leaves, numbered consecutively.

The woodcuts, with which the work abounds, were erroneously supposed by Heinecken to have been the first productions of the graphic art in this country. The *Speculum Mundi*, however, by Caxton, published in 1481, contains twenty-seven wood engravings, and furnishes us with the earliest known English prints published with a date. An almost perfect copy of this first edition of the *Golden Legende*, sold at the Gardner sale in 1854 for £230.

2. The edition of 1483 (small folio):

A very mutilated and otherwise imperfect copy of what was supposed to be the small folio edition of 1483 was sold at the Bright sale for £30. This copy was, however, dated 1486.

As a matter of fact very little is known of this issue, and we have no idea where a specimen is to be seen. Dibdin refers to it in his *Typographica Antiqua* (Ames), but beyond stating that he had never seen a copy, and that he had heard it contained woodcuts but no initials, he gives no particulars.

3. The edition of 1493 (folio).

The first leaf contains the representation of the Saints, as in the large folio edition of 1483; at the head of the leaf this title:

9—2

" Here begynneth the legende named in latyn legenda aurea that is to say in englys | he the golden legende : For lyke as passeth golde in value al other metallys soo thys legende excedeth al other bokes."

On the recto of this first leaf, Caxton's prologue : " The holy and blessed doctour saynt Ierom sayth," etc.

Then follow three leaves of index, and the first numbered folio, commencing :

" The tyme of the advent or comyng of our Lord into this world," etc.

On the recto of leaf No. ccccxxix the following colophon :

" Thus endeth the legc̄de named in latyn legenda aurea " (as before, and terminating as follows) " and now have renewed and fynysshed it at Westmestre the xx day of May The yere of our lord M.ccccCxxxxiii And in the vii yere of the reygne off Kynge henry the VII By me Wyllyam Caxton."

Ccccxxix. folios, numbered, printed with initial letters in double columns.

The colophon is introduced by a very fine initial T, and at the foot is a woodcut of the crucifixion.

The edition has more woodcuts, and the chapters are differently arranged. Caxton died in 1492, and it is probable that although he printed the body of the book, the colophon was executed by Wynkyn de Worde, who affixed Caxton's name out of respect for his master. A copy of this edition, perfect, with the exception of one leaf in MS., sold at the Alchorne sale for £83.

The edition of 1498 (folio).

On the first leaf a large print of God the Father crowned, surrounded with angels. The usual title at the head of the leaf :

" Here begynnyth the legende named in latyn legenda aurea that is to saye in Englysshe," etc. Then on the recto of the same leaf follows Caxton's prologue : " The hooly and blessyd doctour saynt Iherom," etc.

Three leaves of index, and then the first numbered folio : " The tyme of thadvente or comyng of our lord," etc., as before, running on to folio ccclxxxxviii. to the end of the life of St. Erasmus.

Colophon : " Thus endeth the legende named in latyn legenda aurea that is to say in Englysshe the goldē legende. For lyke as golde passeth al other metalles wher in ben conteyned all the hyghe and grete festes of oure lord The festys of our blessyd lady. The lyves passyōs and myracles of many other sayntes hystoryes and actes as all alonge here afore is made mencion whyche werke I dyde accomplysshe and fynysshe att Westmynster the viii daye of Ianeuer the yere of our lorde Thousande CCCCLXxxxviii. And in the xiii yere of the reygne of Kynge Henry the vii By me wynkyn de worde."

This is probably the first impression with which Wynkyn de Worde opened his typographical labours of 1498. The book is truly a magnificent specimen of printing; the woodcuts with which it is embellished are, however, very rude.

Ames gives a description of a specimen of this edition, which has the "lyves and hystoryes" preceding the ordinary text. As will be seen from the above collation, the copy we have examined, and which, with the exception of one or two leaves in MS., is complete, commences on folio primo with "thadvente or comyng of our lord," etc.

Printed as usual in double columns.

The edition of 1503 (folio):

On the first leaf, the woodcut of God the Father, crowned and surrounded by angels. At the head of the leaf:

"Here begynneth the legende named in latyn legenda aurea That is to saye in | Englysse the golden legende. For lyke as passeth golde valewe all other metal | lys So thys legende excelleth all other bookes."

On the recto of this leaf, Caxton's prologue: "The hooly & blessed doctoure saynte Iherome," etc.

One leaf of index.

The first numbered folio: "The tyme of thadvente or comyng of our lorde into this worlde," etc., as before.

Colophon: "Thus endeth the legende named in latyn legenda aurea that is to | saye in Englysshe the golden legende. For lyke as Golde passeth | all other metalles: wherein ben conteyned all the hyghe and grete feestes | of our lorde. The festys of oure blessyd lady. The lyves passyons and | myracles of many other sayntes hystoryes and actes as alle alon | ge here a fore is made mencyon. Whyche werke I dyde accomplysshe | and fynysshe att Tempell baar the xvi daye of Feverer. The yere of | our lorde a Thousande ccccciij And in the xix yere of the reynge | of Kynge Henry the vij By me Iulian Notary."

On the recto of the leaf an ornamental scroll and in the centre:

"Thys empryn | ted at temple bar | re be me Iulyan | Notary dwellyn | ge in saynt clemē | tys parysshe

Underneath is one of the devices of Julian Notary. Folios cclviii., woodcuts forming initial letters, double columns.

The edition of 1512 (folio).

First leaf, woodcut representing an assemblage of saints, with the usual title, "Here begynneth the legende, named in latyn legenda aurea," etc.

This edition has the "Hystoryes shortly taken out of the Byble," which occupy 54 folios. Then follow the "feestes of our lorde Ihesu cryst," on folio primo, the pagination recommencing.

Colophon as usual, and terminating as follows: " Fynyshed the xv daye of Februarye The Yere of our lorde M.CCCCC & XII, the thyrde yere of the reygne of our soueraigne lorde Kynge Henry the eyght. Enprynted &ᶜ by me Wynkyn de Worde."

Folios 406, though numbered only cccc. Double columns. Small woodcuts. The edition of 1527 (folio).

Folio 1 (recto). The woodcut representing an assemblage of saints, and the same as that in the edition of 1483.

Folios 2-53. The lives of certain personages taken from the Bible, beginning with the life of Adam, and ending with that of Judith.

On folio 53 is an index, which is extended to and completely occupies the following folio.

Then follows folio primo and fresh pagination, introducing the advent of our Lord in the usual way, " The tyme of the advent or comynge of our lord in to this worlde," etc.

Colophon : " Thus endeth the legende named in latyn Legĕda aurea | that is to saye in englysshe the golden legende. For lyke | as golde passeth all other metalles so this boke excedeth | all other bokes wherein ben conteyned all the hygh and | grete feestes of our lorde the feestes of our blessed lady | the lyves passyons and myracles of many other sayn | tes hystoryes and actes as all alonge hereafore is made mencyon Whi | che werke hath ben diligĕtly amended in divers places where as grete | nede was. Finysshed the xxvii daye of August the yere of our lord M | CCCCCxxvII the xix yere of the regne of our soverayne lorde kynge | Henry the eyght Imprynted at London in Flete Strete at the sygne of | the soune by Wynkyn de Worde."

On the reverse an ornamental woodcut, and one of the devices of Wynkyn de Worde.

Ccclxxxiv. folios, double columns.

A copy of this edition sold at the Osterly Park sale, May, 1885, for £176.

Another edition of 1527 (?) (folio).

In the British Museum there is an imperfect copy of the *Golden Legende,* which it is exceedingly difficult to identify with any of the above-named editions. The first fifty and the last thirty folios are wanting, and consequently neither the title nor the colophon can be given.

It is thought that the copy bears a close resemblance to the edition of 1527, but not sufficiently so as to form part of that issue. As was often the case in the early era of printing, alterations were made in the text during the progress through the press, but in the instance under discussion the variations are too important and too numerous to suggest any casual alterations such as we refer to.

In all probability when the number of copies of the edition of 1527 were struck off, and the type in process of being broken up, a fresh issue would be made to satisfy the popular demand, and the type reset so far as was necessary. Hence the first portion of the work differs widely from the edition referred to, but the latter portion is almost precisely similar in every respect. In no other way can we explain the close similarity in one part of the book, and the great differences in the other.

THE CHRYSALIS OF A BOOKWORM.

We take this poem from a little volume of graceful verse entitled *Songs and Sonnets*, by Maurice Francis Egan. London: Kegan Paul and Co., 1885.

I read, O friend, no pages of old lore,
Which I loved well, and yet the flying days,
That softly passed as wind through green spring ways
And left a perfume, swift fly as of yore,
Though in clear Plato's stream I look no more,
Neither with Moschus sing Sicilian lays,
Nor with bold Dante wander in amaze,
Nor see our Will the Golden Age restore.
I read a book to which old books are new,
And new books old. A living book is mine--
In age, three years: in it I read no lies,
In it to myriad truths I find no clue—
A tender little child ; but I divine
Thoughts high as Dante's in her clear blue eyes.

THE FIRST EDITION OF THE *PARADISE LOST*.

N the comparatively early days of printing, such as the period at which Milton wrote his *Paradise Lost*, it was an ordinary and, indeed, common practice for authors to make emendations and additions while the process of printing was in full operation.

For this reason textual variations are frequently discovered in books forming part of one and the same edition—a fact well known to those whose delight or duty it is to collate examples of early printed works.

The first edition of the *Paradise Lost* is, like the original issues of the Poems of Skelton and the Plays of Shakespeare, a remarkable instance of the practice to which we refer ; for among the numerous existing copies of that edition there are but few which, in all particulars, prove on examination to be exactly alike.

The alterations in the poem itself are indeed few and unimportant, but the title and preliminary pages have, so far as yet discovered, no less than *nine* distinct variations. The first edition of the *Paradise Lost* assumes, therefore, nine forms at the least—and possibly more.

We have carefully collated seven different copies of the edition, and, with the aid of Mr. Sotheby's work, are enabled to complete the examination of the series.

The first title-page runs as follows :

Paradise lost | A | Poem | written in | Ten Books | By John Milton. | Licensed and Entred according | to Order. | London—Printed, and are to be sold by Peter Parker | under Creed Church neer Aldgate ; And by | Robert Boulter at the Turk's Head in Bishopsgate-street ; | And Matthias Walker, under St. Dunstons Church | in Fleet-street 1667 | .

No prefatory matter, the poem commencing immediately after the title, and ending on the reverse of Vv. 2. Small 4to., pp. 342.

The second title-page :

Same as the above in every respect, save that the author's name, " John Milton," is in large italic type. Small 4to., pp. 342. No prefatory matter.

The third title-page :

Paradise Lost | A | Poem in Ten Books | The Author J.M. | Licensed and entred according | to Order | London | Printed, etc. (as before).

In this variation the date is altered to 1668. Small 4to., pp. 342. No prefatory matter.

The fourth title-page :

The same as the last, only the type in the body of the title is somewhat larger. Dated 1668.

Small 4to., pp. 342. No prefatory matter.

The fifth title-page :

Paradise lost | A | Poem | In | Ten Books | The Author | John Milton | London| Printed by S. Simmons, and to be sold by S. Thomson at | the Bishops-Head in Duck-lane, H. Mortlack at the | White Hart in Westminster Hall, M. Walker under | St. Dunstans Church in Fleet-street, and R. Boulter at | the Turk's Head in Bishopsgate-street 1668 | .

Small 4to., pp. 356. In this variation fourteen pages of preliminary matter are found interpolated between the title-page and the poem, and it is to this that the increase in the number of pages is to be attributed. The additional matter consists of :

(*a*) The three-line advertisement, heading the first page, " *The Printer to the Reader | Courteous Reader,* There was no argument at first in | tended to the Book, but for the satisfaction of many | that have desired it is procured *S. Simons.* |

(*β*) The prose arguments to the several books, occupying 11 pages.

(*γ*) Milton's prose preface, entitled " The Verse," explaining his reasons for abandoning Rhyme. 2 pages.

(*δ*) The Errata. 1 page.

The three-line address alluded to above (*a*) is, of course, ungrammatical, and some copies are found with a corrected five-line address, as follows :

" *The Printer to the Reader. Courteous Reader* There was no Argument at first intended to the Book, but for the satisfaction of many that have desired it I have procur'd it, and withall a reason of that which stumbled many others, why the Poem Rimes not. *S. Simmons.*

The sixth title-page :

The same as the preceding, except that instead of four lines of stars under the author's name, there is an ornament consisting of a combination of thirty-four *fleurs de Lis.*

Small 4to., pp. 356. Preliminary matter the same. Some copies have the three-line address, others the five-line.

The seventh title-page :

Paradise lost | A | Poem | in | ten Books | The Author | John Milton | London | Printed by S. Simmons, and are to be sold by | T. Helder at the Angel in Little Brittain | 1669.

Small 4to., pp. 356. Date at the foot of the page instead of at the end of the last line. Prefatory matter as before. Some copies still retain the three-line address.

The eighth and ninth title-pages :

The same as the preceding, except that the word "Angel" is in italics. A comma will be found after the word "Brittain," instead of a full stop. The only distinction between these title-pages consists in insignificant changes of capital letters and in the pointing.

10

Small 4to., pp. 356. No printer's address to the reader. Date 1669.

So far as the text itself is concerned, the following may be noted :

5th Book, 257th line. Copies dated 1667 and 1669. A new paragraph is begun at this line, and there is no comma after the word "cloud." In the copy dated 1668 the line continues unbroken, and has the comma ; in addition to this the " Errata " directs *in* to be substituted for *with* in the penultimate line of the 3rd Book. In the copy dated 1669 the text is altered in accordance with this direction, and the " Errata " consequently amended.

The reasons which prompted a continual alteration in the verbiage of the title are not so apparent as they would have been if the emendations had occurred in the text itself. In the latter case a desire for improvement would have sufficiently accounted for the change ; but so far as the title-page is concerned, it cannot be pretended that any such motive existed. A reason, however, there must have been, and we suggest the following explanation as not only plausible but probable.

Milton, a Puritan of Puritans, was well known as the author of many furious attacks on the Church ; and worse than all, he posed as an apologist for the judicial murder of Charles I. He hated the censorship of the press—at that time in full vigour—and did not hesitate to express his opinion openly. So notorious was he in this respect that Tomkyns, the deputy of the Archbishop of Canterbury, the supervisor of manuscript, was extremely unwilling to permit the *Paradise Lost* to see the world at all, partly on account of certain passages which he deemed to be subversive of the Word of God, but chiefly, no doubt, on account of the known proclivities of the author.

The suspicious objections of Tomkyns, which were only allayed with the greatest possible difficulty, would seem to have recommended themselves to the printer, Simmons, who accordingly displayed considerable caution in issuing the work. The Court of Star Chamber, with its Writs of Rebellion, had, it is true, been defunct for nearly thirty years ; but for all that State prosecutions of printer, as well as author, were by no means infrequent. What, therefore, the Censor might have overlooked the Crown might at any time discover, or affect to discover, by putting in practice some of those quirks and quibbles by means of which innocent passages were contorted into a totally different meaning to that intended.

On the first four title-pages not the slightest mention is made of Simmons, nor did he issue any prefatory address to the reader. It was only on the fifth title-page and in the fifth issue that these additions were made, and at that time any fear of unpleasant consequences may fairly be thought to have passed away.

The third and fourth title-pages, it will be observed, bore the author's initials (J. M.) only, and this also is probably due to the anxiety of the printer ; for we cannot suppose for a moment that Milton would have deigned to sacrifice his independence even to preserve his safety. The various changes occurring at the foot of the titles in the names of the booksellers were, no doubt, occasioned by the Great Fire, and the necessity of making other business arrangements; and while these various alterations were being made, the opportunity would be seized of effecting the minor differences we have noticed.

These arguments are, of course, based on mere surmise. It may be that Simmons had a passion for alteration, and took advantage of Milton's blindness to gratify it; but in this event, why also did he not try his improving hand on the text? Why not popularize a few of the many lines which he, in common with many others, would doubtless regard as deeply abstruse if not altogether incomprehensible.

We can, in truth, assign no certain reason for the change; but whatever the incidents in this respect, we quite agree that " there are few books respecting the circumstances of whose first publication there is room for a greater variety of curious questions " than Milton's *Paradise Lost.*

THE WODHULL LIBRARY.

 HE Wodhull Library, the property of Mr. J. E. Severne, M.P., which has just been dispersed at Sotheby's, was formed at the end of the last and beginning of the present century by Mr. Michael Wodhull, the translator of *Euripides.* He was born at Thenford on the 15th of August, 1740, his father being John Wodhull, Esq., the head of an old Northamptonshire family. He was first sent to the school of the Rev. William Cleaver, at Twyford, in Buckinghamshire. Wodhull here made the acquaintance of the sons of his tutor, one of whom became Bishop of St. Asaph and another Archbishop of Dublin. The eldest, the Rev. John Cleaver, M.A., was student at Christ Church, Oxford, and was the "******** A.M." to whom Wodhull afterwards addressed one of his epistles. Wodhull next went to Winchester School, and afterwards to Brasenose College, Oxford. In 1754 he inherited, by the death of his father, a large fortune, of which the first use he made was to build a handsome mansion on his estate. In 1761 he married Catherine Milcah, daughter of the Rev. John Ingram, of Wolford, Warwickshire, but had no children. In 1783 he was High Sheriff of Northamptonshire.

Taking advantage of the short peace, he visited the libraries of Paris in 1803, and was one of the English detained by Bonaparte; although he was afterwards released on account of his age. He returned home an invalid and alone, and it was a source of great distress to him to be compelled to leave behind him in France a faithful servant, to whom he was much attached. From that time his bodily infirmities gradually increased, his sight at length failed, and his voice became scarcely audible; but his senses and his memory, which was most singularly retentive, continued unimpaired to the last. He died on November 10, 1816. In politics Mr. Wodhull was a Whig, and opposed to the war against the French Revolutionists; but he never entered into public life, his chief occupation and amusement being the study of books, of which he was celebrated as a collector. He disposed during his life of many which he had purchased; but left behind him above 4,000 volumes, consisting principally of first editions and rare specimens of early printing. A writer in the *Gentleman's Magazine* considers Mr. Wodhull to have been the Orlando of Dibdin's *Bibliomania.* Mr. Wodhull, who attained some note as the first translator into English of the whole of *Euripides,* was the author of *Ode to the Muses,* 1760, 4to. *Epistel to . . . . . . [John Cleaver] A.M., Student of Christ Church,* Lond., 1761, 4to. *Two Odes, i. to Miss Sally Fowler, ii. to the Dryads,* Lond., 1763, 4to. *The Equality of Mankind; a Poem,* Lond., 1766, 4to., of which a new edition was published in 1798 in 8vo. *The Nineteen Tragedies and Fragments of Euripides,* Lond.

1782, 4 vols., 8vo., 21s.; reprinted Lond., 1809, in 3 vols., 8vo. *Poetical Works,* 1804, 8vo.

The sale began January 11. The buyers present represented not only the most prominent English agents and dealers, but America and France. Amongst the best prices were as follows :—Æneas Silvius de Duobus Antibus Eurialo et Lucresia et de Curialium Miseria, with initials finely illuminated in gold and colours, s. l. and a.; Platonis Epistolæ Leonardo Aretino Interprete, s. l. and a. fine copies, in red morocco, gilt edges; 3 vols. in 1, small 4to.; £20 (B. F. Stevens). —Æsopi Fabulæ Gr. et Lat. cum Vita ex Recensione Boni Accursii, 3 parts in 1, first edition, fine copy in green morocco extra, gilt edges, by Mrs. Weir; small 4to.; s. l. and a. sed Mediolani, circa 1480; £20 (B. F. Stevens).—Alcyonii (Petri) Medices Legatus de Exsilio, very fine copy, from the library of Francis I., in old calf, gilt edges, with gold tooling, including crowned F. arms of France, Salamander, fleur-de-lis, beautifully rebacked; small 4to.; Venetiis, Aldus, 1522; £58 (Quaritch).—Aretini (Leonardi Bruni) de Bello Italico adversus Gothos Libri IV., first edition, autograph of " Jacques Le Chandelier, 1550," Fulginei, Em. de Ursinis et J. Numeister, 1470; Justiniani (B.) Oratio habita apud Sixtum IV., very scarce, Romæ, in Domo Joannis Philippi de Lignamine, 1471, very fine copy, from the library of Paul Girardot de Prefond, with his Museum Ticket in letters of gold on red morocco pasted inside the cover, red morocco super extra, broad dentelle borders of gold, silk linings, gilt edges, by Derom; in 1 vol., 4to.; £35 10s. (Quaritch).—Aristotelis Opera et Theophrastus de Historia et de Causis Plantarum, etc., Græce, 6 vol., first edition, fine copy, ruled, in old calf, gilt edges, folio; Venetiis, Aldus, 1495-98; £29 (Nattali).—Aristoteles de Arte Poetica, Gr. et Lat. cum F. Robortelli Explicationibus, fine copy in old brown morocco, covered with gold and silver tooling, comprising Royal Arms of Henry II., with crescent, the crowned H, the interlaced H with DD, interlaced crescents, the bow and quiver with arrows of Diane de Poictiers, the fleur-de-lis, etc., gilt gaufré edges, by P. Roffet Le Faucheux; folio; Florentiæ, L. Torrentinus, 1548; £205 (Quaritch).—Arithmetic. Incommincia una practica molta bona et vtile a ciaschaduno chi vuole vxare larte de labbacho, extremely rare and nearly unique, as the only other copy known is that sold in the Libri sale; small 4to.; Triviso, 1478; £40 (Quaritch).—Athenée, traduit par l'Abbé M. de Marolles, very fine copy, with autograph of M. Folkes (one of those usually termed on large paper), blue morocco extra, covered with fleurs-de-lis and crowned L stamped in gold, gilt edges, from the library of Louis XIV.; 4to.; Paris, 1680; £28 (Bain).— Augustinus (B.) de Vita Christiana et de Singularitate Clericorum, 2 vols. in 1, stained, red morocco, gilt edges; small 4to.; (Coloniæ) Per me Olricum Zel, 1467; £31 (Quaritch).—Auli Gellii Noctes Atticæ, cum Epistola Johannis Andræ Episcopi Aleriensis ad Paulum II., numerous MS. notes, very slightly wormed in margins, else very large copy, ruled, in Russia, by Roger Payne, with Wodhull arms in gold on side; folio; Romæ in Domo Petri de Maximis (Sweynheym and

Pannartz), 1469; £33 (Colm).—Balbi de Janua (Joannis) Summa quæ vocatur Catholicon, sive Grammatica et Lexicon Linguæ Latinæ, 2 vols. in 1, first edition and the fourth book printed with a date, fine copy, with painted capitals, russia extra, gold tooling, by Roger Payne ; folio ; Moguntiæ, J. Gutenberg, 1460; £310 (Quaritch).—Beccaria (C.) dei Delitti e delle Pene, printed on vellum, Didot's beautiful edition, red morocco extra, dentelle borders, gilt edges, by Derome, with arms of M. Paris de Meyzieu in gold on sides, in red morocco case also stamped with his arms ; Parigi, 1780 ; £55 (Quaritch).—Biblia Latina, very fine copy, with beautiful border and initial letter richly illuminated in gold and colours, citron morocco, gilt edges, by Padeloup, very scarce ; folio ; Nurnbergæ, A. Coburger, 1478 ; £43 10s. (Quaritch).—Biblia Latina, Vetus Testamentum secundum LXX Latine redditum et ex Auctoritate Sixti V editum (edidit Antonius Carafa Cardinalis), very fine copy in blue morocco, gilt marbled edges, by Padeloup ; folio ; Romæ in Ædibus Populi Romani (Typis Aldinis), 1588 ; £24 (Toovey).—Bible en Francoys par R. Olivetan aidé de J. Calvin, black letter, last leaf mended, else very fine copy, ruled, in red morocco, borders of gold, gilt edges ; from the M'Carthy Library, with Wodhull arms stamped in gold on side ; folio ; Neufchastel, P. de Wingle dit Pirot Picard, 1535 ; £39 10s. (Quaritch).—Blondi Flavii Forliviensis Italia illustrata, fine manuscript on vellum, with initial letters (first historiated with human figure holding a book), borders and arms of Ruccelai finely illuminated in gold and colours, red morocco extra, gilt edges ; folio ; Sæc. xv. ; £37 (Quaritch).—Boccaccio (Giovanni) il Decamerone, the genuine Giunta uncastrated edition, fine copy in red morocco, borders of gold, silk linings, gilt edges, by Derome le Jeune, with his ticket, in red morocco case ; Firenze, Giunta, 1527 ; £81 (Quaritch).—Breviarium Romanum cum Calendario, beautiful manuscript on vellum, exquisitely written, with Rubrics in blue ink, ornamented with 139 charming miniatures (including signs of the zodiac and murder of Archbishop Becket), 118 borders composed of architectural designs, birds, flowers, fruit, and nondescripts, with almost innumerable initial letters, all richly illuminated in gold and colours, having beneath seven of the largest miniatures, the armorial bearings of the Cardinal of Spain, quartering the arms of Castile and Leon, old calf, lettered Missale ; small 4to. ; Sæc. xv. ; £515 (Quaritch).—Breydenbach (B. de) Grant Voyage de Hierusalem (tiré du Latin par le Frère Nicole Le Huen), fine copy, with folding views of Venice, Parenzo, Candia, Modon, and Rhodes, engraved on copper, the most ancient in any French book, Etruscan calf extra, gilt edges, by Edwards, of Halifax ; small folio ; Lyon, M. Topie de Pymont et J. Heremberck, 1488 ; £48 (Quaritch).—Bruno (Giordano) Speccio de la Bestia trionfante, a magnificent specimen of Boyet's binding in citron morocco, richly ornamented with variegated leathers and gold tooling, double with red leather, gilt marbled edges, in citron morocco case ; Parigi (Londra T. Vautrollier), 1584 ; £360 (Quaritch).—Bruno (Giordano) La Cena de la Ceneri descritta in cinque Dialogi, cuts, beautiful copy, ruled, a magnificent specimen of binding in citron morocco, richly ornamented with variegated leathers and gold tooling, double with bordered red leather, gilt edges, by Monnier, in citron morocco case, s. n. 1584; £365 (Quaritch).—The MS. Cæsar, "De Bello Gallico," folio, fifteenth century, sold for £39 (Quaritch), and the editio princeps, 1469, Sweynheym and Pannartz, with the first and last leaf inlaid; £48 (Quaritch).—Gerson (J.) Collectorium super Magnificat, folio, without place, but Eslingæ, C. Fyner, 1473; £7 (Quaritch). This book is said to contain the earliest printed music.—Gesneri (C.) Historia Animalium, 5 vols., 1551-87, and Nomenclator Aquatilium animantium, 1560, Icones Quadrupedum, etc., 1560, folio, in 4 vols.; £7 10s. (Quaritch).— Gesta Romanorum (Auctore Elimando), sm. folio, without date or place, but Coloniæ, Ulricus Zell, *circa* 1473, fine copy, with painted capitals, considered by Panzer to be the first edition, but Warton thought the one printed at Utrecht by Ketelaer and Leempt, about 1473, earlier, as it contains 151 chapters, while this and subsequent ones have 181; £27 (B. F. Stevens).—Giles de Rome Livre du Gouvernement des Rois et des Princes, translaté de Latin en François par le commandement du Roi Philippe de France, par Henri de Ganchi, manuscript, on vellum, folio, fourteenth century, with fine borders, and historiated letters, among the ornamental work is a figure of the Queen of the Mermaids playing the violin with the bow in her left hand; £24 (Quaritch).—Gratiani Decretum cum Apparatu Bartholomæi Brixiensis, first edition, folio, Argentorati, 1471, the first book printed at Strasburg with a date; £30 10s. (B. F. Stevens).—Gregorii IX. Decretalia cum Glossis, folio, Venetiis, N. Jenson, 1479, with five miniatures and initials illuminated and bound by Roger Payne; £6 10s. (Quaritch).—Gringore (P.), Les Folles Enterprises, black letter, Paris, 1505, woodcuts, title damaged; £6 15s. (Quaritch).—Guidonis de Monte Rocherii Manipulus Curatorum, folio, Paris, 1473, one of the rare early printed books in Paris; £11 (Quaritch).— Guillermi Postilla super Evangelia Dominicalia et super Evangelia de Sanctis, sm. 4to, Paris, 1479, a rare book, unknown to Panzer, Hain, and Brunet, and others; £5 (B. F. Stevens).—Guy de VVarvick Chevalier Dagleterre (*sic*), black letter, with woodcuts, sm. folio, Paris, 1525, fine copy of an exceedingly rare romance of chivalry in prose; £130 (Quaritch). Mr. Wodhull gave £1 11s. 6d. for it at these rooms, in those days called Leigh's, September 12, 1779. A letter from Lord Warwick, dated Hill Street, 1761, is pasted inside the cover thanking him for the sight of the book.—Hesiodi Opera, Gr. et Lat., edidit T. Robinson, largest paper, folio, Oxon., 1737, only ten copies printed, the work of the Sheldon Press; £6 (Quaritch).—Hieronymi (S.) Epistolæ, 2 vols., large folio, Moguntiæ, Schoiffer de Gernszhem, 1470; £18 (Quaritch).—Hieronymo (San) Vitae Epistole Vulgare, folio, Ferrara, 1497, numerous fine woodcuts and initial letters, some leaves mended; £14 (Quaritch).—Homeri Opera, Græce, 2 vols. in 1, first edition, folio, Florentiæ, Sumptibus B. et N. Nerliorum, bound by Derome in blue morocco. This copy is the finest ever sold at auction; £200 (Bain). It cost Mr. Wodhull £15 15s. on August 25, 1770.—The first Aldine Horace, 1501, having painted capitals, and stamped with the Golden Fleece five times in gold on the back, a large copy, as it is styled, though it measured only 6⅛ in., sold for £30 10s. (Quaritch).—Irenici (Francisci) Germania, a work on pedigree, rendered valuable by being Grolier's own copy, a fine folio of 1518, bound in old calf, and tooled in Grolier pattern with his mottoes, but not in fine condition, yet it brought the considerable sum of £62 (Quaritch). On the fly-leaf Mr. Wodhull had written, "Hoblyn's sale, March 23, 1778, £1 1s., and 2s. for repairs."—James V., the New Actis and Constitutionis of Parliament maid by the Rycht Excellent Prince James the Fift Kyng of Scottis, 1540, printed on vellum in black letter, folio, Edinburgh, T. Davidson, 1541, with large woodcuts of coats, the Crucifixion, etc.; £151 (Bain). —Joannis Chrysostomi Homiliæ in Matheum, Georgio Trapezonico Interprete, 1466, and Augustinus (S.) de Arte prædicandi (Argent. ante 1466) in 1 vol., folio; £26 10s. (Quaritch).—Joannis Grammatici in Posteriora resolutoria Aristotelis Comentaria, Græce, folio, Venetiis, Aldus, 1504, with curious impressions of two medals, battle of cavalry, and Orpheus charming the beasts as centre ornaments on the sides and the back ornamented with fleurs-de-lis in gold, being a rare and fine specimen of old Venetian binding in brown morocco; £84 (Quaritch).— Jouvencel (Le) Roman allegori que, etc., par Jean de Breiul, dit le Fleau des Anglois, black letter, woodcuts, folio, Paris, A. Verard, 1493; £10 5s. (Warton).— Justin (Sainct) ses Œuvres en François, par Jan de Maumont, folio, Paris, 1559 (by a curious mistake of the binder this work was put into the old covers of a copy of Vigerii Decachordum, which belonged to Grolier, and is a fine specimen of N. Eve's binding, bearing the title of the work by Vigerius, with the motto of Grolier); £60 (Warton).—Justini Historiæ, fine manuscript, on vellum, folio, fourteenth century, from the Maffei Library; £11 (Quaritch).—Justiniani Institutiones cum glossis, folio, Moguntiæ, Schoyffer, 1472; £18 (Quaritch).—Justiniani Institutiones, printed on vellum, folio, Venetiis, Jacobus de Rubeis, 1476, probably unique, as it was the Pinelli copy purchased in 1789 by Mr. Tyssen for £36, sold in his sale in 1801 for £31 10s. to Mr. Heathcote; and now for £54 (Quaritch).— Lactantii Opera, with contemporary manuscript notes, folio, Romæ, Sweynheym and Pannartz, 1468, fine copy illuminated, and bound by R. Payne; £36 (Quaritch).— La Fontaine (J. de) Contes et Nouvelles en Vers, the Fermiers Généraux edition, with Diderot's notice, 2 vols., Amst. (Paris, Barbou), 1762, with the rare plates; £39 (Bain).—Livii Historiarum Decas Prima, a magnificent manuscript on vellum, folio, fifteenth century, with historiated letters and the Caraccioli arms, brought by Dr. Askew from Palermo; £45 (Quaritch).—Longus, Les Amours Pastorales de Daphnis et Chloe, engravings by Audran from designs by Philip Duke of Orleans, one of the few copies issued before the "Petits Pieds" was finished, but having Scotin's similar plate added, privately printed at the expense of the Regent for presents only, 1718; £16 (Bain).—Lyndewode (W.), Constituciones Provinciales Ecclesiæ Anglicanæ, black letter, Wynkyn de Worde, 1496, with Caxton's small white grounded device at the end, and at the end of tabula, woodcut of a bishop; £30 (H. Stevens).—Mabrian, Histoire singuliere, etc., des quatre filz Aymon, et Cronique du preux et redoubte Prince Mabrian Roy de Hierusalem, etc., black letter, small folio, Paris, no date, but 1525; £22 10s. (Quaritch).—Macrobii Opera, Romæ, 1465, Fenestella de Magistratibus Romanorum, 1465, manuscript on vellum by an Italian scribe of the fifteenth century; £21 (Quaritch).—Macrobii Opera, first edition, folio, Venetiis, N. Jenson, 1472; £12 (Quaritch).—Magic, Picatrix de Magia Veterum, unpublished manuscript on vellum, small 4to., sixteenth century; £12 (Quaritch).—Manfredi (H.), Liber de Homine et Conservatione Sanitatis Italiæ vulgo dictus " Libro del Perche," first edition, folio, Bononiæ, 1474; £15 (Gray).—Mantuani (Babtistæ), Opus Divinum de Purissima Virgine, etc., printed on vellum, small 4to., Paris, 1494, presumed to be unique, as Brunet knew of Croft's copy only, which this is ; £11 5s. (Quaritch).—Marchesini (J.), Mammetractus sive Expositio super Biblia et Legenda Sanctorum, first edition, folio, Moguntiæ, Schoiffer, 1470; £15 10s. (Quaritch).—Marguerites de la Marguerite des Princesses très illustre Royne de Navarre avec la Suyte, 2 vols., Lyon, 1547, woodcuts and autograph of Guyon de Sardière, very fine copy, in blue morocco, by Derome ; £56 (Bain).—Marguerite de Valois son Tombeau faict premièrement en disticques Latins, par les trois sœurs Princesses en Angleterre (Anne, Marguerite, et Jane de Seymour), Paris, 1551; £18 (Bain).—Martialis Epigrammata, first edition, 4to., Venetiis, Vindelinus de Spira, *circa* 1470; £10 10s. (Quaritch).—Meliadus de Leonnoys ses nobles faictz darmes, etc., black letter, folio, Paris, 1528, woodcuts, fine copy, bound by Ruette, with arms of Cardinal Archbishop Berthier de Bezy in gold on sides, and from the Gulston collection, an exceedingly rare book; £130 (Ellis and Scrutton). —Molière, Œuvres, avec des remarques par M. Bret, 6 vols., Paris, 1773, with portrait by Cathelin, and plates by Moreau, fine copy, bound by Derome ; £77 (Quaritch).—Musæi Opusculum de Herone et Leandro, Græce, first edition, small 4to., Venetiis, Aldus, 1494, supposed to be the first book printed by Aldus : in this copy the omitted line on *a* ii. and *b* iii. is supplied in manuscript, said to be in the autograph of Aldus ; £34 (Quaritch).—Mystere des Actes des Apostres, 2 vols., Paris, 1541 ; L'Apocalypse, Paris, 1541, black letter, folio ; 3 vols. in 1, bound by Padeloup ; £32 10s. (Toovey). The Beckford copy, wormed, brought £26 10s.—Orford (Horace Walpole, Earl of), Works, with supplement by E. Edwards, 6 vols., illustrated with portraits, 4to., 1798-1808 ; £12 10s. (B. F. Stevens).—Ovidii Opera, 2 vols. in 1, small folio, Vicentiæ, 1480, fine copy, bound by Derome in citron morocco; £11 (Quaritch).—Ovid, the first Aldine edition, Venetiis, 1502, with autograph cipher by C. M. Cracherode, bound in gilt veau fauve, with arms of Count Hoym in gold on sides ; £17 (Warton).—Ovidii Opera, cura A. Asulani, 3 vols., Venetiis, Aldus, 1533-34, large paper copy with rough leaves ; £15 (Quaritch).—Ovidio Metamorphoseos vulgare, in prosa tradotto da G. de' Bonsignori : first edition, folio, Venetia, 1497, with numerous woodcuts by Zoan Andrea; £36 (Quaritch).—Ovide, Les Metamorphoses en Latin et en

11

François avec des remarques par l'Abbé Banier, 2 vols. in 1, large paper, royal folio, Amst., 1732; £10 10s. (Ellis and Scrutton).—Ovide Metamorphoses, gravées sur les desseins des meilleurs peintres François par les soins des Sieurs Le Mire et Basan, 4to., Paris, 1767; £31 10s. (Bain).—Panzeri (G. W.), Annales Typographici, 11 vols., 4to., Norimbergæ, 1793-1803; £17 (Quaritch).—Papæ (Guidonis) Decisiones Parlamenti Dalph, small folio, Gracionopoli, S. Foretus, 1490, with autograph notes by Peter Eina, Senator of Grenoble, the first book printed at Grenoble, and one of the only two copies known, being mentioned by Beloe, and the other by Colomb de Batines; £58 (Quaritch).—Perceforest, La treselegante delicieuse melliflue et tresplaisante Hystoire du tresnoble victorieux et excellentissime Roy Pereceforest Roy de la grant Bretaigne, fundateur du Franc palais et du Temple du Souuerain Dieu, black letter, folio, Paris, 1531-2; £10 (H. Stevens).—Petrarca Triumphi, a fine manuscript on vellum by an Italian scribe, small 4to., fifteenth century, with the name of the scribe in a Latin verse, "Qui scripsit scribat, semper cum Dño vivat, Vivat in celis Julianus homo fidelis," from Dr. Askew's library; £26 (Ellis and Scrutton).—Petronii Arbitri Satyricon, Paris, 1677, from the La Moignon collection, bound by Padeloup; £9 (B. F. Stevens).

(To be continued.)

REVIEWS.

—◆—

Analogous Proverbs in Ten Languages. By MRS. E. B. MAWR. London : Elliot Stock, 1885. 8vo., pp. 113.

MRS. MAWR has in this little volume arranged a series of English proverbs in alphabetical order, and placed under them corresponding popular phrases, when they were to be found in German, Dutch, Danish, French, Italian, Spanish, Portuguese, Latin and Roumanian. As these are not furnished with literal translations, some acquaintance with nine languages besides English is needed in order to make the fullest use of the book. The chief interest is, however, in the contribution from Roumania—a language and literature of which too little has hitherto been known. Sometimes the analogues given are by no means literal ; thus the Spanish *Mas vale un toma que dos te daré*, is placed under "Fine words butter no parsnips." Generally, however, the parallels are sufficiently exact, and they are always interesting and suggestive. As an example of the style and method of the book, we quote one proverb, which exhibits a familiar moral :—

> They that have no other meat,
> Bread and butter are glad to eat.
> R. Cânele némţului, la nevvie mânânţi si mére padureţe.
> F. Ventre affamé prend tout en gré.
> G. Hunger macht hart Brod zu Honigkuchen.
> I. La fame muta le fave in mandole.
> S. A pan de quinze dias, hambre de tres semanas.
> D. De appetijt en hongersnood,
> Vonden novit kwaad brood.
> Da. Hunger gjer Skovœbler sode.
> P. Quem tem fóme, cardos come.
> L. Nihil contemnit esuriens.

Biographical Lectures. By GEORGE DAWSON, M.A. Edited by G. ST. CLAIR. London : Kegan Paul.

THE late George Dawson was unrivalled as a popular expositor. He had the gift of the improvisatore in the unexpected plane of literary and biographical criticism. He had a keen eye for the salient points, alike of men and books, and a sincere delight in their sympathetic presentation. The lectures which Miss Beauclerc has disinterred from files of old newspapers and other sources will stand tests of criticism before which the bulk of popular addresses would fail utterly. There are some careless phrases which would probably have disappeared had Mr. Dawson himself revised the reports ; but as a whole, they may be accepted as faithful representations of his matter and form. The two most important articles in the volume are not biographical, but deal with the poetry of Coleridge and Wordsworth. The great dead, whose lives are here estimated, range from " Good Queen Bess " to the Prince Consort, and from Swedenborg to Charles Lamb. Dawson's voice was an educational power to the young men who are now passing through middle age, and this volume will convey to a younger generation some of the useful lessons he taught with characteristic individuality and success.

Bibliothèque d'Art Ancien. Hans Holbein. Par JEAN ROUSSEAU. Paris : Jules Rouam. 1885. 4to., pp. 72.

HOLBEIN was born at Augsburg in 1497, his father, Hans Holbein the elder, being a painter in very poor circumstances, and in consequence Holbein had to paint for his living at a very early age. In 1516 he left Augsburg and went, in company with his brother Ambrose, also a painter, to Basel, where he painted the well-known portraits of the Burgomaster Jacob Meyer and his wife. He was employed by the booksellers in designing frontispieces to their publications ; and in this way he illustrated *Aeneae Platonici lib. de immortalitate animae*, Erasmus *declamatio de morte*, St. Augustin *De civitate Deo*, the *Novum Testamentum* of Erasmus, and More's *Utopia.* In 1526 he produced the portrait of his friend and patron Erasmus. During his last years at Basel, Holbein designed and published his celebrated work, the *Dance of Death.* In 1532 he came to London, with a recommendation from Erasmus to Sir Thomas More, for whom he painted a picture of the More family. In 1537 he was first employed by Henry VIII. As the result of Holbein's labours for the King, we have that remarkable series of portraits of the Court of Henry VIII., which is now in the possession of her Majesty. Among the distinguished persons who sat to him for their portraits were Melanchthon, Queen Mary I., Anne of Cleves, Lord Cobham, Henry VIII., Sir Thomas More, Anne Boleyn, Sir Thomas Wyat the poet, and Bishop Fisher. In the work before us M. Rousseau has sketched Holbein's career in an interesting manner, and, in addition, the book is illustrated by a good selection of the portraits and other works of the great master.

Devon Booksellers and Printers in the Seventeenth and Eighteenth Centuries. Supplementary Paper, No. 1. By JOHN INGLE DREDGE, Vicar of Buckland Bremer, Devon. Reprinted from the *Western Antiquary.* Fifty copies ; not published. Plymouth : W. H. Luke, 1885, pp. 41-58.

WE have already expressed our sense of the value of Mr. Dredge's contribution to county bibliography (*Book-Lore*, vol. ii., p. 117), and we need now only express our satisfaction at this early issue of the first of his proposed supplementary papers. The response made to this appeal for additional information is such as to lead him to entertain the hope that he may at length get all the facts necessary on which to base the complete Annals of the Devon Press. We sincerely hope that Mr. Dredge may accomplish this task, for which he is so well fitted.

We have received the following catalogues :—K. W. Hiersemann, 1, Turnerstrasse, Leipzig ; C. W. Palmer, 100, Southampton Row, London, E.C. ; T. Simmons, 164, Parade, Leamington ; R. H. Sutton, 25, Princess Street, Manchester ; Henry Gray, 25, Cathedral Yard, Manchester ; Robson and Kerslake, 23, Coventry Street, Haymarket, London, W. ; James Roche, 1, Southampton Row, London, W.C. ; William Downing, 74, New Street, Birmingham ; Albert Cohn, Berlin (the first part of the collection of the late Fr. Roath) ; Andrew Fredale, Torquay ; Wm. Downing, 74, New Street, Birmingham.

CORRESPONDENCE.

EARLY PARISIAN PRINTERS.

IN the imprint at end of a volume of Legatine and Provincial Constitutions relating to the Church of England, printed at Paris in 1504, the book is stated to be " in unum Codicem Collecta : et a disertissimo ac iuris utriusque peritissimo domino Iohanne Chappuys : recognita et adnotata : Compressa sunt solertissima acuratione atque arte Magistri Wulfgangi Hopitii : impēsis eiusdem : et phissimi bibliopole Iōanis Confluĉtini : in inclyta Parrhisiorum academia A.D. 1504, ad idus Septembris."

The book commences with an address to Wm. Warham, Archbishop of Canterbury, by " Iodocus Badius Ascensius." "Ex officina nostra litteraria in Parrhisiorum academia, ad idus Septembris, 1504."

In this "address" the book is stated to be "recognovissemus : et legitimas etiā epitomatis seu summarius decoranemus diligentissimique bibliopole Wulfgangus Hopit. : et Iōannes Confluĉtinus (quorum ere opus excusoma est), etiā perctissimo iuris utriusque viro : magistro Iohanni Chappaso redintegrāndis et adnotandas conuississent : nosquā illis trapticeni inlicem seu tabellam addridisesseimus," etc., etc.

Who was the actual printer (or printers) of this book, according to this address and imprint ? Is anything known of " Iōanis Confluĉtini "? Was he in partnership with " Wulfgang Hopit "? and did they print on their own account, or "for" " Iodocus Badius Ascensius "?

NOVICE,

A WOODEN LIBRARY.

THE following paragraph is extracted from *The Mirror*, xxiv. (1834), 464 :—

"A singular library exists at Warsenstein, near Cassel ; the books composing it, or rather the substitutes for them, being made of wood, and every one of them is a specimen of some different tree. The back is formed of its bark, and the sides are constructed of polished pieces of the same stock. When put together, the whole forms a box ; and inside of it are stored the fruit, seed, and leaves, together with the moss which grows on the trunk, and the insects which feed upon the tree ; every volume corresponds in size, and the collection altogether has an excellent effect."
Does this still exist ?

T. N. BRUSHFIELD, M.D.

Salterton, Devon.

BONA.

I HAVE a Latin religious work, *Manu ductio ad Cœlum Medullam Continens Sanctorum Patrum et Veterum Philosophorum, Auctore D. Joanne Bona*, etc., dated Coloniæ, MDCLXXXIII. It is the size of an ordinary Prayer-Book, viz., 4½ inches long by 2¾ inches broad, ¾ inch thick, in good condition. Will you kindly inform me in next month's issue the probable value of the same, and where I would be likely to get a purchaser ?

POLYGLOT.

[We are not aware that this volume possesses any special pecuniary value. The best way would be to offer it for sale to a respectable bookseller.—ED.]

BIBLIOPHILE'S KALENDAR.

AT a recent meeting of the Microscopic Section of the Literary and Philosophic Society of Manchester, Mr. Alfred Brothers, F.R.A.S., read a note on "Microscopic Writing," in which he said : "The Lord's Prayer has always been a favourite subject for testing the powers of minute caligraphy. To write the 227 letters within the space covered by the smallest coin is a feat of some difficulty, but that the same number of letters can be engraved on glass within a space so minute as to be almost invisible with the lowest power of the microscope, and the individual letters not defined clearly with an eighth object-glass, may seem incredible. There is, however, in the possession of this Section a slide which contains the Lord's Prayer, written by W. Webb in 1863, within the space of the 405,000th part of an inch. To find this minute speck requires the exercise of much patience, as it is not only necessary to have just the right kind of illumination, but the focus of the lens must be on the true surface of the glass on which the object is written. When once seen with a low power it is not difficult to find with the same power ; but with the half-inch and higher powers it is always a trial of patience even when the position of the object has been carefully registered with a lower power, and you are sure that the object is central in the field. Perhaps with the achromatic condenser some of the difficulty may be removed. It will be remembered that about twenty years ago the late Mr. Rideout presented to the Section a machine for producing minute writing. The instrument was lent by Mr. Rideout to Mr. Dancer, by whom it was recently sent to the Society. It seemed to me that as this instrument was purchased by Mr. Rideout at the Great Exhibition in 1862, it might be the same with which the wonderful piece of writing, or perhaps it should be called engraving, referred to, was executed. I therefore wrote to Mr. Dancer for information on this point. In reply he says : 'The microscopic writing on glass of the Lord's Prayer referred to in your letter was at one time in my possession, and was, I believe, presented by me to the Microscopical Section. It was obtained from Mr. Webb, and he was the same person who exhibited the microscopic writing machine at the Great Exhibition of 1862. Mr. Webb died about ten or fifteen years ago, but I cannot give the exact date. I have a very strong impression that Mr. Rideout obtained the machine from him, which was sent by me to the Society. If able to find Mr. Rideout's letter it may confirm this.' I have not received the letter, but as what Mr. Dancer says confirms the impression I have of what passed at the time, there can be little doubt that the instrument is the one used to produce the writing referred to. Under the microscope I have arranged two other slides of minute writing which have been lent to me by Mr. Armstrong. These are not *very* minute when compared with the one first referred to, and which I have placed under the third microscope where you will see the object with an eighth object-glass. Even with this great amplification the words can scarcely be read, but it can be seen that only greater power is required to make the whole legible. It happens that the covering glass is very thick, so that powers higher than the eighth cannot be used. It will be noticed that the name, ' W. Webb, 1863,' is distinctly legible and very beautifully written. Mr. Armstrong has given me some particulars of Webb's minute writing, from which it appears that he was accustomed to write the Lord's Prayer in spaces of the 500th to the 10,000th of an inch, and, as we have seen, to the 405,000th, and the prices of these slides varied from 2s. 6d. to 70s."

BOOK-LOVERS will be glad of the article in *L'Art*, in which Mr. Max Rooses speaks of Rubens and Moretus, the printer, who at one time were the most famous men of Antwerp. Some fresh details as to the friendship of these two are given from the Plantin-Moretus Archives.

Both Defeated is the title of a small Temperance annual, edited by Mr. T. H. Evans, and published at the National Temperance Publication Depôt. We name it here because it contains as frontispiece a portrait of Thomas Tryon, the Pythagorean, of whose life and writings some account is given.

THE thirty third annual report of the Manchester Public Free Libraries, 1884-85, chronicles another year of progress. The total number of books and periodicals issued during the year was 1,381,149, as against 1,320,393 in the year 1883-84. In the Reference Department the issues were 283,232 in 1884-85, and 278,876 in the preceding year. The Sunday use of the Reference Library decreased slightly, there being an average issue of 265 books each Sunday, against an average of 276 in 1883-84. This decrease is most noticeable in the two classes of Literature and Polygraphy and Politics and Commerce. But when we take all the seven libraries together, we find that the total number of persons who entered the libraries on Sundays in 1884-85 was 245,700, or an average of 4,818 each Sunday. In the previous year the total was 212,150, and the average 4,250. 396,428 books were used in the reading-rooms attached to the branches, and 701,489 books were lent out for home reading. 870 volumes have been added by gift to the Reference Library during the year. Alderman Sir Thomas Baker has presented nearly 500 volumes, including a valuable collection of books and pamphlets illustrating the history of Nonconformity in Manchester. Mr. R. D. Darbishire also has presented a large number of volumes. During the year one branch library has been enlarged, and several lending library catalogues were issued.

IN the *Printing Times* the elaborate *Bibliography of Printing* is brought to a prosperous conclusion. It is an excellent performance.

MR. JOHN BIRD HAWES, the celebrated Cambridge binder, died 17th December, 1885, after a long illness. His death will be regretted by many book-lovers, and especially by those who hail from Cambridge.

WE hear from America of the death of the venerable bibliographer, Mr. John Langdon Sibley, the Librarian Emeritus of Harvard University. He died at his home in Cambridge, Mass. He was the son of Dr. Jonathan and Persis (Morse) Sibley, and was born at Union, Me., December 29, 1804. In the summer of 1819 he entered Phillips Exeter Academy, and was at the beginning of the fall term placed on the Charity Foundation. In 1821 he became a member of Harvard College, and was made president's freshman. At an early period in his college life he began his services in the college library. In his vacations he was employed to write in the library and to render such occasional assistance as the librarian might require. On graduating, in 1825, he entered the divinity school, and was at the same time appointed assistant librarian on a salary of $150, the librarian's salary being then but $300. In May, 1829, Mr. Sibley was ordained as pastor of the First Church in Stow, Mass., where he remained four years. He, however, had formed so strong an attachment to Cambridge that he ill-brooked any other home. For several years after his return he was employed in various kinds of literary labour, and for a part of the time was editor and proprietor of the *American Magazine of Useful and Entertaining Knowledge.* In 1841, when the library was removed from Harvard to Gore Hall, he was again appointed assistant librarian under the management of Dr. T. W. Harris, whom he succeeded in 1856. Mr. Sibley's services to the college library have been invaluable. In addition to his regular official duties he has edited all the triennial (now the quinquennial) catalogues since 1840, and was the editor of the annual catalogue from 1850 to 1870. Mr. Sibley received in 1856 the honorary degree of Master of Arts from Bowdoin College. He had been for nearly forty years among the most active and serviceable members of the Massachusetts Historical Society, and he was also a fellow of the American Academy of Arts and Sciences. His active work in the library ceased in 1877, when he was honoured with the title of Librarian Emeritus, his retirement being caused by his advanced age and temporary loss of sight. At the time of removal to Gore Hall in 1841, the library contained 41,600 volumes, and had from the permanent fund a total income of $250 a year. In 1877, when Mr. Sibley resigned his position, the number of volumes had increased to 164,000, exclusive of an almost equal number of pamphlets, and the permanent fund from $5,000 to $170,000. Much of this increase, both in books and money, was owing to Mr. Sibley's devotion to the interests of the library. All of Mr. Sibley's tastes and acquirements fitted him peculiarly to be in the broadest sense the historiographer of the institution. His first work was published in 1851, being a history of his native place—Union—which is remarkable for the fulness and minuteness of its historical details, its statistics, genealogies, and family records. His second work was printed in the proceedings of the Massachusetts Historical Society, November, 1862, and was entitled *Notices of Account Books of Treasurer of Harvard College, from 1664 to 1752.* His last and most important work consisted of *Biographical Sketches of Graduates of Harvard University.* This was the fruit of an incredible amount of patience and judicious labour, and, while of special value as a record of the College, is second in importance to no contribution to the early history of New England. This extensive and exhaustive work gives a long account of the lives of all graduates of the College from those of the first class in 1642, and is exceedingly interesting. In this grand product of his toil Mr. Sibley has emulated the service which old Anthony Wood performed for his beloved Oxford, though in quite another spirit than that of the crusty and spiteful old memorialist of the English University. For many years Mr. Sibley led, not indeed a solitary or unsocial, but a celibate life, having had rooms in Divinity Hall for thirty-three years, and dwelling in the same room for twenty of them. In 1866 he was most happily married to Miss Charlotte A. Langdon, to whom he had been engaged for more than twenty years. They had no children. At the Alumni dinner in Commencement Week next June, the absence of Mr. Sibley's familiar figure " deaconing off" the Psalm sung after the clearing of the table—as he had done for almost half a century—will be deeply and pathetically regretted.

THE *Library Journal* for Sept.-Oct., 1885, is a double number, and contains the papers read at the Lake George Conference of the American Library Association. Mr. W. E. Foster contributes an interesting paper on " Some Compensations in a Librarian's Life." Dr. Garnett describes the " Method of Printing the British Museum Catalogue." Mr. B. P. Mann, in his paper on " Cataloging Anonymous Works by known Authors," thinks that an anonymous book should be considered as always anonymous, even when the author is known. He says it is the bounden duty of a librarian to "enable you to know, without recourse to a bibliography or a dictionary of anonyms and pseudonyms, if he has or has not in his library the work of which you hold a copy in your hand." But if each book is catalogued under the subject as well as the author's name, it does not matter very much under which heading you put the principal entry, and Mr. Mann's case falls to the ground. This number contains other papers of interest, and also the yearly reports to the Association on subjects interesting to Librarians. The December number includes a discussion of a new method of size notation.

WITH the December issue the *Magazine of American History* closes its fourteenth volume. The number opens with Mr. A. W. Clason's exposition of the part taken by Massachusetts (1788) in the adoption of the Constitution of the United States. A fine portrait of General George B. McClellan is accompanied by a tribute to his memory from the editor. Among the short articles, " The Fight at Fayal," a poem, by Charles K. Bolton; and " Senator Anthony's Gift to Brown University," by Rev. J. C. Stockbridge, are highly entertaining. The January number of the *Magazine of American History* contains an account, by E. H. Goss, of Paul Revere, the hero of the landlord's tale in Longfellow's *Tales of a Wayside Inn.* Revere was a goldsmith and engraver, and some specimens of his pictorial skill are given. The

Civil War papers are continued. Mr. Charles Dimitry contributes an article, entitled "Princess or Pretender." This doubtful person was a lady who resided for many years in Louisiana. She is said to have been the Princess Christine, wife of the Grand Duke Alexis, who by his barbarities made her life so unsupportable that, after a feigned illness and pretended death, she escaped from Russia in 1716. She travelled under an assumed name, and in 1721 settled in Louisiana. A certain Chevalier d'Aubant, who had known the Princess in Europe, had emigrated to Louisiana, and meeting Christine there, married her, and had children. D'Aubant having prospered as a planter, and his health failing, they returned to Europe, where he died. His wife entered a convent, and died about 1771. This is the romance. The truth appears to be that one of the servants of the Princess Christine had settled in Louisiana and met D'Aubant, who, fancying he recognised the features of the princess, married her. The rest of the contents of the *Magazine* are interesting.

WE learn from the report of the Dundee Free Library, 1885, that 291,181 volumes were issued during the year—an increase of 22,404 over the number issued in 1884. The quality of the reading is also improving. For some years there has been a steady decline in the demand for works of a sensational character, whilst novels of a higher and more intellectual type are issued in greater numbers than before.

THE new volume of the *Canterbury Poets* contains the poems of Ralph Waldo Emerson. It is a good thing to have, at so cheap a price, this pretty edition of the great American thinker's verses. Mr. Walter Lewin, the editor, has prefixed a thoughtful introduction, in which is a keen and sympathetic estimate of his position in the realm of poetry.

THE *Massachusetts Magazine* for November last contains an account of the Boston publishing-house of Ticknor and Co.

THE "thirteen" superstition is still rampart in Paris. Some curious proofs of this are given by a correspondent of the *Manchester Evening News*, who says that "there are many streets in French towns where that number does not exist, '12 *bis*' being substituted for it. M. Gustave Claudin, a veteran Paris *Chroniqueur*, always omits it in paging his slips ; when he gets to the end of the 12th slip, he begins the following one : '14th slip—sequel of the 12th.' Théophile Gautier was still more superstitious, for he believed in the 'evil eye,' and as it was currently reported in Paris that Offenbach possessed it, he would never write his name when criticizing his pieces. When it was absolutely necessary to insert the name in his article, the critic sent for a compositor and made him cut out the letters composing it, and paste them on his copy. Another great critic, Paul de Saint-Victor, was persuaded that he would find no ideas in any inkstand but his own. It was a black wooden one which he had bought in Switzerland. He always took that aid to his genius with him when he went on a journey. One of the best living writers, M. Barbey d'Aurevilly, not only works in lace frills and ruffles, but also writes with inks of various colours, so that his copy resembles an illuminated manuscript of the Middle Ages. I need not add that he is not a rapid writer. Sardou is superstitious about his paper, which costs him a penny a slip, and is manufactured purposely for him by a papermaker in the Rue Croix des Petits-Champs. It is very thick and rather rough. The great Dumas also had a special kind of paper to help his inspiration. It was a large blue sheet more than a foot long, and ruled in both directions. He always had a supply in his pockets to be able to work wherever he might be when the inspiration came."

AMONGST the coming book-sales is that of the library of the Rev. Edwin Paxton Hood, which is to begin 5th February.

THE concluding portion of the library of the Rev. John Fuller Russell is particularly rich in books relating to the religious and sectarian history of this country.

THE *Kendal Mercury* is to be commended, not only for having a department of "Notes and Queries," but for giving an index to them. This occupies four columns of the paper of New Year's Day.

DR. AUGUST BLAU contributes to the *Centralblatt für Bibliothekswesen* a "Verzeichniss der Handschriften Kataloge der deutschen Bibliotheken."

BOOKS AND READING.

By WILLIAM E. A. AXON.

(An Address at the Public Library of the Borough of Oldham, 6th February, 1886.)

HO can estimate the influence which books have had upon the lives of men and the history of nations? What warriors have been nurtured on the songs of Homer! How often the fierce life that beats in them has been translated into deeds of blood! How often they have been the springs of mighty enterprises and daring deeds! It is not without reason that the historian tells us that Alexander slept with the poems of Homer beneath his pillow. A song lost James II. his crown, and a pamphlet deprived England of the proudest jewel in her imperial crown—the American colonies. The mighty thinkers are immortal. The words of Plato are still instinct with force and meaning. The imagination of Shakespeare has created a world of human beings who are still full of life and passion, of hope and of heart-break, whilst he has been quietly sleeping beneath the sod for more than two centuries. But if his creations live while their author has passed away to the dust of the fields and the ashes of the earth, we need not say that he is dead, for he lives indeed in the minds and souls of those who find in him the stimulus to endeavour and attainment. A great book packs within itself the sweetness and light of its maker's soul. To his own age and generation Milton was a man whose talents were grudgingly acknowledged, and whose views in politics and religion made him an object of dislike. To us he is the poet who not only ranged over earth, but scaled the very walls of heaven, whose verse peals like the music of a mighty organ set to solemn strains of joy and praise.

A good thought, when once expressed, can never die. It becomes part of the inheritance of the ages. It blooms like a flower by the wayside. The winds of spring kiss it lovingly; it is watered by the summer rains, and when the icy hand of winter comes, there fall from its fairy calyx the seeds which shall rise and repeat its beauty and its perfume to new generations of men.

The influence of literature is one of the mysteries of life. Some careless boy picks up in an idle hour a volume that chance has thrown into his way, and he finds there the spark that kindles the divine flame within his own soul. Some frivolous girl reads in heedless fashion the story of the heroic endeavour of one whose life was a constant effort to good, and all the better instincts of her nature leap into life and action, and fill her with a purpose to fulfil and a mission to perform.

To the untutored mind the very existence of books at all is a mystery. They represent a higher range of intellectual life to which races only attain after long and arduous struggles. Great deeds were done before there lived a poet to celebrate them in his verse, or an historian to record them in his chronicles.

There is an anecdote which shows how strange the possibilities of writing appear to the savages of to-day.

The Rev. John Williams was erecting a mission-house in one of the South Sea Islands. He says, "As I had gone to work one morning without my square, I took up a chip, and with a piece of charcoal wrote upon it a request that Mrs. Williams would send me that article. I called a chief, who was looking after a portion of the work, and said to him, 'Friend, take this; go to our house, and give it to Mrs. Williams.' He was a strange-looking man. He had been a warrior; and, in one of the many battles he had fought, he had lost an eye. Giving me a look of wonder with the other, he said, 'Take that? She will call me foolish, and scold me if I carry a chip to her.' 'No,' I replied, 'she will not. Take it and go at once; I am in haste.' Seeing that I was in earnest he took it, and asked, 'What must I say?' I replied, 'You have nothing to say; the chip will say all I wish.' With a look of surprise and contempt he held up the piece of wood, and said, 'How can this speak? Has this a mouth?' I desired him to take it instantly, and not spend so much time in talking about it. On reaching the house he gave the chip to Mrs. Williams, who read it, threw it away, and went to the tool-chest. The chief, wishing to see the result of this strange affair, followed her closely. On receiving the square from her he said, 'Stay, daughter; how do you know that this is what Mr. Williams wants?' 'Why,' she replied, 'did you not bring me a chip just now?' 'Yes,' said the astonished warrior; 'but I did not hear it say anything.' 'If you did not, I did,' was the reply, 'for it made known to me what he wanted; and all you have to do is to return with it as quickly as possible.' Upon this the chief rushed out of the house, and catching up the piece of wood, he ran through the settlement with the chip in one hand and the square in the other. Holding them up as high as his arms could reach, he shouted as he went, 'See the wisdom of these English people! they can make chips talk; they can make chips talk!'"

It is only familiarity that hides from us the wondrous nature of literature. Here is a book. Its author has been dead two thousand years. The religion in which he believed has fallen amongst the discarded superstitions of the past. The mighty empire of which he was a citizen has been broken to pieces long ago. The civilization which cultured him has been overwhelmed. The towers, the temples, the aqueducts, the mighty symbols of power and skill have either perished, or, if they still remain, awful in decay, are but testimonies against the pride and vanity of those who made them. More enduring than marble pillar or brazen statue, the book lives on. The voice of the author is heard crying across the gulf of time, and the words of warning or exhortation first uttered, it may be, when Nero was making ruthless sport of the tortured Christians, is still heard along the "corridors of time," and still finds an echo in the human soul.

But there are books and books. There are good books and bad books, and books which are no books at all.

It has been estimated that there are ten million books in existence in the world. No library can contain them all. The Manchester Free Library has some seventy thousand volumes. The British Museum may, perhaps, contain a million volumes. Those who have seen the library of the British Museum will have some conception of the immense extent of existing literature from the fact that it would take ten such institutions to hold it. There are probably ten thousand, if not more, editions of the Bible. The books relating to Shakespeare, to the *Imitatio Christi*, to Bunyan, would each form a good-sized library. Dr. Allibone records the works of 46,499 English authors. If you take each as the author of ten volumes, we have 464,990. But since Allibone wrote probably two hundred thousand volumes of English books have been printed. The mass of literature—of printed matter—is increasing yearly. In England we add four or five thousand volumes yearly; in France, as many; in Germany, twice as many.

Yet let us contrast this immense mass of literature with the want of good books in many houses. How many are there who spend freely on handsome furniture and costly food, and whose library consists of a railway-guide, two or three old schoolbooks, several volumes of railway novels, a highly respectable collection of sermons, and a cheap encyclopædia with a good deal of dust on it. What better furniture can you give your homes than the records of the sayings of the wise and the doings of the good? Who but is better for communion with these spirits?

Taking the Manchester Free Library as a good type of the larger city libraries, we may make a little calculation. To read a book that makes serious demands upon the mind is not a quick process. Let us assume that the earnest student will devote on an average ten minutes to each page, and that there are on an average three hundred pages to a volume. At this rate, seventy thousand volumes would need 210,000,000 minutes, or 3,500,000 hours. The Ten Hours Bill is as useful in the study as in the factory. It would therefore take 960 years to read through the books contained in a great city library—a fact to make one regret the days of Methuselah.

Since we cannot either possess or read all books, some process of selection is compulsory. There are good and bad books, and there are books whose worth depends upon what we need from them. Bacon's *Essays* is a good book, and so is the *London Directory*, but their use is not interchangeable. Hence some other method of classification is desirable. The results of all intellectual effort, so far as it is mirrored in literature, can be separated into two broad divisions of Erudition and Ingenuity, of Learning and Genius, or, as De Quincey phrased it, into the literature of fact and the literature of power. The object of a book of information is to impart a certain number of facts. The object of the literature of power or genius is to influence, to convince, to amuse, to move to laughter or tears, to set in motion the springs of human action and endeavour. Books of information may tell of the starry heavens, and the toiling earth—may teach us the processes of machinery, the manner in which our bodies are framed; but the literature of power alone can reveal to us the depths of our own soul, and awaken its responsive power. There is no melody in the Æolian harp until its trembling strings are swept by the vagrant wind.

As to books of information, the boundaries of knowledge have been greatly widened in this generation. A century ago he who had suffused his mind with the thought of Greece and Rome had all that was necessary for either a lover of literature or a professional man of letters. If to this he added some acquaintance with the authors of Spain and Italy, he stood above the level of his peers. Since then we have witnessed a revived interest, not only in classical literature, but in the productions of those languages which have supplanted Greek and Latin as the vehicles of the highest thought. We have witnessed the vigorous development of German literature, essentially informed by the spirit of the present time. We are gradually becoming familiarized with the genius of Scandinavian peoples, and with the novelists and satirists of the Sclavonic race. In the East, too, there has been a corresponding advance. *Ex oriente lux* is still true in a sense, though we are repaying the debt; and the pundits of India may look to Oxford and Berlin for the interpretation of the venerable documents they have kept through centuries of storm and change. The ancient civilizations of Babylon and Assyria have shaken off the dust of centuries, and risen from their desert graves. With all these new conquests it has also been found requisite to re-study much of the old. In our own language what a flood of light has been thrown upon the condition of mediæval England by the publications of the Early English Text Society alone! These have not merely helped us to a better understanding of the past, but have given back to us forgotten poets, not unworthy to take their place in the society of Chaucer and of Spenser. The continual widening of the boundaries of human knowledge and the consequent extension of the sphere of intellectual interest and activity give fresh importance to bibliography, and render acquaintance with its methods indispensable. Centuries ago it was said by the author of Ecclesiastes that "of making many books there is no end." If the literary activity of that age was sufficient to daunt the spirit, what shall we say of the present time, with its myriad newspapers, journals, reviews, and magazines—of an age when the printing-presses of our own country alone produce above a hundred volumes for each day in the year?

The immense field of knowledge, and the growing conviction that education is the best investment for industrial communities, is leading to the multiplication of public libraries. A good library does well for the entire town what each citizen would otherwise have to do imperfectly for himself. The philosophy of the institution has been well explained by the late Professor Jevons, who says :

" The main *raison d'être* of free public libraries, as indeed of public museums, art-galleries, parks, halls, public clocks, and many other kinds of public works, is the enormous increase of utility which is thereby acquired for the community at a trifling cost. If a beautiful picture be hung in the dining-room of a private house, it may perhaps be gazed at by a few guests a score or two of times in the year. Its real utility is too often that of ministering to the selfish pride of its owner. If it be hung in the National Gallery, it will be enjoyed by hundreds of thousands of persons, whose glances, it need hardly be said, do not tend to wear out the canvas. The same principle applies to books in common ownership. If a man possesses a library of a few thousand volumes, by far the greater part of them must lie for years untouched upon the shelves ; he cannot possibly use more than a fraction of the whole in any one year. But a library of five or ten thousand volumes opened free to the population of a town may be used a thousand times as much. It is a striking case of what I propose to call *the principle of the multiplication of utility*, a principle which lies at the base of some of the most important processes of political economy, including the division of labour."

If we take a walk through a public library, we shall find that the books will be of service to persons of every class in the community that have mastered the art of reading. We should find books relating to books, histories of literature, encyclopædias, magazines, transactions of societies, and similar miscellaneous collections. The object of bibliography is to give information as to the books on given subjects, or written in particular countries, or by special bodies of men ; to tell us of the various devices by which the human race in different ages and countries has recorded its thoughts. Bibliography is the aid to every other science, and by its help we find the best that has been written on the particular topic that engages our attention.

We shall find books of philosophy in which the structure of the human mind is investigated ; the delusions to which it is subject ; the methods by which it may be trained to health and sanity ; the ethical relations and developments which it has borne in the long ages of development that have brought about our present civilization. With some familiarity with the history of the human mind in the past, we shall be less liable to be victimized by plausible errors and innovations, for we shall recognise in them ancient foes of human peace and sanity.

The interest of theology is a permanent element in human nature, and in recent years a scientific treatment has been struggling into existence. It was a Frenchman who said that in England we had a hundred religions and only one sauce. *Whitaker's Almanack* records 223 sects as existing in this country, and a

public library should be able to tell us something of the causes that have brought
into existence the Baptists, the Primitive Methodists, and the Salvation Army,
even if it may not give much information about the Alethians, or the Pilgrim
Band.   But if Great Britain is a Christian power, it is also a Mohammedan
power, a Buddhist power, a Pagan power.   The subjects of Queen Victoria
include votaries of all the great religions of the world.   The study of the various
developments and transformations of the religious idea, and of the influence of
churches and sects upon the history and well-being of the human race, has an
importance not to be exaggerated.

A public library should help us to a knowledge of sociology.   The intelligent
study of the subjects belonging to this division is essential to the public life of
to-day.   The statistical method, whether we give it the name of science or not,
has become an important instrument in testing the reality of our progress.   The
death-rate is a matter of greater moment than the rateable value.   Sociology
shows us the experience of the ages in political institutions ; explains the methods
and aims of political economy, the various ramifications of law, and the principles
on which they depend ; the methods of administration both in regard to local
and imperial government, and to the various associations and charities which
spring up by the spontaneous co-operation of like-minded individuals.   Sociology
deals also with the problems of education, and tells us the best that is known as
to its plans and discipline, whether in the elementary school or in the university.
Sociology records also for us the varying customs of different lands and ages, and
celebrates the triumphs of commerce and communications by which men have
been brought into peaceful contact with each other.

Another department of a public library will relate to philology.   Every word
has a history, and some of the homeliest and commonest in our own language
carry us back to a period anterior to the migration of the Indo-European race,
who have since conquered Europe.   The practical importance of modern languages
will be recognised in a manufacturing and commercial community, " whose hand
goes forth to every land."   The science of language, apart from linguistics, is one
of great charm, and it gives a new force and value to words when we know the
processes by which they have been evoked, and by which they have attained
their present status.   The testimony of philology is not always complimentary.
Mr. Crofton's *Gipsy Glossary* reveals the fact that the Romany lads and lasses
give to Lancashire the name of Peerodelingtem, which means the foot-kicking
county.

A public library will contain books of information on natural science.   It is
not required from anyone to enlarge upon the importance or the charm of mathe-
matics.   Astronomy, physics, chemistry, palæontology, biology, botany, zoology,
have many keen students in this district, and here they should find all the help
they need.   Science is the basis of the useful arts, and however much may be
done by the rule of thumb, a safer plan is that which relies upon a mastery of

principles. The useful arts are varied. There is the art of the medical man, of the engineer, of the farmer, of the printer, of the chemist, of the iron-worker, of the textile manufacturer, of the builder. Each of these should find something in a public library to improve him in his respective craft. Then there are the fine arts; and though the flowing colours of the painter cannot be adequately represented, yet the thought that was in his mind, the intellectual element in his picture, can be perpetuated and multiplied by the agency of photography and engraving. There are many who are familiar, and better for their familiarity, with the compositions of Raphael or Thorvaldsen, who will never see the paintings of the one or the sculptures of the other.

History should occupy a large space in a public library. It shows the evolution of man through long centuries of blood and struggle. The "dignity of history" is a mischievous phrase which has led some writers to devote their attention to the squabbles and intrigues of courtiers and courtezans instead of recording the onward march of the people from slavery to liberty, from squalid poverty and hardship to better things. The annals of the empires that have passed away—Egypt, Babylon, Greece, Rome—are picturesque and pathetic, and also contain the prophetic germs of the present. To understand the future we must know the past. Closely allied to history is geography. The English have so much wandering blood in their veins that stories of far-off climes and strange peoples will never lose their attractive charm.

History is the biography of nations, and biography is but the history of the individual. A faithful biography gives the benefit of the experience of another life; it is vicarious wisdom which may be had without the blood and tears it may have cost its former possessor. Few books are more inspiring than good biographies. They teach what men and women have done and can do. Their folly, it may be, but also their strength, their power of self-sacrifice, their readiness to help one another, their sincerity, truth, and endeavour.

Lastly, a public library should contain the best *literature*, the best books to influence the lives and minds of men. What is literature? is a question sometimes asked, and mostly in vain. We can feel life—can we define it? We can be religious—can we say with absolute accuracy what religion is? Literature may be an influence for good with us without our being able to identify it with the rigid accuracy of the mathematician, or the verbal logic of the lexicographer. There is one book that has been, and is, the household book of every English family, which is literature in the highest and best sense. The Authorized Version of the Bible is a noble monument of our mother-tongue. There is a stately rhythm about its sentences that gives the charm of music and the aroma of poetry to its words. Look at its wondrous contents. It contains the workings of very different minds, separated by centuries of time. It contains the records of an ancient race, the traditions of the origin of the world and of the human race, the legends of the birth of the arts; the story of a horde of bondsmen transformed into a mighty nation by the efforts of prophets and patriots. We hear in it the voice of the poet, the supplication of the penitent, the denunciation of the prophet, the exhortation of the preacher. This homely illustration is not spoken from a theological, but from a literary standpoint.

The praise of books has been celebrated by many voices of late. Mr. Alexander Ireland has compiled the *Book-Lover's Enchiridion,* a charming volume of testimonies to the pleasures and advantages of reading. Mr. Frederick Harrison has a volume ready on the *Choice of Books;* Lord Iddesleigh has spoken very charmingly on *Desultory Reading;* Sir John Lubbock has lectured on the *Pleasures of Reading,* and the list he has given of a hundred best books has raised an interesting discussion in the *Pall Mall Gazette.* The list is a very good one, but it is open to criticism. The last "book" named is Scott's novels! These by no process of witchcraft can be counted as one book, and their inclusion raises the list from a hundred to at least one hundred and thirty. Nor, apart from this, is it easy to understand the method by which the figure of one hundred is reached. But apart from this the list is highly suggestive, and whatever may be its omissions it includes nothing that is not excellent. They are, for the most part, books on which time has already passed a favourable verdict.

It will not escape observation that there is not perfect unanimity on the part of the best judges, either as to books or methods. Thus Mr. Lowell has advised that young students should confine themselves to the supreme books in whatever literature, or still better, to choose some one great author and make themselves thoroughly familiar with him. Against this we may place Longfellow's plea for the minor poet :

> Come, read to me some poem,
> Some simple and heartfelt lay
> That shall soothe this restless feeling,
> And banish the thought of day.
>
> Not from the grand old masters,
> Not from the bards sublime,
> Whose distant footsteps echo
> Through the corridors of Time.
>
> For like strains of martial music,
> Their mighty thoughts suggest
> Life's endless toil and endeavour ;
> And to-night I long for rest.
>
> Read from some humbler poet,
> Whose songs gushed from his heart,
> As showers from the clouds of summer,
> Or tears from the eyelids start.
>
> Who, through long days of labour,
> And nights devoid of ease,
> Still heard in his soul the music
> Of wonderful melodies.
>
> Such songs have power to quiet
> The restless pulse of care,
> And come like the benediction
> That follows after prayer.

Then read from the treasured volume
The poem of thy choice,
And lend to the rhyme of the poet
The beauty of thy voice.
And the night shall be filled with music,
And the cares that infest the day
Shall fold their tents, like the Arabs,
And as silently steal away.

We shall most of us agree with Longfellow. The best book is that which fits most closely to the environment. Newton's *Principia* is a better book than Walkinghame's *Arithmetic*, but it would not be a wise proceeding to send the first for use in the lower classes of an elementary school. Some critics allow, others denounce, fiction ; but it responds to a universal sentiment in human nature, and cannot be extirpated. There are some novels, such as *Uncle Tom's Cabin*, that have had a powerful influence upon national destiny. There is one, *Mary Barton*, that in this district at least has preached, with "forty parson power," a lesson of mutual forbearance and mutual respect between the working-classes and their employers. In all ages fiction in one form or another has been the favourite vehicle for the conveyance of moral truth. Yet the object of fiction, whether in the novel or the drama, is not the dogmatic inculcation of morality, but to give that knowledge of the human heart which shall make us wiser, stronger, better, and more tolerant than we were before.

It is not an unpleasant task to suggest courses of reading, but such advice, however excellent, is rarely followed. After all, the safest counsel is to advise the student to read on that which most interests him, and as he finds his knowledge of the subject increase he will find that it is connected with other branches of study, so that at each step forward his mental horizon will widen. That which is undertaken from genuine interest will be more eagerly pursued than that which is adopted as mental task-work. But it is safe to recommend everyone to be thoroughly familiar with at least one book in the highest sphere of literature. Take Milton's *Comus* as an example. It is but a short poem, though one of the most perfect in the language. Anyone who has mastered the vocabulary, the metrical structure, the grammatical peculiarities, the mythological and historical allusions, and has felt the music of the verse and the pathos of the sentiment, has had something of a liberal education, and has incorporated some of the best influences of literature into his mental structure.

To sum up, a public library is an instrument not merely of recreation, but for the rooting up of all forms of ignorance. Ignorance is a prolific mother of vice and crime, and whatever tends to destroy ignorance aims a blow also at the existence of crime. Let us rejoice then at the success of schools and libraries, whence the blessed light of knowledge is diffused into the darkness. "The true university of these days is a collection of books," says Carlyle ; and in a great library what noble teachers we may choose! The best and wisest of all ages are

13

there to give aid and direction, counsel and consolation. The men who have left undying names, who live yet in the loving memory of the "human world at large," are teachers in these universities ; and surely a people who make bosom friends of the wise and good will become better men than they were before, by reason of that companionship. Our English libraries have not hitherto, perhaps, done all the good that lay within their power, because they have hidden their light under a bushel; they have guarded the sacred fountain of literature with jealous care, and have forbidden the poor student and the horny-handed workman to drink at its holy stream. Such is not the spirit of these new town libraries. They open wide their portals to all who wish to drink of the water of knowledge. The spoken word is still an instrument of the education of the nature, but the printed voice is now the chief engine in the dissemination of thought. And not only do books give knowledge, but vision also, which is of infinitely greater worth to those who study them aright :

> They give
> New views of life, and teach us how to live.

"An intelligent class can scarcely ever be, as a class, vicious," says Everett. Those who have tasted the sweets of intellectual pleasures will hardly care to descend to lower and grosser forms of enjoyment, and a people familiar with those lessons of wisdom and truth taught by the mighty dead can hardly fail to be a nation wise, and just, and true.

THE WODHULL LIBRARY.

HE following completes the record of this remarkable sale. The ten days' sale realized altogether £11,973 4s. 6d., and the prices were in striking contrast with those paid by the collector of the library for the treasures now dispersed.

Phalaridis Epistolæ, Francisco Arretino interprete, sm. 4to., Brixiæ, T. Ferrandus, no date, but printed *circa* 1473, and therefore one of the earliest books printed at Brescia ; £10 5s.—Philonis Judæi Opera, Græce, first edition, very large copy, folio, Paris, 1552, in old calf with gold tooling in Grolier style, by Nicholas Eve, much worn ; £13 (Quaritch), having cost Mr. Wodhull only 5s. 6d. in 1798.—Philo Judæus de Divinis decem Oraculis, J. Vœurs interprete, printed on vellum, Lutetiæ, C. Stephanus, 1554, said to be probably unique ; £12 12s. (B. F. Stevens).—Philostrati Vita Apollonii Tyanei, Gr. et Lat., interprete Alemano Rinuccino, Accedit Eusebius contra Hieroclem, etc., two vols. in one, folio, Venetiis, Aldus, 1501-2 ; £7 (Quaritch).—Philostrates (Les Deux), Images ou Tableaux de Platte Peinture et les Statues, mis en François par Blaise de Viganère, avec des épigrammes par T. d'Embry, folio, Paris, 1615, large paper copy, with engravings by J. Isac, L. Gaultier, and T. de Leen ; £6 (B. F. Stevens). —Pianti Devotissimi de la Madona (in Terzine), sm. 4to., Mediolani, without date, but 1469 ; £4 10s.—Pindari Carmina, cum scholiis, Gr. et. Lat., ed. R. West et R. Welsted, folio, Oxon., 1697, large paper ; £3 5s.—Platyna (B. Sacch) de Obsoniis ac honesta Voluptate, folio, Venetiis, 1475, the first edition with a date, and one of the few issued without the printer's name ; £4. The same book, sm. 4to., 1480, In Civitate Austriæ, G. de Flandria, and the first book printed in Friuli ; £2 16s.—Platonis Opera, Græce, first edition, folio, Venetiis, Aldus, 1513, fine large copy, bound by Derome in red morocco ; £15 15s. (Quaritch).— Platonis Opera Omnia, Gr. et Lat., cum notis Jo. Sorrani et H. Stephani, three vols., folio, H. Stephanus, 1568, large paper, and Gulston's copy ; £12 5s. (Bain). Mr. Wodhull's note says, " Ritson's sale at Christie's, 1782, £10 10s."—Plauti Comædiæ emendatæ per Georgium Alexandrinum (Merulam), first edition, folio, Venetiis, Vindolinus de Spira, 1472, fine large copy, with initial letters and arms of the Tornabonii, illuminated in gold and colours, bound in maroon morocco, with arms of Outlawe of Withingham, Norfolk, in gold on sides ; £30 (Quaritch). For this Mr. Wodhull paid Payne £20 in 1798. The reprint of this Plautus, folio, Tarvisii, 1482 ; £3 18s. (Quaritch) ; another Plautus, with Commentary of Lambini, folio, Lutetiæ, 1587 (at end 1576), sold for £2 6s., which had cost Mr. Wodhull £8 8s.—Plynii Naturalis Historia, folio, Venetiis, N. Jenson, 1472, fine copy, with elegant capitals, and with the Bagneri arms, and curious flourish of Jesus, with sporting subjects ; rare, and regarded as the " Glory of Jenson's Press ;"

13—2

£35 (B. F. Stevens).—Plynii Naturalis Historia, with numerous manuscript notes, folio, Romæ, Sweynheym, and Pannartz, 1473; £6 10s. (Quaritch).—Plinio, Historia Naturale, tradocta per C. Landino, folio, Venetiis, N. Jenson, 1476; £4 15s. (Quaritch). This cost Mr. Wodhull eight guineas in 1791.—Plinii Epistolæ cura Juniani Maii, folio, Neapoli, 1476; £16 5s. (B. F. Stevens). Cost Mr. Wodhull £10 10s. at Payne's in 1794.—Plutarch Vitæ Parallelæ, J. A. Campano collectæ et editæ, two vols., first edition, folio, Romæ, without date, but *circa* 1470; £23 (Quaritch).—Plutarchi Parallela, Græce, folio, Venetiis, Aldus, 1519, bound by Derome; £10 10s. (Quaritch).—Poggii Faceciæ, first edition, sm. 4to., Ferrariæ, 1471, Croft's copy; £12 15s. (Quaritch). Cost £2 18s. in Croft's sale, 1783.—Poggii Facetiæ, sm. folio, Lovanii, J. de Westfalia, 1476, a rare and fine edition, unmutilated and unknown to most bibliographers; £9 (Quaritch).—Pol (Sainct), Les Epistres glosees, black-letter, small folio, Paris, A. Verard, 1507, with fourteen paintings and capitals illuminated, and arms of Ratault de Courlay emblazoned in silver, with Lord Shelburne's book-plate of arms, and bought by Mr. Wodhull at the sale of the Marquis of Lansdowne's library, 1803, for £2 7s., now brought £5 1s. (Quaritch).—Poliphili Hypnerotomachia (Italice, F. Columna Auctore), first edition, folio, Venetiis, Aldus, 1499, and an unusually fine and unmutilated copy of this remarkable book, containing the five woodcuts from designs, as is believed, of Vittore Carpaccio, the famous Venetian painter, who was a friend of F. Colonna, himself an architect and Dominican Friar; £5 3s. (Quaritch).—Pomponius Mela de Situ Orbis, MS. on vellum, 4to., fifteenth century: £8 10s. (Quaritch).—Psalterium, Græce, sm. 4to., Venetiis, Aldus, without date, a very rare edition, printed probably in 1497; £8 10s. (Quaritch).—Psalterium cum Calendario in Usum Saram, MS. on vellum, 4to., fifteenth century, with historiated letters and illuminated initial letters; £25 (Quaritch). This interesting MS. belonged to the family of Whetnall, of Kent, and bears their arms, to which the Lady Katherine Whittenhall, buried in the church of St. Thomas of Canterbury, at Padua, was probably related.—Psalterium, MS. on vellum, sm. 4to., fifteenth century; £25 10s. (Ridler). This was bought by Mr. Wodhull in Dr. Askew's sale at Leigh's, 1785, for £1 2s.—Another Psalter, printed on vellum, Paris, 1531, sold for £7 10s.; and another of 1563, Elzevir, bound by Ruette, from the Lamoignon collection, £9 9s.—Ptolomæi Cosmographia, Latine reddita a Jacobo Angelo, folio, Ullmæ, L. Hol, 1482, with the maps; £16 (Quaritch).—Ptolomæi Geographia, M. Serveti, editio secunda, royal folio, Lugduni, 1541; £11 (Harvey).—Pyladæ (J. F. Buccardi), Vocabularium (Carmen), printed on vellum, sm. 4to., Brixiæ, Jacobus Britannicus, 1498; £10 10s. (Sotheran).—Reuchlin (J)., ad Alexandrum VI., pro Philippo Bavariæ Duce Oratio, sm. 4to., Venetiis, Aldus, 1598, which Brunet says is one of the rarest of this press, quoting its price in the Askew sale as 18s., and adding, " Mais aujourd'hui elle vaudrait dix ou peut-être vingt foix ce prix "; £7 15s. (Sotheran).— Rhetores Græci, two volumes, folio, Venetiis, Aldus, 1508-9; Richardi de Bury,

Episcopi Dunelmensis, Philobiblon, first edition, sm. 4to., Coloniæ, 1473, the earliest work on book-collecting, usually ascribed to De Bury, but written at his command by Robert Holkot ; £45 (Quaritch).—Rodorici Zamorensis Speculum Vitæ Humanæ, folio, Romæ, Sweynheym et Pannartz, 1468, first edition ; £25 10s. (H. Stevens). Another edition of the same work, folio, without place or date, but Paris, 1472, and esteemed a rare one ; it had the first leaf mended in the margin ; £4 8s. (Quaritch).—Another in French, Rodorique Hispaignoi Evesque de Zamorensis Miroir, etc., translaté par Frère Julien (Macho), first edition, sm. folio, Lyon, 1477, bound by Derome ; £21 (Quaritch).—Rollenhagii (G)., Emblemata, two vols., sm. 4to., Ultrajecti ex officina C. Passæi, 1611-13, two portraits and 200 engravings by Crispin de Pass ; £16 (Quaritch). These engravings were used for Wither's emblems.—Romant de la Rose ou tout lart damours est enclose (par G. de Lorris et J. de Meung), first edition, black-letter, with coloured woodcuts, folio, without place or date ; the last leaf begins with " Par les Rains sailly le rosier," instead of " Par les Mains saisy le rosier," in the only copy known in the Lyons library, printed by Ulrich Gering, 1479, which has the last leaf supplied in manuscript, dated 1742 ; £32 (Quaritch). Cost Mr. Wodhull, in 1771, three guineas.—Romant de la Rose, par vostre humble Molinet, black-letter, sm. folio, Paris, A. Verard, circa 1510 ; £13 10s. (B. F. Stevens).—Rousseau (J. J., Œuvres Complètes, in 37 vols., 1788-93 ; £16 10s. (Quaritch).—Rudimentum Noviciorum (Epithoma Chronicarum), folio, Lubecæ, 1475, numerous woodcuts in the style of block-books, a curious chronicle, and the first book printed at Lubeck ; £38 (Quaritch).—Rusticæ Rei Scriptores Veteres (Columella, Palladius, Cato, et Terentius Varro), first edition, folio, N. Jenson, 1472 ; £7 10s., (Quaritch).—Sallusti Conjuratio Catilinariæ et Bellum Jugurthinum, fine manuscript on vellum, sm. 4to., fifteenth century ; £10 10s. (Nattali). Cost Mr. Wodhull £1 11s. in 1785.—Senecæ Opera Omnia, first edition, folio, Neapoli, 1475, corner of first leaf facsimiled, else a fine copy ; £9 9s. (Quaritch).—Senecæ Epistolæ, first edition, folio, without place or date, but Argentorato J. Mentelin, cut down to quarto ; £9 (Quaritch).—Senecæ Epistolæ, first edition with a date, folio, Romæ, A. Pannartz, 1475, stained and worn ; £4 10s. (Quaritch).—Seneca Tragediæ cum glossis, folio, manuscript, fourteenth century, in old gilt russia ; £10 (Quaritch). Cost Mr. Wodhull £1 8s. in 1787.—Servetus (M.), de Trinitatis erroribus. Item de Trinitate et de Justicia Regni Christi, two vols. in one, first edition, 1531-2 ; £8 (Quaritch).—Shakespear (W)., Works, edited by Sir T. Hanmer, 4to., Oxford, 6 vols., 1743, four with plates by Gravelot, from designs by Hayman ; £6 5s. (Quaritch).—Solini Rerum Memorabilium Collectaneæ, sm. 4to., without place or date, but Romæ, circa 1475 ; £4 15s. (Nattali).—Solinus de Situ et Memorabilibus Orbis, first edition, sm. folio, Venetiis, N. Jenson, 1473 ; £4 (B. F. Stevens).—Songe du Vergier, du Clerc et du Chevalier, black-letter, folio, Lyon, 1491, woodcuts, fine copy in veau fauve ; £6, cost Mr. Wodhull one guinea, 1796 (B. F. Stevens).—Sozomeni et Evagrii Historiæ Ecclesiasticæ Græce, manuscript, folio, 1524, written for Gibert, Bishop of Verona, and partially collated by Dr. R. Hussey for his edition, quoting it as Codex Severn; £5 15s. (Quaritch). Cost £1 1s. in 1785, in Askew's library.—Sophoclis Tragædiæ Græce, first edition, Venetiis, Aldus, 1502, red morocco, by Kalthæber; £14 (Quaritch). Cost Mr. Wodhull £1 1s. in 1796.—Speed (J.), Theatre of the Empire of Great Britain, with a prospect of the most famous parts of the world, royal folio, 1676, maps, with portrait (by Savery) of the author, and plan of London added; £7 10s. (Quaritch).—Strabonis Geographia Latine, first edition, with a date, folio, Venetiis, V. de Spira, 1472, slightly wormed; £7 (Quaritch). Cost Mr. Wodhull £7 7s.—Straparole (J. F.), Facecieuses Nuicts, two vols. in one, printed on vellum, Paris, 1726, Louis XV.'s copy, bound by Ruette, with the Royal arms; £18 10s. (Rev. Mr. Buckley). For this Mr. Wodhull gave £7 7s. in 1797.—Suetonius de Vita et Moribus Duodecim Principum Romanorum, manuscript, on vellum, by an Italian scribe, sm. folio, fifteenth century, with the Maffei arms; £13 10s. (Quaritch). Cost £2 3s. in 1785.— Taciti Opera, first edition, small folio, Venetiis, V. de Spira, 1468-70, disfigured by attempts to wash out manuscript notes; £4 19s. (Quaritch). Cost Mr. Wodhull £10 10s. in 1798.—Taciti Opera, Paris, 1771, 4 vols., large paper folio; £8 10s. (Quaritch).—Tacitus cum Notis, H. Grotii, Elzevir, 1640; £4 15s. (Quaritch).—Tertulliani Apologeticus, manuscript, on vellum, folio, thirteenth century; £12 10s. (Quaritch). Cost only £1 1s. in 1785.—Tewrdannckh, Die Geuerlicheiten, etc., folio, Nurnberg, Hans Schönsperger, 1517, the first edition of the famous metrical romance of chivalry, written by Melchior Pfinzing, with the 118 woodcuts from designs by Hans Scheufelein, by Jost Negker, coloured, and etching of full-length portrait of Roger Payne, as the binder, inserted. Notwithstanding that the title was pronounced to be in facsimile, exceedingly well done, this rare book brought £6 4s. (B. F. Stevens).—Thomæ Aquinatis (S.) Secunda Secundæ, first edition, folio, without place or date. This appears to be the edition from the press of Mentelin, according to Panzer, but probably by Schoeffer, as it bears an inscription on the last leaf, under the arms of Schoeffer, "Per Johem Fust et Petrum Schoyffer, Anno MCCCCLVII."; £37 (Ellis and Scrutton). The first edition of the same, with a date, folio, Moguntiæ, 1467; £34 (Quaritch).—Thomæ de Aquino (S.) Opus Quarti Scripti, first edition, folio, Moguntiæ, Schoeffer, 1469; £35 (Quaritch).—Thomæ a Kempis Opuscula, sm. folio, without place or date, *circa* 1472, attributed to the press of Lawrence Coster; £5 10s. (Quaritch).—Thucydidis Historia, Græce, manuscript, on bombyx paper, folio, fifteenth century, from Dr. Askew's library, used by Dr. Arnold; £47 (Quaritch). Another manuscript, Thucydides cum scholiis, Græce, folio, fifteenth century; £47 (Quaritch). Both these manuscripts are marked by Dr. Arnold, and mentioned by him, vol. ii. ed. 1832.—Turracremata (Card. J. de), Expositio super toto Psalterio, sm. folio, Poictiers, 1480, in veau marbré, by Derome; £24 (James).—Tyard de Bissy (Pontus de), Œuvres Poetiques, Mantice et Solitaire Premier, 3 vols. in 1, sm. 4to., Paris, 1573, with autograph and manuscript note of Gui-Drummond (W. Drummond, of Hawthornden) ; £16 (Quaritch). —Valturius de Re Militari, first edition, folio, Veronæ, 1472, manuscript notes and woodcuts from designs by Matteo Pasti ; £52 (Quaritch). Another edition of the same with different woodcuts, folio, Veronæ, Boninus de Boninis, 1483 ; £30 (Ellis and Scrutton).—Vandyck portraits, 160, by various well-known engravers, with 12 beauties of Hampton Court (by Lombart) added, and those of Charles I. and Henrietta Maria, royal folio, Anvers, no date ; £52 (Quaritch).—Villon (Francoys), ses Œuvres, Paris, Galiot du Pre, 1532, fine copy, but from bad printing some letters are restored with pen ; £24 (Quaritch).—Of the remarkably fine collection of manuscripts and editions of Virgil, the most interesting were Virgilii Æneis cum Argumentis Ovidii Nasonis, manuscript, on vellum, by an Italian scribe of the fifteenth century, with coat-of-arms and illuminated initial ; £21 (Quaritch). —Vergilius (*sic*), the first Aldine and the first book printed in italic type by Aldus Romanus, and one of the rarest of the Aldines to obtain in fine condition, this being very slightly wormed and mended, else a fine copy, bound in blue morocco by Kalthæber ; £145 (Quaritch). The copy in Sir John Thorold's sale last year, though wormed and having two leaves inlaid, sold for £100.—Virgilii Opera, curante N. Heinsii, large paper, Amst., Elzevir, 1676, in blue morocco, by Padeloup ; £50 (Quaritch).—Voltaire, Œuvres complètes, édition de Beaumarchais, 70 volumes, large paper, plates by Moreau le Jeune, in fine condition ; £31 (Robson). About 1,500 tracts were sold throughout the sale as they came under the alphabetical entries in the catalogue, and only realized small sums, although they must contain matter of interest, as they were collected by Sir Edward Walker, who was Secretary of War to Charles I. After the sale of the library, as announced previously, the collection of autograph letters of Victor Hugo and other interesting memorials belonging to the Hugo family, bound up in a thick quarto volume, was put up and sold for £200 to Messrs. Ellis and Scrutton.

THE ADVENTURES OF JOHN R. JEWITT.

BY RUSHWORTH ARMYTAGE.

N 1815 there appeared a book with the following title, *A Narrative of the Adventures and Sufferings of John R. Jewitt, only Survivor of the Crew of the Ship Boston, during a Captivity of nearly Three Years among the Savages of Nootka Sound, with an Account of the Manners, Mode of Living, and Religious Opinions of the Natives, Illustrated with a Plate representing the Ship in Possession of the Savages.* 12mo., pp. 203, and 2 plates, published at Middleton, Connecticut. It was often reprinted in America, and an edition was published at Edinburgh by Constable, in 1824. John Robert Jewitt, whose adventures this book records, was born on the 21st May, 1783, at Boston, in Lincolnshire, where his father, Edward Jewitt, was a black-smith, with a large business. Being of a somewhat weakly constitution, John was sent to school with the intention of entering the medical profession. Accordingly, at the age of twelve he was sent to an academy at Donnington, then under the care of a Mr. Moses. Here he attained considerable proficiency in writing, reading, and arithmetic, and obtained some knowledge of navigation and surveying; but his progress in Latin was slow, and in a short time he wholly relinquished that study. After two years Mr. Edward Jewitt, thinking that his son had received sufficient education for the profession he intended him for, took him from school in order to apprentice him to a surgeon living at Reasby. But young Jewitt not liking the idea, prevailed on his father to apprentice him to his own trade of blacksmith. Soon afterwards Edward Jewitt removed to Hull, where he soon got a large connection among seafaring folk. Amongst the seamen who employed the Jewitts to do the smith's work in their ship was Captain John Salter, of the ship *Boston*, of Boston, Mass. This gentleman, being of a social turn of mind, soon became acquainted with John Jewitt, and persuaded him to accompany him as armourer on a voyage he was about to make, first to the North-West of America, and afterwards to China. In September, 1802, they set sail, and a twenty-nine days' sail brought them to St. Catherine's, on the coast of Brazil, where they laid in stores. On December 28th they passed Cape Horn, which they had made no less than thirty-six days before, but were repeatedly forced back by contrary winds, experiencing very rough and tempestuous weather in doubling it. After this they had a long spell of fine weather, which lasted until 12th March, 1803, on which day they arrived at Nootka Sound, in Vancouver's Island, where they anchored. On the 13th the King, Maquina, came on board, and seemed very pleased to see the captain, and the crew and natives were mutually agreeable. On the 20th of March the King came on board, and Captain Salter gave him a gun; on the following day Maquina returned the

gun, which he had broken, to the captain, saying that it was *peshak*—that is, bad. Salter was very much offended at this observation, and considering it as a mark of contempt for his present, called the King a liar, adding other opprobrious terms ; and taking the gun from him, said to Jewitt, " John, this fellow has broken this beautiful fowling-piece ; see if you can mend it !" As Maquina understood a few words of English he knew the meaning of the captain's remarks, and though very angry, returned to the shore with his men. The next day Maquina returned to the ship, and having persuaded the captain to send a portion of the crew fishing, he and his men attacked the remainder and killed them ; and when the fishers returned, served them in the same way. Jewitt, who had been working in the hold, on going on to the deck to see what the row was about, was caught by his hair by a savage, who, losing his hold, dropped him, at the same time striking him on the forehead with an axe. Jewitt fell senseless on the floor, and when he recovered, the savages had taken possession of the ship. The King, it seems, knowing that Jewitt was an armourer, ordered his men not to hurt him if they could help it. The King then gave Jewitt the choice between slavery and death. He chose the former, and they then went on shore, where Jewitt heard that another of the crew, named John Thompson, had escaped the massacre, and that the King had decided to kill him ; but Jewitt represented that Thompson was his father, and that if the King was to kill him Jewitt would kill himself ; and so the King, fearing to lose a servant who promised to be of use to him, consented to allow Thompson to live. Thompson and Jewitt's life on shore was far from pleasant. They had, of course, to eat the same food as the natives, cooked in their manner, and with train oil for a relish ; but, as Jewitt observes, hunger will break through stone walls, and they found, at times, that the blubber of sea animals and the flesh of dog-fish made a very acceptable repast.

Thompson had several narrow escapes ; one time he had struck the son of Maquina on the face, and the King was just in the act of loading a musket to shoot Thompson, when Jewitt appeared, and threatened that if his father was killed he would kill himself. This threat again appeased Maquina, who used to say that if John was to die he would kill Thompson. Jewitt resolved to learn the language of the savages, and in a few months was able to make himself well understood, whilst Thompson resolutely declined to attempt to learn it, saying that he hated both them and their cursed lingo, and would have nothing to do with it. Of course the result was that Jewitt soon became liked by the savages, whilst Thompson was disliked ; and it was only the fear of offending John that prevented them from killing him. Jewitt and Thompson gradually began to lose all hope of ever regaining their liberty. On Sunday, whenever the weather permitted, they went to the borders of a fresh-water pond, about a mile from the village, where, after bathing and putting on clean clothes, they would seat themselves under the shade of a beautiful pine, while Jewitt read some chapters in the Bible, and the prayers appointed by the Church for the day, ending their devo-

14

tions with a fervent prayer to the Almighty that He would permit them once more to behold a Christian land.

After a time the King urged Jewitt to get married, saying that as there was no probability of a ship coming to Nootka to release him, that he must consider himself as destined to pass the remainder of his life with them ; that the sooner he conformed to their customs the better; and that a wife and family would render him more contented and satisfied with their mode of living.   Jewitt remonstrated, but Maquina threatened him with death if he should refuse.   Reduced to this extremity, with death on one side and matrimony on the other, Jewitt chose the lesser of two evils, and consented on condition that if he did not fancy any of the Nootka women, he should be permitted to make choice of one from some other tribe.   This being settled, on the next morning Jewitt and Maquina, with about fifty men, set off for A-i-tiz-zart, where Jewitt chose a young girl of about seventeen, the daughter of the chief Upquesta, for his wife.   The marriage cere-monies are described.   Jewitt found his Indian princess both amiable and intelli-gent for one whose limited sphere of observation must necessarily have given rise to but few ideas.   She was extremely ready to agree to anything that he proposed relative to their mode of living, was very attentive in keeping her garments and person neat and clean, and appeared in every respect solicitous to please him. In addition to this, she was the handsomest, with one exception, of all the women in the village.   Yet, in spite of all these charms, Jewitt was discontented, and observes that he could not but view this connection as a chain to bind him down to this savage land and prevent him ever again seeing a civilized country, especially when a few days later the King informed him that in future neither Jewitt nor Thompson should wear their European clothes, and must conform to the native custom.   He afterwards got rid of his wife by sending her back to her father, which was the Nootka method of divorce.   At last a ship—the brig *Lydia*— arrived at Nootka, and by a stratagem Jewitt and Thompson were got on board ; and after a voyage to China, Jewitt arrived at Boston, in Massachusetts.

This is an outline of the work which, although in autobiographical form, was really written by Richard Alsop, of Middleton, in Connecticut, who was the author of several books of poems, and translator of Molina's *History of Chili.* Mr. F. W. Field, in his *Indian Bibliography*, says that " details of the adventures of Jewitt were drawn from him by the indefatigable queries of Alsop, who, after some years, declared that he feared he had done Jewitt but little good in furnish-ing him with a vagabond mode of earning a livelihood, by hawking his book from a wheelbarrow through the country."   Mr. Field considers that "the narrative of Jewitt affords us many new and interesting particulars of the life and habits of the most savage of American aborigines.   It is probably as faithful a portrayal of them as could be made by an unlettered man, after the lapse of several years." But unless Jewitt had forgotten what he learned at school, he was not an entirely unlettered man ; and some of his tales have the appearance of being "seamen's yarns." A somewhat unscrupulous use of Jewitt's adventures was made a few years ago when his narrative, having been slightly altered in form, appeared in the *Boy's Own Paper*, under the title of "A Boston Boy Among Savages." According to Drake's *Dictionary of American Biography*, Jewitt died at Hartford, in Connecticut, on the 21st of January, 1821, aged 57. This is clearly a mistake; as Jewitt was born in 1783, it is evident that if he died in 1821 he was only 37, and that if he was 57 at his death he must have died in 1841.

ON SOME BOOKS WRITTEN IN PRISON.

THESE books are prison-born, a ragged show,
  Yet dowered with light serene and ever pure
  That shall for many centuries endure,
And warm the world with brightest glow.
What bitter tears, what agonizing throe,
  What scorn was theirs, the steadfast few and fit
  Who strove for right and truth with faith and wit,
Nor feared the galling chain of prison woe.

These are the witnesses, of courage high,
  Whose names are on the bead-roll of the years;
Who from the bar of highest heaven look down
  Clad in white robes of saintly purity.
Sweetness they have for toil, and rest for tears,
And as they bore the cross they wear the crown.

WHAT IS A BOOKWORM?

I.

"What is a Bookworm? Tell me, if you can.
I merely mean the insect, not the man."
A reptile whom a wit like Hood might dub
A grub that grubs in Grub Street for its grub.
Versicles from the Portfolio of a Sexagenarian
(Robert Rockliff), Liverpool, 1862.

 HE bookworm has left its mark on literature alike in the literal and figurative acceptance of the phrase. The term bookworm is somewhat vaguely used, and is really applied to a variety of insects. We purpose describing the most important contributions to what may be termed the literature of the bookworm, and, as a beginning, we may refer to the *Report of the British Association for* 1879, which contains an excellent paper by Professor John Obadiah Westwood, M.A., F.R.S., which gives the completest information as to the various species of insects that damage books. From this paper we take the necessary details as to the life-history of the bookworm, by whatever name known to the votaries of science. The caterpillars of the moth *Aglossa pinguinalis*, and also of a species of *Depressaria*, often injure books by spinning their webs between the volumes, gnawing small portions of the paper with which to form their cocoons. A small mite (*Cheyletus eruditus*) is also found occasionally in books kept in damp situations, where it gnaws the paper.

A very minute beetle (*Hypothenemus eruditus*, Westn.) forms its tiny burrows within the binding of books, of which a small portion, with specimens of the beetles, was exhibited.

The small silvery insect (*Lepisma saccharina*) found in closets and cupboards where provisions are kept, also feeds on paper, of which a curious example was exhibited in a framed and glazed print, of which the plain portion was eaten; whilst the parts covered by the printing-ink were untouched. Professor Westwood had been assured that the same fact had been observed in India, where some of the Government's records had been injured in the same manner. This habit of the Lepismæ had not been previously recorded.

The white ants (*Termitidæ*) are a constant source of annoyance in hot and warm climates, eating all kinds of objects of vegetable origin, of which several instances have been recorded. Cockroaches (*Blatta orientalis*) are also equally destructive to books when they fall in their way. The Death-watches (*Anobium pertinax* and *striatum*) do the greatest injury, gnawing and burrowing not only in and through the bindings, but also entirely through the volume, and instances have been recorded where not fewer than twenty-seven folio volumes, placed together on a book-shelf, had been so cleanly drilled through by the larva of this beetle, that a string might be run through the hole made by it, and the volumes raised by the string.

Professor Westwood directed special attention to a *Report of the Commission appointed to inquire into the Causes of the Decay of Wood-carvings (by the Anobia), and the Means of Preventing and Remedying the Effects of such Decay*, which was issued by the Science and Art Department of the Committee of Council on Education, at South Kensington, in 1864. This contains Professor Westwood's account of the life-history of the *Anobia*. He also referred to a previous Parliamentary Report on the National Gallery, with the observations thereon by the late Dr. Waagen, especially with reference to the state of Sebastian del Piombo's picture of the "Raising of Lazarus," which had been attacked by the *Anobia*. The Arabic MSS. in the Cambridge Library, brought from Cairo by Burckhardt, and various Oriental MSS. in the Bodleian Library, were much injured by these insects.

The remedies against the attacks of the *Anobium* upon objects of carved wood must necessarily be of a different character from those used against the bookworms, which are the larvæ of the *Anobia*. In the former case, *saturation* with chloride of mercury dissolved in methylated spirits of wine or other analogous fluid had been found to be efficient; but with respect to books it was necessary to have recourse to *vapourisation*, and experiments were recorded in which objects attacked by the *Anobia* had been placed in a large glass-case made as air-tight as possible, and small saucers, with pieces of sponge saturated with carbolic acid were placed at the bottom of the case; and on the recommendation of Professor Westwood it had been found successful to place the infected volumes in the Bodleian Library in a closed box, with a quantity of benzine in a saucer at the bottom. A strong infusion of colocynth and quassia, chloroform, spirits of turpentine, expressed juice of green walnuts, and pyroligneous acid have also been employed successfully. Fumigation on a large scale may also be adopted by having a room made as air-tight as possible, burning brimstone in it, or filling the room with fumes of prussic acid or benzine.

Dr. Hagen had also suggested that by placing an infected volume under the bell-glass of an air-pump, and extracting the air, the larvæ would be found to be killed after an hour's exhaustion.

This paper, by Professor Westwood, was suggested by one delivered by Dr. Hagen, of Harvard College, Mass., before the American Library Association. Dr. Hagen's paper is printed in the *Library Journal*, vol. iv., pp. 251, 373.

The bookworm, although a destroyer of books, has also been the cause of some literature existing. The earliest of English literary men to write about it was Dr. Thomas Parnell, in whose collected poems will be found the following verses:

THE BOOKWORM.

Come hither, boy ; we'll hunt to-day
The bookworm, ravening beast of prey,
Produc'd by parent Earth, at odds,
As fame reports it, with the gods.
Him frantic hunger wildly drives
Against a thousand authors' lives :
Through all the fields of wit he flies ;
Dreadful his head with clustering eyes,
With horns without, and tusks within,
And scales to serve him for a skin.
Observe him nearly, lest he climb
To wound the bards of ancient time,
Or down the vale of fancy go
To tear some modern wretch below.
On every corner fix thine eye,
Or ten to one he slips thee by !

See where his teeth a passage eat :
We'll rouse him from the deep retreat.
But who the shelter's forc'd to give ?
'Tis sacred Virgil, as I live !

From leaf to leaf, from song to song,
He draws the tadpole form along,
He mounts the gilded edge before,
He's up, he scuds the cover o'er,
He turns, he doubles, there he pass'd,
And here we have him, caught at last.

Insatiate brute, whose teeth abuse
The sweetest servants of the Muse—
Nay, never offer to deny,
I took thee in the fact to fly.
His roses nipt in every page,
My poor Anacreon mourns thy rage ;
By thee my Ovid wounded lies ;
By thee my Lesbia's Sparrow dies ;
Thy rabid teeth have half destroy'd
The work of love in Biddy Floyd ;
They rent Belinda's locks away,
And spoil'd the Blouzelind of Gay.
For all, for every single deed,
Relentless justice bids thee bleed :
Then fall a victim to the Nine,
Myself the priest, my desk the shrine.

Bring Homer, Virgil, Tasso near,
To pile a sacred altar here :
Hold, boy ! thy hand outruns thy wit,
You reach'd the plays that Dennis writ ;
You reach'd me Philips' rustic strain ;
Pray take your mortal bards again.

Come, bind the victim ; there he lies,
And here between his numerous eyes
This venerable dust I lay,
From manuscript just swept away.

The goblet in my hand I take,
For the libation's yet to make :

A health to poets! all their days,
May they have bread, as well as praise ;
Sense may they seek, and less engage
In papers fill'd with party rage.
But if their riches spoil their vein,
Ye Muses, make them poor again.

Now bring the weapon, yonder blade,
With which my tuneful pens are made.
I strike the scales that arm thee round,
And twice and thrice I print the wound ;
The sacred altar floats with red,
And now he dies, and now he's dead.

How like the son of Jove I stand,
This Hydra stretch'd beneath my hand !
Lay bare the monster's entrails here,
To see what dangers threat the year :
Ye gods ! what sonnets on a wench !
What lean translations out of French !
'Tis plain, this lobe is so unsound,
T—— prints, before the months go round.

But hold, before I close the scene,
The sacred altar should be clean.
O had I Shadwell's second bays,
Or, Tate, thy pert and humble lays ?
(Ye fair, forgive me, when I vow
I never miss'd your works till now !)
I'd tear the leaves and wipe the shrine,
That only way you please the Nine :
But since I chance to want these two,
I'll make the songs of Durfey do.

But from the corpse, on yonder pin,
I hang the scales that brac'd it in ;
I hang my studious morning gown,
And write my own inscription down.

This trophy from the Python won
This robe, in which the deed was done,
These, Parnell, glorying in the feat,
Hung on these shelves, the Muses' seat.
Here Ignorance and Hunger found
Large realms of wit to ravage round ;
Here Ignorance and Hunger fell ;
Two foes in one I sent to hell.
Ye poets, who my labours see,
Come share the triumph all with me !
Ye critics, born to vex the Muse,
Go mourn the grand ally you lose !

THE *FAUST* OF CHAMISSO.

N England we associate the name of Faust with that of Goethe almost to the exclusion of our own Marlowe. Yet Germany alone has produced twenty-nine works by various authors who play variations, more or less skilful, upon that wondrous theme which Goethe has touched with the supreme instinct of genius. One of the many *Fausts* came from the pen of Adalbert von Chamisso, and though, compared with Goethe's mighty work, but a sketch, it is not unworthy of attention. He was born on the 27th of January, 1781, and came of a noble family, members of which had lived in the Château of Boncourt, in Champagne, until the Revolution, when the estate was destroyed, and the family left France. They lived in the Netherlands, later in the south of Germany, and in 1796 settled in Berlin. Having lost their estate, two of the sons painted miniature portraits, and thus obtained a small income for the family. Adalbert became one of the Queen of Prussia's pages, and she had him educated in a gymnasium at Berlin. Though he was French in origin, he studied the German language and literature, until he became more German than French. His parents returned to France at the invitation of Napoleon, in 1798, and Adalbert joined the Prussian army, which he left after the peace of Tilsit. Soon after the time that his parents returned to France, he wrote his first German poems; and in 1804, he and Varnhagen von Ense began to edit a *Musen-almanach*, but his editorship only lasted two years. His family had at that time recovered most of their property, and he rejoined them. Whilst in France he taught at a school at Napoléonville, but France was like a strange country to him, and he returned to Germany, where he studied the natural sciences. His best known work was written at the age of thirty-two; it is the story of *Peter Schlemihl*, a man who sold his shadow to the Evil One. This work was published in 1814 by Chamisso's friend, De la Motte Fouqué, and has been translated into many of the European languages. Chamisso published the second edition himself, in 1827, and added to it some poems. In 1814 he began to travel; he accompanied Count Rumjanzow, at the latter's invitation, in an expedition round the world. Many discoveries were made, but they failed in their chief enterprise, which was to discover a north-east passage. He returned from this expedition in 1818. Chamisso went under Captain Kotzebue, who, on his return, wrote an account of the voyage. Chamisso himself wrote *Bemerkungen und Ansichten auf einer Reise um die Welt* (1821). Chamisso then returned again to Berlin, where he became Doctor of Philosophy, a Member of the Royal Academy of Sciences, and Inspector of the Berlin Botanical Gardens. Whilst in this last position he wrote, *Uebersicht der in Norddeutschland vorkommenden nützlichsten und schädlichsten Gewächse, nebst Ansichten über das Pflanzenreich und Pflanzenkunde,*

published in 1827. His interest in the natural sciences, however, did not prevent him from writing more verse ; for his legends and ballads, and many of his smaller poems were written during the last ten years of his life. His death occurred in Berlin, on the 21st of August, 1838. A publication of his collected poems appeared in 1831 at Leipzig, in an octavo volume, and a second edition appeared three years later. There was a complete collection of his works in four octavo volumes, at Leipzig, in 1835, a second edition of which appeared in 1842 in six duodecimo volumes ; the last two volumes of this edition contain Chamisso's life and correspondence, edited by J. E. Hitzig.

With the exception of *Peter Schlemihl*, few of Chamisso's literary works have been translated into English. We have all the more pleasure in calling attention to a version of his *Faust*, which has been printed for private circulation : *Faust, a Dramatic Sketch, by Adalbert von Chamisso* (1803). *Translated from the German by Henry Phillips, jun.* Philadelphia, 1881. Dr. Phillips restricted the issue to one hundred copies. In his prefatory note he observes : " The present poem is one of the twenty-nine *Fausts*, by various authors, which appeared in Germany during the sixty-one years in which Goethe was employed upon his masterpiece. Adalbert von Chamisso, unfortunately best known by his least important work (*Peter Schlemihl*), has sunk into unmerited oblivion ; and under the impression that this poem has never before appeared in our language, I have ventured to translate it, although merely a sketch, not entirely free from obscurities."

Chamisso was a ripe scholar, a naturalist of high rank, and has been characterized as " a hale, hearty, sinewy poet."

The *Faust* of Chamisso is partly monologue and partly dialogue between the too-curious searcher into infinite mysteries and the Good and Evil Spirits who respectively urge and check him in his unhappy career. As a specimen of the work, we give the original of the version of a part of the Good Spirit's choric address to Faust :

CHAMISSO.

Faust ! Faust !
Den seligen Menschen
Gewährte der Vater,
Von allen den Früchten
Des Gartens zu kosten ;
Den seligen Menschen
Verwehrte der Vater
Die einzige Frucht.
Und listig schmeichelnd hob die Schlange sich :
Ihr würdet Göttern gleich, wenn ihr die Frucht,
Die herrliche, zu kosten euch erkühntet,
Die euch der Vater streng verwehrt zu brechen,
Nicht Vater er, der neidische Tyrann !
Faust ! Faust !
Dem kindlichen Menschen,
Die Freuden des Lebens,
Sie knospen ihm alle.
Er weilet, wo duftend

15

Die Rosen ihm blühen,
Die Früchte ihm winken.
Geflügelten Schrittes
Leicht hin über Dornen
Zu schweben, zu eilen,
Gesellt' ihm der Vater
Die holden Gefährten
Den Glauben, die Hoffnung.
Treu ihm in wechselndem Glück.

PHILLIPS' TRANSLATION.

Faust ! Faust !
The once happy man
Our Father did grant
Of Eden's sweet fruits
To pluck as he chose ;
'Twas but one alone
He kept for his own.
With artful flattery raised the snake its head :
" Omniscient ye shall be, and like the Gods,
Should ye but dare to taste that tree forbid
By him ye Father call : an envious soul,
A tyrant he ; no true and loving sire."
Faust ! Faust !
For innocent hearts
All pleasures of life
Are budding forever.
They tarry where blooming
Fresh roses are blowing,
Where fruits ever ripening
Beckoning call
The fleet flying footsteps
O'er barriers to hasten.
As comrades eternal
The Father hath sent him
Firm Faith and strong Hoping—
Mates steadfast in fortune.

COPYRIGHT IN LETTERS.

By J. O. Halliwell-Phillipps, F.R.S.

HE following scrap from Atkyns' *Reports of Cases in Chancery,* 1767, vol. ii. (p. 342), is of interest as giving the leading case as to the law of copyright:

"Pope *v.* Curl, June 17, 1741.

"A motion was made on behalf of Curl the bookseller, upon his having put in his answer to dissolve an injunction, which Mr. Pope had obtained, against his vending a book entitled *Letters from Swift, Pope, and others.*

"*Lord Chancellor* [*Hardwicke*]: The first question is, whether letters are within the grounds and intention of the statute made in the eighth year of Queen Anne, c. 19, entitled An Act for the encouragement of learning, by vesting the copies of printed books in the authors or purchasers of such copies.

"I think it would be extremely mischievous to make a distinction between a book of letters, which comes out into the world, either by the permission of the writer or the receiver of them, and any other learned work.

"The same objection would hold against sermons, which the author may never intend should be published, but are collected from loose papers, and brought out after his death.

"Another objection has been made by the defendant's council, that where a man writes a letter, it is in the nature of a gift to the receiver.

"But I am of opinion that it is only a special property in the receiver, possibly the property of the paper may belong to him; but this does not give a license to any person whatsoever to publish them to the world, for at most the receiver has only a joint property with the writer.

"The second question is, whether a book originally printed in Ireland is lawful prize to the booksellers here.

"If I should be of that opinion, it would have very pernicious consequences, for then a bookseller who has got a printed copy of a book, has nothing else to do but send it over to Ireland to be printed, and then by pretending to reprint it only in England, will by this means entirely evade the Act of Parliament.

"It has been insisted on by the defendant's council, that this is a sort of work which does not come within the meaning of the Act of Parliament, because it contains only letters on familiar subjects, and inquiries after the health of friends, and cannot properly be called a learned work.

"It is certain that no works have done more service to mankind, than those which have appeared in this shape, upon familiar subjects, and which perhaps

15—2

were never intended to be published; and it is this makes them so valuable; for I must confess for my own part, that letters which are very elaborately written, and originally intended for the press, are generally the most insignificant, and very little worth any person's reading.

"The injunction was continued by Lord Chancellor only as to those letters which are under Mr. Pope's name in the book, and which are written by him, and not as to those which are written to him."

REVIEWS.

Sonnets of this Century. Edited and arranged, with a critical introduction on the Sonnet, by WILLIAM SHARP. London : Walter Scott. 12mo., pp. lxxxi-324.

This volume will delight all who cultivate or admire the " sonnet's narrow plot of ground." The selection which Mr. Sharp has made is one of real excellence, and his introductory essay, whilst written with genuine enthusiasm, is full of information, and shows critical insight. The laws of the sonnet are condensed into the form of a decalogue, and we venture to quote the ten absolutely essential rules for a good sonnet, rules to which Mr. Sharp has given the name of the " Ten Commandments of the Sonnet ":

I. The sonnet must consist of fourteen decasyllabic lines.

II. Its octave, or major system, whether or not this be marked by a pause in the cadence after the eighth line, must (unless cast in the Shakespearian mould) follow a prescribed arrangement in the rhyme-sounds, namely, the first, fourth, fifth and eighth lines must rhyme on the same sound ; and the second, third, sixth and seventh on another.

III. Its sestet, or minor system, may be arranged with more freedom ; but a rhymed couplet at the close is *only* allowable when the form is the English, or Shakespearian.

IV. No terminal should also occur in any portion of any other line in the same system ; and the rhyme-sounds (1) of the octave should be harmoniously at variance, and (2) the rhyme-sounds of the sestet should be entirely distinct in intonation from those of the octave. Thus (1) no octave should be based on a monotonous system of nominally distinct rhymes, such as, *sea, futurity, eternity, be, flee, adversity, inevitably, free.*

V. It must have no slovenliness of diction, no weak or indeterminate terminations, no vagueness of conception, and no obscurity.

VI. It must be absolutely complete in itself, *i.e.*, it must be the evolution of *one* thought, or *one* emotion, or *one* poetically apprehended fact.

VII. It should have the characteristic of apparent inevitableness, and in expression be ample, yet reticent. It must not be forgotten that dignity and repose are essential qualities of a true sonnet.

VIII. The continuity of the thought, idea, or emotion must be unbroken throughout.

IX. Continuous sonority must be maintained from the first phrase to the last.

X. The end must be more impressive than the commencement ; the close must not be inferior to, but must rather transcend, what has gone before.

These rules, with the help of genius, will enable a man to write a good sonnet.

The Publishers' Trade List Annual, 1885. Thirteenth Year. New York Office of the *Publishers' Weekly,* 1885, 8vo.

The annual issue of the American catalogue is an evidence of the increasing activity and organization of the Transatlantic book trade. In view of the present discussion as to international copyright, the many entries respecting reprints of English books will be scanned with interest.

The Praise of Gardens : A Prose Cento collected and in Part Englished by Albert F. Sieveking, with *Proem by E. V. B.* London : Elliot Stock. 8vo., 1885, pp. xix-321.

Mr. Sieveking's idea is an ingenious one, and he has worked it out with much industry. Taking the wide sweep of literature between the age of the nineteenth dynasty of Egypt and the present time, he has selected from the authors of many lands their most enthusiastic words spoken in praise of gardens, and of the pleasures to be derived from them. Necessarily these eulogies vary considerably in ability and sincerity, but he must be difficult indeed to please who does not find in this anthology something appropriate and delightful. We have not only Epictetus and Columella, Sir Philip Sidney and Lord Bacon, but Kinglake, Dickens, Mortimer Collins, Ruskin, and many others of the present day. The Hon. Mrs. Boyle has prefixed to the volume a characteristic prose-poem, addressed " to the garden-loving reader."

We have received the following catalogues :—Wm. Downing, 74. New Street, Birmingham ; Albert Cohn, 53, Mohrenstrasse, Berlin ; Wm. Collins, Stroud ; T. Simmons, 164. Parade, Leamington ; J. and J. Leighton, 40, Brewer Street, Golden Square, London ; J. W. Jarvis and Sons, 28, King William Street, London, W.C.

CORRESPONDENCE.

THE "GOLDEN LEGENDE."

I HAVE been reading with interest an article on the "Golden Legende" in this month's *Book-Lore*, as I had occasion last year to examine all the different editions by Caxton, Wynkyn de Worde, and Julian Notary, to compare them with my copy. By internal evidence I was convinced my copy was printed by Wynkyn de Worde, between 1512 and 1527. Having failed to identify this edition, I showed it to Mr. Blades, who very kindly went fully into the subject, and found that imperfect copy at the British Museum, mentioned in the article in *Book-Lore*. He found that they exactly corresponded, and undoubtedly were identical, as my copy is nearly perfect, only wanting folio 1, on which was the woodcut of the Saints in Glory, and the last folio, ccclxxxiii (and the colophon, unluckily). My copy was once Wm. Herbert's, and my grandfather bought it out of Edward's catalogue about 1789.

Yours faithfully,
HENRY SPENCER WALPOLE.

Stagbury, near Banstead, Surrey,
 January 30, 1886.

P.S.—With the exception of the fragment in the British Museum, I believe my copy to be unique, as I can discover no other in any of the great libraries, or in any bibliographical work. It is quite certain it was printed before 1527, so the conjecture in the last paragraph of the article won't hold water.

By-the-bye, the article does not mention an edition printed by Pynson, 1507. The only copy I know of I have seen in the Lambeth Library.

MADEMOISELLE FLORE.

Mademoiselle Flore, artiste du Théâtre de Variétés, *auteur supposé.*
  Ses mémoires. Paris, Le Comptoir des imprimeurs unis, 1845. 3 volumes in 8vo. Réproduit en 1847 par Michel Levy, avec *de nouveau titre* portant, *Deuxième édition.*
  Véritables auteurs, Mesdames Marion du Mersan et Gabriel.
  Renseignement demandé dans *Book-Lore*, Novembre, page 182, *et extrait de Supercheries littéraires devoilées, par Quérard.*

E. R.

PARIS, 25 *Janvier*, 1886.

BIBLIOPHILE'S KALENDAR.

MR. ELLIOT STOCK will shortly publish a volume entitled *The Pleasures of a Book-Worm.* The author, Mr. J. Rogers Rees, has gathered together a series of short Essays on subjects which have an interest for collectors, connoisseurs, and for all those who study the history and peculiar characteristics of books. The subjects treated of are : Concerning Books and Lovers of Books ; Home and Books ; Glimpses of Earthly Paradise ; the Romance and Reality of Dedications ; an Odd Corner in a Book-Lover's Study ; Genius and Criticism, and the Pursuit of Literature in Odd Moments.

THE *Printing Times* has an interesting notice of the first press at Eton. The threatened "improvements" at Eton, it says, have fortunately stopped short of the demolition of a venerable site famous in the annals of English printing. It was in the head-master's house adjoining Weston's Yard that Sir Henry Savile, in 1607, is said to have erected that celebrated press from which issued one of the most magnificent Greek works of which English typography can boast. Of this early Eton press, and its *magnum opus*, a few notes may just now be of interest. Henry Savile, a distinguished Oxford scholar, who, about the year 1580, held the post of Greek tutor to Queen Elizabeth, and was warden of Merton College in 1586, was elected provost of Eton in 1596. Immediately upon taking up residence in this new capacity he is said to have conceived the then gigantic undertaking of collecting and printing the entire works of St. Chrysostom—a feat never before accomplished, and, considering the limited capabilities of the press at that period, a bold project. The scheme, once entertained, was prosecuted with characteristic determination and princely liberality. Vacancies at Eton were filled up by Greek scholars, Savile himself declaring, "Give me the plodding student. If I would look for wits, I would go to Newgate; there be the wits." Manuscripts and printed books were collected from all quarters of Europe. The indefatigable pen of the editor was busy corresponding with the most learned men of his day. The great libraries of France and Germany were ransacked by emissaries from Eton, and Savile himself appears to have made more than one long journey in the course of his labours. James I., always ready to earn the reputation of a patron of letters cheaply, paid a visit to Eton and knighted Savile, graciously permitting him to inform the world of his royal patronage. But the entire expense of the work, amounting to some £8,000, at that time an enormous sum, was wholly defrayed by Sir Henry. The printing began about 1610, John Norton, the King's printer, being employed to execute the work. The beautiful Greek types used are supposed to have been procured abroad, either from the Stephani, of Paris, or from the Wechels, of Frankfort, who are known to have possessed some of the Paris founts. The beauty of these letters appears to have given rise to the rumour circulated at the time, that the Eton *Chrysostom* was printed with silver types. It is stated, that during the course of the impression some of Norton's workmen were tampered with by the publishers of a rival edition of the Father, at that time in progress at Paris. The Eton proofs, as they passed the press, were surreptitiously sent into France, and there copied, letter by letter. "Thus," says Fuller, "two editions of *St. Chrysostom* did together run a race in the world which should get the speed of the other in public sale and acceptance. Sir Henry his edition started first by the advantage of some months. But the Parisian edition came up close to it and outstript it in quickness of sale. But of late the Savillian *Chrysostom* hath much mended its pace, so that very few are left of the whole impression." The edition was completed in 1613, and the excellence of its typography secured for Norton the title of "*In Græcis Regius Typographus*," a distinction already bestowed by Francis I. of France on Henry Stephens, of Paris. The work is comprised in eight great folio volumes, numbering about 7,800 pages, and is to this day looked upon as a masterpiece of Greek typography. It was published at the high price of £9, a sum which Mr. (afterwards Archbishop) Usher declared to be "too high for him to deal withal." Several other Greek works were printed at Eton during and after the printing of the *Chrysostom*; but before Sir Henry Savile's death, which occurred in 1621-2, at the age of seventy-two, its labours had ceased, and its materials were dispersed. Some of the types were seen by Evelyn in his day being used as playthings and counters by the Eton boys, but the remainder were purchased by or presented to the Oxford press. Here they appear for some years to have been fraudulently detained by Turner, the university printer, until Laud moved the heads of colleges to compel their restoration, in 1639. With this incident the Eton Greek types disappear from history, and, beyond the volumes of the *Chrysostom* itself, the head-master's house at Eton is now the only remaining memorial of one of the most famous enterprises of early English typography.

A SINCERE lover of literature and friend of learning has been lost by the death of Mr. Joseph Mayer, F.S.A., on January 20. He was born at Newcastle-under-Lyme, February 23, 1803, settled as a jeweller at Liverpool in 1822, and devoted his labour and fortune to the formation of the Museum presented by him to that town. His earliest study was Greek coins, his collection of which was sold to the French Government in 1844. Antique gems next attracted his chief attention, and his skill and liberality rendered him famous in Europe. His favourite design was to collect in Liverpool a museum of treasures of artistic excellence, in order to educate students in the true principles of beauty. In this he succeeded, and his Egyptian, Abyssinian, and Etruscan collections, chosen with a due regard to art, are justly famed; and he was equally celebrated for his collection of Ivories, of Greek, Roman, and Mediæval gems, and of Wedgwood and of English pottery. With the hope of writing *A History of the Rise and Progress of Art in England from* 1550 *to the Present Time*, he collected between four and five thousand original drawings, between fifteen and twenty thousand early engravings, and above fifty thousand autograph letters of English artists. The number of scientific works for which the world is indebted to Mr. Mayer's generous aid is considerable; the *Inventorium Sepulchrale*, the *Anglo-Saxon Vocabularies*, and the *Diplomatarium Anglicum Ævi Saxonici*, being the most important. When the art of electroplating was discovered by Mr. Thomas Spencer, to this liberal patron of all science did the inventor apply. Under Mr. Mayer's auspices, the first article ever subjected to this process was successfully plated—a spoon, which now lies in the Mayer collection in the Liverpool Museum. In 1860 he raised two companies of volunteers, called the Liverpool Borough Guard, and subsequently raised and clothed at his own expense a third company, in the neighbourhood of Bebington, his residence. In 1865 he made a donation to this Cheshire village of a free library, containing 20,000 volumes, with a handsome edifice, standing in the public walks, which are also a gift of Mr. Mayer. They occupy nearly six acres, and are planted with every variety of flowering shrub that will bear the Cheshire climate. Mr. Mayer was an enthusiastic student of floriculture in its higher forms. In 1870, under the superintendence of Mr. Henry Boyle, M.A., the Victoria Regia was brought to flower beneath the open sky, in his hot-water tanks at Bebington—an achievement never before made, and believed to be possible by very few. In 1869 his grateful townsmen of Liverpool erected a colossal statue of Mr. Mayer in St. George's Hall. It is of Carrara marble, and the work of Signor Giovanni Fontana.

WE regret that by an error of the printer the name of Mr. B. F. Stevens was given on the cover of last month's *Book-Lore* as the author of the account of the Wodhull Sale. Mr. Stevens is in no way responsible for that article.

MISS MARY BOYLE, who wrote a hand-book to Lord Bath's pictures at Longleat, has just completed a *Bibliographical Catalogue of the Portraits at Panshanger,* the seat of Lord Cowper. A few surplus copies have been printed for collectors, and can be had through Mr. Elliot Stock.

READERS of *Book-Lore* will not fail to sympathize with the efforts now being made for the popularization of good literature. It is a matter of surprise that whilst literary classics can be bought in Germany and France at about 2½d. per volume, no similar series was issued in this country. Messrs. Cassell have taken away this reproach by their *National Library*, published in weekly volumes at 3d., under the editorship of Professor Henry Morley. The nature of the series may be judged from the following list : *Warren Hastings,* by Lord Macaulay ; *My Ten Years' Imprisonment,* by Silvio Pellico, translated from the Italian by Thomas Roscoe ; *The Rivals* and *The School for Scandal,* by Richard Brinsley Sheridan ; *The Autobiography of Benjamin Franklin; The Complete Angler,* by Isaac Walton ; *Childe Harold,* by Lord Byron ; *The Man of Feeling,* by Henry Mackenzie ; *Sermons on the Card,* by Bishop Latimer ; *Lives of Alexander the Great and Cæsar,* by Plutarch ; *The Castle of Otranto,* by Horace Walpole ; *Voyages and Travels of Sir John Maundeville; She Stoops to Conquer* and *The Good-Natured Man,* by Oliver Goldsmith ; *Table-Talk,* by Martin Luther ; *Adventures of Baron Trenck,* translated from the German by Thomas Holcroft ; *The Wisdom of the Ancients,* by Lord Bacon ; *Travels in the Interior of Africa,* by Mungo Park ; *Natural History of Selborne,* by Gilbert White ; *The History of Egypt,* by Herodotus ; *A Voyage Round the World,* by Lord Anson, etc. Nor are Messrs. Cassell alone, for it is now announced that Messrs. Routledge propose to issue a series of books at the low price of 3d. each, in a handsome paper cover designed by Mr. Walter Crane, under the title of *Routledge's World Library.* Each volume will consist of 160 pages, royal 16mo., printed in clear type on white paper. The first volume is Anster's translation of Goethe's *Faust.* Besides poetry and the drama, biographies, records of travel, works of history and fiction, and books on social science will be included. The editor is Mr. H. R. Haweis, who quotes Walt Whitman's remark to him, "There is a sea below the sea," which means that "the reading world on the surface of society is as nothing when compared with the reading world beneath the surface."

SHELLEY AND VEGETARIANISM.

N 1824 there was published a periodical entitled *The Medical Adviser*, which was edited by Alexander Burnett, M.D. It was remarkable for its personal attacks upon the fraternity of quack doctors. The first number of this journal is dated December 6, 1823, and contains a squib directed against Shelley and his Pythagorean friends. This is worth reproducing on the ground of its curiosity:

ANIMAL AND VEGETABLE DIET.

That the stomach of man is intended to digest, and his health receive nourishment by animal as well as vegetable diet, is without doubt. We are decidedly omnivorous animals. Neither will the body thrive upon meat alone, nor vegetables alone. Those savages who live on flesh only, and those poor Dutch peasants who seldom see meat upon their tables, are poor squalid-looking beings, and would strongly illustrate our opinions if they were placed alongside of our English butchers, who are a fine strong wholesome set of people in general. It is not animal food which is itself unwholesome, but the improper use of it—too much taken at a time, or perhaps tough and overdone. Let a fair and reasonable portion of underdone meat be taken, with a due portion of vegetables, and it will promote health and strength. Water-drinkers are equally as mistaken as vegetable-dieters; but of this we have spoken in our "advice on drunkenness." The late Percy Bysshe Shelley wrote against animal diet a paper the most absurd and irrational: a parody of which will be found at the end of the following humorous article, handed to us by a correspondent, under the form of a speech by the president. As the article treats of vegetable diet in the way it ought to be treated, we will offer no further arguments against it: and we are in hope that those disciples of the late Mr. Shelley (numerous enough, we know) will take our correspondent's satire as it is meant, namely, to laugh them out of their folly, and thereby add a few years to their lives. The article is supposed to have been reported in a newspaper, and is as follows:

> *Dinner by the Amateurs of Vegetable Diet—Lutophagi and Men whose Heads are not in their Right Places.*

On the —— day of ——, sixty persons, who had lived for more than three years on vegetables and pure water, met for the purpose of felicitating each other on the circumstance of their being still alive. This singular feast excited such an unusual elation of spirits, that it was unanimously resolved that a solemn dinner should be given, to which all the eaters of vegetable diet in the three kingdoms should be invited. One gentleman present observed that some qualifying clause was necessary in this resolution, for that as it was now worded it included all the Scotch and Irish, and a considerable portion of the English peasantry, whose diet was uncontaminated by any carnous admixture. He dwelt largely on the difficulty of bringing such a multitude together, and remarked that if the whole, or even a considerable part, could be assembled, very great terror would be excited in the good city of London and its environs; that such a multitude from its herbiferous habits might justly be regarded as worse than the plague of locusts; that, assuredly, they would eat up everything. Such a measure, he added, would bring upon its adopters the notice of Government, and produce at least a suspension in the Habeas Corpus Act, and an abolition of the right of public meetings. He therefore humbly moved that the word " amateurs " should be substituted for " eaters." Mr. Leigh Hunt, who though not a vegetable man, yet thought himself entitled to speak at this meeting, from his fondness for tea, and the lighter kinds of meats, etc., rose to reply. He agreed with the gentleman who spoke last on the inconvenience that would result from so large a meeting— meetings led him to the right of petition and Parliamentary reform. In alluding to the diet of the peasants, he observed that their privation of animal food was obviously a branch of the borough-mongering system. This, to be sure, was one of its least pernicious results; but it was a result, and as such to be detested: " Timeo Danaos et dona ferentes." He dilated much upon the amiable character of the peasantry. For the Irish peasant in particular he expressed an enthusiastic admiration. To the word "amateurs" he objected as of French growth; commended his own mode of coining words as having a kind of freshness and "springness" about it; and concluded with recommending the word "appetiters " of vegetable diet, as at once being new, expressive, and " unvulgar." The motion, however, passed with the amendment first proposed. The dinner was fixed for the first of the ensuing month, and the place for dining was Hampstead Heath, it being considered that the open air harmonized best with vegetable diet and pure water. Just at this moment Mr. Manchester Hunt arrived out of breath, and bustling into the very centre of the group, begged permission to say a few words, which was granted. He said he felt himself called upon to attend the present meeting for two reasons: the first was, because the object of it was to promote reform, if not in the constitution of the country, at least in the constitution of their bodies. He loved reform in everything, and would support it. Secondly, as the inventor of a vegetable breakfast, which he trusted would go far in reforming the state, not only of the people's health, but also of the treasury. (Some whispered that he meant his own treasury.) As the inventor, he felt confident he would be received and patronized by the meeting. He held in his hand a pound of this breakfast-powder—" grain, pure roasted grain, gentlemen "— and he begged that a fair trial would be given it. He then moved that the party should have a public breakfast as well as a dinner, and that he would supply vegetable powder, which, however, would be on the most reasonable terms. Thus they would have an opportunity of discussing, in the hours between, the virtues of radical reform and roasted grain. He then concluded by distributing his handbills to those around him, declaring that no breakfast-powder was genuine that had not his signature on the package, which, he said, was felony to counterfeit. At the conclusion of Mr. Hunt's address, the greatest confusion arose, and the consequence promised to be fatal to the intended dinner, had not one of the gentlemen present taken Hunt aside, and requested him to withdraw: ingeniously adding an order for twenty pounds of his coffee. This had the desired effect, and the radical gentleman withdrew. When silence was restored, a committee was appointed to cater for the amateurs, and various disputes arose therein, regarding what dishes would be admissible, and what not. The carlines of the season left them no great variety of choice in the vegetable world: some, therefore, contended that fish might be allowed upon a solemn occasion like this; but the proposal was scouted by the rest with the utmost vehemence. One person held out a good while for oysters, asserting that they were to all intents and purposes submarine vegetables; and Mr. Leigh Hunt, who was admitted an honorary member, pleaded hard for shrimps and periwinkles. But his eloquence was spent to no purpose: the Catos of the committee remained unshaken. On the morning of the dinner there was not a vegetable left in Covent Garden Market by nine o'clock. All the greengrocers in the north end of the town were speedily disburdened of their wares, and an immense number of families in the parishes of Pancras and Bloomsbury, in Hampstead, Highgate, and Kentish Town, were left that day without a carrot, cabbage, or potato. An advance took place in the price of vegetables within six miles round, and a turnip was known to fetch five shillings! At five o'clock the tables were spread, and the guests assembled on Hampstead Heath: the late P. B. S. was in the chair; near him sat Dr. L., Mr. R. (the antiquarian), Sir J. S., the Rev. P., and Mr. T., the Pythagorean philosopher; near him was Mr. G., Mr. H., and Mr. L. H., with many others whom it would be tedious to enumerate. We were sorry to observe several of the more rigid amateurs looking very pale and thin, but they all declared that they enjoyed the most perfect health. The dinner was composed of such vegetables as were in season: they were generally boiled or fried, though some few rivals of the gymnosophists preferred their cabbage, etc., etc., in a raw state. One sage in particular we remarked with a dish of clover before him, which he devoured with an avidity worthy of Nebuchadnezzar himself. Like the King of Babylon, he appeared to have served a seven years' apprenticeship to the business. There were not many instances of repletion at this dinner. We are sorry, however, to state that one gentleman was obliged to quit the table very soon, being seized with a fit of the colic, and exhibiting all the symptoms of incipient anasarca—the consequence of an inordinate indulgence in cabbage and toast-and-water. After dinner, tea and Hunt's powder was served up with the dessert; and now began the joyous "rout and revelry." These followers of Pythagoras, however rigid in their adherence to his system of diet, were not very scrupulous observers of his precepts of taciturnity. Tongues wagged on all sides, and arguments rose thick, fast, and fiery. The silent heath resounded, and appeared on a sudden to be metamorphosed into the palace of noise—the temple of discord. How all this might have ended it is hard to say, if the noise had not been suddenly interrupted and drowned by another more powerful din from the opposite side of the heath. This proceeded from a party of brother-amateurs of the long-eared kind, who had just commenced their after-dinner concert and jollification. This interruption proved a seasonable correction to the unphilosophic vociferation of our party, and restored them to a becoming consciousness of their two-legged dignity. The President now arose, and addressed the assembly in the following words:

"It is with the utmost satisfaction that I behold assembled together such

16—2

an illustrious company of enlightened men ; all at least favourable to the principles that dictate our abstinence from animal food, and the majority strict
observers of a vegetable regimen. The depravity of man is undoubtedly to be
sought for in the indulgence of carnivorous appetites. This has been the persua-
sion of the enlightened of all ages. The fact has been darkly hinted at in the
mythology of all religions. The Biblical allegory of the forbidden fruit admits of
no explanation but this. The apple of the fatal tree was nothing, gentlemen, but
a well-dressed beefsteak—whether plain or with oyster sauce is doubtful. The
serpent is a representation of the brute creation. Man is said to have bruised his
head when he devoted the race of animals to death for the gratification of his
unnatural appetite. In return, the heel of man was said to have been bruised by
the serpent ; that is, the indulgence in flesh diet deprived him of his energy, and
reduced him to inactivity, torpor, disease, and death. The fable of Prometheus
may be similarly explained. Prometheus, gentlemen, was a cook of some
celebrity in his day. The gourmands of that time were so delighted with his
culinary preparations that they declared he must have stolen fire from heaven.
But he himself fell the first victim to his own pernicious inventions. A vulture
preyed upon his liver ; that is, he was afflicted with an incurable hepatitis, which
tormented him for many years, and finally put a period to his existence. Such,
gentlemen, is the brief but emphatic account of the origin of cookery—that fatal
science which has taught the knowledge of so many ills—that accursed tree whose
fruit is poison—that exhaustless fountain from which man in every age has drunk
such copious draughts of perdition ! Centuries and centuries have rolled away
since Prometheus discovered his execrable art, and centuries and centuries may
roll away again ere its destructive energies shall cease to operate. To this we
owe the existence of every evil, every crime !

" Animal diet is the parent of madness—madness of criminality and vice. To
this, gentlemen, we owe the existence of superstition, the abuse called government, the injustice of law, and the abomination of marriage—every vice that can
result from the perversion of nature, in our present distempered state of civilization. Yet I confess I entertain some hopes of at least a partial return of natural
diet. When I survey the enlightened assembly around me, I cannot entirely
despair. In each countenance I read the fairest promise of the future dietetic
reformation of mankind. As Prometheus was the introducer of cooked flesh into
the world, so shall Newton be the illustrious restorer of raw vegetables. As in
Adam all eat meat, so in Newton shall all eat cabbage. And who, gentlemen,
that looks upon us that have fed on vegetables for the last three years, can doubt
for a moment of the efficacy of our regimen ? In the whole of our animal economy
there is nothing to offend the most fastidious acumen of philosophical criticism.
We have no superabundant flesh ; no unexpressive roundness—every muscle—
every tendon can be seen.

" There is a ring of thoughtful darkness round our eyes that speaks a true soul
—a soul enlivened by vegetables and pure water ; and there is a hue upon our
cheeks which shames the blush of mutton-eaters. Let us rejoice ! The glorious
era is approaching that will fully develop the perfectability of our natures—the
golden age in which there shall be no such thing as distinction of property, form
of government, institution of law, or establishment of religion ; when there shall
be neither prostitution nor marriage, crime nor punishment, exchange nor
robbery ; when every man shall live under his own vine and fig-tree, and rise

a gentle being from his meal of roots to propagate around him his own unperverted feelings. Gentlemen, I see in you the harbinger of the glorious day—the John the Baptist of the genuine redemption of mankind. Proceed, then, in your frugivorous career—*macte virtute tui.*"

This speech was followed by enthusiastic acclamations, which astonished their quadruped neighbours. Several toasts were then drunk, and many appropriate songs sung. The President gave "A return to nature; or, success to vegetable regimen!" (drunk three times three). Song, "Peas, beans, and cabbage." "The cultivation of grain, and may it quickly supersede pasturage!" was then given. Song, "I wish I was a brewer's horse." Mr. P. B. S. then gave "The memory of Nebuchadnezzar; and may all kings, like him, be speedily sent to graze with their brother brutes!" This toast excited much commotion, but was drunk at last without the adjunct, which it was deemed prudent to omit. Mr. B., of Bible celebrity, observed that, in supposing Nebuchadnezzar to have fed on grass, we are not borne out by the Hebrew text. This he would prove in his intended translation of the Bible. He also took occasion to declare his opinion that the longevity of mankind before the flood was owing to their feeding on vegetables—not on raw meat, as had been erroneously supposed. But these were points, he trusted, would be fully cleared up in his *Treatise on Antediluvian Cherubim.*" Mr. T., the Platonist, proposed a toast, "The reign of Saturn, and speedy restoration of the heathen gods," which, however, was not drunk, as it appeared to interfere with religious toleration. One of the members was now commencing a spirited eulogium upon the pleasures which man must enjoy in a state of nature, when a most overwhelming shower of rain put a stop to his oratory, and proved a sad argument against his doctrine, for the party instantly dispersed to shelter themselves in the best way they could against such natural effects.

This squib may be fittingly supplemented by a quotation from an entertaining volume, the *Personal and Literary Memorials* of Henry Best. In that very miscellaneous collection there is an essay referring to the vegetarianism of Shelley, which we reproduce:

Why should not this

> Spare food, that oft with gods doth diet—

this abstinence from the flesh of animals and vinous spirit, be recommended to wise and good men without reference to penitential mortification? Will anyone forfeit any real happiness by renouncing that agitation of mind excited by the hope of gain or the fear of loss in gaining? Continence in the unmarried, fidelity to a wedded partner, are recognised as moral duties by all who have not set morality at defiance. The advantages to be derived from adherence to the rule of St. Clair, as a plan of wise and virtuous life, may be enjoyed by those who would be indisposed to embrace it, even though not *sub peccato* as a religious observance.

So much has been written—and well written—on the subject of abstinence from animal food, that I spare my reader the fatigue of travelling again over a track where no point of view can be novel to him. I would willingly, however, repress all extravagance on this topic, which in truth has somewhat discredited the herbivorous cause. Dr. Cheyne, for example, says that it was permitted to man to eat flesh after the Deluge, with the design and purpose of shortening human life. This supposition of *malice prepense* on the part of the Almighty is somewhat irreverent; for, although the contraction of the span of our existence was intended, and has been effected, it would be indecorous to imagine that to trick and seduce us to our own destruction by a new and savoury but unwholesome aliment, would be a mean employed to that end.

Ritson, an accomplished scholar and fellow-labourer with the commentators on "our immortal bard," in dissuading us from the slaughter of animals for food, takes occasion to contemplate a royal stag-hunt, and apostrophizes the chief personage of the scene in the rude and disrespectful words, *Siste carnifex!* Now, as the enjoyment of the pleasures of the chase was the object, and not the venison, which might have been procured with less trouble, the abusive term is unfitly applied. Let us be just, and avoid all railing, which may indeed be misinterpreted. Gibbon says in the true spirit and manner of a sensualist, "The paradise of Mahomet excited the indignation, perhaps the envy, of the monks." Let the herbivorous refrain from jactance and reproach that may afford to the flesh-eaters an occasion of retorting, "You only regret that you cannot do as we do."

Nature, by exhibiting to us a panorama of mutual carnage—of beasts of prey, of birds that devour insects, and of fishes that swallow fishes—seems to indicate that man, in feeding on his fellow-animals, does not contravene her laws. The scruples of the believer in the religion of nature, if he feels scruples, may thus be appeased; and Genesis ix. 3 is warrant to those who admit its authority. I quoted this passage to a patient—perhaps he might be called a disciple—of Dr. Lamb, who denied that it gave leave to take away the life of any animal, saying that the following two verses had the force of restricting the permission to the eating flesh of animals that should die of themselves—a permission of which no *gourmand* would avail himself unless of the true pheasant taint. I know not if Dr. Lamb holds the doctrine of the unlawfulness of slaying or shedding the blood of animals. The world is much indebted to him and to his skill and science as a physician; and he has done wonders in persuading so many persons to refrain from the mode of sustaining the human frame, which even in its decent moderate exercise approaches to intemperance, and enters the confines of sensuality. Dr. Lamb, it is known, forbids alcohol, and regards fish as a food even more pernicious to health than the flesh of beasts and birds. He prescribes, too, that the water which we drink should be cleared of its impurities by distillation. May success continue to attend him!—his example and practice, medical and philosophical—encourage hope; at least forbid despair.

Shelley, a poet of greater power of imagination than any that ever rolled the finely frenzied eye, gives, in his notes on "Prometheus Unbound," an animated and forcible dissertation on vegetable diet, together with an extract from Mr. Newton's treatise on that subject. It is amusing with what zest—with what symptoms of a good appetite—Shelley gives a bill of fare of his dinner and dessert. The carnivorous, when told that such a one eats neither flesh nor fish, stare with a roast-beef expression of countenance and cry, "What, then, does he eat?" Shelley's copious list shows that, even in this unfavourable climate, Mother Earth produces what is sufficient to keep alive her rational sons without compelling them to devour all that walk, or fly, or swim on her surface. In point of fact, the poor, who have most need to repair the waste of labour, can procure but very little of that aliment which the rich, the lazy, the luxurious, regard as indispensable to the support of bodies exhausted only by the difficulties of digestion.

For myself, let me be endured in shortly stating that having often passed from the use of one sort of food to the other, I may be considered as having made frequent experiments in this affair, all of them corroborative of the opinion that animal food and alcohol are pernicious, and abstinence from them favourable to our physical, intellectual and moral well-being. I refer to the above-cited authors and to that host of other names that have treated this matter. I am sorry not to be able to quote my old friend Ludovico Cornaro, as he refused no sort of viand not decidedly unwholesome; he only limited himself to twelve ounces of solid and fourteen ounces of liquid *per diem.* This plan he adopted at the age of 40, and in a very infirm state of health; and at the age of 85, he says that he is assured by his own feelings and experience that he shall live to be more than a hundred; and that if he had originally had a good *complexion* he should doubtless attain to 120 years. This use of the word "complexion" is a surprise; etymologically, however, there is no reason why it should not signify the same as *constitution,* since the human frame is *folded together* as well as *built up.*

The fathers of the desert attained to the age of six score on a weight of food that sufficed to Cornaro, but of unleavened bread or biscuit only; and their only drink was the pure element. It is therefore just possible that the noble Venetian lost ten or fifteen years of his life by indulging in flesh and wine. However this be, he began his plan, he says, induced by the observation that, when he consulted physicians, they all aimed at his cure by subtraction, or putting him on short allowance; and he conceived that the art to make men well might also be the art to keep them so. His several treatises form a most novel, singular and astonishing book, the lecture of which is highly gratifying by the sympathy it excites in the happiness of this animated delightful old man.

His remarks on the medical practice of his time may lead us to observe that although the physicians of our day prescribe moderation only in food, and not such a strict unpalatable limitation, yet they replace this milder method by more violent equivalents—disease and the seeds of disease; the first an effort of nature to repel noxious superfluity; second, the deposits of that superfluity are to be removed by subtraction. An amiable man, a physician of high repute, is made to confess that the art of healing can urge its influence no further:

> When patients sick to me apply,
> I physicks, bleeds, and sweats 'em:
> If after that they choose to die,
> What's that to me?
> I. LETTSOM.

Cornaro was visited by many persons with interest and admiration, but he made no converts. Some, he says, even wept with pleasure at beholding the blessedness that temperance had assured to him; his perfect enjoyment of all his senses and faculties; his voice, for he says, " My singing is beautiful "—the simplicity of the old man is not the least amusing of his good qualities—his equal humour; his placid explanation of death, which he felt assured could not, unless by some violent accident, be sudden or immediate. Many promised to follow his example, but, weak of purpose, they yielded to the carnal or carnivorous appetite, and preferred the disease to the remedy.

Dr. Lamb, it seems, has been more fortunate, having induced, it is said, between three and four score persons to eat only of what has not had life, and to drink only distilled water. This success, let it be repeated, forbids despair. Apparently it must be the easiest thing in the world to form a sect. A man has only in the course of twelve months to convince one person of the truth or benefit of a system ; these two in the second year draw over two more ; in the third year, these four enlist four additional recruits ; and according to this geometrical ratio, at the end of ten years 1,024 sectarians are engaged ; in the following ten years the thousand, without reckoning the odd numbers, become 1,000,000, and it will not require ten years more to convert the whole globe. It will be perceived that it is not for nothing that a calculation has been given of the result of doubling the number of grains of wheat at each square of the chess-board. If five years be substituted for one year as the period in which a duplication can be formed of the retainers of a theory, then a century and a half, instead of thirty years, must witness its progress to complete and final triumph in universal adoption.

The utter improbability of success at all proportioned to this extravagant calculation need not deter Dr. Lamb, or any other wise and benevolent man, from doing all the good that may be permitted by the unwillingness of mankind to admit truth or renounce pleasure. Pleasure is always seductive, truth is not always profitable.

A caution shall be added for the use of those few who may adopt a vegetable diet : it is this, not to deem it necessary to make up by quantity for the supposed want of nutritive qualities in their food. Farinaceous vegetables contain more *gluten*, more nourishment in proportion to their weight and volume, than roast-beef itself. If the stomach is sensible of the load committed to it, the load has been too great. By attending to this symptom all may avoid excess, and the pains and perils of digestion.

About a fortnight after I had settled at Florence, in my apartment in the Palazzo Nicolini, in the beginning of July, 1822, at the approach of the hour of retiring to rest, I was detained by the appearance of a coming-on thunderstorm— a sight I always love to witness. I walked about my great hall and along the gallery ; seven large mullioned windows permitted me to enjoy the almost unin-tercepted flashes of lightning, while the spacious rooms re-echoed the thunder. The storm increased in violence, the lightning was no longer forked and darting, but an ἀμφιλαφής ἐμαρμός, almost continuous, that wrapped in flame the statue and orange-trees of the garden, and cast a flashing glare on the bust and armorial shield of the family Nicolini, and on one female figure in marble, larger than life, that stood at the upper end of the gallery. I went to the other side of the apart-ment ; the dome of the Cathedral was illuminated, but it was too near, and the view was much too bounded for it to be picturesque. I returned to the gallery to have a larger *plage cœli*. Opposite to the furthest window of the hall Antoine had set up a high and wide screen to partition off for himself a sort of butler's pantry ; the window not being duly fastened burst open ; the screen fell flat on the floor, and when this loud resounding was past, the wind howled fearfully through the hall. So dreadful was the lightning that I dared not draw nigh to shut the window. I spent more than an hour in the delight of this terrible excite-ment.

On that night, on the coast, at forty miles distance, Percy Bysshe Shelley was shipwrecked. What horrors were endured by the friends who knew of his danger !

What thoughts have since crossed into my own mind! I knew him not, but I admire and pity him.

"But Shelley," say the bigots, who receive their faith from a tyrant and a tigress, "Shelley was an atheist!" True : they who have the boldness to set up altar against altar, to tear the seamless robe of Christ, to distrust His promised help, and to charge His house, the Church, with faithlessness and adultery—these men can be struck with horror at the atheism of Shelley and drive him from among them. Was his heart less warm, was his disinterestedness less sincere, was his consciousness less pure than theirs? A young, an ardent, an impetuous mind rejects control, refuses to submit to an authority which has itself spurned authority; he refuses to acquiesce as a mere formalist in dogmas of whose truth he is unconvinced; he rushes into error, but into error which his example, and that of many others, has proved may be allied with genius, may be compatible with benevolence, may be adorned by the observation of social duty. How is such a man to be reclaimed?

Shame to the self-applauding age and country to which he belonged—the attempt is made by violating, in his regard, the clearest laws, the most sacred right of nature! The Author of Being has established, by the course of His providence, that relation which the parents hold with those who receive from them their existence; and no truth of revealed religion is more clear than the voice which speaks to the heart of the father, impressing sentiments which no other can feel, imposing duties which no other can discharge, exciting gratitude which can be paid to no other, because by no other can it be claimed. Enough, the storm is hushed; let all but the genius of Shelley be silent!

Most of the names mentioned in the squib can be identified. There is John Frederick Newton, the author of the *Return to Nature;* Sir Richard Phillips, the well-known publisher; Joseph Ritson, the antiquary; James Pierrepoint Greaves, the philosophical ascetic; Thomas Taylor, the platonist; Dr. William Lambe, and Sir John Sinclair, the statistician; but who the Rev. P—— is, remains a mystery. The pamphlet by Shelley, to which reference is made, is now one of the rarest of his rarer works.

When *Queen Mab* was published in 1813, it contained several notes, and one of these was lengthy enough to form, with scarcely an alteration, a separate publication. Two copies only are now known to be in existence. One is in the British Museum, and the other belongs to Mr. H. Buxton Forman, our foremost authority on the bibliography of Shelley. The pamphlet was reprinted in its entirety as an article in the *Graham Magazine*, one of the publications in which Sylvester Graham promulgated his theories of the conduct of life. It was also placed as an appendix to Dr. Turnbull's *Manual on Health*, published at New York in 1835. Mr. Forman has included it in his great edition of Shelley, where it will be found at the opening of the second volume. In 1884, a new edition was printed for the Vegetarian Society, and has prefixed a notice, by Mr. H. S. Salt, then of Eton, and Mr. W. E. A. Axon, of Manchester. It seems most likely that Shelley became a vegetarian through his intimacy with the family of Newton, of whom he gives an enthusiastic account. After eight months' trial, he was constrained to bear his testimony; and the result was a pamphlet, of which we now reproduce the original title-page:

A

VINDICATION

OF

NATURAL DIET.

BEING ONE IN A SERIES OF NOTES TO QUEEN MAB
(A PHILOSOPHICAL POEM),

Ιαπετιονιδη, παντων περι μηδεα ειδωσ,
Χαιρεισ πυρ κλειψασ, και εμασ φρενασ ηπεροπευσασ ;
Σοιρ' αυτω μεγα πημα και ανέρμισιν εσσομενοισι.
Τοισδ'εγω αντι πυροσ έωσω κακον, ω κεν απαντεσ
Τερπωνται κατα θυμον, εον κακον αμφαγαπωντεσ.
          ΗΣΙΩΔ. Op. et Dies. 1, 54.

LONDON :
PRINTED FOR J. CALLOW, MEDICAL BOOKSELLER, CROWN COURT,
PRINCE'S STREET, SOHO,
BY SMITH & DAVY, QUEEN STREET, SEVEN DIALS.
1813.

PRICE ONE SHILLING AND SIXPENCE.

     It cannot be said that there is anything strikingly original in Shelley's defence of vegetarianism, though the tract is a very characteristic example of his prose style, and shows how deeply he felt upon this particular subject. He remained to the end of his life practically, if not systematically, vegetarian in his habits. Leigh Hunt has sketched his daily life at Marlow, in 1817 :—

" This was the round of his daily life. He was up early, breakfasted sparingly, wrote this *Revolt of Islam* all the morning ; went out in his boat, or in the woods, with some Greek author or the Bible in his hands ; came home to a dinner of vegetables (for he took neither meat nor wine) ; visited, if necessary, the sick and fatherless, whom others gave Bibles to and no help ; wrote or studied again, or read to his wife and friends the whole evening ; took a crust of bread or a glass of whey for his supper, and went early to bed."

As might be expected in a man of Shelley's temperament, he views the question of diet from the humanitarian side, and the same feeling crops out in other of his writings. It was not with him a question of taste or of cookery, but a problem in whose right solution he saw the prophecy of a happy future for the human race. In impassioned language he has painted a vision of the world from which cruelty and bloodshed should be banished—a picture that may be placed side by side with the Hebrew prophet's vision of that Holy Mountain in which they shall not hurt nor destroy. With Shelley's dream of an ideal world we must conclude this sketch :

" My brethren, we are free ! The fruits are glowing
Beneath the stars, and the night-winds are flowing
O'er the ripe corn. The birds and beasts are dreaming.
　Never again may blood of bird or beast
　Stain with its venomous stream a human feast,
　To the pure skies in accusation steaming ;
　　Avenging poisons shall have ceased
　　　To feed disease and fear and madness ;
　　　The dwellers of the earth and air
　　Shall throng around our steps in gladness,
　　　Seeking their food or refuge there.
Our toil from thought all glorious forms shall cull,
To make this earth, our home, more beautiful ;
And Science, and her sister Poesy,
Shall clothe in light the fields and cities of the free !"

　　　　o　　　o　　　•　　　o　　　o

" Over the plain the throngs were scattered then
　In groups around the fires, which from the sea
Even to the gorge of the first mountain-glen
　Blazed wide and far. The banquet of the free
　Was spread beneath many a dark cypress-tree ;
Beneath whose spires which swayed in the red flame,
　Reclining as they ate, of liberty,
And hope, and justice, and Laone's name,
Earth's children did a woof of happy converse frame.

" Their feast was such as Earth, the general mother,
　Pours from her fairest bosom, when she smiles
In the embrace of Autumn. To each other,
　As when some parent fondly reconciles
　Her warring children, she their wrath beguiles
With her own sustenance ; they relenting weep :—
　Such was this festival, which, from their isles
And continents and winds and oceans deep,
All shapes might throng to share that fly or walk or creep."

These references to Shelley will have a special interest at this moment, when the formation of the Shelley Society is attracting fresh attention to everything connected with the life and writings of that fine genius. The first object of the Society will be the publication *in exact facsimile* of those original editions of Shelley's works which, from their excessive scarcity and consequent prohibitive prices, are practically unprocurable. In addition to these, the Society will issue reprints of early notices and criticisms upon Shelley, some of which are extremely rare, whilst others, being buried in old and forgotten periodical literature, are very difficult of access. The Society's Publications will also include Papers by those who have made Shelley's life, works, and opinions their special study : these, together with reprints of the more important of the later Essays and Reviews, will form a library of the literature of the subject, the advantages of which are self-evident. It is to be hoped it will meet with generous support, and may fairly be commended to the good wishes of the readers of *Book-Lore.*

CHINESE BOOKS AND BOOKMAKERS.

S a pendant to the curious particulars given by M. Jametel, we add some further details from the *North China Herald :*

"The Caliph Omar, in burning the Alexandrian Library, inflicted on posterity a loss that can never be repaired. The volumes contained in that library would naturally embrace many works, copies of which would never afterwards be found. Books that Cicero and Pliny read and mentioned in their writings are many of them hopelessly lost. But for Omar we should have had a good portion of these relics of ancient learning, and should then have been able to form to ourselves a more complete and accurate picture of the ancient world of the Greeks and Romans. In China the destruction of books by the order of the Emperor Ch'in Shih Huang placed modern scholars in a similar position. Many books were destroyed which have not since been recovered. A madman's freak deprived tens of thousands of the pleasure and instruction they might have found in reading books then put out of existence for ever. Yet many books remained. In the time of Liu Hsin, B.C. 9, there were found to be 33,090 sections or chapters of works. The Han dynasty encouraged literature, and restored books to their right place after the brief reign of a fanatical persecutor, who disliked all writings not devoted to divination, medicine, and agriculture. The persecution of literature was undertaken with the object of putting down political discussions, the teaching of history, and popular ballads. The fanatical book-burner hoped that all memories of past dynasties would die out with their chronicles. Is it wonderful that he himself is remembered only to be execrated? The glory of the Han dynasty shows the more brightly in proportion to the thickness of the shade of ignominy that covers his name.

"The encouragement of literature was carried on by the search for old books and the preparation of new copies of all works found. These were presented to the Emperor and preserved in his libraries. Liu Hsiang and his son Liu Hsin were employed as critical editors, and devoted many laborious years to this duty in the first century before Christ. The Han Emperors sympathized with the *literati*, and their popularity was chiefly based on that sympathy. The *literati* have always guided public opinion in China. Whoever controls the sentiment of the *literati* controls the people, and has the patriotism of the country on his side. The roughshod imperialism of the book-burner did not care for policy of this sort. He had his many legions and his supple officers, and was able to keep the peace, so he thought, without a popular policy. His youthful son after his death reaped the disastrous consequences of this unreasonable course. In proportion to the thoroughness of the burning, the scholars who sought for lost literature had so much the more work to do in searching in each department over the whole country for bamboo and wooden tablets, then so precious. But just when the work of the commission was done a time of revolution came. Wang Mang over-turned the dynasty, usurped Imperial power, and the 33,090 chapters were burnt in the ruins of the palaces of Chang An. The scholars had to begin their work afresh in the first century of the Christian era. The great historian Pan Ku was on the new commission. Each Governor was required to send copies of valuable books from his jurisdiction. Special officers were appointed to superintend the making of copies. Books were stored in golden book-cases and marble houses. Catalogues were made, and so it was that in Pan Ku's history it was possible to include in a particular section the titles of all books in the Emperor's possession. Peculiar care was taken to secure a correct copy of the classics by having them engraven on marble monuments in Loyang, the capital city. In the Tang dynasty, some centuries later, the classics were cut again on monumental stones, and set up in the old capital, which had again become the seat of government.

" When printing was invented, in the tenth century, a new field was opened for the encouragement of literature. The Emperor took the lead. He was seconded by the administrators of the provinces, each vying with the other in finding copies of old works to send to the Imperial library, and in engraving useful books for use in the province ruled by him. The printing of Ssŭchuan early became famous. Pien Liang, the capital, naturally took the lead in printing handsome editions of the classics, and all other useful books. The system then in vogue has continued till the present time. Each Governor or Viceroy exhibits his public spirit by promoting the study of the national literature. Learning is not left to the unaided influence of educational institutions, professors, authors and publishers, as in the West. The promotion of literature is considered in China to be a part of the duty of Government. It runs in parallel lines with the examina-tions for degrees. The Government takes care that the books shall be printed which are made the subject of examination in the halls for granting degrees. It is the duty as well as the pride and pleasure of the Viceroys to establish printing depôts in the provincial capitals for the publication of the classics and all useful literature. This is a part of the work of the Government, and the consequence is that printers as a class occupy a lower position in China than in Europe. The working capital is found by the Viceroys. The books are in the possession of the nation. Authors and publishers cannot grow rich by publishing. But rich men in the provinces imitate the Government in the publication of useful books, which appear in the form of libraries, twenty or fifty being printed in succession in uniform shape; and any profit from sales goes to the rich man. This system has its advantages and its disadvantages. The paternal system of Government to which Confucius affixed his *imprimatur* continues to exhibit itself in many forms, and the people have things done for them which they would neglect to do them-selves. But individual energy is kept in check by this system, and no encourage-ment is given to contemporary authorship, such as would pay publishers and authors large profits by its popularity. Hence popular authors do not exist."

IN MEMORIAM.

I.—EDWARD EDWARDS.

BIBLIOGRAPHY has to lament the loss, in the late Edward Edwards, of an earnest and accomplished scholar. Mr. Edwards was a native of London, where he was born in the year 1812. Very little is known of his early career, but his education was good, and he had an acquaintance with the German literature of scholarship that was somewhat rare in those days. He became an assistant in the British Museum, 7th February, 1839, and was employed in the compilation of the *New General Catalogue of the Printed Books*, at an allowance of 8s. 9d. per day for each day actually employed in the work. Mr. Edwards had shown a masterly grasp of the problems of library economy in a printed letter which he addressed in 1836 to Mr. B. Hawes, M.P., and containing "Remarks on the Minutes of Evidence before the Select Committee of 1835." In this, as in his evidence in January, 1836, he asks for greater accessibility for readers, a regular supply of books, so that the institution might not continue to show lamentable gaps in certain periods and classes of literature, a reformation in the state of the catalogues, and a better departmental organization. The great deficiencies of the library in those days as regards foreign literature is insisted upon with emphasis. This tract, with some additions, he reprinted in 1839, about a fortnight before he entered the service of the British Museum.

The catalogue upon which he was employed was the project of Panizzi, whose chief colleagues in this part of his work were Mr. Edwards, Mr. Thomas Watts, Mr. Winter Jones, and Mr. J. Humphreys Parry, afterwards well-known as Serjeant Parry. As Panizzi is credited with a large amount of the autocratic spirit, it is interesting to find that Edwards always bore testimony to the consideration he gave to their opinions when they chanced to diverge from his own. The gentlemen we have named formed the Committee which framed the rules for cataloguing, and Panizzi put matters of dispute to the vote, and loyally bound himself by the votes of the majority when they decided against him. Mr. Edwards was an important witness before each of the Select Committees which, between 1836 and 1850, examined into the management of the national library.

The bent of Mr. Edwards' early studies was not entirely bibliographical. He had some reputation as a numismatist, and in 1837 he edited a handsome folio volume devoted to the "Napoleon Medals," of which representations were given by the process of Achille Colas. This appeared in the spring, and in autumn he printed, for private circulation, *A Descriptive Catalogue of the Medals Struck in France and its Dependencies,* 1789-1830. In this he notes the deficiencies in the series then at the British Museum. His next work was a treatise on *The Administrative Economy of the Fine Arts in England,* which appeared in 1840, when the question of the extent to which the State should interfere or can usefully interfere for the promotion of education and for the encouragement of the fine arts was still a matter upon which there existed great diversity of opinion. Mr. Edwards was a man of popular instincts and sympathies, and took a warm interest in educational matters. He was struck by the poverty of England in regard to public libraries, and in order to test the matter thoroughly he entered upon an elaborate statistical investigation of the subject. He contributed to the *British Quarterly Review* in 1847 a paper on Libraries in London and Paris; he read a paper before the Statistical Society in 1848, and in the same year printed for private circulation, *Remarks upon the Paucity of Libraries Freely Open to the Public in the British Empire.* When Mr. William Ewart secured the appointment of a Select Committee on Public Libraries in 1849, Mr. Edwards was the first and principal witness examined. When it was decided to establish a public library in Manchester, Mr. Edwards was engaged as its first librarian. In that capacity he, in conjunction with the late Mr. James Crossley, prepared the lists and purchased the books which formed the basis of the present city library. There can be no doubt that the character of the collection owes very much to his enlightened views and scholarly tastes. When in Manchester he continued his literary investigations, and in 1855 published a contribution to the local history of the city, dealing, under the title of *Manchester Worthies and their Foundations,* with the endowments of Thomas La Warre, Hugh Oldham, Humphrey Chetham, William Hulme, and John Owens. Mr. Edwards was a man of decided views and quick temper. Difficulties arose which after considerable discussion led to his resignation in 1858 of the position of Chief Librarian. After a brief experience as partner in a bookselling firm, he devoted himself entirely to literature and biography. Before his removal from Manchester there appeared what must be regarded as his most important work, *The Memoirs of Libraries,* published in two large volumes, which it may be noted as a curious circumstance were printed at Leipsic. This book, with all its admitted defects, remains the most considerable contribution that has been made by any Englishman to *Bibliothekwissenschaft.* In 1854 he published a volume of *Chapters of the Biographical History of the French Academy.* In the appendix to this he describes the monastic chronicle entitled *Liber de Hyda,* which he discovered whilst arranging the library of the Earl of Macclesfield. This chronicle he edited (in 1866) for the Rolls Series. The history of management of libraries always had the first claim upon his attention, and in 1864 he issued *Libraries and Founders of Libraries,* which contains the result of much literary and archæological research. He next turned his attention to one of his favourite heroes, and on *The Life of Sir Walter Ralegh,* published in 1868, expended an enormous amount of labour. It includes the first collection ever made of Ralegh's letters, and is based upon patient study of contemporary documents preserved in private, as well as public collections. As a mere piece of by-play he compiled a volume on *Exmouth and its Neighbourhood, Ancient and Modern*, which appeared, but without his name, also in 1869. In the following year he issued *Free Town Libraries, their Formation, Management and History; in Britain, France, Germany, and America*. He made another contribution to literary history in his *Lives of the Founders of the British Museum*, a portly volume published in 1870.

In recent years Mr. Edwards lived in great retirement, from which the kindly efforts that were made failed to draw him. Even the meeting of the Library Association at Oxford did not bring him from this seclusion, although he was then engaged upon some work for the Bodleian Library and Queen's College. He was much gratified by his election in 1882 as honorary member of this Association. His failing health and slender resources gave anxiety to his friends, and the Provost and Fellows of Queen's College, by a memorial under their common seal, petitioned Lord Beaconsfield on his behalf for a pension.

This document states so carefully the literary claims of Mr. Edwards, that it may be well to reproduce the essential parts of it:

" We, the Provost and Scholars of the Queen's College, in the University of Oxford, wish to bring before your notice the name of Edward Edwards, Esquire, formerly an assistant in the Department of Printed Books in the British Museum, afterwards Principal Librarian of the Free Libraries of the City of Manchester, and lately employed in cataloguing the library of Queen's College. We desire to pray that her Majesty will be graciously pleased to confer upon Mr. Edwards the honour of a pension in recognition of services rendered by him to literature; and we would ask you to consider his claims in the hope that you may think it well to advise her Majesty to grant this petition. Mr. Edwards' literary work has been chiefly in the departments of bibliography and of history. He has made a special study of the history and economy of libraries. Upon the history of libraries his *Memoirs of Libraries* (published in 1859) is, as we believe, the standard English authority; the discussion of practical library arrangements which follows the historical part of the book is, for the most part, the only English treatise upon its subject, and his treatment of systems of cataloguing and classification has an independent value besides its value as the summing up of long discussions. He has also dealt with this last subject in his *Comparative Table of Schemes for the Classification of Human Knowledge*, and *Comparative Table of the Principal Schemes for the Classification of Libraries, with a Special Report on a Classed Catalogue for the Manchester Free Library* (1855). When an assistant in the British Museum, he spent much labour in collecting statistics concerning Public Free Libraries in Europe. In April, 1849, he was examined before a Select Committee of the House of Commons appointed to consider the question of Public Libraries, and his evidence and tables, and other statements prepared by him, make up a considerable part of the volume of Report and Minutes published by that Committee. He has contributed further to the knowledge of this subject by his *Notes upon the Public Libraries of the United States of North America* (1856), containing minute historical and statistical details, and *History of Free Libraries at Home and Abroad* (1869) ; with the historical and biographical side of his subject he has dealt in *Libraries, and Founders of Libraries,* and *Lives of Founders and Benefactors of the British Museum* (1870.)   To English history Mr. Edwards has done good service by his *Life of Sir Walter Ralegh, together with his Letters, now for the first time Collected*—in which work a history of Ralegh was, for the first time, based upon a careful comparison of the original documents.   This book is described to us by the Regius Professor of Modern History in this University as a monument of patient and persevering research, marked by a sound historical discrimination.   Mr. Edwards' chief independent historical works besides this, are *Chapters in the History of the French Academy,* and some biographical articles in the Eighth Edition of the *Encyclopædia Britannica.*   But he has edited, under the direction of the Master of the Rolls, *Liber Monasterii de Hyda,* supplying indices, an introduction, and other illustrative appliances.   Mr. Edwards' part of this work the Regius Professor speaks of as thoroughly good, being accurate and scholar-like.   Mr. Edwards has also given aid to the student of history by his *Synoptical Tables of the Records of the Realm, with an Historical Preface;* and by his editions of *The Great Seals of England,* and *The Napoleon Medals* (1837), and his *Descriptive Catalogue of a Series of French Medals in the Cabinet of the British Museum* (1838).   In literary discussions of his day he has taken part by publishing various essays, *Remarks on the Ministerial Plan of a Central University Examining Board* (1836), *The Economy of the Fine Arts in England* (1840), *Letter on the Present State of the Education Question* (1846).   We believe Mr. Edwards, after many years of literary labour, to have slight permanent sources of income, or none, but to be dependent upon such temporary engagements as that which he accepted from this College in 1870, and is now terminating.   As his connection with them has been temporary, and formed for a definite purpose only, the members of this College—while sensible of the valuable services they have received from him—are not likely to devote any part of the College revenues hereafter to the assistance of Mr. Edwards.   With the University he has had no connection.   Mr. Edwards was born in 1812.   His health is, we fear, precarious, and he has long suffered from deafness.   He is married, but has no children.   Under these circumstances we venture to hope that after considering the services rendered to the cause of learning by him, you will be able to advise her Majesty to confer upon Mr. Edwards a pension as a mark of her Royal favour."

This application was also backed up by Alderman Curtis, the Mayor of Manchester, and by Sir Thomas Baker, Chairman of the Free Libraries Committee.   The memorial was not immediately successful; but in 1883, on the recommendation of Mr. Gladstone, the Queen granted a Civil List pension of £80 to Mr. Edwards.   In these later years Mr. Edwards was resident at Niton, Isle of Wight, and was devoting himself to the preparation of a new edition of his *Memoirs of Libraries.*   The greater part of this was written, and some of it was in type, early last year, but it was the author's desire in the revision to bring the data down to the midsummer of 1885.   He spoke with great confidence of having his book out by the October of last year; but in this a sanguine disposition led him to underestimate the difficulties in the way.   We are glad to learn that, possibly by some prophetic instinct, Mr. Edwards had arranged for the revision of the proofs by a competent friend.

The end came suddenly and peacefully. On the Sunday morning of February 7th, Mr. Edwards was found dead in his bed at St. Catherine's Lodge, Niton, Isle of Wight.

Below we give a list of his writings, which, if not quite exhaustive, probably does not omit anything of great importance :

The Napoleon Medals: A Complete Series of the Medals struck in France, Italy, Great Britain, and Germany, from the Commencement of the Empire in 1804 to the Restoration in 1815, engraved by the process of Achilles Collas, with Historical and Biographical Notices. Edited by Edward Edwards. London, 1837, fol., pp. x-167 ; 40 plates.

A Brief Descriptive Catalogue of the Medals struck in France and its Dependencies between the Years 1789 and 1830, contained in the Cabinet of the British Museum, with the deficiencies noted. By the Editor of "The Napoleon Medals." London, 1837 [not printed for sale], 8vo., not paged.

Remarks on the "Minutes of Evidence" taken before the Select Committee on the British Museum, with an Appendix containing heads of inquiry respecting the improvement of the Museum, etc., etc. By Edward Edwards, Esq. Second edition, with a Postscript on the results of the inquiry. London : not printed for sale [1839], 8vo. [First edition, 1836.]

The Administrative Economy of the Fine Arts in England. By Edward Edwards, of the British Museum. London, 1840, 8vo., pp. 376.

Public Libraries in England and Paris. Reprinted from No. XI. of the "British Quarterly Review." London, 1847, 8vo., pp. 48.

Statistical View of the Principal Public Libraries of Europe and America. By Edward Edwards, Esq., of the British Museum. Third edition, corrected, with additional tables and illustrative plans. London, 1849, fol., pp. vi-48, [1st and 2nd editions published in 1848.]

Remarks on the Paucity of Libraries freely Open to the Public in the British Empire ; together with a Succinct Statistical View of the Existing Provision of Public Libraries in the several States of Europe. . . . By Edward Edwards, Esq., of the British Museum. Second edition, enlarged. London : for private circulation. 1849, 8vo., pp. 38.

Three Reports on the Origin, Formation, and First Year's Working of the Manchester Free Library ; with an Introduction on the results and defects of the Public Libraries Act of 1850. By Edward Edwards, Esq., Manchester : Cave and Sever. 1853, 8vo., pp. xiv-48.

Questions and Answers relating to the Educational Condition of those Persons whose taste for Literature and disposition to Self-Improvement has been sufficiently strong to lead them to make use of the Manchester Free Public

Library; and to the Number of Persons who frequent that Institution. [Signed] Edward Edwards, Principal Librarian. Manchester, March 1st, 1853.

Manchester Worthies and their Foundations; or, Six Chapters of Local History; with an Epilogue, by way of moral. By Edward Edwards. Manchester: J. Galt and Co. 1855, 8vo., pp. 88.

Special Report on the Plan, Preparation, and Printing of a Classed Catalogue of the Reference Department of the Manchester Free Library. By Edward Edwards. August, 1855. Manchester: Cave and Sever. 1855, 8vo., pp. 22.

Manchester Free Libraries: A Letter to Sir John Potter, M.P. . . . accompanying the re-circulation of a Special Report on the Plan, Preparation, and Printing of a Classed Catalogue of the Reference Department. Manchester: Cave and Sever. 1857, 8vo., pp. 19.

Trübner's Bibliographical Guide to American Literature. Compiled and edited by Nicholas Trübner. London: Trübner and Co., 1859, 8vo. Contains an Account of the Public Libraries of the United States, by Edward Edwards.

Memoirs of Libraries: including a Handbook of Library Economy. By Edward Edwards. London [Leipsic printed]: Trübner and Co., 1859, 8vo., 2 vols.

Notes on the Results of the "Libraries Acts" of 1850 and 1855. By Edward Edwards. (Transactions of the National Association for the Promotion of Social Science, 1860.) Pp. 855 and 885.

Libraries and Founders of Libraries. By Edward Edwards. London: Trübner and Co., 1864, 8vo., pp. xix-507.

Chapters of the Biographical History of the French Academy. With an appendix, relating to the unpublished Monastic Chronicle entitled "Liber de Hyda." By Edward Edwards. London, 1864, 8vo., pp. iv-176.

Synoptical Tables of the Records of the Realm. With an Historical Preface. By Edward Edwards. London, 1865, fol., pp. xxviii-44.

Liber Monasterii de Hyda; comprising a Chronicle of the Affairs of England, from the Settlement of the Saxons to the Reign of King Cnut; and a Chartulary of the Abbey of Hyde, in Hampshire, A.D. 455-1023. Edited by Edward Edwards, Esq. London, 1866, 8vo., pp. cxiv-468. Rolls Series.

The Life of Sir Walter Ralegh. Based on contemporary documents preserved in the Rolls House, the Privy Council Office, Hatfield House, the British Museum, and other manuscript repositories, British and Foreign. Together with his letters, now first collected. By Edward Edwards. Macmillan and Co., 1868, 8vo., 2 vols.

Exmouth and its Neighbourhood, Ancient and Modern. Being Notices Historical,

Biographical, and Descriptive, of a Corner of South Devon. Exmouth, 1868, 8vo., pp. viii-362.

Free Town Libraries: their Formation, Management, and History, in Britain, France, Germany, and America. Together with brief notices of Book-Collectors, and of the respective places of deposit of their surviving collections. By Edward Edwards. London: Trübner and Co., 1869, 8vo., pp. xiv-371-[262].

Lives of the Founders of the British Museum; with Notices of its Chief Augmentors and other Benefactors, 1570-1870. By Edward Edwards. London: Trübner and Co., 1870, 8vo., pp. x-780.

A Handbook to the Literature of General Biography. By Edward Edwards and the Rev. Charles Hole, B.A. Part I. Ventnor: G. H. Brittain, 250 copies printed; 1885, 8vo., pp. 56. 32.

Mr. Edwards, it has been remarked, was not a man who made a large figure in the eye of the public, and his writings were not of the popular kind; but they were highly appreciated by the specialists to whom they were addressed. He not only aided in the needed reformation of the British Museum, but to his persistent and intelligent advocacy the nation owes in a great measure the establishment of the modern free libraries under civic control. These institutions came before the era of compulsory education; and it may well be that in the future, with the general spread of elementary instruction, they will have even more importance than they have had in the past, as instruments by which the best that has been said on any topic is made accessible to all.

WILLIAM E. A. AXON.

II.—HENRY BRADSHAW.

IT fell to the lot of the present writer to be one of several guests invited by the late Mr. Henry Bradshaw to occupy rooms at King's College, Cambridge, during the Conference of the Library Association in September, 1882. There were too many guests, and the time was too crowded with the business of the Conference, to afford much opportunity for intimate communion between Mr. Bradshaw and the librarians and other friends who enjoyed his hospitality; but surely no man ever so speedily made himself loved as he did in those few short days. There was no mistaking his open-heartedness, his unaffected pleasure in meeting the members of the Association. Everyone was at his ease at once, and rejoiced at the evident delight which the President was taking in his duties. He seemed, too, to have an intuitive knowledge of each one's predilections or studies, and he found time for a cheery chat with even the shyest of us. His presence at the head of the breakfast-table or at dinner in Hall gave an additional grace to the meal. Then his evident and justifiable pride in the splendid library under his charge was delightful; and the manner in which he conducted the meetings, both public and private, of the Association was admirable. Yet there was apparent an exceeding modesty in the man, and a desire to receive what was good to be learned from others. When the members separated, there were many who felt they were parting from an old friend, and not the acquaintance of a week, and all looked forward to meeting again at future annual conferences.

To these guests the news of his unexpected death gave a painful shock, hardly less severe than that felt by his more intimate friends. Only the truest grief could call forth such tributes as have found expression in the various obituary notices which have appeared. Take for example the following, from the pen of an intimate friend, which was published in a Cambridge paper:

"In the death of Mr. Bradshaw, his College, the University, and the world of science have suffered an irreparable loss; but in the minds of his friends, the many who knew him and loved him, this feeling will be, for the present at least, overpowered by the sense of the personal blow which they have sustained. It is the man and the friend, the judicious counsellor, the sympathetic listener, the unselfish worker for others, ever ready to place his time and the stores of his knowledge, as well as his judgment and experience, at the disposal of those who applied to him, whom most of us will regret more even than the world will regret the scholar, so much of whose learning has, alas! perished with him. To old and young, graduate and undergraduate, Englishman and foreigner, he ever extended the same ready hand of sympathy and aid. There is hardly a student in the fields of learning which he made peculiarly his own who has not at some time or other come to him for guidance, and found more than he asked, or could have hoped to find; but his heart warmed to genuine workers in any field, and men of learning, whatever was their pursuit, recognised in him a comrade. Nor is it only such men who will have cause to regret him. A man of strong feelings, capable both of warm attachments and hearty dislikes, he had the faculty of binding to him most of those with whom he came in contact with the bonds of an affection such as it is given to few men to arouse. Many men have been more widely known, many could boast of a longer list of acquaintances; but there are few who have had more real friends, few over whose grave will be shed more genuine tears."

Henry Bradshaw, who died peaceably in his rooms at King's College, Cambridge, on February 12th, is said to have come from Quaker ancestors. He was born about 1832, and was educated at Eton and King's College. He took his B.A. degree in 1854, and proceeded M.A. three years later. His official connection with the University Library began in 1856, when he was appointed assistant-librarian under Mr. J. Power. In 1859 he took the superintendence of the Manuscript Department, and in 1867 he succeeded the Rev. J. E. B. Mayor as University Librarian, by the unanimous choice of the electors to that office. He was one of the Senior Fellows of his College, having gained his fellowship in 1856. In 1882 he filled the office of President of the Library Association of the United

Kingdom, and, as has already been stated, conducted the meetings of the Conference at Cambridge in that year.

The articles which have been given in the *Athenæum* of February 20th, the
Academy of February 20th and 27th, and *Nature* for February 18th, afford
materials for an estimate of Mr. Bradshaw's place both in his University and in
the library world; and we cannot do better than refer our readers to those
notices. From them it will be seen how invigorating was his influence on successive generations of Cambridge men, and what great weight his opinions had
on the course of University and College politics. His sympathies were at once
broad and deep, his views being "widened by the very variousness of men's
characters;" and all reasonable development or healthy change in the University
or elsewhere received from him due recognition and encouragement.

In his own special office as librarian, he set a high ideal before himself, and
an admirable example to others. A librarian's primary duty was, he would say,
" in the widest sense to save the time of those who sought his services." " He
should know so much of the contents of manuscripts and books that he can
recognise what will help others in their researches; he has not to study for
himself." He laid wide plans for the improvement of the University Library,
both in its regulations and its catalogues. He acquired wonderful stores of
knowledge in his retentive memory, and opened those stores freely to all who
chose to make use of them. He had a method of his own in collating and
cataloguing incunabula and manuscripts—a method which is described by Mr.
Hessels in the *Academy*, and worked out in some of his own pamphlets.

The titles of his published writings will show some of the veins of bibliographical research in which he worked.

The following is a list of the papers he contributed to the Cambridge
Antiquarian Society, and are printed in their *Antiquarian Communications :*

On the Recovery of the long-lost Waldensian Manuscripts. 1862.
Two [Early] Lists of Books in the University Library. 1862.
An Early University Statute concerning Hostels. 1863.
On two hitherto unknown Poems by John Barbour, author of the " Brus." 1866.
A View of the State of the University in Queen Anne's Reign. 1866.
On the Earliest English Engravings of the Indulgence known as the " Image of
Pity." 1867.
An Inventory of the Staff in the College Chambers (King's College), 1598.
1868.
On the Engraved Device used by Nicolaus Gotz, of Sletzstat, the Cologne
Printer, in 1474. 1870.
Note on a Book printed at Cologne by Gotz in 1477.
On Two Engravings on Copper by G. M., a Wandering Flemish Artist of the
XV.-XVIth century. 1870.

On Three Engravings on Copper fastened into the Cambridge Copy of the
Utrecht Breviary of 1514.

On the Engravings fastened into the Lambeth Copy of the Salisbury Primer, or
Horæ, printed by Wynkyn de Worde about 1494.

On the Oldest Written Remains of the Welsh Language. 1871.

On the Collection of Portraits belonging to the University before the Civil War.
1872.

Notes of the Episcopal Visitation of the Archdeaconry of Ely in 1685. 1875.

On the A B C as an Authorised School-book in the Sixteenth century. 1875.

Note on the Various Spellings of the Name of St. Erasmus in the Trinity Parish
Accounts. 1879.

The following are the titles of a series of octavo pamphlets, which he called
" Memoranda :"

1. The Printer of the Historia S. Albani. 1868.

2. A Classified Index of the Fifteenth Century Books in the Collection of
M. J. de Meyer, which were sold at Ghent in November, 1869. 1870.

3. List of the Founts of Type and Woodcut Devices used by Printers in Holland
in the Fifteenth Century. 1871.

4. The Skeleton of Chaucer's Canterbury Tales : an Attempt to Distinguish the
Several Fragments of the Work as left by the Author. 1868 (not published
till 1871).

5. Notice of a Fragment of the Fifteen Oes and other Prayers Printed at
Westminster by W. Caxton, about 1490-91, preserved in the Library of the
Baptist College, Bristol. 1877.

6. The University Library. Papers contributed to the *Cambridge University
Gazette*, 1869. Published 1881.

7. Address at the Opening of the Fifth Annual Meeting of the Library
Association of the United Kingdom, Cambridge, Sept. 5, 1882. With an
Appendix. 1882.

The Appendix to this admirable address contains :

I. Some Account of the Organization of the Cambridge University
Library.

II. Notes on Local Libraries considered as Museums of Local Authorship and Printing.

III. A Word on Size-Notation as distinguished from Form-Notation.

These papers are included also in the Transactions of the Library
Association.

8. The Early Collections of Canons, commonly known as the Hibernensis. A
Letter addressed to Dr. F. W. H. Wasserschleben, Privy Councillor, Professor of Law in the University of Giessen. 1885.

The above include nearly all that he published himself; but many of the results of his studies will be found embodied in the works of other scholars, to whom he communicated them without stint.

Two subjects to which he had devoted some attention in recent years were Irish bibliography and the history of bookbinding. On the former, he read a valuable paper at the Dublin Meeting of the Library Association in 1884. Concerning binding, he must have left many interesting notes. He spared no trouble in prosecuting his researches. In September, 1884, he journeyed as far as Manchester to see a lot of books, which promised well. Writing afterwards, he said :

"We had a very satisfactory day's exploration at Mr. Cornish's. The books are, as you say, not in good condition, but my friend and I were especially interested in early English bindings, and it is very seldom indeed that you can see so many specimens together. One can *learn* from them when in poor condition, as well as when fresh."

Much more than he ever published is left in manuscript; and we cordially echo the hope which has been expressed, that as many of his writings as may be available for publication should be given to the world without delay.

C. W. SUTTON.

III.—HENRY STEVENS, OF VERMONT.

Death has been making a raid on the bibliographers, and has carried off at one fell swoop three of the best-known workers in that field. Mr. Edward Edwards, the pioneer of the Free Library movement; Mr. Henry Bradshaw, the learned and lovable librarian of the University of Cambridge; and Mr. Henry Stevens, the American bibliographer, have all recently passed away.

Henry Stevens, of Vermont, as he delighted to style himself, though a lover of his country to the core, was not of the type usually regarded as American. His somewhat bulky frame, his large head, full face, and large warm heart, gave one more the impression of the best stamp of middle-class Englishmen than anything else. He also spoke the English language as it is known to us, and was wont to warn his friends against any countryman of his who spoke of himself as an *Amurican.* Mr. Stevens was full of humour, and abounded in anecdote. His Noviomagian Programmes are delightfully redolent of quip and crank. The one for 1879 explains that "Noviomagus in Britain is the only old Roman Station founded by Cæsar somewhere between London and the sea, whose site is not now generally known. It never was a rotten borough, though for some centuries buried in forgetfulness. It is now under the administration of fifteen Associated Fellows of the Royal Society of Antiquaries, whose pleasure and occupation it is to look after and maintain its pristine eminence and original strategic importance.

For further particulars see *Antoninus Pius* and the *Lost Books of Livy*." But the Noviomagians appear to have considered their duty done by dining together once a year. Mr. Stevens figures on the "Roll of Honour" as "The American Minister and Secretary of State."

His *Recollections of Mr. James Lenox*, for whose great library he collected books for more than a quarter of a century, are crowded with bibliographical lore and racy anecdote. The paper, a somewhat lengthy one, is printed in the *Transactions of the Library Association of the United Kingdom*, at the Liverpool meeting. Some autobiographical details are therein given. Stevens says of himself: "In July, 1845, a young man from Vermont, at the age of twenty-six, I found myself in London, a self-appointed missionary, on an antiquarian and historical book-hunting expedition, at my own expense and on my own responsibility, with a few Yankee notions in my head and an ample fortune of nearly forty sovereigns in my pocket. I had contrived by the light of pine-knots and dips to pick up some education among the Green Mountains, with a little Latin and less Greek; had passed the year 1839 in Middlebury College; 1840 at Washington as a well-paid clerk in the Treasury Department; 1841-3 in Yale College, where a B.A. degree was won; 1844 in Harvard Law School under Story; all the while dabbling in books and manuscripts by way of keeping the pot boiling. During vacations and holidays, I had for five years scouted through the New England and Middle States, prospecting in out-of-the-way places for historical nuggets, mousing through public and private libraries and old homestead garrets. . . . In this way the acquaintance of many of the chief authors and book-lovers of the country was made, and sufficient experience, it was thought, had been acquired to try the happier hunting-fields of the Old World, its libraries, its archives, its book-stalls, and its old homesteads."

Once launched in London, this adventurous young man soon made the acquaintance of those who dealt in books, and those whose love of books was as keen as his own. He began at once to purchase heavily for the American market, to supply the British Museum with books printed in America, a branch in which the great national library was sadly lacking at that time. He became acquainted in the way of business with Mr. Jas. Lenox in 1845, and from that time for more than twenty-five years he continued to supply that gentleman with those valuable book rarities which now form the Lenox Library. This library has been generously bequeathed by its founder to the City of New York.

Becoming firmly established as a seller of old books in London, Mr. Stevens acquired a large *clientèle* and a host of friends, both in this and in his native country; and was quite content, in spite of his patriotic leanings, to remain amongst us for the goodly space of over forty years. During that time his pen has been almost as active as his book-hunting. He has compiled much, but his work is not the kind of thing that renders a man famous. It is not literature—it is, in a sense, better than literature, for it is that which renders literature possible.

The following are some of his more important works:

1. History of Printing for the Use of the Blind, in all Languages and Systems. 1851.
2. An Account of the Proceedings at the Dinner given by Mr. George Peabody to the Americans connected with the Great Exhibition. 1851.
3. Catalogue of my English Library. Collected and described by Henry Stevens, G[reen] M[ountain] B[oy], F.S.A.
4. American Bibliographer. 1854.
5. Catalogue Raisonné of English Bibles, etc. 1855.
6. Historical Nuggets: Bibliotheca Americana, or a Descriptive Account of my Collection of Rare Books relating to America. 1858 and 1862. 2 vols.
7. A Catalogue of American Books in the Library of the British Museum. 1859 and 1862.
8. Historical and Geographical Notes on the Earliest Discoveries in America, 1453-1530. 1869.
9. Photo-Bibliography. 1878.
10. The Bibles in the Caxton Exhibition. 1878.
11. Who Spoils our New English Books? 1884. Reprinted from the *Transactions of the Library Association.*
12. Recollections of James Lenox. In the *Transactions of the Library Association.* 1884.
13. Recollections of Sir A. Panizzi: a Paper read at the Dublin meeting of the Library Association.

The librarian, the book-lover, and the literary man owe him more than they can readily repay. As he was fond of a Shakespearian quotation, we may conclude by saying of him—

" A merrier man
Within the limits of becoming mirth
I never spent an hour's talk withal."

WILLIAM ROBERT CREDLAND.

REVIEWS.

Kaffir Folk-Lore: a Selection from the Traditional Tales current among the People Living on the Eastern Border of the Cape Colony; with copious explanatory notes. By GEO. MCCALL THEAL. 2nd edition. London: Swan, Sonnenschein, Le Bas, and Lowry, 1886.

MR. THEAL'S book attracted the attention of folk-lorists on its first appearance, and received warm and well-deserved praise. We are glad to find that a second edition has been asked for. The stories are very quaint, and the first of them contains at least a partial parallel to the tale of "Beauty and the Beast." We commend Mr. Theal's book to the attention of our readers.

The Best Hundred Books. Pall Mall extra, Nov. 24. London: *Pall Mall Gazette* Office. 8vo., pp. 32.

THE list prepared by Sir John Lubbock, and in which he included the one hundred books that he thought best worth reading, has given rise to many communications, of which the most notable are included in this pamphlet. The letters vary in interest, perhaps the best of all being that written by Mr. William Morris. None of the lists will fully satisfy, and even a perfect catalogue of the best books would not be implicitly followed by even the most devoted student; but the discussion which has taken place will have the good effect of directing fresh attention to many excellent books.

Silex Scintillans: Sacred Poems and Private Ejaculations. By HENRY VAUGHAN, Silurist. Being a facsimile of the first edition, published in 1650, with an introduction by the Rev. WILLIAM CLARE, B.A., Adelaide. London: Elliot Stock, 1885. 12mo., pp. 13-110.

To say that Henry Vaughan was a favourite poet of Wordsworth, and one to whom the author of the *Ode on the Intimations of Immortality* was deeply indebted, is sufficient to claim for the Silurist a place in the affections of all lovers of literature. It is good, therefore, that Mr. Clare should have reproduced in facsimile this little volume in which Vaughan first made his claim to a place in the English Parnassus. It has been reserved for our own generation to acknowledge his genius. The *Silex Scintillans* first appeared in 1650, and some unsold copies, with slight modification, formed the basis of the first part of the enlarged edition of 1655. No edition was published between that date and 1847. The seventeenth century had but two editions of Vaughan; the nineteenth has had six.

Popular County Histories. A History of Devonshire, with Sketches of its Leading Worthies. By R. N. WORTH, F.G.S. London: Elliot Stock, 1886. 8vo., pp. x-347.

MR. WORTH has written a very readable history of the important county of Devon. Taking each large town he has sketched its history, with that of the adjoining villages. The introduction of printing is thus noticed: "That Devonshire should be one of the first counties in England into which the art of printing was introduced, is due to the enterprise and zeal for learning of the monks of Tavistock, in their later mended ways. Only two works of this early Tavistock press now exist; but as the first of these is dated 1525, and the second 1534, they must have produced much more than these two fragments. The earliest is a copy of Boethius's *Consolations of Philosophy*, as translated by Walton, of Osney; 'Emprented in the exempt Monastery of Tauestok, in Denshyre, By me, Dan Thomas Rychard, Monke of the sayde Monastery. To the instant desire of the ryght Worshypful esquyer, Mayster Robert Langdon.' The other extant publication of the Tavistock press is a copy of the *Statutes of the Stannaries.*" Mr. Worth has paid special attention to the worthies of the county. Devonshire men, as is well known, took a leading part in the discoveries and adventures of the Elizabethan period, and such names as Sir Humphrey Gilbert, Sir Walter Raleigh, and the Hawkinses would add lustre to the roll of natives of any county of England. And it was not only in seamanship that Devonians distinguished themselves, as is testified by the long lists of authors and artists who were either born in the county or had very intimate relations with it. Amongst the authors we may mention the following: John Reynolds, one of the translators of the Authorised Version of the Bible; Tom D'Urfey, the wit and song-writer; Simon Ockley, the historian; Sir John Bowring; Sir Walter Raleigh; Dean Buckland; Sir William Pole; Toplady, the author of the hymn "Rock of Ages;" Samuel Taylor Coleridge; Sir J. T. Coleridge; Hannah Cowley, the dramatist; Sir John Fortescue, author of *De Laudibus Legum Angliæ;* Thomas Westcote, an antiquary, and author of the *View of Devonshire in* 1630; John de Garland, an eleventh-century poet, who is supposed to have been born at Garland; John Gay, the poet; John Jewell, Bishop of Salisbury, who was born at Bowden Farm, in the parish of

Berry Narbor, in an old house yet standing, and of whom Mr. Worth states that "His sermons, in blackletter, may yet be seen chained up as of yore in some of the churches of the West ;" Shebbeare, the author of *Chrysal ;* Edward Capern, the Devonshire Burns, the postman poet ; Henry de Bracton, Chief Justiciary under Henry III., and the writer of the celebrated *De Legibus et Consuetudinibus Angliæ ;* Joseph Glanvill, F.R.S., author of *Saducismus Triumphatus ;* Matthew Tindal, the Deist ; Bryant, the mythologist ; John Kitto, D.D. ; Nathaniel Foster, a translator of Plato ; Dr. Wolcot ; John Prince, author of the *Worthies of Devon ;* Edward Lye, the Anglo-Saxon scholar ; Benjamin Kennicott, the Hebraist ; Robert Herrick, the author of *Hesperides ;* William Gifford ; and John Ford, the dramatist. The Devonshire artists include Sir Joshua Reynolds, James Northcote, Samuel Prout, Benjamin Robert Haydon, Samuel Hart, and Sir Charles Lock Eastlake. Sir Joshua Reynolds was born at Plympton, and never forgot his native town, of which he was, in 1733, mayor. On this occasion he gave the town his portrait, painted by himself ; but in 1832 the grateful and enlightened Corporation sold it to the Earl of Egremont, for £150 ! Mr. Worth is to be congratulated on the very interesting book he has produced.

Zichronoth ; or, Reminiscences of a Student of Jewish Theology. Written in Hebrew Rhymed Prose, and accompanied by an Essay in English on the Rise and Progress of Hebrew Poetry in Post-Biblical Times. By the Rev. Dr. [J.] CHOTZNER. London : David Nutt, 1885. 8vo., pp. xvi-84.

DR. CHOTZNER'S *Zichronoth* can only appeal to a limited circle of scholars, Hebrew and English ; but it is an essay in a department of literature that is gradually attracting more attention. The metrical form of Hebrew he traces chiefly to the *Hagadah*, but when the temple service was suspended the public worship of the synagogue took its place. The simple ritual was supplemented by discourses based upon some portion of the *Halachah* or the *Hagadah*. These were poetical in form, and in this way arose a considerable liturgical literature, mingled with history, legend, and philosophy. The earlier and simpler forms were gradually modified by contact with the Arabs, from whom they adopted rhymes, metres, and prosodial rules. The greatest of the mediæval poets of the race of Israel was Juda Halevy, of whose many successors a few are named by Dr. Chotzner. Post-Biblical Hebrew literature is a study which may be commended alike for its novelty and interest. Dr. Chotzner's little volume deserves a warm welcome.

We have received the following catalogues :—W. Spencer, 27, New Oxford Street, London, W. ; H. T. Wake, Wingfield Park, Fritchley, near Derby ; Walter Scott, 7, Bristo Place, Edinburgh ; Henry Gray, 25, Cathedral Yard, Manchester ; C. Herbert, 319, Goswell Road, London, E.C. ; James Wilson, 35, Bull Street, Birmingham ; Robson and Kerslake, 23, Coventry Street, Haymarket, London, W. ; James Fawn and Son, 18, Queen's Road, Bristol ; Edward Howell, Church Street, Liverpool ; J. and J. P. Edmond and Spark, Aberdeen ; Albert Sutton, 130, Portland Street, Manchester ; James Roche, 1, Southampton Row, Holborn, London, W.C. ; James Miles, Boar Lane, Leeds ; K. W. Hiersemann, 1, Turnersstrasse, Leipzig ; Charles Lowe, Broad Street Corner, Birmingham.

CORRESPONDENCE.

THE "BEST HUNDRED BOOKS."

THERE has lately been a very interesting discussion in the columns of the *Pall Mall Gazette* on the subject of the "best hundred books," and the various communications have since been issued, with additions, in a handy pamphlet form. Sir John Lubbock's list was freely criticized, and many additions and some subtractions were suggested, but his final list is substantially the same as that first given.

On looking at this list, and at the numerous letters from men who are more or less authorities on the subject, one cannot help feeling somewhat surprised at some of the names put forward, as well as at some of the omissions. Most of the writers mention the name of Charles Lamb, but the thousands of lovers of the gentle " Elia " will be grieved to find that Sir John Lubbock disregards their favourite, while at the same time he can find room for Smiles's *Self-Help*. Surely the glorification of the men who began life with half-a-crown in their pockets, and worked their way up to the possession of many half-crowns, could be better spared than Lamb's inimitable wit and pathos, better spared than, for instance, "The Praise of Chimney-Sweepers," or the "Dissertation upon

Roast Pig," or " Mrs. Battle's Opinions on Whist," or—but we might name every individual essay, for " Elia's " friends love them all.

Another favourite book with many generations of readers does not seem to have been mentioned by any of the writers—we mean Burton's *Anatomy of Melancholy*, a perfect storehouse of learning and humour, emphatically a " quaint and curious volume of forgotten lore." Among the essayists no one has suggested the name of the late Dr. John Brown, the author of " Rab and his Friends," and many other sketches and essays penetrated with wisdom and humour, and filled with a fine humanity.

Another complaint we would make has reference to the undue space devoted to the classic authors of Greece and Rome. But a small number of us, comparatively, ever obtain sufficient mastery of the ancient languages to be able to thoroughly enjoy Æschylus and Homer and Cicero and Tacitus in their own tongues, while in translations much of the beauty and much of the value of the originals must be hopelessly lost. Would it not be well for Sir John Lubbock, or for any of the other authorities who have taken part in this discussion, in advising the great mass of readers as to what to read, not to lay so much stress upon the classics, but to put forward more prominently the distinguished names in our own literature, many of which are altogether ignored by Sir John, and others only casually mentioned by a few of his critics? In our " hundred " we should like to include Sir Thomas Browne and Thomas Fuller ; and for the sake of some of the old dramatists, Marlowe, Ben Jonson, Beaumont and Fletcher, Shirley, Congreve, Wycherley, Etherege, none of whom are mentioned by Sir John Lubbock ; we would willingly part with the " Ramayana," the " Apostolic Fathers," or even with Comte's " Positive Philosophy." Again, the fiction section of a list seems incomplete that omits all mention of Fielding and Smollett, and, to the books given, we would add for our own delectation Charlotte Brontë's *Jane Eyre* and *Shirley*, and perhaps her sister's gloomy but powerful *Wuthering Heights;* while for Bulwer Lytton's *Last Days of Pompei* we would venture to suggest the substitution of some of Mrs. Gaskell's tales.

It seems somewhat strange, too, nowadays, to find in a list which includes Gray and Southey, that Coleridge, Shelley, and Keats are conspicuous only by their absence.

We humbly submit that readers might derive more benefit from the study of such authors as we have named, than from reading some of the works that have been suggested in the various lists —such second-rate history, for example, as Miss Strickland's *Queens of England*, or such second-rate fiction as Kingsley's *Hereward*.

However, in matters of this kind it is doubtless impossible to please all tastes ; each reader must choose for himself. Happily the wells of literature are deep and inexhaustible ; let everyone who thirsteth therefor approach and drink without stint.

G. L. A.

BIBLIOPHILE'S KALENDAR.

THE increasing interest taken in the sonnet is evidenced not only by the number of volumes and dissertations devoted to it, but also by the greater number of writers who venture upon its fascinating but dangerous ground. Mrs. Clara Swain Dickins, who has hereditary claims to consideration as the daughter of Charles Swain, has issued a volume of *Sonnets, Sacred and Secular* (London : Simpkin, Marshall and Co.). The mastery she shows over this difficult form is very considerable, but the thoughts sometimes lack clearness of expression. As a specimen we quote the sonnet on—

THE READER.

One fully lovely at life's loveliest age
A book o'erleaned. I watched her reading so ;
One hand amid her ringlets pressed her brow,
The other held an ever half-turned page
That had the force or sweetness to engage
Her being utterly ; she did not know
That she did me, the watcher, too endow
With her pleasure whether gay or sage.
Within her eyes, upon her cheeks was signed
The vivid meaning of a changeful mood,
Till half from lip to lap the book declined,
Her own life standing where but story stood,
Ere it the pictured happiness resigned
To her believing, beauteous womanhood.

WE learn from the *Academy* that Mr. Clement Boase has printed for private circulation seventy-five copies of a catalogue of the books and pamphlets in his library, "by certain of those in the fellowship of the apostles since their restoration in 1835, with an appendix of the publications *contra* Irvingism." The list is not constructed on the principles of orthodox bibliography, but its usefulness will be readily acknowledged. It forms a very good basis for such a superstructure on Irvingism and its professors as that treated by Joseph Smith in his admirable catalogues of books written by, or against, the members of the Society of Friends. The chief Irvingite writers are John B. Cardale, who died a few years ago ; Thomas Carlyle, the advocate ; Henry Drummond, the well-known banker and politician ; and Edward Irving himself ; and the lists of their works as given by Mr. Boase must be all but complete. About twelve hundred publications, in all, are entered in his catalogue.

IN the *Western Antiquary* Mr. J. R. Chanter gives an account of an episode in the life of Shelley, whose *Letter to Lord Ellenborough* was printed at Barnstaple. The printer became alarmed at the inquiries of the authorities as to a radical placard which the poet had caused to be distributed. His servant, Daniel Hill, was imprisoned for posting them in the neighbourhood.

WE have received the *Catalogue of the Library of the Grimsby Mechanics' and Literary Institution*, which has been compiled by Mr. W. G. B. Page in a manner well adapted to be of service to those for whose use it is intended.

FROM Mr. Walter Scott, of London and Newcastle, we have received a new volume of the Canterbury Poets, which will familiarize the claims of Walt Whitman to many to whom he has hitherto been but a name, if even that. Mr. Ernest Rhys contributes an appreciative introduction. Mr. Rhys is also the editor of a new venture due to the enterprise of Mr. Scott, under the title of *The Camelot Classics*. He is about to issue a series dealing with the prose literature of Britain, and the first volume is devoted to Malory's *History of King Arthur and the Quest of the Holy Grail*. This book is interesting in itself as well as on account of the service it has rendered to our poets who have found in it a mine from which to dig manifold riches.

THE annual report for 1884-85 of the Leeds Free Public Library shows that the total issues have increased from 652,594 in 1883-84, to 752,486, being an increase of 99,892 in one year. The system of branch libraries as in practice in Leeds might be adopted with advantage by many other towns. There are twenty-seven of these branches in different parts of the borough ; they are kept in schoolrooms, and the cost for attendance and rent is very slight.

- WE take the following observations on typographical facsimiles from the *Globe* of February 1 : " The publication, by Mr. Elliot Stock, of a facsimile of the first edition of Henry Vaughan's *Silex Scintillans*, reminds us of the comparative rarity of such productions. This is pre-eminently the period of the practical, and the everyday reader does not see the wisdom of repro-ducing the more or less crabbed typography of our earlier printers. Let us have all the great works of literature, he says, but let us have them in a modern garb. Let the paper and binding, as well as the type, be of the best available ; let our literary treasures be enshrined in a casket worthy of them and of us. And, of course, that is a very right and proper feeling, and one which will no doubt continue to prevail, making the number of facsimiles few in the future as in the past and the present. And certainly it would be possible to carry the fondness for exact reproduction to an extreme. It would be folly for the lover of books to confine himself—if he were able—to facsimiles of original editions. Those editions are often palpably obscure and obviously incorrect. They require, in most cases, considerable elucidation, and, in certain instances, they have been wholly repudiated by their authors. Some writers, indeed, have been as eager in their efforts to suppress the first 'heir of their invention' as they were, in the first place, to give it currency. Still, for the literary enthusiast there must always be something attractive about the facsimile of the first issue of a favourite classic. He would much prefer, of course, a copy of the original edition ; but, if he cannot get that, it is something to have it in facsimile form—something to have the text in a shape precisely similar to that in which it first appeared. The spelling may be excru-ciating, and the punctuation all wrong ; but there, at any rate, is the classic as it first showed itself, misprints and all ; and that is a boon for which the student cannot be too grateful."

IN *L'Art* there have been some interesting notices of Rubens as a book-collector, to which we may again refer at greater length.

WE have received from the Newton (Massachusetts) Free Library the report for last year. There is an interesting reference to the possibility of co-operation between the public school and the public library. This we may quote :—"It has been for a number of years a question of interesting discussion among the managers and officers of public libraries, especially during the sessions of the American Library Association, how, not simply to keep the free library from becoming an embarrassment and injury to school children, but how, with the co-operation of the teachers, to make it a positive aid, and to create, if possible, among them a taste for improving literature. A very successful experiment of this character has been tried for the last three months in connection with the Newton Free Library. The plan, as yet, has been introduced into but a portion of the schools, but will be at once into the others. Masters and teachers offer us their heartiest co-operation, and are warm in their expressions of interest and confidence in the undertaking. The principal of the Bigelow School, Mr. H. C. Sawin, writes, in a note to the Superintendent, 'I am very glad to welcome the public library as an ally to the public school. In years past I have considered it antagonistic to the interests of the pupils, believing, with Dr. Taylor, of Andover, that "scholars, while attending school, have no time for desultory reading ;" but the efforts of the friends both of the library and the school, in Worcester, Providence, Boston, and more recently in our own city, are making the library one of the most efficient aids in the mental development of the young. The plan recently adopted and put in practice, of furnishing the teachers with a number of books relating to the subjects taught in the schools, will accomplish the twofold object of illustrating and giving interest to the regular school-work, and of guiding the pupil in the art of reading well. Mr. James Russell Lowell says, in his recent address, " I sometimes think that our public schools undertake to teach too much, and that the older systems, which taught the three R's, and taught them well, leaving natural selection to decide who should go farther, is better." In educational work there is no sign more hopeful than the new relation of the public library to the public school, making it possible for the instructor of youth to teach the first and most important of the three R's more successfully. Hoping that the results of your efforts to aid the schools in their work will be all that can be desired, so that you will be encouraged to devise yet more liberal things for them, I remain sincerely yours.' Each public school teacher receives ten cards upon which to draw books for his class from the library. The teacher sends to the library a list of topics which are being studied in the class, and asks that some works suited to the grade of the pupils may be sent to the school. The following list was received from a grammar-school master :—' Please send me books on Mound Builders, Early Discoveries, Columbus, North American Indians, Colonial History, U. S. Constitution, U. S. Coinage, John Smith, Insects, China and Japan.' Another teacher asks for books upon South America, as that is the portion of the globe which they have reached in their geography ; and still another seeks for books upon Asia. Books are especially desired upon animals, particularly stories about them, for the younger classes. Works upon physics, geology, mineralogy, poetry, history, biography—in short, any possible helps which the library can afford, are freely offered and zealously used. To give some idea of the character of the new reading among our school-children, we append, at the close of the report, a list of the books which have already been placed in circulation among them. There have been many books of travel, science, history and biography, written and compiled within a short period, especially for the reading of young people and children. These works are finely illustrated, and are calculated to arrest the attention of young readers, and to lend fresh interest and value to the study of their text-books. Many of the books are used by the teachers as rewards for good lessons, the children being permitted to take them home, or to read them in school after the lessons are completed. The librarian makes a personal visit to the schools, invites a short meeting with the teachers, and explains the method of working with the library. This has never failed to awaken the interest of the teachers, and often arouses enthusiasm in the work. The immediate good accomplished in quickening the interest of pupils in their school studies, is but a small part of the beneficial results that must follow such an effort, if perseveringly continued. More than in any other way will a generation be trained up to relish and demand something besides a fictitious and sensational literature. The children discover what interesting books there are in the library, they copy the numbers upon their own cards, and we find them selecting these for their home reading. The teachers eagerly avail themselves of the opportunity afforded by their additional cards. One teacher tells us of a lad who had never accomplished anything in school until aroused by the inspiration of the illustrative books, in which he became greatly interested. Superintendent Emerson assures us of the enthusiasm awakened among the teachers of the schools over the new plan of reference books from the library. During the year the arrangement which has been so successfully effected in a few of the schools will be introduced throughout the city. In the three months in which the delivery to the schools has been made, 568 books have been issued to them. But six of the schools have as yet been visited, and some of those not until November, showing that the teachers generally have availed themselves of the privilege."

MYTHICAL MONSTERS.

 NE by one the various domains of human thought are being brought within the purview of scientific investigation, and even the poetic visions of primeval people are being subjected to the reign of law. The latest attempt of this nature has been made by Mr. Charles Gould, whose handsome volume on *Mythical Monsters*, published by Messrs. W. H. Allen and Co., is perhaps the first systematic attempt to show that in the stories of dragons and "chimæras dire" we have, not the creations of a disordered fancy, but the distorted remembrance of animals that had a real existence in the bygone ages of the world. "For me," he says, "the major part of these creatures are not chimeras, but objects of rational study. The dragon, in place of being a creature evolved out of the imagination of Aryan man by the contemplation of lightning flashing through the caverns which he tenanted, as is held by some mythologists, is an animal which once lived and dragged its ponderous coils, and perhaps flew; which devastated herds, and on occasions swallowed their shepherd ; which, establishing its lair in some cavern overlooking the fertile plain, spread terror and destruction around, and, protected from assault by dread or superstitious feeling, may even have been subsidized by the terror-stricken peasantry, who, failing the power to destroy it, may have preferred tethering offerings of cattle adjacent to its cavern to having it come down to seek supplies from amongst their midst.

"To me the specific existence of the unicorn seems not incredible, and, in fact, more probable than that theory which assigns its origin to a lunar myth. Again, believing as I do in the existence of some great undescribed inhabitant of the ocean depths, the much-derided sea-serpent, whose home seems especially to be adjacent to Norway, I recognise this monster as originating the myths of the midgard serpent which the Norse Elder Eddas have collected, this being the contrary view to that taken by mythologists, who invert the derivation, and suppose the stories current among the Norwegian fishermen to be modified versions of this important element of Norse mythology. I must admit that, for my part, I doubt the general derivation of myths from 'the contemplation of the visible workings of external nature.' It seems to me easier to suppose that the palsy of time has enfeebled the utterance of these oft-told tales until their original appearance is almost unrecognisable, than that uncultured savages should possess powers of imagination and poetical invention far beyond those enjoyed by the most instructed nations of the present day; less hard to believe that these wonderful stories of gods and demigods, of giants and dwarfs, of dragons and monsters of all descriptions, are transformations than to believe them to be inventions." (P. 3.)

Mr. Gould rightly points out that the natural attitude of disbelief on the first hearing of remarkable stories is frequently not justified by further investigations, and even Fernando Mendez Pinto, whom Congreve styled a "liar of the first magnitude," although a credulous repeater of much doubtful stuff told him in the various countries he visited, was not altogether the untrustworthy narrator he

THE SEA-SERPENT ATTACKING A VESSEL.—FROM "OLAUS MAGNUS."

has been supposed to be. Within our own day travellers' tales have been denounced as inventions, only to be triumphantly vindicated by further inquiry. These considerations bespeak a careful hearing to Mr. Gould's ingenious attempt to show that the mythical monsters of poetry and tradition are but a distorted record of animals now extinct, that once lived and were a terror on the earth. Such an inquiry cannot fail to have interest for the readers of *Book Lore*, who in the course of their explorations of our older literature must often have come within sight of

Gorgons and Hydras, and Chimæras dire !

The geological record shows beyond dispute the former existence of vast animal forms, beside which those of living species are but of pigmy proportions.

Whilst the mammoth and the dodo are universally extinct, local changes have driven the bear and the wolf within comparatively recent historic periods from Britain. Without following Mr. Gould through his dissertation on the antiquity of the human race, it seems clear that man was the contemporary of the mammoth, the woolly rhinoceros, and a variety of other species now extinct. Mr. Gould has some interesting speculations as to the existence of communication between the Old World and the New in the earlier ages of the world, and he points out a variety of analogous customs, such as the couvade, scalping, etc.

THE DRAGONS OF MOUNT PILATE.—FROM THE "MUNDUS SUBTERRANEUS," OF ATHANASIUS KIRCHER.

Mr. Gould speaks in detail of the sea-serpent, and gives from Olaus Magnus the wonderful picture which we reproduce, the unicorn, the Chinese phœnix, and the dragon ; we shall confine our attention to the last-named, as the best known and most characteristic of mythical monsters. There are innumerable references to dragons in older literature ; and in some cases the name was doubtless applied to boas, pythons, and other large serpents, who, when undisturbed monarchs of the forest, may have attained proportions not now realized. Yet Dr. Gardiner mentions a Brazilian water-boa, forty feet long, that devoured a horse. Many references to winged serpents, and to the dragon in classical periods, are passed in review. The calendar of saints includes no less than seven dragon-slayers. The fossil remains found in China are uniformly described as dragons' bones, and as such enter into the pharmacopœia of the Celestial Empire.

As late as the time of Aldrovandus, European naturalists included the dragon in their account of the fauna of the world. Athanasius Kircher tells the story of the fight of Gozione with the dragon of the Drachenfeldt, which forms the basis of one of Schiller's fine poems. By the courtesy of the publishers, we reproduce also the picture of the dragons of Mount Pilate, as described by Kircher. Mr. Gould has added a considerable amount of dragon lore from Chinese writers. The inhabitants of the Middle Kingdom have given to this monster an important place, alike in literature and in art. From the data still subsisting in books and monuments, Mr. Gould believes that the dragon had a real existence, and was "a long terrestrial lizard, hibernating and carnivorous, with the power of constricting with its snake-like body and tail; possibly furnished with wing-like expansions of its integuments, after the fashion of *Draco volans*, and capable of occasional progress on its hind-legs alone, when excited in attack. It appears to have been protected by armour and projecting spikes, like those found in *Moloch horridus* and *Megalania prisca*, and was possibly more nearly allied to this last form than to any other which has yet come to our knowledge. Probably it preferred sandy, open country to forest land; its habitat was the highlands of Central Asia, and the time of its disappearance about that of the Biblical Deluge, discussed in a previous chapter.

"Although terrestrial, it probably, in common with most reptiles, enjoyed frequent bathing; and when not so engaged, or basking in the sun, secluded itself under some overhanging bank or cavern.

"The idea of its fondness for swallows, and power of attracting them, mentioned in some traditions, may not impossibly have been derived from these birds hawking round and through its open jaws in pursuit of the flies attracted by the viscid humours of its mouth. We know that at the present day a bird, the trochilus of the ancients, freely enters the open mouth of the crocodile, and rids it of the parasites affecting its teeth and jaws." (P. 259.)

Apart from the main purpose of the book, there is plenty of interesting reading in Mr. Gould's volume. Thus, in referring to Victor Hugo's narrative of the fight with the devil-fish, he points out that Hokosai, the famous Japanese artist, has a picture of a fisherman attacked by an octopus; and that a Japanese ivory carver has represented a woman who, whilst bathing, has become enmeshed in the grasp of an octopus, and is vainly struggling to free herself from the peril of a cruel death.

MY FRIEND, THE CATALOGUE.

BY J. J. OGLE.

MONG books which are no books Charles Lamb included *catalogues*, and the stigma which some folk perceive in this dictum of that genial *littérateur* is still thought to belong to all catalogues. Be it so, then. There are many good things besides books, and certainly library catalogues are not among the least of them. The Catalogue is the jackal to the book-lion. Instances are known of his providing him with food on which he has grown to bulk and importance. Whether he provide food or not, he almost always introduces visitors to the king of the literary forest. If the book may not grow without meat, certainly he cannot live, in the best sense, without appreciative visitors. The Catalogue, then, is an important creature.

Ay; but you say, "He is dull and uninteresting as a suddenly rich coal-factor, though he too is important." Let us see. That depends upon yourself. Have you the knack of drawing out of him his wonderful treasures of information, of worming yourself into his state secrets, of securing his guidance into the most beautiful paradises of fairyland? There are who have, and these do not find him dull.

Only study his ways a little, and you will be astonished at finding what an excellent fellow he is. Ah, I hear you now! You are saying to yourself: "That fellow not dull! That creature with the blurred face excellent! I don't know where you see it!" But study his features. You will be repaid for the trouble, which after all is no trouble. There is order there. Looking through the glasses of ignorance you have not perceived it; but it is true, nevertheless, that every feature is well formed, regular, and, if not beautiful, at least pleasing. He has, too, a wonderful faculty for raising a smile on the face of any friend of his. So the sooner you enroll yourself as his friend the better for you. The Catalogue is a most catholic person, and his catholicity comes out in his choice of friends and in his tastes. "Choice," did I say? Nay; for he has no choice—all is fish that comes to his net. Among his friends are numbered the most learned *savant* and the village schoolboy, Chinese mandarin and Virginian negro, emperor and nihilist, pope and scripture-reader. At any of his favourite haunts you may introduce yourself to him sans ceremony. You will be welcome as the daylight, and he will extend the same courtesy to you as to the Queen.

His simplicity, you will find, is perfectly captivating. Learned as he is, he still retains an immense veneration for the alphabet. This peculiarity is the secret of his marvellous memory, for every fact or item of knowledge is connected in his mind with a certain position in the alphabet. Ask him about anything, and he will answer with great brevity. He has too many things to mind to say much about each, but he will generally tell you where you may learn more. Thus a friend of mine, wishing to know something about meteorology, ascertained from this courteous Catalogue the names of a large number of recent books specially dealing with the subject. This he had expected; but the Catalogue told him much more, for he put him on the track of information in such unlooked-for publications as Chambers's *Book of Days;* Conferences held in connection with the Special Loan Collection, South Kensington; Goethe's *Naturwissenschaftliche Correspondenz,* and Lloyd's *Miscellaneous Papers.* Besides this, the Catalogue was good enough to suggest that, if my friend wished, he would supply information on various subdivisions of the subject and on allied subjects, such as atmosphere, physiography, storms, weather, winds, the barometer, and the thermometer. Perhaps now it is apparent why a consultation with the Catalogue is provocative of good-humour.

His respect for dates almost equals his veneration for *Alpha Beta.* Do you want to know when an obscure writer published his treatise on the Nativity, or which was the earliest of the many books written by the Rev. So-and-so? He will do his best to aid you, and his best is often the best you can get.

Of editions and editors of the great ancient and modern classics he has a long inventory, and his notes and cursory remarks upon many of these are not only curious and interesting, but often important.

You wish to trace the history of a periodical that has several times changed its name in consequence of repeated marriages with other periodicals? Ask the Catalogue. Ten to one he knows all about it, and will readily tell you what you want to know.

The Catalogue has his prejudices—who has not? He has a mortal aversion to calling things by wrong names. "Knickerbocker" publishes a *History of New York;* "Boz" issues some *Sketches* from the press; "H. H." writes some *Poems,* and gives them to the world. "Ah, ah!" says he; "you, Knickerbocker, Boz, H. H., you don't deceive *me!* I will hold you up to public notice, you pseudonymous rascals!" And so Washington Irving, Charles Dickens, and Helen Hunt Jackson are made known as the authors of their respective works.

Protean changes of title are frequently exposed by this relentless foe to deception. In telling of one title, he will notify the fact that it is a re-issue or an adaptation of such a book with another title. Thus one learns from him that a book in Arabic entitled *The Pearl of the Seas* is simply an adaptation of the English Defoe's *Robinson Crusoe;* and that *Pen Pictures of Modern Authors* is a reprint on large paper of Vol. II. of *The Literary Life,* with illustrations added.

Many books are published with misleading titles, and many more with non-descriptive titles. The class of such the Catalogue is anxious to indicate. So people are warned that *Proserpina* is not a work on mythology, nor a poem, but a book on botany; and that *The American Register* is a journal devoted to the interests of the Democratic party.

It is to be hoped that henceforth no reader of this plea for my friend the Catalogue will scorn him or say hard things about him, and that many who have not yet known him will hasten to make his acquaintance.

"*A BOOKSELLER OF THE LAST CENTURY.*"

OHN NEWBERY has found in his successor a fitting annalist. Mr. Charles Welsh has inherited the traditions of the firm, and on various occasions has shown not only his literary faculty, but his interest in the bibliographical history of the last century. The firm of Newbery and Harris had a special instinct for juvenile literature, but its chief fame now arises from its connection with Goldsmith. In *A Bookseller of the Last Century*, Mr. Welsh has given a good account of the life of John Newbery, the founder of the firm, and of the books he published. He has also added some account of the later Newberys. The volume is handsomely printed and illustrated.

John Newbery was the son of Robert Newbery, a small farmer, of Waltham St. Lawrence in Berkshire. The family is stated by Mr. Welsh (on the authority of a pedigree belonging to the family) to have traced its descent from Ralph Newberie, a London publisher and printer, who was master of the Stationers' Company in 1598 and 1601. Ralph Newberie bequeathed in 1633 a small property to the poor of Waltham St. Lawrence, and some of his descendants resided in Berkshire; but the pedigree of the family in the *Visitation of Worcestershire*, 1682-83, does not mention any of the family as then residing in Waltham, so that it is quite possible that John Newbery was descended not from Ralph himself, but from one of his brothers or uncles. Robert Newbery the farmer had two sons—Robert, also a farmer, whose son Francis became a bookseller, and John. John was born in 1713, and was baptized on the 19th July. Having had an ordinary education he was anxious to become a tradesman; and when about the age of sixteen he engaged himself as an assistant to a Reading "merchant," who was probably William Carnan the printer, proprietor and editor of one of the earliest of provincial newspapers, *The Reading Mercury and Oxford Gazette*. In 1737 William Carnan died, appointing Newbery one of his executors, and shortly afterwards his widow married John Newbery, who was about six years her junior. Newbery continued the business at Reading for three or four years longer, and then removed to London, before which, however, he made a tour through England for the benefit of his Reading business. Mr. Welsh gives some interesting extracts from his private memorandum-book in which he entered each day's journeyings, the miles he travelled, the inns at which he lay, and all the notable sights that were seen. At Derby he noticed a curious and very useful machine, viz., a Ducking Stool, for the benefit of scolding wives. "A plan of this instrument," continues Mr. Newbery, "I shall procure and transplant to Berkshire, for the good of my native county!" Returning to Reading he entered vigorously into his business. The earliest book known with his imprint is dated Reading, 1740; and in 1743 he purchased for £100 the right of selling Hooper's "Female Pills" for fourteen years. About 1744 Newbery commenced a business in London, at Devereux Court, without Temple Bar, but the following year removed to the Bible and Sun, near the Chapter House, in St. Paul's Churchyard. Here his trade increased to such an extent that he sold his Reading business, and devoted himself solely to London. In 1746 he purchased the right of selling Dr. James's celebrated "Fever Powder," and he also sold other patent medicines in large quantities. Newbery's principal claim to notice, however, is his attempt to provide the children of that time with literature suitable to their years and understanding. Newbery was the first publisher who introduced a juvenile library, and gave children books in a more permanent form than the popular chap-books of the period. These books were bound in "flowered and gilt dutch paper," and illustrated with "bad pictures," all for the sum of one penny. And by an ingenious system of puffing, Newbery made these pamphlets advertise each other. Thus in the *Blossoms of Morality*, the chapter entitled the "Book of Nature" opens, "My dear papa," said young Theophilus to his father, "I cannot help pitying those poor little boys whose parents are not in a condition to purchase them such a nice gilded library, as that with which you have supplied me from my good friends at the corner of St. Paul's Churchyard. Surely such unhappy boys must be very ignorant all their lives, for what can they learn without books?" The father, while agreeing, proceeds to point out that there is room for infinite study in the "Book of Nature." And in others of Newbery's publications occur passages of which the following are good examples: "Pulled one of Mr. Newbery's books out of his pocket, he read;" and "Taking Mr. Newbery's *Valentine's Gift* out of her pocket." Newbery was quite a genius in advertising his own books and medicines, and they occur in his books in the most unexpected places, as when, in *Goody Two Shoes*, little Margery's father was "seized with a violent fever in a place where Dr. James's 'Fever Powder' was not to be had, and where he died miserably." But although Newbery's children's books had made him famous, he "left no field of literature untried in his publishing ventures. A glance at the catalogue of books he published will show that theology, fiction, prose and poetry, scientific and educational works, music, and indeed every department of literature is represented."

The connection of Newbery with Dr. Goldsmith was very close. They first became associated about 1757 or 1758. The Doctor compiled or revised a large number of books and pamphlets for the enterprising bookseller. The *Vicar of Wakefield* appeared in 1766, and the title-page states that it was at "Salisbury, printed by B. Collins, for F. Newbery, in Pater-Noster-Row, London." This was Francis, the nephew of John Newbery, and the well-known story of Dr. Johnson finding Goldsmith arrested for debt by his landlady, and selling the MS. of the *Vicar of Wakefield* to effect his release, has often been repeated. But an entry discovered by Mr. Welsh shows that a third of the copyright had been sold to Mr. B. Collins in 1762 for £21. How the enigma thus propounded is to be solved is difficult to decide.   Mr. Austin Dobson, in the preface to the excellent facsimile edition of the *Vicar of Wakefield*, has contributed something to its elucidation; Mr. Welsh offers an explanation, and various correspondents of the *Athenæum* and the *Academy* have tried to throw light upon what still remains a literary puzzle.

Mr. John Newbery died 22nd December, 1767, aged fifty-four.   The publications of the firm from 1740 to 1800 have been carefully catalogued by Mr. Welsh, and this list, though not quite complete, is an important addition to bibliography. Altogether Mr. Welsh may be congratulated on the fresh interest he has given to the shrewd but kindly man of business, who lives in the pages of Goldsmith as the philanthropic bookseller of St. Paul's Churchyard.

ON READING SIR JOHN MANDEVILLE'S VOYAGES AND TRAVELS.

SONNET ACROSTIC.

J OHN MANDEVILLE of marvels did indite,
O f dragons fierce and many a monstrous thing,
H ow Phœnix from the fire can rise and sing ;
N ow Syria and now Cathay's wonders bright,

M ake up the burden of his trav'ler's song.
A non he speaks of that faint-hearted knight—
N ever shall it be askèd what he hight—
D ared not to kiss the loathly dragon long,
E ven though he knew it but a damsel fair,
V exed and transformed by magic to that shape.
I n Mandeville we feel the past once more,
L ook as he looked on earth, and sea, and air ;
L ist then unto his marvels, so escape
E ven from the present, and the past restore.

THE *BOOK OF MORMON.*

HE *Book of Mormon* is one of the curiosities of literature, and as such merits some attention from the readers of *Book-Lore*. It is a remarkable instance of a new religion and a new form of government flourishing in spite of adverse conditions and of the hostility, overt and covert, of the nation in whose midst it has become an *imperium in imperio,* and based wholly upon a literary imposture so gross and glaring as to be apparently beneath the contempt of anyone of education. It is not sixty years since the *Book of Mormon* was first printed, and it is now the " sacred book" of a church whose most notorious doctrine and practice—polygamy—it flatly and emphatically condemns. Mormonism is now attracting the indignant attention of the American people, and how to deal with it is one of the grave public questions of the day.

There never was any great doubt as to the real origin of the *Book of Mormon,* and the recent appearance of *New Light on Mormonism,* by Mrs. Ellen E. Dickinson, published at the close of last year by Messrs. Funk and Wagnalls, of New York, may be said to make the matter as clear as the history of a theological and literary fraud can ever be made. It has frequently been asserted that the founders of the " Church of the Latter-day Saints " had obtained the substance of their pretended revelation from an historical romance written by the Rev. Solomon Spaulding, M.A.; and the opinion is so generally received that Dr. Allibone treats Joseph Smith, the prophet, simply as the corrupter of Spaulding's romance. Mrs. Dickenson is the grand-niece of this clerical novelist, and has obtained from his daughter, Mrs. M. S. M'Kinstry, a sworn statement of the circumstances so far as they are known to her. Spaulding, who was born in 1761, and educated at Dartmouth College, after preaching for a few years retired from the ministry on account of ill-health. He appears to have been a man of imaginative temperament, and deeply impressed with a fanciful theory that has frequently been promulgated, and which sees in the Indian tribes of the American continent the remnant and descendants of the lost ten tribes. Those who are familiar with Field's *Indian Bibliography,* or with the literature which it records, will know that various authors have seriously urged this view. During a residence in Ohio the excavation of an earth-mound containing skeletons and other relics of prehistoric man appears to have excited Spaulding's imagination, and he began to write and read to his family and friends a visionary chronicle of the peopling of America by the missing remnants of the chosen people. This literary effort, to which he gave the title of the *Manuscript Found,* made him a man of some distinction in the neighbourhood. Acting, doubtless, on the traditional advice of friends, he sought to have his book published, and offered it to a Pittsburg printer, who, however, declined to speculate in the matter, but said to the author, " Polish it up, finish it, and you will make money out of it." It is suggested that whilst there the MS. was copied by Sidney Rigdon, who was then in the office, and who was afterwards one of the early associates of Joseph Smith. That dubious prophetical personage vainly tried in 1825 to induce Mr. Thurlow Weed, then of Rochester, New York, to print his pretended revelation. In effect it did not appear until 1830, when it was printed at Palmyra, New York. This was eighteen years after Spaulding's romance was written, and fourteen years after his death. Mrs. M'Kinstry has still a vivid recollection of hearing her father read portions of his tale, and the names Mormon, Moroni, and Nephi are still fresh in her mind. Of the general identity of Spaulding's romance and Smith's pretended revelation there appears to be no doubt. It may be a matter of regret that it is impossible to compare them more closely. The *Manuscript Found*, if not irretrievably lost, is at all events not available for examination. Joseph Smith, whose character was none of the best, saw in the wild story of the ex-clergyman the materials out of which to construct a new religion, and fearlessly made use of them. One of the recollections of Thurlow Weed is, that when he was publishing the *Rochester Telegraph*, a man who introduced himself as Joseph Smith, of Palmyra, New York, called upon him and stated that he had been directed by a vision to a spot he described, where in a cavern he found what he called a " Golden Bible." Weed declined to have anything to do with the matter, and the book was published in Palmyra. The first edition is now very rare. Mrs. Dickenson gives the following transcript of the original title (p. 266) :

The Book of Mormon. An account written by the hand of Mormon from plates taken from the plates of Nephi. Wherefore it is an abridgement of the Record of the people of Nephi; and also of the Lamenites; written to the Lamenites which are a remnant of the House of Isreal; and also to Jew and Gentile; written by way of commandment and also of the spirit of Prophesy and of Revelation, written and sealed up, and hid up unto the Lord, that they might not be destroyed; to come forth by the gift and power of God unto the interpretation thereof; sealed by the hand of Morini and hid up unto the Lord, to come forth in due time by the way of Gentiles, the interpretation thereof by the gift of God; an abridgement taken from the Book of Ethen. Also which is a record of the people of Jared which were scattered at the time, the Lord confounded the language of the people when they were building a tower to get to Heaven; which is to show unto the remnant of the House of Isreal [sic] how great things the Lord hath done for their fathers, and that they may know the covenants of the Lord, that they are not cast off forever; and also to the convincing of the Jew and the Gentile that Jesus is the Christ, the Eternal God, *manifesting Himself unto all nations. And now if there be fault, it be the mistake of man; wherefore condemn not the things of God, that ye may be found spotless at the Judgment seat of Christ. By Joseph Smith, Junior, Author and Proprietor.* Palmyra : Printed by E. D. Grandin, for the Author. 1830."

The third American edition was published at Nauvoo, Illinois, in 1841. The first European edition was reproduced from the second American edition. It was printed at Liverpool in 1841, in English, Danish, French, German, Italian, and Welsh. There have been various editions issued since, both by the Latter-Day Saints of the Salt Lake, and by the section of the Mormon Church known as Josephites, who repudiate the doctrine of polygamy, and denounce Brigham Young as having foisted that infamy upon the original doctrine laid down in the *Book of Mormon.* The only alteration in the title-pages of the later issues is that the words "author and proprietor" are omitted, and the volume is simply said to be " Translated by Joseph Smith, jun." The *Book of Mormon* has prefixed to it two declarations. In the first, Oliver Cowdery, David Whitmer, and Martin Harris, " the three witnesses," declare that the engravings upon the plates had been shown to them by "an angel of God" who " came down from heaven" for that express purpose. The second testimony is signed by eight witnesses, three of whom belonged to Smith's family and four to Whitmer's family, who all declare that they have " seen and *hefted* and know for a surety that the said Smith has got the plates." The educational status of the witnesses may be judged by their use of the interesting dialect word *hefted* for handled. That Joseph Smith had something which his illiterate colleagues regarded as having been written centuries before by the prophets of the Hebrew remnant may well be true ; but it needs no great critical acumen to see that the *Book of Mormon* is an ignorant parody of the English of the Authorized Version. Whatever may have been the character of Smith, there is no reason to think that Whitmer was other than an honest fanatic. He was a Pennsylvanian, born in 1805, and, after joining the Latter-Day Saints, followed the fortunes of the sect until, driven from Ohio by persecution, it found a refuge in Missouri. But he did not join in the migration to Utah. The probable reason is that he disapproved of the "doctrine of polygamy," which was not originally a part of the creed, and which, the "Josephite" section of the Mormons declare, has been foisted upon the Church since the death of the " Prophet." They have, at all events, the authority of the *Book of Mormon.* Nothing can be plainer than the manner in which polygamy is denounced by " Jacob, the brother of Nephi." When the Latter-Day Saints moved on towards the Great Salt Lake Whitmer stayed at Richmond, in Missouri, where he became an influential citizen, having a seat in the Council, and filling the office of Mayor. A happy marriage, of which he passed the golden anniversary, may explain his stubborn resistance to the later matrimonial theories of Mormonism. Whitmer, who died in December last, in his early days had his share of religious fanaticism, but his moral sense revolted from the baseness of the successors of the " Prophet" Smith.

As to the style of the *Book of Mormon,* a single extract may suffice : " Behold, I have written upon these plates the very things which the brother of Jared saw, and there never was greater things made manifest than that which was made manifest unto the brother of Jared ; wherefore the Lord hath commanded me to write them ; and I have written them. And he commanded me that I should seal them up ; and he also hath commanded that I should seal up the interpretation thereof; wherefore I have sealed up the interpreters, according to the commandment of the Lord. For the Lord said unto me, They shall not go forth unto the Gentiles until the day that they shall repent of their iniquity, and become clean before the Lord; and in that day that they shall exercise faith in me, saith the Lord, even as the brother of Jared did, that they may become sanctified in me, then will I manifest unto them the things which the brother of Jared saw, even to the unfolding unto them all my revelations, saith Jesus Christ, the Son of God, the Father of the heavens and of the earth, and all things that in them are."

The book, as a whole, is tiresome and uninteresting. Mrs. Dickenson's *New Light*, though not displaying any great literary skill, is an important contribution to the annals of a great delusion and imposture, which must ever remain one of the most curious episodes in the religious and political development of the age.

INCENT BOURNE, the best-known of modern Latin poets, was one who simply followed a track in which many scholars of preceding generations had distinguished themselves; but, like the heroes who lived before Agamemnon, the greater part of them are now forgotten, at least as Latin poets. Nor, perhaps, is our loss great on the whole. Congratulatory odes to royal visitors, and panegyrics prefixed to annotated editions of the Classics hardly survive in interest the persons whom they were intended to honour. Short poems of another type, such as the *Carmina Quadragesimalia*, recited in the School of Natural Philosophy by Christ Church men, are often neat and epigrammatic—better, one may frankly allow, than elegiacs upon similar themes which are done in our public schools now.

Two volumes of these Lent Verses were printed at the Sheldonian Theatre, in 1723 and 1748 respectively. Fugitive pieces by many a scholar, whose name afterwards became conspicuous in Church or State, were circulated in manuscript or sometimes in print, and an effort was occasionally made by some University man of taste and enterprise to collect and preserve the best of these poems and verses. So in Popham's *Selecta Poemata Anglorum*, 1779, we find Dr. South's poem " On the Power of Music," Dr. Wm. King's " Epitaph on Beau Nash," Warton's *Mons Catharinæ*, Gray's " Ode to West," and many other pieces of note.

An earlier and equally interesting compilation of this kind is *Musarum Anglicanarum Analecta* in two volumes, of which the first seems to have been printed separately in 1691 (at least that is the date of the Vice-Chancellor's *Imprimatur* in the second edition). This was issued, together with a second volume, from the Sheldonian Theatre, in 1699. The present writer has not been able to discover any trace of the first edition, but the Preface to the second volume states that it was surreptitiously edited in London without the Author's consent, and that many of the poems were mutilated.* This second volume is dedicated by Addison, one of the principal contributors, to Charles Montague, Chancellor of the Exchequer, afterwards Lord Halifax. The poem to which attention is now to be drawn is the last but two in the first volume, occupying from page 221 to page 244. It contains about 500 lines. It is evidently a reprint of a rare tract [Brit. Mus. 11,900 e. 4], of which the full title and preface are as follows :

° " . . . . . illis parum invidentes, qui opera adeo mutila et furtiva Typis mandârunt, ut deformes partus aut non agnoverint ipsi Parentes, aut agnitis erubuerint."

AUCTIO DAVISIANA.

Oxonii habita

Per ⟨ **Gulielmum Cooper,** ⟩ Bibliop. *Lond.*
   ⟨ **Edvar. Millingtonum** ⟩

Spissis indigna THEATRIS
Scripta pudet recitare, & nugis addere pondus.
Hor.

LONDINI,
Prostant venales apud Jacobum Tonson 1689.

The Publisher | To The | READER.

THESE *Verses were designed at first for the entertainment of such onely who were upon the place where the Scene lay: The many private hints and relations to particular passages will not allow them to be thoroughly* understood *by any other sort of Reader: However allowance being made for this, and (the Author's modesty would have added,) for other faults it is hoped they will not be unacceptable: the ingenious Gentlemen concerned, will excuse the Publisher for doing them Justice, though without their leave.*

Jacob Tonson.

This tract is a quarto, and contains iv and 15 pp. In comparing it with the Oxford reprint, the latter is found faithfully to reproduce the few errors of the former, and by the omission of one line and the alteration of another, seriously to vitiate the sense in two passages. These will be noticed where they occur. In one particular, however, we are indebted to the Oxford editor. He gives us the clue to the *dramatis personæ,* who in the first edition were so many cyphers. The author's name is concealed in both, but fortunately this important question is settled for us on the unimpeachable authority of Anthony Wood.* It was George Smalridge. After giving the title, as above, he remarks : ' This excellent *Latin* Poem was written on the Sale of the Books of *Rich. Davis,* an ancient Bookseller of *Oxon,* which were exposed to Sale by way of Auction in a large Stone Fabric, opposite to *St. Michael's* Church in *Oxon,* near the North Gate of the City, commonly called *Bocardo.*" Bishop Smalridge is now chiefly known by his sermons, of which sixty were printed as recently as 1852. He took some

---

° *Ath. Oxon.,* ed Tanner, ii. 1,055.

small part in the controversial writings of 1687 concerning Church Government.* Hearne's short notice of him is worth reprinting, especially as he belonged to the "sneaking party:" "1706, April 27.—Dr. Smalridge, of Christ Church, was born at Lichfield. His father was a dyer, and had more children, and was but very poor, as I am informed by one who lived in the place seven years. This Dr. Smalridge is a man of admirable strong parts, great elocution, and good learning."† He is said to have owed his education to Ashmole. He took his B.A. degree June 15, 1686; his M.A., July 4, 1689; D.D., 1700; was successively Canon and Dean of Christ Church, having been for a short time Dean of Carlisle. His preferment was rapid, and in 1714 he was consecrated Bishop of Bristol, and soon afterwards appointed Almoner to Queen Anne. He died 1719. Mr. Overton‡ remarks that he was Atterbury's successor in one preferment after another, the "Favonius" of the *Tatler*, and according to Robert Nelson, in his *Life of Bishop Bull*, "the great favourite of all learned and good men throughout the nation." Mr. Overton thinks that the great merit of Smalridge's sermons is the "singularly luminous and smooth style in which they are written."

It appears, then, that the *Auctio Davisiana* is the only performance of its class produced by its author; but an anecdote told by Hearne§ is evidence that there was a vein of humour in his seriousness. When Dean of Christ Church he went one night to the play, to hear *Cato* acted; and the presence of a man of his order and dignity excited the ridicule of some ladies, in whose hearing the Dean remarked to an acquaintance: "Sure the ladies, by laughing so, think themselves to be at church"—a remark which completely silenced them. When Hearne's collections have been printed in full by the Oxford Historical Society, it is likely that some further particulars of general interest about Bishop Smalridge may be gathered up: the first volume adds little to what we have already said, except, perhaps, his high opinion of Dr. Grabe, whom he presented for his Doctor's degree. It is time to pass to the persons represented in this small drama. They are six Christ Church men—Arthur Keye, Waller Bacon, Ed. Stradling, George Dixon, Christopher Codrington, and William Woodward. Of these, one—and, so far as the present writer can ascertain, one only—became famous, Christopher Codrington. He won a singular renown in his own day, and a posthumous glory second to few Oxford men, as a soldier, philanthropist and collector of books—a striking combination. His military exploits in the Netherlands, which were a passport to the favour of William III., may be now forgotten; but his splendid benefactions to his College of All Souls and to the Gospel Propagation Society keep his memory very fresh.

The reader who wishes to study the life of Codrington may be referred to his biography in Professor Burrows's *Worthies of All Souls*, pp. 324-336—a most

---

° *Animadversions on the Eight Theses, etc.* Oxon., 1687.
† *Reliqu. Hearn.*, 2nd edition, i. 106.　　　　‡ *Life in the English Church*, 85, 254.
§ *Reliquiæ*, ii. 163.

interesting sketch, showing the very high estimation which his own University, and learned men generally, had formed of this young man's talents. Books were dedicated to him ; the Muses mourned his departure to the wars ; he was selected to express the joy of the University at William III.'s visit. If Addison had written his encomium of this Sovereign in English instead of Latin, his eulogy on Codrington would be better known than it is. Three lines out of this paragraph, which are inscribed on the west side of All Souls' Library, may be rudely Englished thus :

> Skilled in the various arts, and decked with all
> Minerva's lore, thee Oxford to fierce Mars
> Reluctant gave, and boasts her noble son.[*]

He was no doubt a liberal patron to booksellers and bookmakers. His name is among the five-guinea subscribers to Tonson's *Dryden's Virgil ;* and a " cut " in that work is duly dedicated to him. Hearne, in 1706, believed his library to contain 12,000 volumes, and valued it at £6,000. Professor Burrows, speaking of him as a student, says that very little of his poetry has come down to our time. He only names some verses addressed to Sir Samuel Garth on that author's *Dispensary.* Rose's *Biographical Dictionary* credits him with the authorship of some poems in the *Musæ Anglicanæ.* As the present writer has not seen the edition of 1741, he cannot tell whether any of those left anonymous in 1699 are there attributed to him ; but the only poem in the collection to which his name is appended in this edition is that now under discussion, of which he was not the author. Any piece published by him during his undergraduate days (1685-1689) would have been noticed by Wood. Professor Burrows's remark seems to be to the point here : " A reputation is sometimes made, and justly made, without much to show for it, in print." The sentiments which Smalridge puts into his mouth, when asked to take the part of Millington, the fluent ranter, if genuine, may have checked his pen, though matter and words would have come readily enough.

> Diis habeo grates, modici me quodque pusilli
> Finxerunt animi, pauca atque modesta loquentem.

His stores of learning have survived, as generations of readers in the Codrington Library could testify, but the collector himself is mute. He died in Barbadoes, at the early age of forty-four, having spent most of his time, after resigning the office of Governor, " in contemplation and study."

The other collocutors may be dismissed very briefly. Woodward takes the part of Cooper in the description of the auction. Stradling was no doubt of the same family as Sir Edward Stradling, of St. Donat's Castle, Glamorganshire, who was well skilled in British antiquities, and died, aged eighty, in 1609.

---

[*] Quem varias edoctum artes, studiisque Minervæ
Omnibus ornatum Marti Rhedicina furenti
Credidit invita, et tanto se jactat Alumno.—*Mus. Anglic.,* ii. 6.

Having no male issue, his estate went to his next kinsman, Sir John Stradling, Kt., who was made a Baronet. His son, Sir E. Stradling, Bart., was a Colonel in Charles I.'s army, and was buried in Jesus College, Oxford, 1644. Our friend must have been his grandson.*

These characters are managed by Smalridge with great skill ; and are so well sustained, that we may fancy them clever portraits, with just so much caricature as to satisfy the mock-heroic cast of the piece. There is not only an evenly sustained level of humour, with much variety of incident, but an intimate acquaintance with the best Latin poets, and not a little ingenuity in adapting their trite sayings to the purpose of the speaker.

There seems no doubt that the particular auction which is here celebrated is that of 1686. In *Notes and Queries* (5th S., xii., 1879) there is much curious information, in successive numbers, on the subject of Book-auctions. "Fama" says that an auction took place in Feb., 167⅚, apud "Theatrum Sheldonianum," and that others followed, catalogues of Richard Davis's books being issued in parts— i., ii., and appendix in 1686, iii. in 1688, and iv. in 1692. He refers also to an auction conducted by Bowman, in Oxford, in 1687, and says that Millington was selling Dr. Edm. Castell's Library at Cambridge, on June 30th, 1686. Bodley contains a catalogue of rare books sold at Oxford in the School of Moral Philosophy on June 20, 1700. Perhaps Mr. Lawler will devote a chapter some day to early auctions at the Universities. One would have fancied, from the mention of bowls and tennis and the dog-days, that Cooper's and Millington's auction in question had been held in June, rather than in either April or October.†

As an actual record of the sale, Smalridge's poem has probably no great value ; a limited number of typical books are offered, and a discussion ensues on each. Nor, probably, can the prices be taken as historical ; yet the general impression is very graphic and lifelike. Poor Davis—bankrupt in his old age— with wasted form and shambling gait, is portrayed with a regretful and almost loving touch ; the medley of buyers and spectators ; the aristocratic hauteur of the Christ Church gentlemen-commoners, chafing at the strong plebeian element, yet keen to watch and to purchase ; the dull pomposity of Cooper, with his heavy blunders, the vivacious effrontery of Millington—all these form a series of pictures, truthful photographs, of an eye-witness. Making allowance for some exaggeration of their peculiarities of manner and address, we may suppose that the worthy auctioneers are very faithfully drawn. They were not popular with the book-selling fraternity, and Tonson's short preface, printed above, is in the same key with the preface to Clavel's Catalogue, which takes some pains to

---

* Wood, *Ath. Oxon.*, i. 350 ; *Fasti*, ii. 144. Collins's *Peerage* (ed. 1735), iv. 399, 400. His great-uncle was Chaplain to Dr. Sheldon when Bishop of London, and in 1672 Dean of Chichester. He died in 1688, and was buried in Westminster Abbey.—Wood, *Ath. Oxon.*, ii. 822.
† *Book-Lore*, ii. 6.

prove that the public pay more for books at an auction than by purchasing in the regular way of trade, and that a lottery is, on the whole, more profitable. It is impossible here to give any particulars of the auctions in which these two brethren figured together and separately. Some information may be culled from the 1879 volumes of *Notes and Queries;* and from an earlier volume of the same periodical (2nd Series, xi. 464) may be copied Millington's epitaph:

> Underneath this marble stone
> Lives (*sic*) the famous Millington :
> A man who through the world did steer,
> I' th' station of an auctioneer.
> A man with wondrous sense and wisdom blest,
> Whose qualities are not to be exprest.

The translation that follows has been undertaken with considerable diffidence,[*] and with a sincere wish that author or editor had consulted the interests of both contemporaries and posterity by giving some short notes of explanation. Many of the allusions are quite out of the translator's depth, and his notes are frequently tentative rather than explanatory. Unquestionably there are materials in Oxford itself for throwing light on several points of doubt which may occur to the reader of these lines; and younger men in Oxford seem disposed to try if they cannot wipe off the reproach that the history of the University in all its later epochs remains yet to be written. A single question may be asked here: Why is Davis called Tryphon? The Greek τρυφῶν means literally, "one who lives delicately, a dainty or voluptuous man," in which literal sense the name would seem applicable to Davis only on the *lucus a non lucendo* principle. But Tryphon is also a proper name of various literary persons, artists, surgeons, and others, as may be seen more at large in Smith's *Biographical Dictionary.*

Davis was a fairly active publisher of theological, learned, and loyal works, but he was not himself a printer. Among Dr. Bliss's *Books Printed at Oxford* (Catalogue, vol. ii.), the first published by Davis (in conjunction with T. Robinson) is J. Reading's *Guide to the Holy City*, in 1651; the last, H. Foulis's *History of the Wicked Plots . . . of our Pretended Saints*, in 1674.[†] He was associated with A. Royston in various issues of the four volumes, folio, of Hammond's collected works, his name appearing on the title-pages till 1684. He presented to the world many of the Hon. Robert Boyle's philosophical writings (Clavel's Catalogue credits him with nine), and in 1685 he published the same author's well-known tract, *Of the High Veneration, etc.* Four Latin treatises

---

[*] " *That* is epigrammatic and witty in Latin, which would be perfectly insipid in English . . . If a Latin poem is neat, elegant, and musical, it is enough ; but English readers are not so easily satisfied."—Cowper's *Letters*, ed. Hayley (1812), i. 314.

[†] In the writer's copy of this book, which lately belonged to Bishop Wordsworth, of Lincoln, a contemporary hand has written, *ex dono Bibliopolæ Ric. Davis.* Some good customer, doubtless.

issued from his house in Hilary Term, 1683. It is possible that, like Moses Pitt, he ruined himself by undertaking books which could only command a limited sale among the learned. In this last-named list of Clavel's, several other books are said to have been *sold* by him, including *Livii Opera*, Amsterdam, in one vol., 12mo.

From the description of his shop in the poem, one would judge that his stock was large and varied. In translating that portion, and, indeed, other parts also, a doubt has sometimes been felt about the author's precise meaning ; but, at the risk of encumbering the page with notes and references, every serious point of difficulty has been mentioned, and, as the original could not well be printed in parallel columns, the more obvious imitations of the Latin poets have been pointed out for the sake of classical readers who do not possess an edition of *Musæ Anglicanæ.* Those who are better acquainted with the Oxford and the general literature of this period may be so kind as to supply points of information in which the translator is deficient, and to correct errors into which he has without doubt fallen. It will be understood that the original has no notes whatever. The translator's aim has been to follow the original as literally as is consistent with a fair attention to English idiom, but some few passages are paraphrased and condensed.

With respect to the prices bid for books, the Latin expressions of value are reduced, it is hoped correctly, to their English equivalents ; but of course the higher value of money at the end of the seventeenth century must be borne in mind as a set-off against the extremely low prices given for many of the lots.

The translator may crave some allowance for shortcomings on the ground that the work has been done at stray times, snatched from more serious occupations, and at a distance from any public library.

[K. Arthur Keye. B. Waller Bacon. S. Edward Stradling. D. George Dixon. C. Christopher Codrington. W. William Woodward, Esquires, of Christ Church.]

A. O the vanity of human wishes! O the changeableness of fate, and its settled unkindness to us! Alas! through how many accidents and dangers do we mortals rush on! Where is the man, whose lot has been uniformly happy, whom vain hopes have not befooled and made wretched? So, fickle Fortune, dost thou ever love to jest, to take what thou hadst just given, to exchange mirth for misery.

B. Why, O Chrysippus, are you uttering here these words redolent of the schools, these copious suggestions from your reading in Crantor and Epictetus?*

S. Come, say what are your sad tidings?

° Horace (*Ep.*, i. 2, 4) classes Crantor with Chrysippus as a moral philosopher. Epictetus' maxim was " Suffer and abstain (from evil)."

D. Is it an accident?

C. Does any Heaven-sent misfortune oppress you?

W. Why are you silent? Why stretch you your eyes and hands to Heaven in bewilderment, and refuse to disclose what is locked up in your breast?

D. If I am not mistaken, he is in love. Phyllis is holding him in suspense, and torturing him with a slow fire.* While she was kind, and did not turn a deaf ear to his complaints, then the Fates spun his life-thread calmly,† the days passed merrily, nor was the Deity then implacable. But when Venus turned her back, when Phyllis changed her mind and encouraged‡ his rival Alexis, and despised our friend's love, from that moment Fortune became his foe. Hence his deadly hatred of bitter Fate, his censure of the capricious gods.

B. Or perhaps he is now coming back from the smooth lawn where the youths play at bowls;§ here, while hope beguiled the toil, he has fought a battle against superior luck and skill. Now he is grieving over lost coins and an empty pocket.

S. Nay, I shrewdly suspect that you (*to* K.) have been for some days expecting a horse, promised by your fond mother, to carry you to your father's place and your country-home; but your father does not care to send either horse or servant, lest a man be lacking in the harvest-field and a nag in the waggon. Hence these groans and upbraidings of stern Fate.

K. You (*to* S.) are not a *Calchas*,‖ nor has he (*to* D.) nor any one of you greater skill; for though there is a variety in your mistakes, you all are equally mistaken. Another (but do not sneer at me)—another misfortune disturbs my mind. The large house of Davis has fallen; it was,¶ it *was*, I say, distinguished, a glorious temple of the Muses; but now the barbarous creditor is laying all waste, the Muses are expelled, and the shop goes begging.** If after this anyone is rash enough to believe that his good fortune will last, if he dares to put his trust in the fickle goddess, let him look at these wares scattered, these Penates turned out, and thyself, little Tryphon, harried by the mighty Fates.††

C. Here then is the upshot of all this opening flourish! I should have thought he was weeping for the fate of Priam.‡‡ It turns out to be a broker!§§

W. A memorable matter indeed, worthy of the tragic buskin of Sophocles. The stars mingle with the shades! the constellations with the infernal regions! The gods and goddesses are all in a flurry! A bookseller is bankrupt!‖

S. Who can escape Lachesis, when the Fates managed to catch even *Him*, when that mite of a manikin¶¶ could not elude the savage Parcæ?

---

* Hor. *Carm.*, i. 13, 8. † Tibull., i. 8, 1. ‡ Virg. *Ecl.*, i. 28.
  § "Molli qua sphæra vireto
    Exercet juvenes."
‖ *I.e.*, an augur—Virg. *Æn.*, ii. 182, etc.
¶ Or, "it has been," *i.e.*, "it is no longer;" as *Æn.*, ii. 325. ** Juv. *Sat.*, iii. 16.
†† Virg. *Æn.*, ii. 182. ‡‡ Cf. Hor. *Ar. Poet.*, 137, 138. §§ *Ib.*, 22.
‖‖ Juv. *Sat.*, vii. 129. ¶¶ "Tantillus Homuncio."

B. I saw (a wonder that the slender form did not escape my sight)—I saw the tiny pigmy walking along through the streets. Just as decrepitude, lingering on through countless ages, had sapped the strength of Tithonus, so Tryphon's withered knees totter* slowly on. His veins are knotted with the chilled blood. The muscles are contracted, and he looks shorter as he walks, not too well propped by a slender stick.† Such was the man. So he stepped, so looked.‡

K. Laugh, if you will; but I, joking apart, am serious in my distress. The time was, I remember, when all his shop-front was covered with engraved busts of heroes and numerous sheets of paper, when parchments§ hung thick on the walls. Within used to stand a thousand shelves, a thousand bookcases, a thousand compartments, and a corresponding number of volumes ranged neatly along them. But now the house, once so proud with its many badges and inscriptions,‖ stands a gazing-stock (horrible sight !), with disgraceful placards, and in the very entrance a manuscript catalogue¶ seems to charge its lord for being a runaway and exile.

D. So the bee on the plain of Hybla, flitting up and down over the strawberry and crocus, sucks the sweet juices from one flower and another, and presses in a great store of honey.** Soon some malignant spirit hostile to bees, some sour-faced imp, taking the shape of a drone or of a spotted lizard, rifles her hoards ; at once all her labour is ruined, and the bee herself.

W. Yet hope is not utterly at an end, nor is Tryphon so hateful to Heaven and the gods, but that some comfort is left for him in his broken condition, since a refuge is open to the unhappy man. Go now, Fortune, and give the rein to all thy storms. An auction stands to oppose thee,†† and it will recoup the mischief of Fate. Come on then, and let us duly sing in alternate strains what is the manner of selling, what laws and regulations the auction observes, how the purchasers are arranged, what is the place, and any other incidents which can be fitly rendered in verse.

S. There is a spot well known to our naughty‡‡ citizens. The ignorant crowd call it Northgate, but scholars style it *Bocardo*.§§ Not far from here is a house sometimes devoted to tender dances,‖‖ where with joyous steps youths and maidens are wont to trip through the days.

C. (*to* S.) Among whom we have seen thee as a partner.

S. Now there is another state of things. It is crammed full with a multitude of books. Dancer gives place to bookseller. Twice each day, with a large

---

* Virg. *Æn.*, v. 432.   † Cf. Juv., iii. 193.   ‡ Virg. *Æn.*, iii. 490.
§ "Chartæ."   ‖ "Titulis," cf. Juv. *Sat.*, v. 110.
¶ "Chirographus index." Perhaps the public notice of the sale.
** Virg. *Georg.*, iv. 163.   †† Or, "an auction is set up opposite."   ‡‡ "Improbulis."
§§ There are two views of Bocardo, the old City Prisons, in the *Antiquary*, vol. i., p. 73.
‖‖ See above, the extract from Wood. The "Clarendon Rooms," near this spot, have witnessed some interesting book-auctions, notably that of Professor Conington's Library, November 8, 1870.

thronging crowd, rival gownsmen are hurrying here from every side, all who are learned in books :—

C. Or who would be thought learned.

K. Sheldon's threshold* is neglected, and his next-door neighbour Bodley. Now for some time the chains have not rattled,† and the schools have been deserted. No one walks round the empty courts. The reader, alas! like Thracian Orpheus, commits his opinions to wood or to dumb stones.

B. I was strolling along the way :—

S. (*to* B.) Lazily, as your custom is.‡

B. Where the youth are wont to throw the ball and to ply it with alternate strokes, as it rebounds from the opposing walls.§ There were no active players, no applauding spectators. Nowhere could you see coats put down in the dust. All round was a gloomy silence and profound desolation.

S. No doubt the idle crowd is flocking within these walls, when they have lunched roughly but substantially at a charge of three halfpence,‖ or when breakfast has taken off the edge of their morning appetite.¶ A kind of procession is made, and all, when the door is open, rush in together and seize a seat. All have equal distinction, the same benches. No one has a better form than another, nor a seat of greater dignity. You may find in the front row and sitting next to a doctor, one who on the far-off hills of Cornwall used either to keep his sheep, though himself not their master, or to goad on the oxen toiling after another man's plough.

D. You are right, for there was one who clung close round my shoulders and arms like a second Pylades in his affection for Orestes, some low-born clownish fellow with his gown split in two, brought up to Oxford in the same waggon with bacon or barley. His coarse-textured felt-hat actually shone, and his moist locks diffused around his head a perfume of grease; his gown glistened wondrously.

K. Please spare the ears and noses of gentlemen, and do not offend the chaste Muses with unsavoury verses.

D. But to no purpose do so many tassels give a distinction to my dress,** if

---

* "Limina Sheldoni," the lately erected theatre. It was opened July 9, 1669.

† Probably an allusion to the barriers which separated the listeners from the disputants, or reciters, in the schools. Cf. Juv. *Sat.*, iii. 304.

‡ Hor. *Sat.*, i. 9. 1.

§ Loggan represents a fives-court in the space between Merton and Corpus Colleges, which men would pass in going to the river. See "Ludus Pilæ Palmariæ," in Popham's *Selecta Poemata*, p. 23.

¶ "Prandia cum male pasti obolis constantia ternis ceperunt." Obscure : "male pasti" must be imitated from Virgil's serpent "mala gramina pastus" (*Æn.*, ii. 471), "fed on poisonous herbs."

¶ "It was the custom for colleges, and indeed for most other people, till towards the middle of the seventeenth century, to dine at ten or eleven o'clock in the forenoon."—*Oxoniana*, i. 231. "Will you go and show me that pretty *Banqueting-house* for Curates?—I mean the *Three-penny Ordinary*, for I can go no higher."—*The Curates' Conference*, 1641, in *Harl. Misc.*, i. 484.

** "Plurima sed frustra variat mihi fimbria vestem." Probably in allusion to the gentleman-commoner's cap and gown. Cf. *Oxoniana*, i. 230. These menial offices performed by the servitors survived till a few years ago. Now their status is raised to that of Exhibitioners. A comic poem, my next neighbour is one who waits behind me as a servitor at dinner, whom I order to bring my cup or to take away my plate and what remains of the course.

B. O unlucky me, that I was not sitting next to you on that bench! Not that I had any bench to sit on. My ribs were ground between a cook on one side and a lamp-seller* on the other—the very scum of the mob; for even such as these press in with us as buyers, and there are seated on the same bench philosophers, bakers, doctors, head-cooks,† physicians, and quacks and medicine-vendors. All are seated; the rostrum is mounted. But who—that the course of events may explain itself better—who of you will represent the person of Millington, and also afterwards that of Cooper?

K. *Them!* Who would, or could?

C. *and* W. No one; by Hercules, no one!

N. Do you (*to* W.), pray, since you have a grave countenance, and a venerable appearance, not unworthy of Cato—do you take the part of Cooper, who is a man of such wonderful and notable gravity. You (*to* C.) will not disdain the part of Millington, for you are a pleasant fellow, humorous and sharp in your sayings.

W. I play Cooper! Do you see me displaying, as I get up, a monstrous paunch? Have I that admirable breadth of visage?‡ Tell me—am I a mayor, or a bumpkin, or an alderman? §

C. And I have no better hope of sustaining my part. I thank the gods that they made me of moderate ability and a retiring temper, slow and quiet of speech. He has a Stentor's lungs, consummate impudence—a very wind-bag, whose hollow bellows‖ blow lies; while I (being what I am) have not learnt to lie.¶ If a book is bad, I cannot pile encomiums on it—prefer Wither** to Virgil, or thee, Merlin, to

by G. Adams, student of Christ Church, styled *Jus Pilei Oxoniensis* in this collection (*Musæ Anglicanæ*, ii. 105-114), speaks of one variety of hat in very much the same language that we find above:

  B. Alter adhuc restat rigido subtemine crassus,
    Qui pinguis nitet, et ventos contemnit et imbres;
    Talem haud gestabis. (A. Talem nec forcipe tangam.)
  C. Sed tanges olim cum legum ænigmata disces.

For much curious information on this subject see *Archæologia*, vol. xxiv., pp. 168-189; *Oxoniana*, i. 20.

        In tecto qui sedetis
        Sublimi vel profundo,
        Qui pileo gaudetis
        Quadrato vel rotundo,

says Tom Warton, if he be the author of *A Companion to the Guide, and a Guide to the Companion*, with its clever supplementary skit on congratulatory odes.

  * "Lychniopola," perhaps "link-seller."   † Juv. *Sat.*, ix. 109.
  ‡ "Spatiuno admirabile vultus." Cf. Juv. *Sat.*, iv. 39.
  § "Numnam Prætor ego? vel Bubo? vel Aldermannus?"
  ‖ Juv. *Sat.*, vii. 111.   ¶ "Mentiri nescio," etc. Juv. *Sat.*, iii. 41.
  ** In the *Jus Pilei Oxoniensis*, A. says

        Et patria quoties jacuit neglectus in aulâ
        Quarlus, et ingentis carmen sublime *Witheri*,
        Arripui fervens, et pernox sæpe relegi.

the Sybils. But if you like some amusement, so let it be agreed. Let him (*to* W.) take his part; I will not be wanting in mine.

W. Since you wish me to play the fool, I will not be obstinate. I will settle my countenance to the best of my power, and in such strains (myself insensible to shame) will I hammer out some wretched lines, as Bavius or Mævius wrote,* or as Cooper himself, if he could write verses, would perpetrate.

B. Then you (*to* C.) must take your trumpet, and in the tune of Papinian,† or in such bombast as he employs to whom the *gens Claudia* gives his name,‡ you must roll out grand words and mingle thunders with your notes.

S. (*to* C.) But take care not to break down the benches with your loud shouting.§

D. Or that Sheldon's solid block‖ does not fall headlong.

Q.¶ Now come, let us have an introductory address to commend the famous wares.

B. We are ready to buy.

S. Or at least to look on.

W. I will begin. But do you (*to* C.), brother, prompt me if I hesitate; for you have always a better flow of words. You, O Athenians, hope of the Britons——

C. Add "and glory."

W. "And glory." (*To* C.) What next?

C. "Flower of the Gown."

W. And flower of Gownsmen, favour me with silence, and lend your kind attention.

To which C. replies:

> . . . . "At multum tibi debet Apollo
> Qui stripidum memoras tantâ cum laude Witherum."

º Virg. *Ecl.*, iii. 90. *Jus Pilei Oxoniensis*, p. 107.
† "*Modulamine Papiniano.*" The allusion here is obscure. The celebrated jurist, Papinian, does not seem to have been a man to "blow his own trumpet." *Papinianistæ* was a title sometimes given to students-in-law, who in their third year's course studied the writings of Papinian (Du Lange). Students who had approached the end of their course might be disposed to brag. Perhaps some one can offer a better explanation.
‡ Claudian, "the last of the Latin classic poets," wrote little besides panegyrics on the great people of his time.
§ Juv. *Sat.*, vii. 86.
‖ It may be questioned whether the Sheldonian theatre is intended here, or the statue of Sheldon which adorns its southern *façade*. The theatre was opened in 1679, and Oxford poets of this period are loud in the praises of its munificent founder. Corbet Owen's Pindaric Ode, *In Theatrum Sheldonianum*, is in *Musæ Anglic.*, t. i., pp. 99-128. Among the first lines are:

> Quousque defixi stupemus
> *Saxei* saxa, *plumbeique* plumbum?

These may have suggested the above. Gilbert Sheldon was the most popular ecclesiastic of his day, certainly in his own University (where he had been Warden of all Souls, and was ejected in the Commonwealth), probably in England. (Burrows' *Worthies of all Souls*, 183, *etc.*) Dr. Simon Ford addressed to him, when Archbishop of Canterbury, his charming Latin poem on fishing (*Musæ Anglic.*, i. 129), and claims him as a disciple of the gentle art.
¶ Q. (*sic*), prob. K.

C. Go on in your own valour. I will not add another word.

W. If my memory serves me right, it is now twelve years since auction-sales—long known to the French, and very well known to the Belgians, though late—at length reached our shores. London received them with applause, and Cambridge gave a favourable echo. May I venture to hope that you, too, will approve? Here are books for you. There is no need for me to praise them—or, indeed, of any orator. I am not a good speaker——

K. That is true.

W. But I claim both in word and deed to be called an honest man, and steady to my promises. Nor, if Nature has refused Cooper a very sharp wit, has the jade made him a trickster and a liar.* It remains for me to beg—kindly excuse my asking it—that I may keep my head covered, so as not to catch a bad cold.

C. Do not be afraid, Bollanus,† but trust in your thick brain. Could any blow, any illness, affect this head? Then I could believe that flints were soft and steel porous.

W. I am waiting to hear your pleasure. What is your wish?

K. By all means we assent.

B. Cover your head.

S. Put on your hat.

D. Why not?

W. For your great kindness I return my deep thanks; nor for a moment while this head survives, while the breath of life directs my limbs, shall anyone prove me unmindful or thoughtless of the favour. Listen, all of you; silence and attention while I read out aloud the conditions under which the auction is held. *He who bids the highest sum for a book shall have it. If any dispute arises, it rests with you to decide it.‡ Whatever volumes are imperfect, let them be restored.§ When the third blow has been struck, it is irrevocable.* Come, then. First I offer for sale a Bible printed in the Hebrew language. Who will name a sum? If you have any heartfelt religion, if your faith rests on an unshaken foundation, you will give £20.‖

K. I have a due regard for religion, but I have taken no oath as a convert to the circumcised, that I would turn over the Bible in an unknown tongue, and revere what I cannot understand. This work, these books the Jew Apella may pore over—not I.¶ My good parents taught me better.

° Cf. Virg. *Æn.*, ii. 79, 80.   † Hor. *Sat.*, i. ix. 11.

‡ "Decidere vos penes esto." No doubt this means—the lot shall be put up again, if you cannot settle the question. See Mr. Lawler's article in *Book-Lore*, ii 3.

§ This line, omitted in the *Musæ Anglic.*, is supplied from the original edition. Probably "saucia" means mutilated in any way, "restituuntor," let them be returned to the auctioneers.

‖ "Vicenas libras." Properly £20 each (volume), the numeral being distributive ; but it is certainly used for "viginti" as "undenas" is afterwards for "undecim," etc. ; and this Bible must have been in one volume from the sequel.

¶ Hor. *Sat.*, i. v. 100.

B. Nay, but I am neither a Jew nor bound to Antichrist; yet his own language is not more familiar to any man * than all the sacred sounds of Greek, Arabian, Italian, Chaldean, Hebrew, Assyrian, Æthiopian, or Memphitic Copt are to me. I am a man who prefers drawing water from the very fountain-head, rather than leading it down in a long canal.† Consequently (if I may praise myself), I have read the Targum and Masora,‡ Onkelos and Kimchi, whose very names (*to* K.) terrify you; Rabbinical commentators—all that the Kabbala has tied up in knots and hidden in dark riddles. So I will willingly give three shillings. But first let me examine the volume, and look carefully, for fear it may be torn somewhere, or have some pages missing.

W. Will one of you hand him the book? (*To* B.) Examine it.

B. What is this? I withdraw my bid. The title is missing, and the first page. Before the introduction, and at the very beginning,§ is written *Finis.* You scoundrel! (*to* W.) You dare to thrust on us an imperfect book! You expect to cheat the learned youth!

S. Is this the way you know Arabic? Is this how you understand Hebrew? You have indeed read Kimchi to good purpose! No doubt you have got the Kabbala by heart, when you clearly do not know that the Orientals, reversing our order, begin at the right-hand and proceed to the left in reading—go along an unusual track, and move backwards!

W. But you (*to* S.), how much do you bid?

S. To his three I add one more.

D. Well! I, although (for I ought not to be ashamed to tell the truth) the strange form and abnormal character of this new type perplexes me, and is disagreeable to my eyes, yet, that due honour may be paid to what is holy and reverence to the sacred language, I offer six shillings.

W. No one more? No one? *Once, twice, thrice has sounded the hammer.*‖ *The blow cannot be recalled.*

C. Where now is religion gone? Where veneration for the gods? the gods, I say! Some playwright will command a higher price than Moses.

W. Look! here are twice ten volumes of Suarez¶ for you.

C. A book itself a library.

W. Who can carry off such large spoils?

(*To be continued.*)

---

* Juv. *Sat.*, i. 17.
† Cf. Hor. *Sat.*, i. 1, 46.
‡ He pronounces it Māsōrā.
§ Vir. *Æn.*, ii. 469.
‖ *Buxum.* Cooper's hammer was made of boxwood. Millington applies to his own the Homeric line, ἐσσυμένη δὲ κλαγγὴ γένετ᾽ ἀργυρέοιο βιοῖο, but for all that one may question its being a silver hammer.
¶ Francis Suarez, the celebrated Spanish Jesuit, *ob.* 1615. His works fill twenty-three volumes, folio.

REVIEWS.

Prize Translations, Poems and Parodies. London, 1881, 8vo., pp. 90.

Prizes and Proximes for Prose and Verse Translation, with some original Poems. London, 1882, 8vo., pp. viii-115.

Essays in Translation and other Contributions, reprinted from the "Journal of Education." London, 1885, 8vo., pp. xv-200.

THE three volumes named above have all been published at the office of the *Journal of Education*, and are the result of the literary competitions in that periodical. The contests have attracted great interest, and it is an open secret that some distinguished people have been amongst the unsuccessful. The late Mark Pattison was one of these. The three volumes contain many very charming translations, and a close examination of them throws much light upon the theory and practice of the art of translation. To give an adequate rendering of a poem in another language is perhaps as much an ethical as a literary triumph. To students and for general readers these collections may be warmly recommended.

Saxon Lyrics and Legends, after Aldhelm. By LOCHNELL. London : Field and Tuer. 12mo., pp. 114.

AS Aldhelm's English songs have all perished, there is no fear that this volume can be taken for anything but what it is, a clever imitation in modern language of the spirit and form of Anglo-Saxon poetry. The absence of rhyme is decidedly felt, but there is a certain rhythmical motion, and some of the legends here told were well worth re-telling.

Madame Roland. By MATHILDE BLIND. London : W. H. Allen. 1886, 8vo., pp. vi-255.

MISS BLIND has had a congenial task in detailing the stormy life and heroic death of Madame Roland. The material is ample, and includes some that is quite fresh. No previous attempt can claim the completeness that has been attained by Miss Blind, who has now presented to the English public a sufficient portrait of this able, sincere, and unfortunate woman.

The Early Life of Anne Boleyn : a Critical Essay. By J. H. ROUND, M.A. London : Elliot Stock. 8vo., pp. 47.

THERE has been ample controversy as to the life and character of that beautiful lady from whose eyes the poet, if not the historian, declares the "gospel light" first beamed upon the royal "Defender of the Faith." Mr. Round has shown much acuteness in his attempt to clear up some of the doubts and mysteries in the earlier life of the lady who ascended the throne of England only to find it but the stepping-stone to the scaffold.

Sub-Mundanes ; or, the Elementaries of the Cabala : being the history of Spirits. Reprinted from the text of the Abbé de Villars, Physio-Astro-Mystic, wherein is asserted that there are in existence on earth rational creatures besides man. With an illustrative appendix from the work "Demoniality," or "Incubi and Succubi," by the Rev. Father Sinistrari, of Ameno. Privately printed only for subscribers. Bath, 1886, 4to., pp. 136.

UNDER this fresh title there has been issued a handsome reprint of the English translation of *Le Comte de Gabalis*, the well-known Rosicrucian romance of the Abbé de Montfaucon de Villars. The author is believed to have drawn much of his inspiration, if not his absolute material, from the *Chiave del Gabinetto* of Borri, who, in turn, embodied in his work the floating Rosicrucian tradition and some of the fancies of Paracelsus. De Villars' book was printed at Paris in 1670, and ten years later there appeared an English translation now reprinted. When Pope wrote the *Rape of the Lock* he took from *Le Comte de Gabalis* the fairy machinery by which that charming poem is distinguished. This led to a renewed interest in the work, and it appeared with a London imprint both in the original and in an English version. Pope is not the only poet who has found material in it. Charles Mackay's *Salamandrine* was suggested by it, and in the introduction he has pointed out other signs of indebtedness in the literature of Germany. The present handsome reprint appears to be intended for the lovers of occult literature, and some portions of the original French have been discreetly left untranslated.

Bolton Bibliography, and Jottings of Book-Lore : with notes on local authors and printers. By JAS. C. SCHOLES. Manchester : Henry Gray. 1886, 12mo., pp. 247.

BOLTON has not achieved any great fame as an intellectual centre, but this little volume shows that it is not destitute of literary associations. It would be well if every town had some one who, with the enthusiasm and patience displayed by Mr. Scholes, would chronicle the doings of the printers and authors of the locality. Much curious information is lost for want of intelligent annalists. At Lostock, in the neighbourhood of Bolton, there is believed to have been a private printing-press, at which, in the seventeenth century, a number of Roman Catholic books were printed. From that time Bolton has had a fair share of ecclesiastics, sectaries, rhymers, a d miscellaneous writers. Mr. Scholes has made the most of his subject, and the book contains a great deal of information respecting some of the byways of literature.

Les Artistes Célèbres : François Boucher. Par André Michel. Paris : Librairie de l'Art. 1886, 8vo., pp. 144.

THE graceful, if somewhat artificial, pictures of Boucher are well-known to the lovers of eighteenth-century literature, and they will welcome this charming monograph in which M. Michel has detailed the life and works of the French artist. The text, clear and satisfactory in itself, is further illustrated by forty-four engravings.

Strambotti e Sonnetti dell' Altissimo. Per Cura di RODOLFO RENIER. Torino : Società Bibliofila. 1886, 8vo., pp. xlvii-75.

To be a Florentine poet and to be called " L' Altissimo " by the popular voice of Dante's city might seem a sure presage of enduring fame ; but the verses of Cristoforo. *poeta fiorentino*, are not reprinted in obedience to the public demand, but only in a restricted edition for lovers of the book-lore of the Renaissance. We hope that some copies may find their way into English libraries, and that we shall soon see a renewed interest in Italian literature, once so popular in this country and now so strangely neglected. Recent attempts to naturalize certain forms of Italian verse ought to send readers to that language in which they may be seen in full flower.

Dickensiana, a Bibliography of the Literature relating to Charles Dickens and his Writings. Compiled by FRED. G. KITTON. London : George Redway. 8vo., pp. xxxii-510.

THE title-page is sufficiently explanatory of the scope of this volume, which contains information indispensable to all Dickens's collectors and is interesting to all who admire the great novelist. Mr. Kitton has relieved the inevitable " dryness " of a list of titles by copious quotations and annotations, so that the book will appeal to many beside the sworn adepts of bibliography.

WE have received the following catalogues : C. W. Holdich and Sons, 11, Queen Street, Hull ; Henry Turrill, 280, High Street, Lincoln ; Thomas Simmons, 164, Parade, Leamington ; W. Webber, Dial Lane, Ipswich ; Charles Lowe, Broad Street Corner, Birmingham ; Albert Sutton, 130, Portland Street, Manchester ; Walter Scott, 7, Bristo Place, Edinburgh ; James G. Commin, 230, High Street, Exeter ; Jonathan Nield, 29, Bath Street, Bristol ; Andrew Iredale, Torquay ; William Smith, 97, London Street, Reading ; J. W. Jarvis and Son, 28, King William Street, Charing Cross, London ; Macmillan and Bewes, Cambridge ; B. Stretten, 7, London Lane, Hackney ; Richard H. Sutton, 25, Princess Street, Manchester ; W. Downing, 74, New Street, Birmingham.

◆◇◆

CORRESPONDENCE.

BOOKWORMS.

LAST week I was looking over some old papers which I had not disturbed for some time, when, on pulling them open, I broke a white cocoon, spun between the leaves and made up of small bits of paper gnawed off. I could not, however, identify the worm inside with either of those described in your article on bookworms last month. It was about three-quarters of an inch long, and very fat creamy white ; in fact, just such a maggot as one sees in cheese or fruit.

It is now spinning another cocoon, in a japanned box, and when the moth comes out I will let you know for certain what it is. This is the first of its kind I ever met with.

H. S. WYNDHAM.

Thornton Heath, Surrey.

WILLIAM HAZLITT.

PERHAPS it may not be without interest to mention a *Defence of Mr. Hazlitt against the Misrepresentations of the Quarterly Review,* which appeared in the *Academic,* No. X., June 1, 1821, p. 185.

This was a Liverpool publication, and of great rarity. It is not named in Mr. Ireland's capital Bibliography.

M.

BIBLIOPHILE'S KALENDAR.

THE fifth volume of Mr. G. L. Gomme's *Gentleman's Magazine Library* is devoted to Archæology, and contains the papers contributed to the magazine on Geologic, and Prehistoric Remains, Early Historic Remains, Sepulchral Remains, and Encampments and Earthworks. Under these heads Mr. Gomme has gathered from the pages of the *Gentleman's Magazine* records of many important discoveries made in Great Britain during a period of nearly 140 years. These accounts of discoveries are most important, and even the immature theories deduced by some of the old contributors to the *Gentleman's Magazine* are not uninstructive, as marking the gradual advance in the scientific treatment of the subjects up to our own time. Mr. Gomme has added to this volume, as to the former issues of the collection, useful notes, among which may be named a comparison, in tabular form, of the cave remains and flint and bronze implements recorded in the volume, with the great authorities on those subjects.

THE *Northamptonshire Notes and Queries* has a notice of Robert Holcot from the pen of Mr. W. E. Buckley.

WE have received the report of the Librarian of the Maimonides Library, District No. 1, I.O.B.B., New York, 1886. Mr. Max Cohen, the librarian, in the course of his interesting statement, states that he is making a collection of books on education.

THE *Library Journal* contains in full the address of Mr. J. R. Lowell at the opening of the public library at Chelsea, Mass.

THE contributor's point of view is well expressed in some verses by Bessie Chandler, which appear in *Harpers' Bazaar*, and which we quote :

A HUMBLE CONTRIBUTOR'S APPEAL.

Though I sometimes write a story,
　Or a poem now and then,
Not from any hope of glory
　Do I touch the flowing pen.
On Parnassus fair and sunny
　I have never sought to climb ;
It is just for sordid money
　That I ramble into rhyme.
Not a rustling crown of laurel
　Is the object of my verse ;
No ; its only aim and moral
　Is a rustling in my purse.
Yet how oft my little chickens
　Flutter back like weary things,
With a note that plays the dickens
　Neatly tied beneath their wings !
Then I smooth each ruffled feather,
　Here and there a wing I clip,

Meanwhile gathering stamps together
　To prepay another trip.
One hot summer, nearly frantic
　For the sea, I wrote a rhyme,
Which I sent to the *Atlantic*—
　Where I didn't go that time.
But hope springs as green and weedy
　As fresh pusley after rain,
And because I'm really needy
　I will try my luck again.
Now I want a winter bonnet,
　One that costs a pretty bit ;
Do you think that song or sonnet
　From my head can cover it ?
Think, ye editorial creatures,
　Of my pate all unprotected,
Of my pinched and frost-nipped features,
　And send word I'm not—rejected.

LADY WILLIAM WARREN VERNON has presented to the Dante Museum of Florence copies of the important works written by her father, the late Lord Vernon, on the great Italian poet.

THE Rev. J. D. Stockbridge is engaged upon a catalogue of the Harris Collection of American Poetry, lately devised to Brown University by Senator Anthony.

MR. WM. HENRY BURR, of Washington, is the author of a work on " Bacon and Shakespere," and " proving " that Bacon wrote the sonnets ascribed to the latter.

THE Eighth Annual Report of the Librarian of the Borough of Wigan has recently been issued. The donations, which slightly exceed in number the average of previous years, include the privately printed *Bibliotheca Lindesiana*, presented by the Earl of Crawford and Balcarres, and a collection of books given by Mrs. Fisher. We are glad to learn that the Borough Council have authorized the librarian, Mr. H. T. Folkard, to proceed with the publication of a Catalogue to the Reference Library. An instalment is expected to be issued before the close of this year, and it will doubtless add greatly to the value of the library. The issues from the Reference Department during the year have been 11,186, those from the Lending Library, 62,691 volumes, while the attendance at the News Room on Sundays alone has been 10,573.

THE want of a British Biographical Dictionary had long been felt in England when Mr. Leslie Stephen, assisted by a large number of competent writers, commenced the *Dictionary of National Biography*, the first volume of which was issued early last year. This magnificent work is to be completed in about fifty volumes, and the last of which is expected to be in the hands of the public about the year 1897. The six volumes that have been issued include the names from Abbadie to Browell, and give some idea of the probable value of what is really a gigantic undertaking. Every deceased Englishman, Irishman, and Scotchman who has written anything, done anything, or been anything of importance, is, or ought, according to plan, to be included ; all of the articles are signed by the authors, who are required to give the authorities for the statements made. Mr. Leslie Stephen had calculated that the letters A and B would occupy seven volumes, but in point of fact that quantity will be exceeded by a very trifling amount, probably by less than 100 pages ; and it is expected that D will conclude the first quarter of the work. Mr. Stephen has hitherto been able to issue a volume regularly every three months, and it is to be hoped that he will not be obliged by the remissness of contributors to delay the publication of this valuable work, which has so long been hoped for, and which has now such a good prospect of completion within a reasonable time.

THE *Hull Quarterly and East Riding Portfolio*, which came to an untimely end in October, 1885, after an existence of two years, contains many articles of interest to East Yorkshire folk. Among the matters of more general importance we may mention a long discussion on the authenticity of the "Johnson MSS." In 1875, Mr. W. A. Gunnell, of Hull, published a selection from a mass of manuscripts purporting to have been written by a family of Johnsons, who formerly resided in Hull. The publication of these MSS. occasioned much controversy among the *literati* of the town, some of whom denied the authenticity of the MSS., whilst others as stoutly defended them. But no one having any acquaintance with the history of the English language could regard them as anything but impudent and clumsy forgeries. In addition to these amusing discussions there are also lives of Sir Henry Vane the younger, Bishop John Alcock, and an account of Dante Rossetti, the poet. The magazine was ably edited during its short career by Mr. W. G. B. Page, of the Subscription Library, Hull.

MR. W. G. B. PAGE is preparing for publication a book in two volumes, *The Booksellers' Signs of London, from the Earliest Time.* The work will contain an alphabetical list of upwards of 600 of the shop signs of the booksellers of London, together with the names of the occupiers of the various shops, in chronological order, and biographical notices of the booksellers.

UNDER the title *Quest and Vision*, Mr. W. J. Dawson, the author of the *Vision of Souls*, will publish a volume of studies on some of the poets of the present century, among others on Shelley, Wordsworth, George Eliot, Matthew Arnold, James Thomson, Tennyson and Browning.

THE *Cambridge Review* contains an article by Mr. G. J. Gray on Cambridge University periodicals. The list is carefully prepared, and the author asks for further notes on the subject.

DR. E. REYER contributes to the *Centralblatt für Bibliothekswesen* an interesting paper on American libraries.

M. HENRI BORDIER is the author of a *Description des Peintures et autres Ornemens contenus dans les Manuscrits grecs de la Bibliothèque nationale*, which has been published in Paris. The French National Library claims to have the largest collection in the world of Greek MSS. Whilst the Vatican has 3,560, the British Museum 716, and the Escurial 586, the Bibliothèque Nationale has 4,600.

THE *Library Journal* contains the first part of an elaborate and hypercritical attack upon Mr. Melvil Dewey's new edition of his *Bibliography*. The proposed building for the Library of Congress is illustrated.

THE New York *Book Buyer* contains a second article on American book-plates.

THE *Pall Mall Gazette* says that among the instances of what he quaintly calls false wit, Addison mentions the productions of authors who were at infinite pains to write whole Iliads in which some one letter or elementary word was throughout conspicuous by its absence. A book of the kind, prompted not by a desire to be witty, but by the fierce indignation of the linguistic purist, has just made its appearance in France. It is called *Contes sans qui ou que*, and this title is literally borne out, for neither word, whether as relative or conjunction, is used at all. In his preface, M. Chennevières, the author, discourses on his hatred to these "tyrants and vermin" of the French language, and says that he hopes to popularise his peculiarity till relatives are exterminated from France.

FROM *Shorthand* for April we learn that soon after it was mooted that a Phonographic Jubilee was to be held next year in recognition of the lifelong labours of Mr. Isaac Pitman, it was proposed, on the initiative of Dr. Westby-Gibson, Vice-President of the Shorthand Society, that advantage should be taken of that London gathering in 1887 to hold concurrently an International Congress, representing all persons interested in shorthand, gentlemen of the press, and

... professionally or otherwise and a committee will be formed, so that the matter may be fairly started and carried through with every prospect of a successful issue. In the meantime, letters on the subject may be addressed to Dr. Westby-Gibson, 10, Great Coram Street, Russell Square, London. W.C.

INDEX.